Henry James

Henry James OM (15 April 1843 – 28 February 1916) was an American-British author regarded as a key transitional figure between literary realism and literary modernism, and is considered by many to be among the greatest novelists in the English language. He was the son of Henry James Sr. and the brother of renowned philosopher and psychologist William James and diarist Alice James.

He is best known for a number of novels dealing with the social and marital interplay between émigré Americans, English people, and continental Europeans. Examples of such novels include The Portrait of a Lady, The Ambassadors, and The Wings of the Dove. His later works were increasingly experimental. In describing the internal states of mind and social dynamics of his characters, James often made use of a style in which ambiguous or contradictory motives and impressions were overlaid or juxtaposed in the discussion of a character's psyche.(Source: Wikipedia)

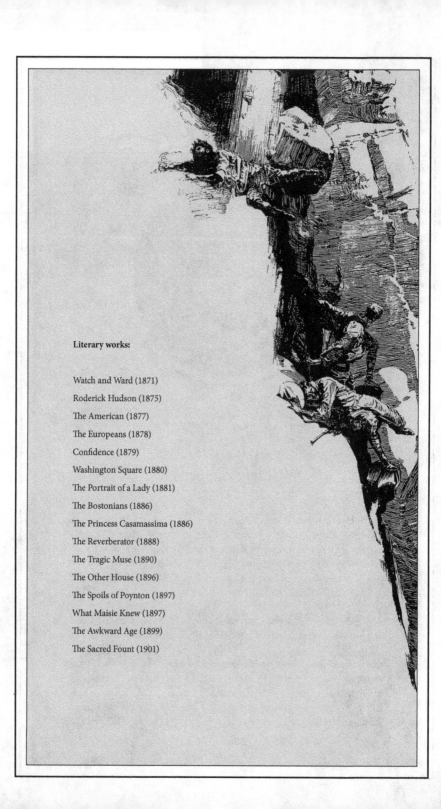

Literary works:

Watch and Ward (1871)

Roderick Hudson (1875)

The American (1877)

The Europeans (1878)

Confidence (1879)

Washington Square (1880)

The Portrait of a Lady (1881)

The Bostonians (1886)

The Princess Casamassima (1886)

The Reverberator (1888)

The Tragic Muse (1890)

The Other House (1896)

The Spoils of Poynton (1897)

What Maisie Knew (1897)

The Awkward Age (1899)

The Sacred Fount (1901)

THE
WORKS
OF
HENRY JAMES
VOL. 25 (OF 36)

THE LETTERS OF
HENRY JAMES
(VOLUME I)

THE LESSON OF THE MASTER

An Imprint of Moon Classics LLC

A Wholly Owned Subsidiary of Queenior LLC

A Melodragon Company

First Printing: 2020

ISBN 978-1-6627-1596-9 (Paperback)

ISBN 978-1-6627-1597-6 (Hardcover)

Published by Moon Classics

www.moonclassics.com

Contents

THE
WORKS
OF
HENRY JAMES
VOL. 25 (OF 36)

THE LETTERS OF HENRY JAMES (VOLUME I)

INTRODUCTION

WHEN Henry James wrote the reminiscences of his youth he shewed conclusively, what indeed could be doubtful to none who knew him, that it would be impossible for anyone else to write his life. His life was no mere succession of facts, such as could be compiled and recorded by another hand; it was a densely knit cluster of emotions and memories, each one steeped in lights and colours thrown out by the rest, the whole making up a picture that no one but himself could dream of undertaking to paint. Strictly speaking this may be true of every human being; but in most lives experience is taken as it comes and left to rest in the memory where it happens to fall. Henry James never took anything as it came; the thing that happened to him was merely the point of departure for a deliberate, and as time went on a more and more masterly, creative energy, which could never leave a sight or sound of any kind until it had been looked at and listened to with absorbed attention, pondered in thought, linked with its associations, and which did not spend itself until the remembrance had been crystallised in expression, so that it could then be appropriated like a tangible object. To recall his habit of talk is to become aware that he never ceased creating his life in this way as it was lived; he was always engaged in the poetic fashioning of experience, turning his share of impressions into rounded and lasting images. From the beginning this had been his only method of dealing with existence, and in later years it even meant a tax upon his strength with which he had consciously to reckon. Not long before his death he confessed that at last he found himself too much exhausted for the 'wear and tear of discrimination'; and the phrase indicates the strain upon him of the mere act of living. Looked at from without his life was uneventful enough, the even career of a man of letters, singularly fortunate in all his circumstances. Within, it was a cycle of vivid and incessant adventure, known only to himself except in so far as he himself put it into words. So much of it as he left unexpressed is lost, therefore, like a novel that he might have written, but of which there can now be no question, since its only possible writer is gone.

Fortunately a great part of it survives in his letters, and it is of these that his biography must be composed. The material is plentiful, for he was at all times a copious letter-writer, overflowing into swift and easy improvisation to his family and to the many friends with whom he corresponded regularly. His letters have been widely preserved, and several thousands of them have passed through my hands, ranging from his twenty-fifth year until within a few days of his last illness. They give as complete a portrait of him as we can now hope to possess. His was a nature in which simplicity and complexity were very curiously contrasted, and it would need all his own power of fusing innumerable details into coherency to create a picture that would seem sufficient to those who knew him. Yet even his letters, varied as they are, give full expression to one side of his life only, the side that he shewed to the world he lived in and loved. After all the prodigal display of mind that is given in these volumes, the free outpouring of curiosity and sympathy and power, a close reader must still be left with the sense that something, the most essential and revealing strain, is little more than suggested here and there. The daily drama of his work, with all the comfort and joy it brought him, does not very often appear as more than an undertone to the conversation of the letters. It was like a mystery to which he was dedicated, but of which he shrank from speaking quite openly. Much as he always delighted in sociable communion, citizen of the world, child of urbanity as he was, all his friends must have felt that at heart he lived in solitude and that few were ever admitted into the inner shrine of his labour. There it was nevertheless that he lived most intensely and most serenely. In outward matters he was constantly haunted by anxiety and never looked forward with confidence; he was of those to whom the future is always ominous, who dread the treachery of apparent calm even more than actual ill weather. It was very different in the presence of his work. There he never knew the least failure of assurance; he threw his full weight on the belief that supported him and it was never shaken.

That belief was in the sanctity and sufficiency of the life of art. It was a conviction that needed no reasoning, and he accepted it without question. It was absolute for him that the work of the imagination was the highest and most honourable calling conceivable, being indeed nothing less than the actual creation of life out of the void. He did not scruple to claim that except through art there is no life that can be known or appraised. It is the artist who takes over the deed, so called, from the doer, to give it back again in the form in which it can be seen and measured for the first time; without the brain that is able to close round the loose unappropriated fact and render all its aspects, the fact itself does not exist for us. This was the standard below which Henry James would never allow the conception of his office to drop, and he had the reward of complete exemption from any chill of misgiving. His life as a creator of art, alone with his work, was one of unclouded happiness. It might be hampered and hindered by external accidents, but none of them could touch the real core of his security, which was his faith in his vocation and his knowledge of his genius. These certainties remained with him always, and he would never trifle with them in any mood. His impatience with argument on the whole aesthetic claim was equally great, whether it was argument in defence of the sanctuary or in profanation of it. Silence, seclusion, concentration, he held to be the only fitting answer for an artist. He disliked the idea that the service of art should be questioned and debated in the open, still more to see it organised and paraded and publicly celebrated, as though the world could do it any acceptable honour. He had as little in common with those who would use the artistic profession to persuade and proselytise as with those who would brandish it defiantly in the face of the vulgar.

Thus it is that he is seldom to be heard giving voice to the matters which most deeply occupied him. He preferred to dwell with them apart and to leave them behind when he emerged. Sometimes he would drop a word that shewed what was passing beneath; sometimes, on a particular challenge, or to one in whom he felt an understanding sympathy, he would speak out with impressive authority. But generally he liked to enter into other people's thought and to meet them on their own ground. There his natural kindliness and his keen dramatic interest were both satisfied at once. He enjoyed friendship, his letters shew how freely and expansively; and with his steady and vigilant eye he watched the play of character. He was insatiable for anything that others could give him from their personal lives. Whatever he could seize in this way was food for his own ruminating fancy; he welcomed any grain of reality, any speck of significance round which his imagination could pile its rings. It was very noticeable how promptly and eagerly he would reach out to such things, as they floated by in talk; it was as though he feared to leave them to inexpert hands and felt that other people could hardly be trusted with their own experience. He remembered how much of his time he had spent in exploring their consciousness when he spoke of himself as a confirmed spectator, one who looked on from the brink instead of plunging on his own account; but if this seemed a pale substitute for direct contact he knew very well that it was a much richer and more adventurous life, really, than it is given to most people to lead. There is no life to the man who does not feel it, no adventure to the man who cannot see the whole of it; the greatest share goes to the man who can taste it most fully, however it reaches him. Henry James might sometimes look back, as he certainly did, with a touch of ruefulness in reflecting on all the experience he had only enjoyed at second hand; but he could never doubt that what he had he possessed much more truly than any of those from whom he had taken it. There was no hour in which he was not alive with the whole of his sensibility; he could scarcely persuade himself that he might have had time for more. And indeed at other moments he would admit that he had lived in the way that was at any rate the right way for him. Even his very twinges of regret were not wasted; like everything else they helped to swell the sum of life, as they did to such purpose for Strether, the 'poor sensitive gentleman' of *The Ambassadors*, whose manner of living was very near his creator's.

These letters, then, while they shew at every point the abundant life he led in his surroundings, have to be read with the remembrance that the central fact of all, the fact that gave everything else its meaning to himself, is that of which least is told. The gap, moreover, cannot be filled from other sources; he seems to have taken pains to leave nothing behind him that should reveal this privacy. He put forth his finished work to speak for itself and swept away all the traces of its origin. There was a high pride in his complete lack of tenderness towards the evidence of past labour—the notes, manuscripts, memoranda that a man of letters usually accumulates and that shew him in the company of his work. It is only to the stroke of chance which left two of his novels unfinished that we owe the outspoken colloquies with himself, since published, over the germination of those stories—a door of entry into the presence of his imagination that would have been summarily closed if he had lived to carry out his plan. And though in the prefaces to the collected edition of his works we have what is perhaps the most comprehensive statement ever made of the life of art, a *biographia literaria* without parallel for fulness and elaboration, he was there dealing with his books in retrospect, as a critic from without, analysing and reconstructing his own creations; or if he went further than this, and touched on the actual circumstances of their production, it was because these had for him the charm of an old romance, remote enough to be recalled without indiscretion. So it is that while in a sense he was the most personal of writers—for he could not put three words together without marking them as his own and giving them the very ring of his voice—yet, compared with other such deliberate craftsmen as Stevenson or Gustave Flaubert, he baffles and evades curiosity about the private affairs of his work. If curiosity were merely futile it would be fitting to suppress the chance relic I shall offer in a moment—for it so happens that a single glimpse of unique clarity is open to us, revealing him as no one saw him in his life. But the attempt to picture the mind of an artist is only an intrusion if it is carried into trivial and inessential things; it can never be pushed too far, as Henry James would have been the first to maintain, into a real sharing of his aesthetic life.

The relic in question consists of certain pencilled pages, found among his papers, in which he speaks with only himself for listener. They belong to the same order as the notes for the unfinished novels, but they are even more informal and confidential. Nothing else of the kind seems to have survived; the schemes and motives that must have swarmed in his brain, far too numerously for notation, have all vanished but this one. At Rye, some years before the end, he began one night to feel his way towards a novel which he had in mind—a subject afterwards abandoned in the form projected at first. The rough notes in which he casts about to clear the ground are mostly filled with the mere details of his plan—the division of the action, the characters required, a tentative scenario. These I pass over in order to quote some passages where he suddenly breaks away, leaves his imaginary scene, and surrenders to the awe and wonder of finding himself again, where he has so often stood before, on the threshold and brink of creation. It is as though for once, at an hour of midnight silence and solitude, he opened the innermost chamber of his mind and stood face to face with his genius. There is no moment of all his days in which it is now possible to approach him more closely. Such a moment represented to himself the pith of life—the first tremor of inspiration, in which he might be almost afraid to stir or breathe, for fear of breaking the spell, if it were not that he goes to meet it with a peculiar confidence.

I take this up again after an interruption—I in fact throw myself upon it under the *secousse* of its being brought home to me even more than I expected that my urgent material reasons for getting settled at productive work again are of the very most imperative. Je m'entends—I have had a discomfiture (through a stupid misapprehension of my own indeed;) and I must now take up projected tasks—this long time *entrevus* and brooded over, with the firmest possible hand. I needn't expatiate on this—on the sharp consciousness of this hour of the dimly-dawning New Year, I mean; I simply make an appeal to all the powers and forces and divinities to whom I've ever been loyal and who haven't failed me yet—after all: never, never yet! Infinitely interesting— and yet somehow with a beautiful sharp poignancy in it that makes it strange and rather exquisitely formidable, as with an unspeakable deep agitation, the whole artistic question that comes up for me in the train of this idea ... of the *donnée* for a situation that I began here the other day to fumble out. I mean I come back, I come back yet again and again, to my only seeing it in the dramatic way—as I can only see everything and anything now; the way that filled my mind and floated and uplifted me when a fortnight ago I gave my few indications to X. Momentary side-winds—things of no real authority—break in every now and then to put their inferior little questions to me; but I come back, I come back, as I say, I all throbbingly and yearningly and passionately, oh mon bon, come back to this way that is clearly the only one in which I can do anything now, and that will open out to me more and more, and that has overwhelming reasons pleading all beautifully in its breast.

What really happens is that the closer I get to the problem of the application of it in any particular case, the more I get *into* that application, so that the more doubts and torments fall away from me, the more I know where I am, the more everything spreads and shines and draws me on and I'm justified of my logic and my passion.... Causons, causons, mon bon—oh celestial, soothing, sanctifying process, with all the high sane forces of the sacred time fighting, through it, on my side! Let me fumble it gently and patiently out— with fever and fidget laid to rest—as in all the old enchanted months! It only looms, it only shines and shimmers, *too* beautiful and too interesting; it only hangs there too rich and too full and with too much to give and to pay; it only presents itself too admirably and too vividly, too straight and square and vivid, as a little organic and effective Action....

Thus just these first little wavings of the oh so tremulously passionate little old wand (now!) make for me, I feel, a sort of promise of richness and beauty and variety; a sort of portent of the happy presence of the elements. The good days of last August and even my broken September and my better October come back to me with their gage of divine possibilities, and I welcome these to my arms, I press them with unutterable tenderness. I seem to emerge from these recent bad days—the fruit of blind accident—and the prospect clears and flushes, and my poor blest old Genius pats me so admirably and lovingly on the back that I turn, I screw round, and bend my lips to passionately, in my gratitude, kiss its hands.

To the exaltation of this wonderful unbosoming he had been brought by fifty years of devout and untiring service. Where so little is heard of it all, the amount of patience and energy that he had consecrated to it might easily be mistaken. His immense industry all through his crowded London years passes almost unnoticed, so little it seems to conflict with this life in the world, his share in which, with the close friendships he formed and the innumerable relations he cultivated, could have been no fuller if he had had nothing to do but to amuse himself with the spectacle. In one way, however, it is possible to divine how heavily the weight of his work pressed on him. The change that divides the general tone and accent of his younger and middle age from that of his later years is too striking to be overlooked. The impression is unmistakeable that for a long while, indeed until he was almost an old man, he felt the constant need of husbanding and economising his resources; so that except to those who knew him intimately he was apt to seem a little cold and cautious, hesitating to commit himself freely or to allow promiscuous claims. Later on all this was very different. There were certain habits of reserve, perhaps, that he never threw off; all his friends remember, for example, how carefully he distinguished the different angles of his affection, so to call them—adjusting his various relations as though in fear lest they should cross each other and form an embarrassing complexity. Yet any scruples or precautions of this sort that still hung about him only enhanced the large and genial authority of his presence. There seemed to have come a time when after long preparation and cogitation he was able to relax and to enjoy the fruit of his labour. Not indeed that his labour was over; it never was that, while strength lasted; but he gave the effect of feeling himself to be at length completely the master of his situation, at ease and at home in his world. The new note is very perceptible in the letters, which broaden out with opulent vigour as time goes on, reaching their best comparatively late.

That at last he felt at home was doubtless indeed the literal truth, and it was enough to account for this ample liberation of spirit. His decision to settle in Europe, the great step of his life, was inevitable, though it was not taken without long reflection; but it was none the less a decision for which he had to pay heavily, as he was himself very well aware. If he regarded his own part as that of an onlooker, the sense in which he understood observation was to the highest degree exacting. He watched indeed, but he watched with every faculty, and he intended that every thread of intelligence he could throw out to seize the truth of the old historic world should be as strong as instruction, study, general indoctrination could make it. It would be useless for him to live where the human drama most attracted him unless he could grasp it with an assured hand; and he could never do this if he was to remain a stranger and a sojourner, merely feeding on the picturesque surface of appearances. To justify his expatriation he must work his own life completely into the texture of his new surroundings, and the story of his middle years is to be read as the most patient and laborious of attempts to do so. Its extraordinary success need hardly be insisted on; its failure, necessary and foredoomed, from certain points of view, is perhaps not less obvious. But the great fact of interest is the sight of him taking up the task with eyes, it is needless to say, fully open to all its demands, and never resting until he could be certain of having achieved all that was possible. So long as he was in the thick of it, the task occupied the whole of his attention. He took it with full seriousness; there never was a scholar more immersed in research than was Henry James in the study of his chosen world. There were times indeed when he might be thought to take it even more seriously than the case required. The world is not used to such deference from a rare critical talent, and it certainly has much less respect for its own standards than Henry James had, or seemed to have. His respect was of course very freely mingled with irony, and yet it would be rash to say that his irony preponderated. He probably felt that this, in his condition, was a luxury which he could only afford within limits. He could never forget that he had somehow to make up to himself for arriving as an alien from a totally different social climate; for his own satisfaction he had to wake and toil while others slept, keeping his ever-ready and rebellious criticism for an occasional hour of relief.

The world with which he thus sought to identify himself was a small affair, by most of our measurements. It was a circle of sensibilities that it might be easy to dismiss as hypertrophied and over-civilised, too deeply smothered in the veils of artificial life to repay so much patient attention. Yet the little world of urbane leisure satisfied him because he found a livelier interest, always, in the results and effects and implications of things than in the groundwork itself; so that the field of study he desired was that in which initial forces had travelled furthest from their prime, passing step by step from their origin to the level where, diffused and transformed, they were still just discernible to acute perception. It is not through any shy timidity that so often in his books he requires us to infer the presence of naked emotion from the faintest stirrings of an all but unruffled surface; it is because these monitory signals, transmitted from so far, tell a story that would be weakened by a directer method. The tiny movement that is the last expression of an act or a fact carries within it the history of all it has passed through on the way—a treasure of interest that the act, the fact in itself, had not possessed. And so in the social scene, wherever its crude beginnings have been left furthest behind, wherever its forms have been most rubbed and toned by the hands of succeeding generations, there he found, not an obliteration of sharp character, but a positive enhancement of it, with the whole of its past crowded into its bosom. The kind of life, therefore, that might have been thought too trifling to bear the weight of his grave and powerful scrutiny was exactly the life that he pursued for its expressive value. He clung to civilisation, he was faithful throughout to a few yards of town-pavement, not because he was scared by the rough freedom of the wild, but rather because he was impatient of its insipidity. He is very often to be heard crying out against the tyrannous claims of his world, when they interfere with his work, his leisure, his health; but at the moment of greatest revulsion he never suggests that the claims may be fraudulent after all, or that this small corner of modernity is not the best and most fruitful that the age has to shew.

It must be a matter of pride to an English reader that this corner happened to be found among ourselves. Henry James came to London, however, more by a process of exhaustion than by deliberate choice, and plenty of chastening considerations for a Londoner will appear in his letters. If he elected to live among thick English wits rather than in any nimbler atmosphere, it was at first largely because English ways and manners lay more open to an explorer than the closer, compacter societies of the mainland. Gradually, as we know well, his affection was kindled into devoted loyalty. It remained true, none the less, that with much that is common ground among educated people of our time and place he was never really in touch. One has only to think of the part played, in the England he frequented, by school and college, by country-homes, by church and politics and professions, to understand how much of the ordinary consciousness was closed to him. Yet it is impossible to say that these limitations were imposed on him only because he was a stranger among strangers; they belonged to the conditions of his being from much further back. They were implied in his queer unanchored youth, in which he and his greatly gifted family had been able to grow in the free exercise of their talents without any of the foundations of settled life. Henry James's genius opened and flourished in the void. His ripe wisdom and culture seemed to have been able to dispense entirely with the mere training that most people require before they can feel secure in their critical outlook and sense of proportion. There could be no better proof of the fact that imagination, if only there is enough of it, will do the work of all the other faculties unaided. Whatever were the gaps in his knowledge—knowledge of life generally, and of the life of the mind in particular—his imagination covered them all. And so it was that without ever acquiring a thousand things that go to the making of a full experience and a sound taste, he yet enjoyed and possessed everything that it was in them to give.

His taste, indeed, his judgment of quality, seems to have been bestowed upon him in its essentials like a gift of nature. From the very first he was sure of his taste and could account for it. His earliest writing shews, if anything, too large a portion of tact and composure; a critic might have said that such a perfect control of his means was not the most hopeful sign in a young author. Henry James reversed the usual procedure of a beginner, keeping warily to matter well within his power of management—and this is observable too in his early letters—until he was ready to deal with matter more robust. In his instinct for perfection he never went wrong—never floundered into raw enthusiasms, never lost his way, never had painfully to recover himself; he travelled steadily forward with no need of guidance, enriching himself with new impressions and wasting none of them. He accepted nothing that did not minister in some way to the use of his gifts; whatever struck him as impossible to assimilate to these he passed by without a glance. He could not be tempted by any interest unrelated to the central line of his work. He had enough even so, he felt, to occupy a dozen lives, and he grudged every moment that did not leave its deposit of stuff appropriate to his purpose. The play of his thought was so ample and ardent that it disguised his resolute concentration; he responded so lavishly and to so much that he seemed ready to take up and transform and adorn whatever was offered him. But this in truth was far from the fact, and by shifting the recollection one may see the impatient gesture with which he would sweep aside the distraction that made no appeal to him. It was natural that he should care nothing for any abstract speculation or inquiry; he was an artist throughout, desiring only the refracted light of human imperfection, never the purity of colourless reason. More surprising was his refusal, for it was almost that, of the appeal of music—and not wordless music only, but even the song and melody of poetry. It cannot be by accident that poetry scarcely appears at all in such a picture of a literary life as is given by his letters. The purely lyrical ear seems to have been strangely sealed in him—he often declared as much himself. And poetry in general, though he could be deeply stirred by it, he inclined to put away from him, perhaps for the very reason that it meant too forcible a deflection from the right line of his energy. All this careful gathering up of his powers, in any case, this determined deafness to irrelevant voices, gave a commanding warrant to the critical panoply of his later life. His certainty and consistency, his principle, his intellectual integrity—by all these the pitch of his opinions, wherever he delivered them, reached a height that was unforgettably impressive.

I have tried to touch, so far as possible, on the different strains in Henry James's artistic experience; but to many who read these letters it will be another aspect altogether that his name first recalls. They will remember how much of his life was lived in his relations with his countless friends, and how generously he poured out his best for them. But if, as I have suggested, much of his mind appears fitfully and obscurely in his letters, this side is fully irradiated from first to last. Never, surely, has any circle of friendship received so magnificent a tribute of expressed affection and sympathy. It was lavished from day to day, and all the resources of his art were drawn upon to present it with due honour. As time goes on a kind of personal splendour shines through the correspondence, which only becomes more natural, more direct a communication of himself, as it is uttered with increasing mastery. The familiar form of the letter was changed under his hand into what may really be called a new province of art, a revelation of possibilities hitherto unexplored. Perfect in expression as they are, these letters are true extemporisations, thrown off always at great speed, as though with a single sweep of the hand, for all their richness of texture and roundness of phrase. At their most characteristic they are like free flights of virtuosity, flung out with enjoyment in the hours of a master's ease; and the abundance of his creative vigour is shewn by the fact that there should always be so much more of it to spare, even after the exhausting strain of his regular work. But the greater wonder is that this liberal gesture never became mechanical, never a fixed manner displayed for any and all alike, without regard to the particular mind addressed. Not for a moment does he forget to whom he is speaking; he writes in the thought of his correspondent, always perceptibly turning to that relation, singled out for the time from all the rest. Each received of his best, but some peculiar, inalienable share in it.

If anything can give to those who did not know him an impression of Henry James's talk, it will be some of the finest of these later letters. One difference indeed is immediately to be marked. His pondering hesitation as he talked, his search over the whole field of expression for the word that should do justice to the picture forming in his mind—this gives place in the letters to a flow unchecked, one sonorous phrase uncoiling itself after another without effort. Pen in hand, or, as he finally preferred, dictating to his secretary, it was apparently easier for him to seize upon the images he sought to detach, one by one, from the clinging and populous background of his mind. In conversation the effort seemed to be greater, and save in rare moments of exceptional fervour—no one who heard him will forget how these recurred more and more in the last year of his life, under the deep excitement of the war—he liked to take his time in working out his thought with due deliberation. But apart from this, the letters exactly reflect the colour and contour of his talk—his grandiose courtesy, his luxuriant phraseology, his relish for some extravagantly colloquial turn embedded in a Ciceronian period, his humour at once so majestic and so burly. Intercourse with him was not quite easy, perhaps; his style was too hieratic, too richly adorned and arrayed for that. But it was enough to surrender simply to the current of his thought; the listener felt himself gathered up and cared for—felt that Henry James assumed all the responsibility and would deal with the occasion in his own way. That way was never to give a mere impersonal display of his own, but to create and develop a reciprocal relation, to both sides of which he was more than capable of doing the fullest justice. No words seem satisfactory in describing the dominance he exerted over any scene in which he figured—yet exerted by no over-riding or ignoring of the presence of others, rather with the quickest, most apprehending susceptibility to it. But better than by any description is this memory imparted by the eloquent roll and ring of his letters.

He grew old in the honour of a wide circle of friends of all ages, and of a public which, if small, was deeply devoted. He stood so completely outside the evolution of English literature that his position was special and unrelated, but it was a position at last unanimously acknowledged. Signs of the admiration and respect felt for him by all who held the belief in the art of letters, even by those whose line of development most diverged from his—these he unaffectedly enjoyed, and many came to him. None the less he knew very well that in all he most cared for, in what was to him the heart and essence of life, he was solitary to the end. However much his work might be applauded, the spirit of rapt and fervent faith in which it was conceived was a hermitage, so he undoubtedly felt, that no one else had perceived or divined. His story of the Figure in the Carpet was told of himself; no one brought him what he could accept as true and final comprehension. He could never therefore feel that he had reached a time when his work was finished and behind him. Old age only meant an imagination more crowded than ever, a denser throng of shapes straining to be released before it was too late. He bitterly resented the hindrances of ill-health, during some of his last years, as an interruption, a curtailment of the span of his activity; there were so many and so far better books that he still wished to write. His interest in life, growing rather than weakening, clashed against the artificial restraints, as they seemed, of physical age; whenever these were relaxed, it leaped forward to work again. The challenge of the war with Germany roused him to a height of passion he had never touched before in the outer world; and if the strain of it exhausted his strength, as well it might, it gave him one last year of the fullest and deepest experience, perhaps, that he had ever known. It wore out his body, which was too tired and spent to live longer; but he carried away the power of his spirit still in its prime.

NOTE

The best thanks of the editor are due to Henry James's family, and particularly to his niece, Mrs. Bruce Porter, for much valuable help. Mrs. Porter undertook the collecting and copying of all the letters addressed to correspondents in America; and it is owing to her that the completion of these volumes, inevitably hindered by the war, has not been further delayed.

I. FIRST EUROPEAN YEARS (1869-74)

THE letters in this section take up the story of Henry James's life at the exact point to which he brought it in the second instalment of his reminiscences, *Notes of a Son and Brother*. It will be remembered that the third volume, *The Middle Years*, of which only a fragment was written, opens with his arrival in England in February 1869; and the first letter here printed is dated from London a few days later. But in evoking his youth it was no part of Henry James's design to write a consecutive tale, and the order of dates and events is constantly obscured in the abundance of his memories. For convenience, therefore, a brief summary may be given of the course of his early years.

Henry James was born on April 15, 1843, at 2 Washington Place, New York. He was the second child of his parents, the elder by a year being his brother William. The younger members of the family were Wilkinson ('Wilky'), Robertson ('Bob'), and Alice. Their father Henry James the elder, was a man whose striking genius has never received full justice except at the hands of his illustrious sons, though from them with profound and affectionate admiration. He was the most brilliant of a remarkable group of many brothers and sisters, whose portraits, or some of them, are sketched in *A Small Boy and Others*. Originally of Irish descent, the James family had been settled for a couple of generations in the State of New York, and in particular at Albany. The founder of the American branch had been a prosperous man of business, whose successful career left him in a position to bequeath to his numerous descendants a fortune large enough to enable them all to live in complete independence of the commercial world. Henry James the elder has been sometimes described as 'the Reverend,' but in fact he never occupied any position but that of a detached philosopher, lecturer, man of letters. To his brothers and their extensive progeny he was a trusted and untiring moral support of a kind that many of them distinctly needed; the bereavements of the family were many, their misfortunes various, and his genial charity and good faith were an inexhaustible resource. His wife was Mary Walsh. She too belonged to a substantial New York family, of Scotch origin, several members of which are commemorated in *A Small Boy*. Her sister Katharine was for many years an inmate of the elder Henry's household, and to the end of her life the cherished friend of his children.

The second Henry James has left so full and vivid a portrait of his father that it is unnecessary to dwell on the happy influences under which the family passed their youth. The 'ideas' of the head of the house, as his remote speculations were familiarly known at home, lay outside the range of his second son; but in the preface to a collection of papers, posthumously issued in 1884, they are sympathetically expounded and appraised by William James, whose adventurous mind, impatient of academic rules and forms, was more akin to his father's, though it developed on quite other lines. It is natural to speak of the father as a Swedenborgian, for the writings of Swedenborg had been the chief source of his inspiration and supplied the tincture of his thought. He did not, however, himself admit this description of his point of view, which indeed was original and unconventional to the last degree. It was directed towards an ideal, to use William James's words, of 'the true relation between mankind and its Creator,' elaborated and re-affirmed in book after book, and always in a style so peculiarly vivacious and attractive that it is difficult to explain the indifference with which they were received and which has allowed them to fall completely forgotten. To the memory of his father's courageous spirit, his serene simplicity and luminous humour, none of which ever failed in the face of repeated disappointment, the younger Henry, years later, devoted his beautiful tribute of art and piety.

His recollections of childhood began, surprisingly enough, when he was little more than a year old. In the summer of 1844 the parents carried their two infants, William and Henry, for a visit to Europe, an adventure not altogether lost upon the younger; for he actually retained an impression of Paris, a glimpse of the Place Vendôme, to be the foundation of all his European experience. His earliest American memories were of Albany; but the family were soon established in Fourteenth Street, New York, which was their home for some ten years, a settlement only broken by family visits and summer weeks by the sea. The children's extraordinarily haphazard and promiscuous education went forward under various teachers, their father's erratic rule having apparently but one principle, that they should stay nowhere long enough to receive any formal imprint. To Henry at least their schooling meant nothing whatever but the opportunity of conducting his own education in his own way, and he made the utmost of the easy freedom they enjoyed. He was able to stare and brood to his heart's content, and thus to feed his imagination on the only pasturage it required.

In 1855 the whole household migrated to Europe for a visit of three years. This, the grand event of Henry's childhood, was really the determination of his whole career; for he then absorbed, once for all, what he afterwards called the 'European Virus'—the nostalgia for the old world which made it impossible for him to rest in peace elsewhere. All this time was one long draught of romance; though indeed as an initiation into the ways of French and English life it could hardly have been a more incoherent enterprise. True to his law, the head of the household planted the young family in one place only to sweep them away as soon as they might begin to form associations there. The summer of 1855 was spent at Geneva, then the classic spot for the acquisition of the 'languages,' according to the point of view of New York. But Geneva was abandoned before the end of the year, and the family settled in London for the winter, at first in Berkeley Street, afterwards in St. John's Wood. For any real contact with the place, this was a blank interlude; the tuition of a young Scotchman, later one of R. L. Stevenson's masters, seems to have been the solitary local tie provided for the children. By the middle of 1856 they were in Paris, and here they were able to use their opportunities a little more fully. Of these one of the oddest was the educational 'Institution Fezandié,' which they attended for a time. But there was more for them to learn at the Louvre and the Luxembourg, and it was to this time that Henry James afterwards ascribed his first conscious perception of what might be meant by the life of art. In the course of the two following years they twice spent some months at Boulogne-sur-mer, returning each time to Paris again. During the second visit to Boulogne Henry was laid low by the very serious attack of typhus that descends on the last page of *A Small Boy*.

35

In 1858 the family was rushed back to America for a year at Newport; but they were once more at Geneva for the winter of 1859-60. Here Henry was at first put to the strangest of all his strange educational courses, at the severely mathematical and commercial 'Institution Rochette.' But presently pleading for humaner studies, he was set free to attend lectures at the Academy, where at sixteen, for the first time and after so many arid experiences, he tasted instruction more or less adapted to his parts. Needless to say it did not last long. In the following summer the three elder boys were sent as private pupils to the houses of certain professors at Bonn. By this time William's marked talent for painting had decided his ambition; and it was quite in line with the originality of the household that they should at once return to America, leaving Paris behind them for good, in order that William might study art. Henry alone of them, by his account, felt that their proceedings needed a great deal of explanation. The new experiment, as short-lived as all the rest, was entered upon with ardour, and the family was re-established at Newport in the autumn of 1860. The distinguished master, William Hunt, had his studio there; and for a time Henry himself haunted it tentatively, while his brother was working with a zeal that was soon spent.

If we may trust his own report, Henry James had reached the age of seventeen with a curiously vague understanding of his own talent. No doubt it is possible to read the 'Notes' too literally; and indeed I have the fortunate opportunity of giving a side-light upon this period of his youth which proves as much. But if he was not quite the indeterminate brooder he depicts, he was far from rivalling the unusual precocity and decision of his brothers, and he was only now beginning to take real stock of his gifts. He had been provided with almost none of the sort of training by which he might have profited; and it is not to be supposed that his always indulgent parent would have neglected the taste of a literary son if it had shewn itself distinctly. He had been left to discover his line of progress as best he might, and his advance towards literature was slow and shy. Yet it would seem that by this time he must have made up his mind more definitely than he suggests in recalling the Newport years. The side-light I mentioned is thrown by some interesting notes sent me by Mr. Thomas Sergeant Perry, who made the acquaintance of the family at

Newport and was to remain their lifelong friend. His description shews that Henry James had now his own ambitions, even if he preferred to nurse them unobtrusively.

The first time I saw the James boys (writes Mr. Perry) was at the end of June or early in July 1858, shortly after their arrival in Newport for a year's stay. This year of their life is not recorded by H. J. in his 'Notes of a Son and Brother,' or rather its memories are crowded into the chronicle of the longer stay of the family in America, beginning with 1860. Mr. Duncan Pell, who knew Mr. James the father, told his son and me that we ought to call on the boys; and we did, but they were out. A day or two later we called again and found them in. We all went together to the Pells' house and spent the evening in simple joys.

I have often thought that the three brothers shewed that evening some of their characteristic qualities. I remember walking with Wilky hanging on my arm, talking to me as if he had found an old friend after long absence. When we got to the house and the rest of us were chattering, H. J. sat on the window-seat reading Leslie's Life of Constable with a certain air of remoteness. William was full of merriment and we were soon playing a simple and childish game. In 'A Small Boy and Others' H. J. speaks of Wilky's 'successful sociability, his instinct for intercourse, his genius for making friends,' and these amiable traits shewed themselves that evening as clearly as his other brother's jollity. Very soon afterwards H. J. with his two younger brothers entered the school where I was studying, that of the Rev. W. C. Leverett, who is mentioned in the 'Notes.' I recall H. J. as an uninterested scholar. Part of one day in a week was devoted to declaiming eloquent pieces from 'Sargent's Standard Speaker,' and I have not forgotten his amusement at seeing in the Manual of English Literature that we were studying, in the half page devoted to Mrs. Browning, that she had married R. Browning, 'himself no mean poet.' This compact information gave him great delight, for we were reading Browning. It was then too that he read for the first time 'The Vicar of Wakefield' and with great pleasure.

It was at that time that we began to take long walks together almost every afternoon along the Cliffs, over the beaches to the Paradise Rocks, to the Point, or inland, wherever it might be. A thousand scrappy recollections of the strolls still remain, fragments of talk, visions of the place. Thus it was near the Lily Pond that we long discussed Fourier's plan for regenerating the world. Harry had heard his father describe the great reformer's proposal to establish universal happiness, and like a good son he tried to carry the good news further. At another time, he fell under the influence of Ruskin; he devoted himself to the conscientious copying of a leaf and very faithfully drew a little rock that jutted above the surface of the Lily Pond. These artistic gropings, and those in Hunt's studio where he copied casts, were not his main interest. His chief interest was literature. We read the English magazines and reviews and the Revue des Deux Mondes with rapture. We fished in various waters, and I well remember when W. J. brought home a volume of Schopenhauer and showed us with delight the ugly mug of the philosopher and read us amusing specimens of his delightful pessimism. It was W. J. too who told us about Renan one cool evening of February when the twilight lingers till after six. H. J. in his books speaks without enthusiasm of his school studies, but he and I read together at Mr. Leverett's school a very fair amount of Latin literature. Like Shakespeare he had less Greek.

The departure of the James family to Geneva in October 1859 was a grievous blow. They returned, however, with characteristic suddenness the next September and came at once to Newport. During their stay abroad H. J. and I had kept up a lively correspondence. Most unfortunately all his letters, which I had faithfully preserved, were destroyed during one of my absences in Europe, and among them a poem, probably the only thing of the kind he ever tried, a short narrative in the manner of Tennyson's 'Dora.' He had entirely forgotten it, very naturally, when he said in his 'Notes': 'The muse was of course the muse of prose fiction—never for the briefest hour in my case the presumable, not to say the presuming, the much-taking-for-granted muse of rhyme, with whom I had never had, even in thought, the faintest flirtation.'

After his return to America in 1860, the question what he should do with his life became more urgent. Of course it was in literature that he took the greatest interest. One task that he set himself was translating Alfred de Musset's 'Lorenzaccio,' and into this version he introduced some scenes of his own. Exactly what they were I do not recall, though I read them with an even intenser interest than I did the original text. He was continually writing stories, mainly of a romantic kind. The heroes were for the most part villains, but they were white lambs by the side of the sophisticated heroines, who seemed to have read all Balzac in the cradle and to be positively dripping with lurid crimes. He began with these extravagant pictures of course in adoration of the great master whom he always so warmly admired.

H. J. seldom entrusted these early efforts to the criticism of his family— they did not see all he wrote. They were too keen critics, too sharp-witted, to be allowed to handle every essay of this budding talent. Their judgments would have been too true, their comments would have been too merciless; and hence, for sheer self-preservation, he hid a good part of his work from them. Not that they were cruel, far from it. Their frequent solitude in foreign parts, where they had no familiar companions, had welded them together in a way that would have been impossible in America, where each would have had separate distractions of his own. Their loneliness forced them to grow together most harmoniously, but their long exercise in literary criticism would have made them possibly merciless judges of H. J.'s crude beginnings.

The following anecdote will shew what I mean. Mr. James the father was getting out a somewhat abstruse book called 'Substance and Shadow, or Morality and Religion in their Relation to Life.' W. J. amused himself and all the family by designing a small cut to be put on the title page, representing a man beating a dead horse. This will illustrate the joyous chaff that filled the Jameses' house. There was no limit to it. There were always books to tell about and laugh over, or to admire, and there was an abundance of good talk with no shadow of pedantry or priggishness. H. J.'s spirits were never so high as those of the others. If they had been, he still would have had but little chance in a conflict of wits with them, on account of his slow speech, his halting choice of words and phrases; but as a companion in our walks he was delightful. He had plenty of humour, as his books shew, and above all he had a most affectionate heart. No one ever had more certain and more unobtrusive kindness than he. He had a certain air of aloofness, but he was not indifferent to those who had no claim upon him, and to his friends he was most tenderly devoted. Those who knew him will not need to be assured of that.

The Civil War, which presently broke upon the leisurely life of Newport, went deep into the mind and character of Henry James; but his part in it could only be that of an onlooker, for about this time an accidental strain developed results that gave him many years of uncertain health. He had to live much in the experience of his brothers, which he eagerly did. The two youngest fought in the war, Wilky receiving a grave wound of which he carried the mark for the rest of his life—he died in 1883. Henry went to Harvard in 1862, where William, no longer a painter but a man of science, had preceded him the year before. By the beginning of 1864 the rest of the family had settled in Boston, at Ashburton Place, whence they finally moved out to Cambridge in 1866. This was the end of their wanderings. For the remainder of his parents' lives Cambridge was Henry's American home and, with the instalment there of his brother William, the centre of all the family associations. But the long connection with New England never superseded, for Henry at least, the native tie with New York, and he was gratified when his name was at last carried back there again, many years afterwards, by another generation.

In Boston and Cambridge Henry James at length touched a purely literary circle. The beginning of such fruitful friendships as those with Professor C. E. Norton and Mr. W. D. Howells meant his open and professed dedication to literature. The Harvard Law School left as little direct impression on him as any of his other exposures to ordinary teaching, but at last he had finished with these makeshifts. His new friends helped him into his proper channel. Under their auspices he made his way into publication and became a regular contributor of criticism and fiction to several journals and reviews. There followed some very uneventful and industrious years, disturbed to some extent by ill-health but broken by no long absences from Cambridge. His constant companion and literary confidant was Mr. Howells, who writes to me that 'people were very much struck with his work in the magazine'—the *Atlantic*

Monthly, of which this friend was at that time assistant editor—'but mostly not pleased with it. It was a common thing to hear them say, "Oh, yes, we like Mr. James very much, but we cannot bear his stories".' Mr. Howells adds: 'I could scarcely exaggerate the intensity of our literary association. It included not only what he was doing and thinking himself in fiction, and criticism of whatever he was reading, but what other people were trying to do in our American magazines.' Beneath these activities we are to imagine the deep preoccupation, growing and growing, of the idea of a possible return to Europe. It is not very clear why the satisfaction of his wish was delayed for as long as it was. His doubtful health can hardly have amounted to a hindrance, and the authority of his parents was far too light and sympathetic to stand in his way. Yet it is only by the end of 1868, as I find from a letter of that time, that a journey to Europe has 'ceased to look positively and aggressively impossible.' Thereafter things move more quickly, and three months later he arrives at the great moment, memorable ever afterwards, of his landing at Liverpool.

From this point the letters speak for themselves, and only the slenderest commentary is required. He went first to London, where the hospitable Nortons had been installed on a visit for some while. These good friends opened the way to many interesting impressions for him, but he was only briefly in London at this time. For health's sake he spent three weeks alone at Great Malvern, in some sort of hydropathic establishment, among very British company. He writes of his great delight in the beauty of the place, and how he is 'gluttonised on British commonplace' indoors. After a tour which included Oxford and Cambridge and several English cathedrals, he had a few weeks more of London, and then passed on to Switzerland. He was at Geneva by the end of May, from where he writes that he is 'very well—which has ceased to be a wonder.' The Nortons joined him at Vevey. He left them in July for a small Swiss tour before making the great adventure of crossing the Alps for the first time. By Venice and Florence he reached Rome in November. He gave himself up there to rapturous and solitary wanderings: 'I see no people, to speak of, or for that matter to speak to.' In December he was at Naples for a fortnight, and then returned northwards by Assisi, Perugia, Genoa, Avignon, to Paris. Italy had made the deep and final impression on him for which he was so well prepared; 'already,' he writes, 'I feel my bows beneath her weight settle comfortably into the water.... Out of Italy you don't know how vulgar a world it is.' Presently he was in England and at Malvern again, everywhere saturating himself in the sense of old history and romance, to make the most of an opportunity which he did not then hope to prolong. 'It behoves me,' he writes to Professor Norton, 'as a luckless American, diabolically tempted of the shallow and the superficial, really to catch the flavour of an old civilization (it hardly matters which) and to strive to raise myself, for one brief moment at least, in the attitude of observation.' At the end of April 1870 he sailed for America.

After a year of Europe his hunger for the old world was greater than ever, but he had no present thought of settling there permanently. For two years he resumed the quiet life of his American Cambridge, busily engaged on a succession of sketches, reviews, and short stories of which only one, 'A Passionate Pilgrim,' survives in the collected edition of his works. 'I enjoy America,' he says in a letter of 1870, 'with a poignancy that perpetually surprises me'; but 'the wish—the absolute sense of need—to see Italy again' constantly increases. He spends 'a quiet, low-toned sort of winter, reading somewhat, writing a little, and "going out" occasionally.' He wrote his first piece of fiction that was long enough to be called a novel—'Watch and Ward,' afterwards so completely disowned and ignored by him that he always named as his first novel Roderick Hudson, of four years later. But the memory of Italy had fatally shaken his rest, and there began a long and anxious struggle with his sense of duty to his native land. In his letters of this time the attitude of the 'good American' remains resolute, however. 'It's a complex fate, being an American,' he writes, early in 1872, 'and one of the responsibilities it entails is fighting against a superstitious valuation of Europe.' It was still as a tourist and a pilgrim only that he crossed the Atlantic again, with his sister and aunt (Miss Katharine Walsh), in May 1872.

He came with a definite commission to contribute a series of 'Transatlantic Sketches' to the American *Nation*, and the first material was gathered in an English tour that ranged from Chester to North Devon. Still with his sister and aunt he wandered for three months in Switzerland, North

Italy and Bavaria, settling upon Paris, now alone, for the autumn. It was here that he began his intimacy with J. R. Lowell, in afternoon walks with him between mornings of work and evenings at the Théâtre Français. He declares that he saw no one else in Paris—his mind was firmly set upon Italy. To Rome he went for the first six months of 1873, where he was now at home enough among ancient solitudes to have time and thought for social novelty. Thirty years later, in his life of William Wetmore Story, he revived the American world of what was still a barely modernised Rome, the world into which he was plunged by acquaintance with the sculptor and his circle. Now and thenceforward it was not so much the matter for sketches of travel that he was collecting as it was the matter for the greater part of his best-known fiction. The American in Europe was to be his own subject, and he began to make it so. The summer months were mainly spent at Homburg, which was also to leave its mark on several of his tales. His elder brother joined him when he returned to Rome, but William contracted a malaria, and they moved to Florence early in 1874. Here Henry was soon left alone, in rooms on Piazza Sta. Maria Novella, for some months of close and happy concentration on Roderick Hudson. The novel had already been engaged by Mr. Howells for the *Atlantic Monthly*, and its composition marks the definite end of Henry James's literary apprenticeship. He had arrived at it by wary stages; of the large amount of work behind him, though much of it was of slight value, nothing had been wasted; every page of his writing had been in the direct line towards the perfect literary manners of his matured skill. But hitherto he had written experimentally and to occasion; he was now an established novelist in his own right.

He returned to America in the autumn of 1874, after some summer wanderings that are shewn by the 'Transatlantic Sketches' to have taken him through Holland and Belgium. But it happens that at this point there is an almost empty gap of a year and more in his surviving correspondence, and it is not possible to follow him closely. He disappears with the still agitating question upon his hands—where was he to live?—his American loyalty still fighting it out with his European inclination. The steps are lost by which the doubt was determined in the course of another year at home. It is only certain that when he next came to Europe, twelve months later, it had been quieted for ever.

TO MISS ALICE JAMES.

H. J.'s lodging in Half Moon St., and his landlord, Mr. Lazarus Fox, are described, it will be remembered, in *The Middle Years*. He had arrived in London from America a few days before the date of the following letter to his sister. Professor Charles Norton, with his wife and sisters, was living at this time in Kensington.

7 Half Moon St., W.

March 10th [1869].

Ma sœur chérie,

I have half an hour before dinner-time: why shouldn't I begin a letter for Saturday's steamer?... I really feel as if I had lived—I don't say a lifetime—but a year in this murky metropolis. I actually believe that this feeling is owing to the singular permanence of the impressions of childhood, to which any present experience joins itself on, without a broken link in the chain of sensation. Nevertheless, I may say that up to this time I have been crushed under a sense of the mere magnitude of London—its inconceivable immensity—in such a way as to paralyse my mind for any appreciation of details. This is gradually subsiding; but what does it leave behind it? An extraordinary intellectual depression, as I may say, and an indefinable flatness of mind. The place sits on you, broods on you, stamps on you with the feet of its myriad bipeds and quadrupeds. In fine, it is anything but a cheerful or a charming city. Yet it is a very splendid one. It gives you here at the west end, and in the city proper, a vast impression of opulence and prosperity. But you don't want a dissertation of commonplaces on London and you would like me to touch on my own individual experience. Well, my dear, since last week it has been sufficient, altho' by no means immense. On Saturday I received a visit from Mr. Leslie Stephen (blessed man) who came unsolicited with the utmost civility in the world and invited me to dine with him the next day. This I did, in company with Miss Jane Norton. His wife made me very welcome and they both appear to much better effect in their own premises than they did in America. After dinner he conducted us by the underground railway to see the beasts in the Regent's Park, to which as a member of the Zoological Society he has admittance 'Sundays.' ... In the evening I dined with the invaluable Nortons and went with Chas. and Madame, Miss S. and Miss Jane (via underground railway) to hear Ruskin lecture at University College on Greek Myths. I enjoyed it much in spite of fatigue; but as I am to meet him some day through the Nortons, I shall reserve comments. On Wednesday evening I dined at the N.'s (toujours Norton, you see) in company with Miss Dickens—Dickens's only unmarried daughter—plain-faced, ladylike (in black silk and black lace,) and the image of her father. I exchanged but ten words with her. But yesterday, my dear old sister, was my crowning day—seeing as how I spent the greater part of it in the house of Mr. Wm. Morris, Poet. Fitly to tell the tale, I should need a fresh pen, paper and spirits. A few hints must suffice. To begin with, I breakfasted, by way of a change, with the Nortons, along with Mr. Sam Ward, who has just arrived, and Mr. Aubrey de Vere, *tu sais,* the Catholic poet, a pleasant honest old man and very much less high-flown than his name. He tells good stories in a light natural way. After a space I came home and remained until 4-1/2 p.m., when I had given rendez-vous to C.N. and ladies at Mr. Morris's door, they going by appointment to see his shop and C. having written to say he would bring me. Morris lives on the same premises as his shop, in Queen's Square, Bloomsbury, an antiquated ex-fashionable region, smelling strong of the last century, with a hoary effigy of Queen Anne in the middle. Morris's poetry, you see, is only his sub-trade. To begin with, he is a manufacturer of stained glass windows, tiles, ecclesiastical and medieval tapestry, altar-cloths, and in fine everything quaint, archaic, pre-Raphaelite—and I may add, exquisite. Of course his business is small and may be carried on in his house: the things he makes are so handsome, rich and expensive (besides being articles of the very last luxury) that his *fabrique* can't be on a very large scale. But everything he has and does is superb and beautiful. But more curious than anything is himself. He designs with his own head and hands all the figures and patterns used in his glass and tapestry, and furthermore works the latter, stitch by stitch, with his own fingers—aided by those of his wife and little girls. Oh, ma chère, such a wife! *Je n'en reviens pas*—she haunts me still. A figure cut out of a missal—out of one of Rossetti's or Hunt's pictures—to say this gives but a faint idea of her, because when such an image puts on flesh and blood, it is an apparition of fearful and wonderful intensity. It's hard to say whether she's a grand synthesis of all the pre-Raphaelite pictures ever made—or they a 'keen analysis' of her—whether she's an original or a copy. In either case she is a wonder. Imagine a tall lean woman in a long dress of some dead purple stuff, guiltless of hoops (or of anything else, I should say,) with a mass of crisp black hair heaped into great wavy projections on each of her temples, a thin pale face, a pair of strange sad, deep, dark Swinburnian eyes, with great thick black oblique brows, joined in the middle and tucking themselves away under her hair, a mouth like the 'Oriana' in our illustrated Tennyson, a long neck, without any collar, and in lieu thereof some dozen strings of outlandish beads—in fine complete. On the wall was a large nearly full-length portrait of her by Rossetti, so strange and unreal that if you hadn't seen her you'd pronounce it a distempered vision, but in fact an extremely good likeness. After dinner (we stayed to dinner, Miss Grace, Miss S. S. and I,) Morris read us one of his unpublished poems, from the second series of his un-'Earthly Paradise,' and his wife, having a bad toothache, lay on the sofa, with her handkerchief to her face. There was something very quaint and remote from our actual life, it seemed to me, in the whole scene: Morris reading in his flowing antique numbers a legend of prodigies and terrors (the story of Bellerophon, it was), around us all the picturesque bric-a-brac of the apartment (every article of furniture literally a 'specimen' of something or other,) and in the corner this dark silent medieval woman with her medieval toothache. Morris himself is extremely pleasant and quite different from his wife. He impressed me most agreeably. He is short, burly, corpulent, very careless and unfinished in his dress, and looks a little like B. G. Hosmer, if you can imagine B. G. infinitely magnified and fortified. He has a very loud voice and a nervous restless manner and a perfectly unaffected and business-like address. His talk indeed is wonderfully to the point and remarkable for clear good sense. He said no one thing that I remember, but I was struck with the very good judgment shown in everything he uttered. He's an extraordinary example, in short, of a delicate sensitive genius and taste, saved by a perfectly healthy body and temper. All his designs are quite as good (or rather nearly so) as his poetry: altogether it was a long rich sort of visit, with a strong peculiar flavour of its own.... Ouf! what a repulsively long letter! This sort of thing won't do. A few general reflections, a burst of affection (say another sheet), and I must close.... Farewell, dear girl, and dear incomparable all—

Your H.

TO HIS MOTHER.

7 Half Moon St., W.

March 26, 1869.

My dearest Mother,

...This will have been my fifth weekly bundle since my arrival, and I can't promise—or rather I forbear to threaten—that it shall be as hugely copious as the others. But there's no telling where my pen may take me. You see I am still in what my old landlord never speaks of but as 'this great metropolis'; and I hope you will believe me when I add, moreover, that I am in the best of health and spirits. During the last week I have been knocking about in a quiet way and have deeply enjoyed my little adventures. The last few days in particular have been extremely pleasant. You have perhaps fancied that I have been rather stingy-minded towards this wondrous England, and that I was [not] taking things in quite the magnanimous intellectual manner that befits a youth of my birth and breeding. The truth is that the face of things here throws a sensitive American back on himself—back on his prejudices and national passions, and benumbs for a while the faculty of appreciation and the sense of justice. But with time, if he is worth a copper, the characteristic beauty of the land dawns upon him (just as certain vicious chilblains are now dawning upon my poor feet) and he feels that he would fain plant his restless feet into the rich old soil and absorb the burden of the misty air. If I were in anything like working order now, I should be very sorry to leave England. I should like

47

to settle down for a year and expose my body to the English climate and my mind to English institutions. But a truce to this cheap discursive stuff. I date the moment from which my mind rose erect in impartial might to a little sail I took on the Thames the other day in one of the little penny steamers which shoot along its dirty bosom. It was a grey, raw English day, and the banks of the river, as far as I went, hideous. Nevertheless I enjoyed it. It was too cold to go up to Greenwich. (The weather, by the way, since my arrival has been horribly damp and bleak, and no more like spring than in a Boston January.) The next day I went with several of the Nortons to dine at Ruskin's, out of town. This too was extremely pleasant. Ruskin himself is a very simple matter. In face, in manner, in talk, in mind, he is weakness pure and simple. I use the word, not invidiously, but scientifically. He has the beauties of his defects; but to see him only confirms the impression given by his writing, that he has been scared back by the grim face of reality into the world of unreason and illusion, and that he wanders there without a compass and a guide—or any light save the fitful flashes of his beautiful genius. The dinner was very nice and easy, owing in a great manner to Ruskin's two charming young nieces who live with him—one a lovely young Irish girl with a rich virginal brogue—a creature of a truly delightful British maidenly simplicity—and the other a nice Scotch lass, who keeps house for him. But I confess, cold-blooded villain that I am, that what I most enjoyed was a portrait by Titian—an old doge, a work of transcendent beauty and elegance, such as to give one a new sense of the meaning of art.... But, dearest mammy, I must pull up. Pile in scraps of news. Osculate my sister most passionately. Likewise my aunt. Be assured of my sentiments and present them to my father and brother.

Thy HENRY jr.

TO HIS MOTHER.

Florence, Hôtel de l'Europe.

October 13th, 1869.

My darling Mammy,

...For the past six weeks that I have been in Italy I've hardly until within a day or two exchanged five minutes' talk with any one but the servants in the hotels and the custodians in the churches. As far as meeting people is concerned, I've not as yet had in Europe a very brilliant record. Yesterday I met at the Uffizi Miss Anna Vernon of Newport and her friend Mrs. Carter, with whom I had some discourse; and on the same morning I fell in with a somewhat seedy and sickly American, who seemed to be doing the gallery with an awful minuteness, and who after some conversation proposed to come and see me. He called this morning and has just left; but he seems a vague and feeble brother and I anticipate no wondrous joy from his acquaintance. The 'hardly' in the clause above is meant to admit two or three Englishmen with whom I have been thrown for a few hours.... One especially, whom I met at Verona, won my affections so rapidly that I was really sad at losing him. But he has vanished, leaving only a delightful impression and not even a name—a man of about 38, with a sort of quiet perfection of English virtue about him, such as I have rarely found in another. Willy asked me in one of his recent letters for an 'opinion' of the English, which I haven't yet had time to give—tho' at times I have felt as if it were a theme on which I could write from a full mind. In fact, however, I have very little right to have any opinion on the matter. I've seen far too few specimens and those too superficially. The only thing I'm certain about is that I like them—like them heartily. W. asked if as individuals they 'kill' the individual American. To this I would say that the Englishmen I have met not only kill, but bury in unfathomable depths, the Americans I have met. A set of people less framed to provoke national self-complacency than the latter it would be hard to imagine. There is but one word to use in regard to them—vulgar, vulgar, vulgar. Their ignorance—their stingy, defiant, grudging attitude towards everything European—their perpetual reference of all things to some American standard or precedent which exists only in their own unscrupulous wind-bags—and then our unhappy poverty of voice, of speech and of physiognomy—these things glare at you hideously. On the other hand, we seem a people of *character*, we seem to have energy, capacity and intellectual stuff in ample measure. What I have pointed at as our vices are the elements of the modern man with *culture* quite left out. It's the absolute and incredible lack of *culture* that strikes you in common travelling Americans. The pleasantness of the English, on the other side, comes in a great measure from the fact of their each having been dipped into the crucible, which gives them a sort of coating of comely varnish and colour. They have been smoothed and polished by mutual social attrition. They have manners and a language. We lack both, but particularly the latter. I have seen very 'nasty' Britons, certainly, but as a rule they are such as to cause your heart to warm to them. The women are at once better and worse than the men. Occasionally they are hard, flat, and greasy and dowdy to downright repulsiveness; but frequently they have a modest, matronly charm which is the perfection of womanishness and which makes Italian and Frenchwomen—and to a certain extent even our own—seem like a species of feverish highly-developed invalids. You see Englishmen, here in Italy, to a particularly good advantage. In the midst of these false and beautiful Italians they glow with the light of the great fact, that after all they love a bath-tub and they hate a lie.

16th, Sunday. I *have* seen some nice Americans and I still love my country. I have called upon Mrs. Huntington and her two daughters—late of Cambridge—whom I met in Switzerland and who have an apartment here. The daughters more than reconcile me to the shrill-voiced sirens of New England's rock-bound coast. The youngest is delightfully beautiful and sweet—and the elder delightfully sweet and plain—with a plainness *qui vaut bien des beautés....*

Maman de mon âme, farewell. I have kept my letter three days, hoping for news from home. I hope you are not paying me back for that silence of six weeks ago. Blessings on your universal heads.

Thy lone and loving exile,

H. J. jr.

TO WILLIAM JAMES.

Hôtel d'Angleterre, Rome.

Oct. 30th [1869].

My dearest Wm.

...The afternoon after I had posted those two letters I took a walk out of Florence to an enchanting old Chartreuse—an ancient monastery, perched up on top of a hill and turreted with little cells like a feudal castle. I attacked it and carried it by storm—i.e. obtained admission and went over it. On coming out I swore to myself that while I had life in my body I wouldn't leave a country where adventures of that complexion are the common incidents of your daily constitutional: but that I would hurl myself upon Rome and fight it out on this line at the peril of my existence. Here I am then in the Eternal City. It was easy to leave Florence; the cold had become intolerable and the rain perpetual. I started last night, and at 10-1/2 o'clock and after a bleak and fatiguing journey of 12 hours found myself here with the morning light. There are several places on the route I should have been glad to see; but the weather and my own condition made a direct journey imperative. I rushed to this hotel (a very slow and obstructed rush it was, I confess, thanks to the longueurs and lenteurs of the Papal dispensation) and after a wash and a breakfast let myself loose on the city. From midday to dusk I have been roaming the streets. Que vous en dirai-je? At last—for the first time—I live! It beats everything: it leaves the Rome of your fancy—your education— nowhere. It makes Venice—Florence—Oxford—London—seem like little cities of pasteboard. I went reeling and moaning thro' the streets, in a fever of enjoyment. In the course of four or five hours I traversed almost the whole of Rome and got a glimpse of everything—the Forum, the Coliseum (stupendissimo!), the Pantheon, the Capitol, St. Peter's, the Column of Trajan, the Castle of St. Angelo—all the Piazzas and ruins and monuments. The effect is something indescribable. For the first time I know what the picturesque is. In St. Peter's I stayed some time. It's even beyond its reputation. It was filled with foreign ecclesiastics—great armies encamped in prayer on the marble plains of its pavement—an inexhaustible physiognomical study. To crown my day, on my way home, I met his Holiness in person—driving in prodigious purple state—sitting dim within the shadows of his coach with two uplifted benedictory fingers—like some dusky Hindoo idol in the depths of its shrine. Even if I should leave Rome tonight I should feel that I have caught the keynote of its operation on the senses. I have looked along the grassy vista of the Appian Way and seen the topmost stone-work of the Coliseum sitting shrouded in the light of heaven, like the edge of an Alpine chain. I've trod the Forum and I have scaled the Capitol. I've seen the Tiber hurrying along, as swift and dirty as history! From the high tribune of a great chapel of St. Peter's I have heard in the papal choir a strange old man sing in a shrill unpleasant soprano. I've seen troops of little tonsured neophytes clad in scarlet, marching and countermarching and ducking and flopping, like poor little raw recruits for the heavenly host. In fine I've seen Rome, and I shall go to bed a wiser man than I last rose—yesterday morning....

A toi,

H. J. jr.

TO WILLIAM JAMES.

'Minny Temple' is the beloved young cousin commemorated in the last pages of *Notes of a Son and Brother*. The news of her death came to H. J. at Malvern almost immediately after the following letter was written.

Great Malvern.

March 8th, 1870.

Beloved Bill,

You ask me in your last letter so 'cordially' to write home every week, if it's only a line that altho' I have very little to say on this windy March afternoon, I can't resist the homeward tendency of my thoughts. I wrote to Alice some eight days ago—raving largely about the beauty of Malvern, in the absence of a better theme: so I haven't even that topic to make talk of. But as I say, my thoughts are facing squarely homeward and that is enough.... Now that I'm in England you'd rather have me talk of the present than of pluperfect Italy. But life furnishes so few incidents here that I cudgel my brains in vain. Plenty of gentle emotions from the scenery, etc.; but only man is vile. Among my fellow-patients here I find no intellectual companionship. Never from a single Englishman of them all have I heard the first word of appreciation and enjoyment of the things here that I find delightful. To a certain extent this is natural: but not to the extent to which they carry it. As for the women, I give 'em up in advance. I am tired of their plainness and stiffness and tastelessness—their dowdy beads and their lindsey woolsey trains. Nay, this is peevish and brutal. Personally (with all their faults) they are well enough. I revolt from their dreary deathly want of—what shall I call it?—Clover Hooper has it—intellectual grace—Minny Temple has it—moral spontaneity. They live wholly in the realm of the cut and dried. 'Have you ever been to Florence?' 'Oh yes.' 'Isn't it a most peculiarly interesting city?' 'Oh yes, I think it's so very nice.' 'Have you read *Romola*?' 'Oh yes.' 'I suppose you admire it.' 'Oh yes, I think it so very clever.' The English have such a mortal mistrust of anything like criticism or 'keen analysis' (which they seem to regard as a kind of maudlin foreign flummery) that I rarely remember to have heard on English lips any other intellectual verdict (no matter under what provocation) than this broad synthesis—'so immensely clever.' What exasperates you is not that they can't say more, but that they wouldn't if they could. Ah, but they are a great people for all that.... I re-echo with all my heart your impatience for the moment of our meeting again. I should despair of ever making you know how your conversation m'a manqué or how, when regained, I shall enjoy it. All I ask for is that I may spend the interval to the best advantage—and you too. The more we shall have to say to each other the better. Your last letter spoke of father and mother having 'shocking colds'—I hope they have melted away. Among the things I have recently read is father's *Marriage* paper in the *Atlantic*—with great enjoyment of its manner and approval of its matter. I see he is becoming one of our prominent magazinists. He will send me the thing from *Old and New*. A young Scotchman here gets the *Nation* sent him by his brother from N.Y. Whose are the three French papers on women? They are 'so very clever.' A propos—I retract all those brutalities about the Engländerinnen. They are the mellow mothers and daughters of a mighty race. But I *must* pull in. I have still lots of unsatisfied curiosity and unexpressed affection, but they must stand over. Farewell. Salute my parents and sister and believe me your brother of brothers,

H. JAMES jr.

TO HIS FATHER.

Great Malvern

March 19th, '70.

Dear Father,

...The other afternoon I trudged over to Worcester—through a region so thick-sown with good old English 'effects'—with elm-scattered meadows and sheep-cropped commons and the ivy-smothered dwellings of small gentility, and high-gabled, heavy-timbered, broken-plastered farm-houses, and stiles leading to delicious meadow footpaths and lodge-gates leading to far-off manors—with all things suggestive of the opening chapters of half-remembered novels, devoured in infancy—that I felt as if I were pressing all England to my soul. As I neared the good old town I saw the great Cathedral tower, high and square, rise far into the cloud-dappled blue. And as I came nearer still I stopped on the bridge and viewed the great ecclesiastical pile cast downward into the yellow Severn. And going further yet I entered the town and lounged about the close and gazed my fill at that most soul-sustaining sight—the waning afternoon, far aloft on the broad perpendicular field of the Cathedral spire—tasted too, as deeply, of the peculiar stillness and repose of the close—saw a ruddy English lad come out and lock the door of the old foundation school which marries its heavy gothic walls to the basement of the church, and carry the vast big key into one of the still canonical houses—and stood wondering as to the effect on a man's mind of having in one's boyhood haunted the Cathedral shade as a King's scholar and yet kept ruddy with much cricket in misty meadows by the Severn. This is a sample of the meditations suggested in my daily walks. Envy me—if you can without hating! I wish I could describe them all—Colwell Green especially, where, weather favouring,

I expect to drag myself this afternoon—where each square yard of ground lies verdantly brimming with the deepest British picturesque, and half begging, half deprecating a sketch. You should see how a certain stile-broken footpath here winds through the meadows to a little grey rook-haunted church. Another region fertile in walks is the great line of hills. Half an hour's climb will bring you to the top of the Beacon—the highest of the range—and here is a breezy world of bounding turf with twenty counties at your feet—and when the mist is thick something immensely English in the situation (as if you were wandering on some mighty seaward cliffs or downs, haunted by vague traditions of an early battle). You may wander for hours—delighting in the great green landscape as it responds forever to the cloudy movements of heaven—scaring the sheep—wishing horribly that your mother and sister were—I can't say *mounted*—on a couple of little white-aproned donkeys, climbing comfortably at your side. But at this rate I shall tire you out with my walks as effectually as I sometimes tire myself.... Kiss mother for her letter—and for that villainous cold. I enfold you all in an immense embrace.

Your faithful son,

H.

TO CHARLES ELIOT NORTON.

Professor Norton and his family were still at this time in Europe. Arthur Sedgwick was Mrs. Norton's brother.

Cambridge, (Mass.)

Jan. 16, '71.

My dear Charles,

If I had needed any reminder and quickener of a very old-time intention to take some morning and put into most indifferent words my frequent thoughts of you, I should have found one very much to the purpose in a letter from Grace, received some ten days ago. But really I needed no deeper consciousness of my great desire to punch a hole in the massive silence which has grown up between us....

Cambridge and Boston society still rejoices in that imposing fixedness of outline which is ever so inspiring to contemplate. In Cambridge I see Arthur Sedgwick and Howells; but little of any one else. Arthur seems not perhaps an enthusiastic, but a well-occupied man, and talks much in a wholesome way of meaning to go abroad. Howells edits, and observes and produces—the latter in his own particular line with more and more perfection. His recent sketches in the *Atlantic*, collected into a volume, belong, I think, by the wondrous cunning of their manner, to very good literature. He seems to have resolved himself, however, [into] one who can write solely of what his fleshly eyes have seen; and for this reason I wish he were "located" where they would rest upon richer and fairer things than this immediate landscape. Looking about for myself, I conclude that the face of nature and civilization in this our country is to a certain point a very sufficient literary field. But it will yield its secrets only to a really *grasping* imagination. This I think Howells lacks. (Of course *I* don't!) To write well and worthily of American things one need even more than elsewhere to be a *master*. But unfortunately one is less!... I myself have been scribbling some little tales which in the course of time you will have a chance to read. To write a series of good little tales I deem ample work for a life-time. I dream that my life-time shall have done it. It's at least a relief to have arranged one's life-time....

There is an immensity of stupid feeling and brutal writing prevalent here about recent English conduct and attitude—innocuous to some extent, I think, from its very stupidity; but I confess there are now, to my mind, few things of more appealing interest than the various problems with which England finds herself confronted: and this owing to the fact that, on the whole, the country is so deeply—so tragically—charged with a consciousness of her responsibilities, dangers and duties. She presents in this respect a wondrous contrast to ourselves. We, retarding our healthy progress by all the gross weight of our maniac contempt of the refined idea: England striving vainly to compel her lumbersome carcase by the straining wings of conscience and desire. Of course I speak of the better spirits there and the worst here....

We have over here the high natural light of chance and space and prosperity; but at moments dark things seem to be almost more blessed by the dimmer radiance shed by impassioned thought.... But I must stay my gossiping hand....

TO HIS PARENTS.

This next visit to Europe had begun in the spring of 1872. He had reached Germany, in the company of his sister and aunt, by way of England, Switzerland and Italy.

Heidelberg,

Sept. 15th, '72.

Dear Father and Mother,

I think I should manifest an energy more becoming a child of yours if I were to sustain my nodding head at least enough longer to scrawl the initial words of my usual letter: we are travellers in the midst of travel. You heard from me last at Innsbrück—or rather, I think, at Botzen, just before, a place beautiful by nature but most ugly by man; and [we] came by an admirable five hours' run through the remnant of the Tyrol to Munich, where we spent two rather busy days. It's a singular place and one difficult to write of with a serious countenance. It has a fine lot of old pictures, but otherwise it is a nightmare of pretentious vacuity: a city of chalky stucco—a Florence and Athens in canvas and planks. To have come [thither] from Venice is a sensation! We found reality at last at Nüremburg, by which place, combined with this, it seemed a vast pity not to proceed rather than by stupid Stuttgart. Nüremburg is excellent—and comparisons are odious; but I would give a thousand N.'s for one ray of Verona! We came on hither by a morning and noon of railway, which has not in the least prevented a goodly afternoon and evening at the Castle here. The castle (which I think you have all seen in your own travels) is an incomparable ruin and holds its own against any Italian memories. The light, the weather, the time, were all, this evening, most propitious to our visit. This rapid week in Germany has filled us with reflections and observations, tossed from the railway windows on our course, and irrecoverable at this late hour. To me this hasty and most partial glimpse of Germany has been most satisfactory; it has cleared from my mind the last mists of uncertainty and assured me that I can never hope to become an unworthiest adoptive grandchild of the fatherland. It is well to listen to the voice of the spirit, to cease hair-splitting and treat one's self to a good square antipathy—when it is so very sympathetic! I may 'cultivate' mine away, but it has given me a week's wholesome nourishment.

Strasbourg. We have seen Strasbourg—a palpably conquered city—and the Cathedral, which beats everything we have ever seen. Externally, it amazed me, which somehow I hadn't expected it to do. Strasbourg is gloomy, battered and painful; but apparently already much Germanized. We take tomorrow the formidable journey to Paris....

Yours in hope and love,

H. JAMES jr.

TO W. D. HOWELLS.

Mr. Howells's novel, just published, was *A Chance Acquaintance.* An allusion at the end of this letter recalls the great fire that had recently devastated the business quarter of Boston.

Berne, June 22d [1873].

My veritably dear Howells,

Your letter of May 12th came to me a week ago (after a journey to Florence and back) and gave me exquisite pleasure. I found it in the Montreux post-office and wandered further till I found the edge of an open vineyard by the lake, and there I sat down with my legs hanging over the azure flood and broke the seal. Thank you for everything; for liking my writing and for being glad I like yours. Your letter made me homesick, and when you told of the orchards by Fresh Pond I hung my head for melancholy. What is the meaning of this destiny of desolate exile—this dreary necessity of having month after month to do without our friends for the sake of this arrogant old Europe which so little befriends us? This is a hot Sunday afternoon: from my window I look out across the rushing Aar at some beautiful undivided meadows backed by black pine woods and blue mountains: but I would rather be taking up my hat and stick and going to invite myself to tea with you. I left Italy a couple of weeks since, and since then have been taking gloomy views of things. I feel as if I had left my "genius" behind in Rome. But I suppose I am well away from Rome just now; the Roman (and even the Florentine) lotus had become, with the warm weather, an indigestible diet. I heard from my mother a day or two since that your book is having a sale—bless it! I haven't yet seen the last part and should like to get the volume as a whole. Would it trouble you to have it sent by post to Brown, Shipley & Co., London? Your fifth part I extremely relished; it was admirably touched. I wished the talk in which the offer was made had been given (instead of the mere résumé), but I suppose you had good and sufficient reasons for doing as you did. But your work is a success and Kitty a creation. I have envied you greatly, as I read, the delight of feeling her grow so real and complete, so true and charming. I think, in bringing her through with such unerring felicity, your imagination has *fait ses preuves....* I should like to tell you a vast deal about myself, and I believe you would like to hear it. But as far as vastness goes I should have to invent it, and it's too hot for such work. I send you another (and for the present last) travelling piece—about Perugia etc. It goes with this, in another cover: a safe journey to it. I hope you may squeeze it in this year. It has numbers (in pages) more than you desire; but I think it is within bounds, as you will see there is an elision of several. I have done in all these months since I've been abroad less writing than I hoped. Rome, for direct working, was not good—too many distractions and a languefying atmosphere. But for "impressions" it was priceless, and I've got a lot duskily garnered away somewhere under my waning (that's an *n*, not a *v*) *chevelure* which some day may make some figure. I shall make the coming year more productive or retire from business altogether. Believe in me yet awhile longer and I shall reward your faith by dribblings somewhat less meagre.... I say nothing about the Fire. I can't trouble you with ejaculations and inquiries which my letters from home will probably already have answered. At this rate, apparently, the Lord loveth Boston immeasurably. But what a grim old Jehovah it is!...

My blessing, dear Howells, on all your affections, labours and desires. Write me a word when you can (B. & S., London) and believe me always faithfully yours,

H. JAMES jr.

TO MISS GRACE NORTON.

Florence, Jan. 14th, '74.

Dear Grace,

...I have been jerked away from Rome, where I had been expecting to spend this winter, just as I was warming to the feast, and Florence, tho' very well in itself, doesn't go so far as it might as a substitute for Rome. It's like having a great plum-pudding set down on the table before you, and then seeing it whisked away and finding yourself served with wholesome tapioca. My brother, after a month of great enjoyment and prosperity at Rome, had a stroke of malaria (happily quite light) which made it necessary for him to depart, and I am here charitably to keep him company. I oughtn't to speak light words of Florence to you, who know it so well, and with reason love it so well: and they are really words from my pen's end simply and not from my heart. I have an inextinguishable relish for Florence, and now that I have been back here a fortnight this early love is beginning to shake off timidly the ponderous shadow of Rome.... Just as I was leaving Rome came to me Charles's letter of Dec. 5th, for which pray thank him warmly. I gather from it that he is, in vulgar parlance, taking America rather hard, and I suppose your feelings and Jane's on the matter resemble his own. But it's not for me to blame him, for I take it hard enough even here in Florence, and though I have a vague theory that there is a way of being contented there, I am afraid that when I go back I shall need all my ingenuity to put it into practice. What Charles says about our civilization seems to me perfectly true, but practically

I don't feel as if the facts were so melancholy. The great fact for us all there is that, relish Europe as we may, we belong much more to that than to this, and stand in a much less factitious and artificial relation to it. I feel forever how Europe keeps holding one at arm's length, and condemning one to a meagre scraping of the surface. I have been nearly a year in Italy and have hardly spoken to an Italian creature save washerwomen and waiters. This, you'll say, is my own stupidity; but granting this gladly, it proves that even a creature addicted as much to sentimentalizing as I am over the whole *mise en scène* of Italian life, doesn't find an easy initiation into what lies behind it. Sometimes I am overwhelmed with the pitifulness of this absurd want of reciprocity between Italy itself and all my rhapsodies about it. There is certainly, however, terribly little doubt that, practically, for those who have been happy in Europe even Cambridge the Brilliant is not an easy place to live in. When I saw you in London, plunged up to your necks in that full, rich, abundant, various London life, I knew that a day of reckoning was coming and I heaved a secret prophetic sigh. I can well understand Charles's saying that the memory of these and kindred things is a perpetual private [? pang]. But pity our poor bare country and don't revile. England and Italy, with their countless helps to life and pleasure, are the lands for happiness and self-oblivion. It would seem that in our great unendowed, unfurnished, unentertained and unentertaining continent, where we all sit sniffing, as it were, the very earth of our foundations, we ought to have leisure to turn out something handsome from the very heart of simple human nature. But after I have been at home a couple of months I will tell you what I think. Meanwhile I aspire to linger on here in Italy and make the most of it—even in poor little overshadowed Florence and in a society limited to waiters and washerwomen. In your letter of last summer you amiably reproach me with not giving you personal tidings, and warn me in my letters against mistaking you for the *Nation*. Heaven forbid! But I have no *nouvelles intimes* and in this solitary way of life I don't ever feel especially like a person. I write more or less in the mornings, walk about in the afternoons, and doze over a book in the evenings. You can do as well as that in Cambridge....

TO HIS MOTHER.

Florence,

May 17th, 1874.

Dearest Mother,

...The days pass evenly and rapidly here in my comfortable little dwelling on this lively (and also dusty) old Piazza Sta. Maria Novella. (The centre of the square is not paved and the dust hovers over it in clouds which compel one to live with closed windows. But I remove to my bedroom, which is on a side-street and very cool and clean.) Nothing particular happens to me and my time is passed between sleeping and scribbling (both of which I do very well,) lunching and dining, walking, and conversing with my small circle of acquaintance.... Tell Willy I thank him greatly for setting before me so vividly the question of my going home or staying. I feel equally with him the importance of the decision. I have been meaning, as you know, for some time past to return in the autumn, and I see as yet no sufficient reason for changing my plan. I shall go with the full prevision that I shall not find life at home *simpatico*, but rather painfully, and, as regards literary work, obstructively the reverse, and not even with the expectation that time will make it easier; but simply on sternly practical grounds; i.e. because I can find more abundant literary occupation by being on the premises and relieve you and father of your burdensome financial interposition. But I shrink from Willy's apparent assumption that going now is to pledge myself to stay forever. I feel as if my three years in Europe (with much of them so *maladif*) were a very moderate allowance for one who gets so much out of it as I do; and I don't think I could really hold up my head if I didn't hope to eat a bigger slice of the pudding (with a few more social plums in it, especially) at some future time. If at the end of a period at home I don't feel an overwhelming desire to come back, it will be so much gained; but I should prepare myself for great deceptions if I didn't take the possibility of such desire into account. One oughtn't, I suppose, to bother too much about the future, but arrange as best one can with the present; and the present bids me go home and try and get more things published. What makes the question particularly difficult to decide is that though I should make more money at home, American prices would devour it twice as fast; but even allowing for this, I should keep ahead of my expenses better than here. I know that when the time comes it will be unutterably hard to leave and I shall be wondering whether, if I were to stay another year, I shouldn't propitiate the Minotaur and return more resignedly. But to this I shall answer that a year wouldn't be a tenth part enough and that besides, as things stand, I should be perplexed where to spend it. Florence, fond as I have grown of it, is worth far too little to me, socially, for me to think complacently of another winter here. Here have I been living (in these rooms) for five weeks—and not a creature, save Gryzanowski, has crossed my threshold—counting out my little Italian, who comes twice a week, and whom I have to *pay* for his conversation! If I knew any one in England I should be tempted to go there for a year, for there I could work to advantage—i.e. get hold of new books to review. But I can't face, as it is, a year of British solitude. What I desire now more than anything else, and what would do me more good, is a *régal* of intelligent and suggestive society, especially male. But I don't know how or where to find it. It exists, I suppose, in Paris and London, but I can't get at it. I chiefly desire it because it would, I am sure, increase my powers of work. These are going very well, however, as it is, and I have for the present an absorbing task in my novel. Consider then that if nothing extremely unexpected turns up, I shall depart in the autumn. I have no present plans for the summer beyond ending my month in my rooms—on the 11th of June. I hope, dearest mammy, that you will be able to devise some agreeable plan for your own summer, and will spend it in repose and comfort.... Has the trunk reached Quincy St.? Pray guard jealously my few clothes—a summer suit and a coat, and two white waistcoats that I would give much for here, now. But don't let Father and Willy wear them out, as they will serve me still. Farewell, sweet mother. I must close. I wrote last asking you to have my credit renewed. I suppose it has been done. Love abounding to all. I will write soon to Willy. I wrote lately to A.

Yours ever,

H.

II. PARIS AND LONDON:(1875-1881)

AFTER another uneventful American year at Cambridge (1874-5,) during which Roderick Hudson was running its course in the *Atlantic Monthly*, Henry James came to Europe again with the clear intention of staying for good. His first idea was to settle in Paris. There he would find the literary world with which he had the strongest affinity, and it does not seem to have occurred to him at the time to seek a European home anywhere else. His knowledge of England was still very slight, and he needed something more substantial to live and work upon than the romance of Italy. In Paris he settled therefore, in the autumn of 1875, taking rooms at 29 Rue du Luxembourg. He began to write The American, to contribute Parisian Letters to the *New York Tribune*, and to frequent the society of a few of his compatriots. He made the valued acquaintance of Ivan Turgenev, and through him of the group which surrounded Gustave Flaubert—Edmond de Goncourt, Alphonse Daudet, Guy de Maupassant, Zola and others. But the letters which follow will shew the kind of doubts that began to arise after a winter in Paris—doubts of the possibility of Paris as a place where an American imagination could really take root and flourish. He found the circle of literature tightly closed to outside influences; it seemed to exclude all culture but its own after a fashion that aroused his opposition; he speaks sarcastically on one occasion of having watched Turgenev and Flaubert seriously discussing Daudet's *Jack*, while he reflected that none of the three had read, or knew English enough to read, *Daniel Deronda*. During a summer stay at Etretat these doubts increased, and when he went back to Paris in the autumn of 1876 he had already begun to feel the tug of an inclination towards London. His brother William seems to have given the final impulse which sent him over, and before the end of the year he was in London at last.

He took rooms at 3 Bolton Street, just off Piccadilly, and at first found the change from 'glittering, charming, civilised Paris' rather rude. But within a few weeks he was deep in London, with doors unnumbered opening to him and a general welcome for the rising young novelist from America. Letter after letter was sent home with accounts of the visits and dinner-parties which were soon his habitual round. He quickly discovered that this was his appointed home and set himself deliberately to cultivate it. But his relief at finding a place of which he could really take possession was entirely compatible with candid criticism. Letter after letter, too, is filled with caustic reflections on the minds and manners of the English; and as the following pages contain not a few of these, so it should here be pointed out that his correspondence was the only outlet open to these irrepressible sentiments, and that they must be seen in due proportion with the perfect courtesy of appreciation that he always shewed to his well-meaning hosts. He was very much alone in his observing detachment during these years. 'I wish greatly,' he writes to Miss Norton about this time, 'you and Charles were here, so that I might have some one to say the things that are in me too; I mean the things about England and the English—the feelings, impressions, judgments, emotions of every kind that are being perpetually generated, and that I can't utter to a single Briton of them all with the smallest chance of being understood.... The absence of a sympathetic, compatriotic, intelligent spirit, like yours, is my greatest deprivation here, and everything is corked up.'

But whatever the shortcomings of the English might be, London life closed round him and held him fast. He would break away for an occasional excursion abroad, or he would carry his work into seaside lodgings for the end of the summer. Otherwise he clung to London, with such country visits as sprang naturally from his numerous relations with the town and were simply an extension of these. During the years covered by the present section he spent some weeks in Rome towards the end of 1877, three months in Paris in the autumn of 1879, and two in Italy again, at Florence and Naples, in the following spring. By 1881 he was sufficiently acclimatised in London to feel the need of escaping from the 'season,' then so much more organised and exacting an institution than it has since become; he went to Venice in March and did not return till July. But these were the only variations from the life of a 'cockney *convaincu*,' as he admitted himself to be. The wonder is that he found time under such conditions to accomplish the large amount of work he still put forth year by year. In spite of health that continued somewhat uncertain, he was able to concentrate upon his writing in the midst of all distractions. Daisy Miller, The Europeans, Confidence, Washington Square, and the Portrait of a Lady, all belong to the first five years of his London life, besides an unbroken stream of shorter pieces—fiction, picturesque sketches, reviews of books—contributed to several English and American periodicals. Time slipped by, and he began to wait upon the right opportunity for a long visit to his own country. It was not indeed that he felt himself to be losing touch with it; his appetite for American news was unassuageable, and by means of a correspondence as copious as ever he jealously preserved and cherished every possible tie with his old home. But he turned to his own family, then as always afterwards, with an affection stimulated by his unfathered state in England. His parents were growing old, his elder brother (who had married in 1878) was beginning to enjoy and exhibit the maturity of his genius, and it was more than time for a renewal of associations on the spot. By the autumn of 1881 he had finished The Portrait of a Lady, the longest and in every way the most important of his works hitherto, and he could also feel that his grounding in London, so to call it, was solid and secure. After six years of absence he then saw America again.

TO HIS FATHER.

29 Rue du Luxembourg.

April 11th [1876].

Dear Father,

...The slender thread of my few personal relations hangs on, without snapping, but it doesn't grow very stout. You crave chiefly news, I suppose, about Ivan Sergeitch [Turgenev], whom I have lately seen several times. I spent a couple of hours with him at his room, some time since, and I have seen him otherwise at Mme. Viardot's. The latter has invited me to her musical parties (Thursdays) and to her Sundays *en famille*. I have been to a couple of the former and (as yet only) one of the latter. She herself is a most fascinating and interesting woman, ugly, yet also very handsome or, in the French sense, *très-*

belle. Her musical parties are rigidly musical and to me, therefore, rigidly boresome, especially as she herself sings very little. I stood the other night on my legs for three hours (from 11 till 2) in a suffocating room, listening to an interminable fiddling, with the only consolation that Gustave Doré, standing beside me, seemed as bored as myself. But when Mme. Viardot does sing, it is superb. She sang last time a scene from Gluck's *Alcestis*, which was the finest piece of musical declamation, of a grandly tragic sort, that I can conceive. Her Sundays seem rather dingy and calculated to remind one of Concord 'historical games' etc. But it was both strange and sweet to see poor Turgenev acting charades of the most extravagant description, dressed out in old shawls and masks, going on all fours etc. The charades are their usual Sunday evening occupation and the good faith with which Turgenev, at his age and with his glories, can go into them is a striking example of that spontaneity which Europeans have and we have not. Fancy Longfellow, Lowell, or Charles Norton doing the like, and every Sunday evening! I am likewise gorged with music at Mme. de Blocqueville's, where I continue to meet Emile Montégut, whom I don't like so well as his writing, and don't forgive for having, à l'avenir, spoiled his writing a little for me. Calling the other day on Mme. de B. I found with her M. Caro, the philosopher, a man in the expression of whose mouth you would discover depths of dishonesty, but a most witty and agreeable personage. I had also the other day a very pleasant call upon Flaubert, whom I like personally more and more each time I see him. But I think I easily—more than easily—see all round him intellectually. There is something wonderfully simple, honest, kindly, and touchingly inarticulate about him. He talked of many things, of Théo. Gautier among others, who was his intimate friend. He said nothing new or rare about him, except that he thought him after the Père Hugo the greatest of French poets, much above Alfred de Musset; but Gautier in his extreme perfection was unique. And he recited some of his sonnets in a way to make them seem the most beautiful things in the world. Find in especial (in the volume I left at home) one called *Les Portraits Ovales*.... I went down to Chartres the other day and had a charming time—but I won't speak of it as I have done it in the Tribune. The American papers over here are *accablants*, and the vulgarity and repulsiveness of the Tribune, whenever I see it, strikes me so violently that I feel tempted to stop my letter. But I shall not, though of late there has been a painful dearth of topics to write about. But soon comes the *Salon*.... I am very glad indeed that Howells is pleased with my new tale; I am now actively at work upon it. I am well pleased that the *Atlantic* has obtained it. His own novel I have not read, but he is to send it to me.

Your home news has all been duly digested. Tell Willy that I will answer his most interesting letter specifically; and say to my dearest sister that if she will tell me which—black or white—she prefers I will send her gratis a fichu of écru lace, which I am told is the proper thing for her to have.

Ever, dearest daddy, your loving son,

H. JAMES jr.

TO W. D. HOWELLS.

The 'story' was *The American*, which began to appear in *The Atlantic Monthly* in June, 1876.

29 Rue du Luxembourg, Paris.

May 28th [1876].

Dear Howells,

I have just received (an hour ago) your letter of May 14th. I shall be very glad to do my best to divide my story so that it will make twelve numbers, and I think I shall probably succeed. Of course 26 pp. is an impossible instalment for the magazine. I had no idea the second number would make so much, though I half expected your remonstrance. I shall endeavour to give you about 14 pp., and to keep doing it for seven or eight months more. I sent you the other day a fourth part, a portion of which, I suppose, you will allot to the fifth.

My heart was touched by your regret that I hadn't given you "a great deal of my news"—though my reason suggested that I could not have given you what there was not to give. "La plus belle fille du monde ne peut donner que ce qu'elle a." I turn out news in very small quantities—it is impossible to imagine an existence less pervaded with any sort of *chiaroscuro*. I am turning into an old, and very contented, Parisian: I feel as if I had struck roots into the Parisian soil, and were likely to let them grow tangled and tenacious there. It is a very comfortable and profitable place, on the whole—I mean, especially, on its general and cosmopolitan side. Of pure Parisianism I see absolutely nothing. The great merit of the place is that one can arrange one's life here exactly as one pleases—that there are facilities for every kind of habit and taste, and that everything is accepted and understood. Paris itself meanwhile is a sort of painted background which keeps shifting and changing, and which is always there, to be looked at when you please, and to be most easily and comfortably ignored when you don't. All this, if you were only here, you would feel much better than I can tell you—and you would write some happy piece of your prose about it which would make me feel it better, afresh. *Ergo*, come—when you can! I shall probably be here still. Of course every good thing is still better in spring, and in spite of much mean weather I have been liking Paris these last weeks more than ever. In fact I have accepted destiny here, under the vernal influence. If you sometimes read my poor letters in the *Tribune*, you get a notion of some of the things I see and do. I suppose also you get some gossip about me from Quincy St. Besides this there is not a great deal to tell. I have seen a certain number of people all winter who have helped to pass the time, but I have formed but one or two relations of permanent value, and which I desire to perpetuate. I have seen almost nothing of the literary fraternity, and there are fifty reasons why I should not become intimate with them. I don't like their wares, and they don't like any others; and besides, they are not *accueillants*. Turgenev is worth the whole heap of them, and yet he himself swallows them down in a manner that excites my extreme wonder. But he is the most loveable of men and takes all things easily. He is so pure and strong a genius that he doesn't need to be on the defensive as regards his opinions and enjoyments. The mistakes he may make don't hurt him. His modesty and naïveté are simply infantine. I gave him some time since the message you sent him, and he bade me to thank you very kindly and to say that he had the most agreeable memory of your two books. He has just gone to Russia to bury himself for two or three months on his estate, and try and finish a long novel he has for three or four years been working upon. I hope to heaven he may. I suspect he works little here.

I interrupted this a couple of hours since to go out and pay a visit to Gustave Flaubert, it being his time of receiving, and his last Sunday in Paris, and I owing him a farewell. *He* is a very fine old fellow, and the most interesting man and strongest artist of his circle. I had him for an hour alone, and then came in his "following," talking much of Emile Zola's catastrophe—Zola having just had a serial novel for which he was handsomely paid interrupted on account of protests from provincial subscribers against its indecency. The opinion apparently was that it was a bore, but that it could only do the book good on its appearance in a volume. Among your tribulations as editor, I take it that this particular one is not in store for you. On my way down from Flaubert's I met poor Zola climbing the staircase, looking very pale and sombre, and I saluted him with the flourish natural to a contributor who has just been invited to make his novel last longer yet....

Your inquiry "Why I don't go to Spain?" is sublime—is what Philip van Artevelde says of the Lake of Como, "softly sublime, profusely fair!" I shall spend my summer in the most tranquil and frugal hole I can unearth in France, and I have no prospect of travelling for some time to come. The Waverley Oaks seem strangely far away—yet I remember them well, and the day we went there. I am sorry I am not to see your novel sooner, but I applaud your energy in proposing to change it. The printed thing always seems to me dead and done with. I suppose you will write something about Philadelphia—I hope so, as otherwise I am afraid I shall know nothing about it. I salute your wife and children a thousand times and wish you an easy and happy summer and abundant inspiration.

Yours very faithfully,

H. JAMES, jr.

TO WILLIAM JAMES.

Etretat,

July 29th [1876].

Dear Wm.

...I have little to tell you of myself. I shall be here till August 15-20, and shall then go and spend the rest of the month with the Childes, near Orléans (an ugly country, I believe,) and after that try to devise some frugal scheme for keeping out of Paris till as late as possible in the autumn. The winter there always begins soon enough. I am much obliged to you for your literary encouragement and advice—glad especially you like my novel. I can't judge it. Your remarks on my French tricks in my letters are doubtless most just, and shall be heeded. But it's an odd thing that such tricks should grow at a time when my last layers of resistance to a long-encroaching weariness and satiety with the French mind and its utterance has fallen from me like a garment. I have done with 'em, forever, and am turning English all over. I desire only to feed on English life and the contact of English minds—I wish greatly I knew some. Easy and smooth-flowing as life is in Paris, I would throw it over tomorrow for an even very small chance to plant myself for a while in England. If I had but a single good friend in London I would go thither. I have got nothing important out of Paris nor am likely to. My life there makes a much more succulent figure in your letters, my mention of its thin ingredients as it comes back to me, than in my own consciousness. A good deal of Boulevard and third-rate Americanism: few retributive relations otherwise. I know the Théâtre Français by heart!

Daniel Deronda (Dan'l himself) is indeed a dead, though amiable, failure. But the book is a large affair; I shall write an article of some sort about it. All desire is dead within me to produce something on George Sand; though perhaps I shall, all the same, mercenarily and mechanically—though only if I am forced. *Please make a point of mentioning,* by the way, whether a letter of mine, upon her, exclusively, *did* appear lately in the Tribune. I don't see the T. regularly and have missed it. They misprint sadly. I never said, e.g., in announcing her death, that she was '*fearfully* shy': I used no such vile adverb, but another—I forget which.

71

I am hoping from day to day for another letter from home, as the period has come round.... I hope your own plans for the summer will prosper, and health and happiness be your portion. Give much love to Father, and to the ladies.

Yours always,

H. JAMES jr.

TO WILLIAM JAMES.

H. J. had by this time been settled in London for some three months.

Athenaeum Club, Pall Mall.

March 29th, '77.

Dear Wm.

...London life jogs along with me, pausing every now and then at some more or less succulent patch of herbage. I was almost ashamed to tell you through mother that I, unworthy, was seeing a bit of Huxley. I went to his house again last Sunday evening—a pleasant, easy, no-dress-coat sort of house (in our old Marlboro' Place, by the way). Huxley is a very genial, comfortable being—yet with none of the noisy and windy geniality of some folks here, whom you find with their backs turned when you are responding to the remarks that they have made you. But of course my talk with him is mere amiable generalities. These, however, he likes to cultivate, for recreation's sake, of a Sunday evening. (The thundering Spencer I have not lately seen here.) Some mornings since, I breakfasted with Lord Houghton again—he invites me most dotingly. Present: John Morley, Goldwin Smith (pleasanter than my prejudice against him,) Henry Cowper, Frederick Wedmore, and a monstrous cleverly, agreeably talking M.P., Mr. Otway. John Morley has a most agreeable face, but he hardly opened his mouth. (He is, like so many of the men who have done much here, very young-looking.) Yesterday I dined with Lord Houghton—with Gladstone, Tennyson, Dr. Schliemann (the excavator of old Mycenae, etc.) and half a dozen other men of 'high culture.' I sat next but one to the Bard and heard most of his talk, which was all about port wine and tobacco: he seems to know much about them, and can drink a whole bottle of port at a sitting with no incommodity. He is very swarthy and scraggy, and strikes one at first as much less handsome than his photos: but gradually you see that it's a face of genius. He had I know not what simplicity, speaks with a strange rustic accent and seemed altogether like a creature of some primordial English stock, a thousand miles away from American manufacture. Behold me after dinner conversing affably with Mr. Gladstone—not by my own seeking, but by the almost importunate affection of Lord H. But I was glad of a chance to feel the 'personality' of a great political leader—or as G. is now thought here even, I think, by his partisans, ex-leader. That of Gladstone is very fascinating—his urbanity extreme—his eye that of a man of genius—and his apparent self-surrender to what he is talking of, without a flaw. He made a great impression on me—greater than any one I have seen here: though 'tis perhaps owing to my naïveté, and unfamiliarity with statesmen....

Did I tell you that I had been to the Oxford and Cambridge boat-race? But I have paragraphed it in the *Nation*, to which I refer you. It was for about two minutes a supremely beautiful sight; but for those two minutes I had to wait a horribly bleak hour and a half, shivering, in mid-Thames, under the sour March-wind. I can't think of any other adventures: save that I dined two or three days since at Mrs. Godfrey Lushington's (they are very nice *blushing* people) with a parcel of quiet folk: but next to a divine little Miss Lushington (so pretty English girls can be!) who told me that she lived in the depths of the City, at Guy's Hospital, whereof her father is administrator. Guy's Hospital—of which I have read in all old English novels. So does one move all the while here on identified ground. This is the eve of Good Friday, a most lugubrious day here—and all the world (save 4,000,000 or so) are out of London for the ten days' Easter holiday. I think of making two or three excursions of a few hours apiece, to places near London whence I can come back to sleep: Canterbury, Chichester etc. (but as I shall commemorate them for lucre I won't talk of them thus).

Farewell, dear brother, I won't prattle further.... Encourage Alice to write to me. My blessings on yourself from your fraternal

H. J. jr.

TO MISS GRACE NORTON.

3 Bolton St., Piccadilly.

August 7th, 1877.

Dear Grace,

...I feel now more at home in London than anywhere else in the world— so much so that I am afraid my sense of peculiarities, my appreciation of people and things, as *London* people and things, is losing its edge. I have taken a great fancy to the place; I won't say to the people and things; and yet these must have a part in it. It makes a very interesting residence at any rate; not the ideal and absolutely interesting—but the relative and comparative one. I have, however, formed no intimacies—not even any close acquaintances. I incline to believe that I have passed the age when one forms friendships; or that every one else has. I have seen and talked a little with a considerable number of people, but I have become familiar with almost none. To tell the truth, I find myself a good deal more of a cosmopolitan (thanks to that combination of the continent and the U.S.A. which has formed my lot) than the average Briton of culture; and to be—to have become by force of circumstances—a cosmopolitan is of necessity to be a good deal alone. I don't think that *London*, by itself, does a very great deal for people—for its residents; and those of them who are not out of the general social herd are potentially deadly provincial. I have become in all these years as little provincial as possible. I don't say it from fatuity and I may say it to you; and yet to be so is, I think, necessary for forming here many close relations. So my interest in London is chiefly that of an observer in a place where there is most in the world to observe. I see no essential reason however why I should not some day see much more of certain Britons, and think that I very possibly may. But I doubt if I should ever marry—or want to marry—an English wife!

This is an extremely interesting time here; and indeed that is one reason why I have not been able to bring myself to go abroad, as I have been planning all this month to do. I can't give up the morning papers! I am not one of the outsiders who thinks that the "greatness" of England is now exploded; but there mingles with my interest in her prospects and doings in all this horrible Eastern Question a sensible mortification and sadness. She has not resolutely played a part—even a wrong one. She has been weak and helpless and (above all) unskilful; she has drifted and stumbled and not walked like a great nation. One has a feeling that the affairs of Europe are really going to be settled without her. At any rate the cynical, brutal, barbarous pro-Turkish attitude of an immense mass of people here (I am no fanatic for Russia, but I think the Emperor of R. might have been treated like a gentleman!) has thrown into vivid relief the most discreditable side of the English character. I don't think it is the largest side, by any means; but when one comes into contact with it one is ready to give up the race!

I saw the Lowells and can testify to their apparent good-humour and prosperity. It was a great pleasure to talk with Lowell; but he is morbidly Anglophobic; though when an Englishman asked me if he was not I denied it. I envied him his residence in a land of colour and warmth, of social freedom and personal picturesqueness; so many absent things here, where the dusky misery and the famous "hypocrisy" which foreign writers descant so much upon, seem sometimes to usurp the whole field of vision. But I shall in all probability go abroad myself by Sept. 1st: go straight to our blessed Italy. I hope to be a while at Siena, where you may be sure that I shall think of you....

Yours always, dear Grace, in all tender affection,

H. JAMES jr.

TO MISS GRACE NORTON,

Paris, Dec. 15th [1877].

Dear Grace,

I hoped, after getting your letter of October 15th, to write you from Siena, but I never got there. I only got to Rome (where your letter came to me,) and in Rome I spent the whole of the seven weeks that I was able to give to Italy. I have just come back, and am on my way to London, whither I find I gravitate as toward the place in the world in which, on the whole, I feel most at home. I went directly to Rome some seven weeks since, and came directly back; but I spent a few days in Florence on my way down. Italy was still more her irresistible ineffable old self than ever, and getting away from Rome was really no joke. In spite of the "changes"—and they are very perceptible—the old enchantment of Rome, taking its own good time, steals over you and possesses you, till it becomes really almost a nuisance and an importunity. That is, it keeps you from working, from staying indoors, etc. To do those things in sufficient measure one must live in an ugly country; and that is why, instead of lingering in that golden climate, I am going back to poor, smutty, dusky, Philistine London. Florence had never seemed to me more lovely. Empty, melancholy, bankrupt (as I believe she is), she is turning into an old sleeping, soundless city, like Pisa. This sensible sadness, with the glorious weather, gave the place a great charm. The Bootts were there, staying in a villa at Bellosguardo, and I spent many hours in their garden, sitting in the autumn sunshine and staring stupidly at that never-to-be-enough-appreciated view of the little city and the mountains....

I have had an autumn of things rather than of people, and have not much to relate in regard to human nature. Here in Paris, for a few days, I find I know really too many people—especially as they are for the most part acquaintances retained for the sake of social decency rather than of strong sentiment. They consume all my time, so that I can't even go to the Théâtre Français! In Rome I found the relics and fragments of the ancient American group, which has been much broken up—or rather broken down. But neither in its meridian nor in its decline has it had any very irresistible charms. The chief quality acquired by Americans who have lived thirty years in Europe seems to me a fierce susceptibility on the subject of omitted calls.

Public matters here, just now, are more interesting than private—and in France indeed are as interesting as can be. Parliamentary government is really being put to the test, and bearing it. The poor foolish old Marshal has at last succumbed to the liberal majority, and has apparently no stomach to renew his resistance. Plevna is taken by the Russians and England is supposed to be dreadfully snubbed. But one is only snubbed if one feels it, and it remains to be seen how England will take the Russian success. But one has a feeling now—to me it is a very painful one—that England will take anything; that over-cautious and somewhat sordid counsels will always prevail. On the continent, certainly, her ancient "prestige" is gone; and I almost wish she would fight in a bad cause, if only to shew that she still can, and that she is not one vast, money-getting Birmingham. I really think we are assisting at the political decadence of our mighty mother-land. When so mealy-mouthed an organ as the *Times* is correctly held to represent the sentiment of the majority, this *must* be. But I must say that even the "decline" of England seems to me a tremendous and even, almost, an inspiring spectacle, and if the British Empire is once more to shrink up into that plethoric little island, the process will be the greatest drama in history!

This will reach you about Xmas-time, and I imagine you reading it at a window that looks out upon the snow-laden pines and hemlocks of Shady Hill. That white winter light that is sent up into a room from the deep snow is something that one quite loses the memory of here; and yet, as I think of it now, it is associated in my mind with all kinds of pleasant and comfortable indoor scenes. I am afraid that, for you, the season will have no great animation; but you will, I suppose, see a good deal of infantine exhilaration about you....

TO WILLIAM JAMES.

8 Bolton St., W.

May 1st, '78.

Dear William,

...There were many interesting allusions in your letter which I should like to take up one by one. I should like to see the fair Hellenists of Baltimore; and I greatly regret that, living over here, my person cannot profit by my American reputation. It is a great loss to have one's person in one country and one's glory in another, especially when there are lovely young women in the case. Neither can one's glory, then, profit by one's person—as I flatter myself, even in your jealous teeth, that mine might in Baltimore!! Also about my going to Washington and its being my 'duty,' etc. I think there is much in that; but I can't whisk about the world quite so actively as you seem to recommend. It would be great folly for me, à peine established in London and getting a footing here, to break it all off for the sake of going to spend four or five months in Washington. I expect to spend many a year in London—I have submitted myself without reserve to that Londonizing process of which the effect is to convince you that, having lived here, you may, if need be, abjure civilization and bury yourself in the country, but may not, in pursuit of civilization, live in any smaller town. I am still completely an outsider here, and my only chance for becoming a little of an insider (in that limited sense in which an American can ever do so) is to remain here for the present. After that—a couple of years hence—I shall go home for a year, embrace you all, and see everything of the country I can, including Washington. Meanwhile, if one will take what comes, one is by no means cut off from getting impressions here.... I know what I am about, and I have always my eyes on my native land.

I am very glad that Howells's play seemed so pretty, on the stage. Much of the dialogue, as it read, was certainly charming; but I should have been afraid of the slimness and un-scenic quality of the plot. For myself (in answer to your adjuration) it has long been my most earnest and definite intention to commence at play-writing as soon as I can. This will be soon, and then I shall astound the world! My inspection of the French theatre will fructify. I have thoroughly mastered Dumas, Augier, and Sardou (whom it is greatly lacking to Howells—by the way—to have studied:) and I know all they know and a great deal more besides. Seriously speaking, I have a great many ideas on this subject, and I sometimes feel tempted to retire to some frugal village, for twelve months, where, my current expenses being inconsiderable, I might have leisure to work them off. Even if I could only find some manager or publisher sufficiently devoted to believe in this and make me an allowance for such a period, I would afterwards make a compact and sign it with my blood, to reimburse him in thousands. But I shall not have to come to this, or to depend upon it.

I received a few days since your article on H. Spencer, but I have not yet had time to read it. I shall very presently attack—I won't say understand it. Mother speaks to me of your articles in Renouvier's magazine—and why have you not sent me those? I wish you would do so, punctually. I met Herbert Spencer the other Sunday at George Eliot's, whither I had at last bent my steps. G.H. Lewes introduced me to him as an American; and it seemed to me that at this fact, coupled with my name, his attention was aroused and he was on the point of asking me if I were related to you. But something instantly happened to separate me from him, and soon afterwards he went away. The Leweses were very urbane and friendly, and I think that I shall have the right *dorénavant* to consider myself a Sunday *habitué*. The great G.E. herself is both sweet and superior, and has a delightful expression in her large, long, pale equine face. I had my turn at sitting beside her and being conversed with in a low, but most harmonious tone; and bating a tendency to *aborder* only the highest themes I have no fault to find with her....

We expect to hear at any hour that war has broken out; and yet it may not be. It will be a good deal of a scandal if it does—especially if the English find themselves fighting side by side with the bloody, filthy Turks and their own Indian Sepoys. And to think that a clever Jew should have juggled old England into it! The papers are full of the Paris exhibition, which opens today; but it leaves me perfectly incurious. Blessings on all from yours fraternally,

H. JAMES jr.

TO MISS ALICE JAMES.

H. J. was at this time contributing a series of articles on English life and letters to the American *Nation*.

Tillypronie, Aberdeen.

Sept. 15th, 1878.

Dearest Sister,

On this howling stormy Sunday, on a Scotch mountainside, I don't know what I can do better than give you a little old-world news. I have had none of yours in some time; but I venture to interpret that as a good sign and to believe that peace and plenty hovers over Quincy Street. I shall continue in this happy faith and in the belief that you are gently putting forth your strength again, until the contrary is proved. Behold me in Scotland and very well pleased to be here. I am staying with the Clarks, of whom you have heard me speak and than whom there could not be a more tenderly hospitable couple. Sir John caresses me like a brother, and her ladyship supervises me like a mother.... I have been here for four or five days and I feel that I have done a very good thing in coming to Scotland. Once you get the hang of it, and apprehend the type, it is a most beautiful and admirable little country—fit, for 'distinction' etc., to make up a trio with Italy and Greece. There is a little very good company in the house, including my brilliant friend Lady Hamilton Gordon, and every day has brought with it some pretty entertainment. I wish I could relate these episodes in detail; but I shall probably do a little of it in mercenary print. On the first day I went to some Highland sports, given by Lord Huntly, and to a sumptuous lunch, in a coquettish marquee, which formed an episode of the same. The next day I spent roaming over the moors and hills, in company with a remarkably nice young fellow staying in the house, Sidney Holland, grandson of the late Sir Henry (his father married a daughter of Sir Chas. Trevelyan, sister of my friend Mrs. Dugdale). Nothing can be more breezy and glorious than a ramble on these purple hills and a lounge in the sun-warmed heather. The real way to enjoy them is of course supposed to be with an eye to the grouse and partridges; but this is, happily, little of a shooting house, though Holland keeps the table—one of the best in England (or rather in Scotland, which is saying more)—supplied with game. The next day I took part in a cavalcade across the hills to see a ruined castle; and in the evening, if you please, stiff and sore as I was, and am still, with my exploits in the saddle, which had been sufficiently honourable, I went to a ball fifteen miles distant. The ball was given by a certain old Mr. Cunliffe Brooks, a great proprietor hereabouts and possessor of a shooting-lodge with a ball-room; a fact which sufficiently illustrates the luxury of these Anglo-Scotch arrangements. At the ball was the famous beauty Mrs. Langtry, who was staying in the house and who is probably for the moment the most celebrated woman in England. She is in sooth divinely handsome and it was 'extremely odd' to see her dancing a Highland reel (which she had been practising for three days) with young Lord Huntly, who is a very handsome fellow and who in his kilt and tartan, leaping and hooting and romping, opposite to this London divinity, offered a vivid reminder of ancient Caledonian barbarism and of the roughness which lurks in all British amusements and only wants a pretext to explode. We came home from our ball (where I took out two young ladies who had gone with us for a polka apiece) at four a.m., and I found it difficult on that morning, at breakfast, to comply with that rigid punctuality which is the custom of the house.... Today our fine weather has come to an end and we are closely involved in a ferocious wet tornado. But I am glad of the rest and quiet, and I have just bolted out of the library to escape the 'morning service,' read by the worthy Nevin, the American Episcopal chaplain in Rome, who is staying here, to which the dumb and decent servants are trooping in. I am fast becoming a good enough Englishman to respect inveterately my own habits and do, wherever I may be, only exactly what I want. This is the secret of prosperity here—provided of course one has a certain number of sociable and conformable habits, and civil inclinations, as a starting-point. After that, the more positive your idiosyncrasies the more positive the convenience. But it is drawing toward lunch, and I can't carry my personality quite so far as to be late for that.

I have said enough, dear sister, to make you see that I continue to see the world with perhaps even enviable profit. But don't envy me too much; for the British country-house has at moments, for a cosmopolitanised American, an insuperable flatness. On the other hand, to do it justice, there is no doubt of its being one of the ripest fruits of time—and here in Scotland, where you get the conveniences of Mayfair dovetailed into the last romanticism of nature— of the highest results of civilization. Such as it is, at any rate, I shall probably have a little more of it.... Scotland is decidedly a thing to see and which it would have been idiocy to have foregone. Did I tell you I was now London correspondent of the *Nation*? Farewell, dearest child and sister. I wish I could blow you a little of the salubrity of bonnie Scotland. The lunch-bell is striking up and I hurry off with comprehensive blessings.

Ever your faithfullest

H. J. jr.

TO WILLIAM JAMES.

The brief allusion at the end of this letter to two memorable visits will recall the picture he long afterwards made of them, and of the lady who inducted him, in *The Middle Years*. The closing paragraph of *Daisy Miller*, it may be mentioned, gives a glance at the hero's subsequent history and a hint that he became 'much interested in a clever foreign lady.' The story about to appear in the *Cornhill* was *An International Episode*.

Devonshire Club, St. James's, S.W.

Nov. 14th, '78.

My dear William,

...I was much depressed on reading your letter by your painful reflections on *The Europeans*; but now, an hour having elapsed, I am beginning to hold up my head a little; the more so as I think I myself estimate the book very justly and am aware of its extreme slightness. I think you take these things too rigidly and unimaginatively—too much as if an artistic experiment were a piece of conduct, to which one's life were somehow committed; but I think also that you're quite right in pronouncing the book 'thin' and empty. I don't at all despair, yet, of doing something fat. Meanwhile I hope you will continue to give me, when you can, your free impression of my performances. It is a great thing to have some one write to one of one's things as if one were a third person, and you are the only individual who will do this. I don't think however you are always right, by any means. As for instance in your objection to the closing paragraph of *Daisy Miller*, which seems to me queer and narrow, and as regards which I don't seize your point of view. J'en appelle to the sentiment of any other story-teller whatsoever; I am sure none such would wish the paragraph away. You may say—'Ah, but other *readers* would.' But that is the same; for the teller is but a more developed reader. I don't trust your judgment altogether (if you will permit me to say so) about *details*; but I think you are altogether right in returning always to the importance of subject. I hold to this, strongly; and if I don't as yet seem to proceed upon it more, it is because, being 'very artistic,' I have a constant impulse to try experiments of form, in which I wish to not run the risk of wasting or gratuitously using big situations. But to these I am coming now. It is something to have learned how to write, and when I look round me and see how few people (doing my sort of work) know how (to my sense,) I don't regret my step-by-step evolution. I don't advise you however to read the two last things I have written—one a thing in the Dec. and Jan. *Cornhill*, which I will send home; and the other a piece I am just sending to Howells. They are each quite in the same manner as *The Europeans*.

I have written you a letter after all. I am tired and must stop. I went into the country the other day to stay with a friend a couple of days (Mrs. Greville) and went with her to lunch with Tennyson, who, after lunch, read us Locksley Hall. The next day we went to George Eliot's.

Blessings on Alice. Ever your

H. J. jr.

TO HIS MOTHER.

3 Bolton St., W.

January 18th [1879].

My dearest Mother,

I have before me your letter of December 30th, with its account of your Christmas festivities and other agreeable talk, and I endeavour on this 'beastly' winter night, before my carboniferous hearth, to transport myself into the family circle.

Mrs. Kemble has returned to town for the winter—an event in which I always take pleasure, as she is certainly one of the women I know whom I like best. I confess I find people in general very vulgar-minded and superficial— and it is only by a pious fiction, to keep myself going, and keep on the social harness, that I succeed in postulating them as anything else or better. It is therefore a kind of rest and refreshment to see a woman who (extremely annoying as she sometimes is) gives one a positive sense of having a deep, rich, human nature and having cast off all vulgarities. The people of this world seem to me for the most part nothing but *surface*, and sometimes—oh ye gods! such desperately poor surface! Mrs. Kemble has no organized surface at all; she is like a straight deep cistern without a cover, or even, sometimes, a bucket, into which, as a mode of intercourse, one must tumble with a splash. You mustn't judge her by her indifferent book, which is no more a part of her than a pudding she might make.... Please tell William and Alice that I received a short time since their kind note, written on the eve of their going to Newport, and complimenting me on the first part of the *International Episode*. You will have read the second part by this time, and I hope that you won't, like many of my friends here (as I partly know and partly suspect,) take it ill of me as against my 'British entertainers.' It seems to me myself that I have been very delicate; but I shall keep off dangerous ground in future. It is an entirely new sensation for them (the people here) to be (at all delicately) *ironised* or satirised, from the American point of view, and they don't at all relish it. Their conception of the normal in such a relation is that the satire should be all on their side against the Americans; and I suspect that if one were to push this a little further one would find that they are extremely sensitive. But I like them too much and feel too kindly to them to go into the satire-business or even the light-ironical in any case in which it would wound them—even if in such a case I should see my way to it very clearly. Macmillan is just on the point of bringing out Daisy Miller, The International Episode, and Four Meetings in two little big-printed volumes, like those of the *Europeans*. There is every reason to expect for them a very good success, as Daisy M. has been, as I have told you before, a really quite extraordinary hit. I will send you the new volumes.... Farewell, dearest Mother. I send my filial duty to father, who I hope is worrying comfortably through the winter (I am afraid that since you wrote you have had severe weather)—and looking and listening always for a letter, remain your very lovingest

H. JAMES jr.

TO MISS GRACE NORTON.

The 'short novel' he was now just finishing was *Confidence*.

3 Bolton St., W.

Sunday a.m., June 8th [1879].

My dear Grace,

...It is difficult to talk to you about my impressions—it takes a great deal of space to generalise; and (when one is talking of London) it takes even more to specify! I am afraid also, in truth, that I am living here too long to be an observer—I am sinking into dull British acceptance and conformity. The other day I was talking to a very clever foreigner—a German (if you can admit the "clever")—who had lived a long time in England, and of whom I had asked some opinion. "Oh, I know nothing of the English," he said, "I have lived here too long—twenty years. The first year I really knew a great deal. But I have lost it!" That is getting to be my state of mind and I am sometimes really appalled at the matter of course way of looking at the indigenous life and manners into which I am gradually dropping! I am losing my standard— my charming little standard that I used to think so high; my standard of wit, of grace, of good manners, of vivacity, of urbanity, of intelligence, of what makes an easy and natural style of intercourse! And this in consequence of my having dined out during the past winter 107 times! When I come home you will think me a sad barbarian—I may not even, just at first, appreciate your fine points! You must take that speech about my standard with a grain of salt—but excuse me; I am treating you—a proof of the accusation I have brought against myself—as if you were also a dull-eyed Briton. The truth is I am so fond of London that I can afford to abuse it—and London is on the whole such a fine thing that it can afford to be abused! It has all sorts of superior qualities, but it has also, and English life, generally, and the English character have, a certain number of great plump flourishing uglinesses and drearinesses which offer themselves irresistibly as pin-cushions to criticism and irony. The British mind is so totally un-ironical in relation to itself that this is a perpetual temptation. You will know the things I mean—you will remember them—let that suffice. Non ragioniam di lor!—I don't suppose you will envy me for having dined out 107 times—you will simply wonder what can have induced me to perpetrate such a folly, and how I have survived to tell the tale! I admit that it is enough for the present, and for the rest of the summer I shall take in sail. When the warm weather comes I find London evenings very detestable, and I marvel at the powers of endurance of my fellow "factors," as it is now the fashion to call human beings—(actors—poor blundering unapplauded Comedians would be a better name). Would you like a little gossip? I am afraid I have nothing very lively in hand; but I take what comes uppermost. I am to dine tonight at Sir Frederick Pollock's, to meet one or two of the (more genteel) members of the Comédie Française, who are here just now, playing with immense success and supplying the London world with that invaluable boon, a topic. I mean the whole Comédie is here *en masse* for six weeks. I have been to see them two or three times and I find their artistic perfection gives one an immense lift out of British air. I took with me one night Mrs. Kemble, who is a great friend of mine and to my sense one of the most interesting and delightful of women. I have a sort of notion you don't like her; but you would if you knew her better. She is to my mind the first woman in London, and is moreover one of the consolations of my life. Another night I had with me a person whom it would divert you to know—a certain Mrs. Greville (a cousin, by marriage, of the Greville Papers:) the queerest creature living, but a mixture of the ridiculous and the amiable in which the amiable preponderates. She is crazy, stage-struck, scatter-brained, what the French call *extravagante*; but I can't praise her better than by saying that though she is on the whole the greatest fool I have ever known, I like her very much and get on with her most easily.... I am just finishing a short novel which will appear presently in six numbers of Scribner. This is to say please don't read it in that puerile periodical (where its appearance is due to—what you will be glad to hear—large pecuniary inducements,) but wait till it comes out as a book. It is worth being read in that shape. I have asked you no questions—yet I have finished my letter. Let my blessing, my tender good wishes and affectionate assurances of every kind stand instead of them. Divide these with Charles, with your mother, with the children, and believe me, dear Grace, always very faithfully yours,

H. JAMES jr.

TO W. D. HOWELLS.

H.J.'s forthcoming story in the *Cornhill* was *Washington Square*.

3 Bolton Street, W.

Jan. 31st [1880].

My dear Howells,

Your letter of Jan. 19th and its enclosure (your review of my *Hawthorne*) came to me last night, and I must thank you without delay for each of them....

Your review of my book is very handsome and friendly and commands my liveliest gratitude. Of course your graceful strictures seem to yourself more valid than they do to me. The little book was a tolerably deliberate and meditated performance, and I should be prepared to do battle for most of the convictions expressed. It is quite true I use the word provincial too many times—I hated myself for't, even while I did it (just as I overdo the epithet "dusky.") But I don't at all agree f with you in thinking that "if it is not provincial for an Englishman to be English, a Frenchman French, etc., so it is not provincial for an American to be American." So it is not provincial for a Russian, an Australian, a Portuguese, a Dane, a Laplander, to savour of their respective countries: that would be where the argument would land you. I think it is extremely provincial for a Russian to be very Russian, a Portuguese very Portuguese; for the simple reason that certain national types are essentially and intrinsically provincial. I sympathize even less with your protest against the idea that it takes an old civilization to set a novelist in motion—a proposition that seems to me so true as to be a truism. It is on manners, customs, usages, habits, forms, upon all these things matured and established, that a novelist lives—they are the very stuff his work is made of; and in saying that in the absence of those "dreary and worn-out paraphernalia" which I enumerate as being wanting in American society, "we have simply the whole of human life left," you beg (to my sense) the question. I should say we had just so much less of it as these same "paraphernalia" represent, and I think they represent an enormous quantity of it. I shall feel refuted only when we have produced (setting the present high company—yourself and me—for obvious reasons apart) a gentleman who strikes me as a novelist—as belonging to the company of Balzac and Thackeray. Of course, in the absence of this godsend, it is but a harmless amusement that we should reason about it, and maintain that if right were right he should already be here. I will freely admit that such a genius will get on *only* by agreeing with your view of the case—to do something great he must feel as you feel about it. But then I doubt whether such a genius—a man of the faculty of Balzac and Thackeray—*could* agree with you! When he does I will lie flat on my stomach and do him homage—in the very centre of the contributor's club, or on the threshold of the magazine, or in any public place you may appoint!—But I didn't mean to wrangle with you—I meant only to thank you and to express my sense of how happily you turn those things.—I am greatly amused at your picture of the contributing blood-hounds whom you are holding in check. I wish immensely that you would let them fly at me—though there is no reason, certainly, that the decent public should be bespattered, periodically, with my gore. However my tender (or rather my very tough) flesh is prescient already of the Higginsonian fangs. Happy man, to be going, like that, to see your plays acted. It is a sensation I am dying (though not as yet trying) to cultivate. What a tremendous quantity of work you must get through in these years! I am impatient for the next *Atlantic*. What is your *Cornhill* novel about? I am to precede it with a poorish story in three numbers—a tale purely American, the writing of which made me feel acutely the want of the "paraphernalia." I *must* add, however (to return for a moment to this), that I applaud and esteem you highly for not feeling it; i.e. the want. You are certainly right—magnificently and heroically right—to do so, and on the day you make your readers—I mean the readers who know and appreciate the paraphernalia—do the same, you will be the American Balzac. That's a great mission—go in for it! Wherever you go, receive, and distribute among your wife and children, the blessing of yours ever,

H. JAMES jr.

TO CHARLES ELIOT NORTON.

3 Bolton Street, W.

Nov. 13th, 1880.

My dear Charles,

...I wish you could take a good holiday and spend it in these countries. I have got to feel like such an old European that I could almost pretend to help to do you the honours. I am at least now a thoroughly naturalised Londoner—a cockney "convaincu." I am attached to London in spite of the long list of reasons why I should not be; I think it on the whole the best point of view in the world. There are times when the fog, the smoke, the universal uncleanness, the combined unwieldiness and flatness of much of the social life—these and many other matters—overwhelm the spirit and fill it with a yearning for other climes; but nevertheless one reverts, one sticks, one abides, one even cherishes! Considering that I lose all patience with the English about fifteen times a day, and vow that I renounce them for ever, I get on with them beautifully and love them well. Our dear Vasari, I fear, couldn't have made much of them, and they would have been improved by a slight infusion of the Florentine spirit; but for all that they are, for me, the great race—even at this hour of their possible decline. Taking them altogether they are more complete than other folk, more largely nourished, deeper, denser, stronger. I think it takes more to make an Englishman, on the whole, than to make anyone else—and I say this with a consciousness of all that often seems to me to have been left out of their composition. But the question is interminable, and idle into the bargain. I am passing a quiet autumn. London has not yet waked up from the stagnation that belongs to this period. The only incident of consequence that has lately occurred to me was my dining a few days since at the Guildhall, at the big scrambling banquet which the Lord Mayor gives on the 9th November to the Cabinet, foreign ministers, etc. It was uncomfortable but amusing—you have probably done it yourself. I met Lowell there, whom I see, besides, with tolerable frequency. He is just back from a visit to Scotland which he appears to have enjoyed, including a speech-making at Edinburgh. He gets on here, I think, very smoothly and happily; for though he is critical in the gross, he is not in the detail, and takes things with a sort of boyish simplicity. He is universally liked and appreciated, his talk enjoyed (as well it may be, after some of their own!) and his poor long-suffering wife is doing very well. I therefore hope he will be left undisturbed by Garfield to enjoy the fruition of the long period of discomfort he has passed through. It will be in the highest degree indecent to remove him; though I wish he had a pair of secretaries that ministered a little more to the idea of American brilliancy. Lowell has to do *that* quite by himself....

Believe me always faithfully yours,

H. JAMES jr.

TO HIS MOTHER.

Mentmore, Leighton Buzzard,

November 28th, 1880.

Dearest mammy,

...This is a pleasant Sunday, and I have been spending it (from yesterday evening) in a very pleasant place. 'Pleasant' is indeed rather an odd term to apply to this gorgeous residence, and the manner of life which prevails in it; but it is that as well as other things beside. Lady Rosebery (it is her enviable dwelling) asked me down here a week ago, and I stop till tomorrow a.m. There are several people here, but no one very important, save John Bright and Lord Northbrook, the last Liberal Viceroy of India. Millais, the painter, has been here for a part of the day, and I took a walk [with him] this afternoon back from the stables, where we had been to see three winners of the Derby trotted out in succession. This will give you an idea of the scale of Mentmore, where everything is magnificent. The house is a huge modern palace, filled with wonderful objects accumulated by the late Sir Meyer de Rothschild, Lady R.'s father. All of them are precious and many are exquisite, and their general Rothschild-ish splendour is only equalled by their profusion....

I have spent a good part of the time in listening to the conversation of John Bright, whom, though I constantly see him at the Reform Club, I had never met before. He has the repute of being often "grumpy"; but on this occasion he has been in extremely good form and has discoursed uninterruptedly and pleasantly. He gives one an impression of sturdy, honest, vigorous, English middle-class liberalism, accompanied by a certain infusion of genius, which helps one to understand how his name has become the great rallying-point of that sentiment. He reminds me a good deal of a superior New Englander—with a fatter, damper nature, however, than theirs.... They are at afternoon tea downstairs in a vast, gorgeous hall, where an upper gallery looks down like the colonnade in Paul Veronese's pictures, and the chairs are all golden thrones, belonging to ancient Doges of Venice. I have retired from the glittering scene, to meditate by my bedroom fire on the fleeting character of earthly possessions, and to commune with my mammy, until a supreme being in the shape of a dumb footman arrives, to ventilate my shirt and turn my stockings inside out (the beautiful red ones imparted by Alice—which he must admire so much, though he doesn't venture to show it,) preparatory to my dressing for dinner. Tomorrow I return to London and to my personal occupation, always doubly valued after 48 hours passed among *ces gens-ci*, whose chief effect upon me is to sharpen my desire to distinguish myself by personal achievement, of however limited a character. It is the only answer one can make to their atrocious good fortune. Lord Rosebery, however, with youth, cleverness, a delightful face, a happy character, a Rothschild wife of numberless millions to distinguish and demoralize him, wears them with such tact and bonhomie that you almost forgive him. He is extremely nice with Bright, draws him out, defers to him etc., with a delicacy rare in an Englishman. But, after all, there is much to say—more than can be said in a letter—about one's relations with these people. You may be interested, by the way, to know that Lord R. said this morning at lunch that his ideal of the happy life was that of Cambridge, Mass., "living like Longfellow." You may imagine that at this the company looked awfully vague, and I thought of proposing to him to exchange Mentmore for 20 Quincy Street.

I have little other personal news than this, which I have given you in some detail, for entertainment's sake.... I embrace you, dearest mother, and also your two companions.

Ever your fondest

H. JAMES jr.

TO MRS. FANNY KEMBLE.

Hôtel de la Ville, Milan.

March 24th, '81.

My dear Mrs. Kemble,

Your good letter of nearly four weeks ago lies before me—where it has been lying for some days past—making me think of you so much that I ended by feeling as if I had answered it. On reflection I see that I haven't, however—that is, not in any way that you will appreciate. Shall you appreciate a letter from Milan on a day blustering and hateful as any you yourself can lately have been visited with? I have been spending the last eight days at this place, but I take myself off—for southern parts—to-morrow; so that by waiting a little I might have sent you a little more of the genuine breath of Italy. But I can do that—and I shall do it—at any rate, and meanwhile let my Milanese news go for what it is worth. You see I travel very deliberately, as I started for Rome six weeks ago, and I have only got thus far. My slowness has had various causes; among others my not being in a particular hurry to join the little nest of my compatriots (and yours) who cluster about the Piazza di Spagna. I have enjoyed the independence of lingering in places where I had no visits to pay—and this indeed has been the only charm of Milan, which has seemed prosaic and winterish, as if it were on the wrong side of the Alps. I have written a good deal (not letters), and seen that mouldering old fresco of Leonardo, which is so magnificent in its ruin, and the lovely young Raphael in the Brera (the Sposalizio) which is still so fresh and juvenile, and Lucrezia Borgia's straw-coloured lock of hair at the Ambrosian Library, and several other small and great curiosities. I have kept pretty well out of the Cathedral, as the chill of Dante's frozen circle abides within it, and I have had a sore throat ever since I left soft San Remo. On the other hand I have also been to the Scala, which is a mighty theatre, and where I heard Der Freyschütz done à l'italienne, and sat through about an hour and three quarters of a ballet which was to last three. The Italians, truly, are eternal children. They paid infinitely more attention to the ballet than to the opera, and followed with breathless attention, and an air of the most serious credulity, the interminable adventures of a danseuse who went through every possible alternation of human experience on the points of her toes. The more I see of them the more struck I am with their having no sense of the ridiculous.

It must have been at Marseilles, I think, that I wrote you before; so that there is an hiatus in my biography to fill up. I went from Marseilles to Nice, which I found more than usually detestable, and pervaded, to an intolerable pitch, with a bad French carnival, which set me on the road again till I reached San Remo, which you may know, and which if you don't you ought to. I spent more than a fortnight there, among the olives and the oranges, between a big yellow sun and a bright blue sea. The walks and drives are lovely, and in the course of one of them (a drive) I called upon our friends the George Howards, who have been wintering at Bordighera, a few miles away. But he was away in England getting himself elected to Parliament (you may have heard that he has just been returned for East Cumberland,) and she was away with him, helping him. The idea of leaving the oranges and olives for that! I saw, however, a most delightful little maid, their eldest daughter, of about

15, who had a mixture of shyness and frankness, the softness of the papa and the decision of the mother, with which I quite fell in love. I didn't fall in love with Mrs. William Morris, the strange, pale, livid, gaunt, silent, and yet in a manner graceful and picturesque, wife of the poet and paper-maker, who is spending the winter with the Howards; though doubtless she too has her merits. She has, for instance, wonderful aesthetic hair. From San Remo I came along the rest of the coast to Genoa, *not* by carriage however, as I might have done, for I was rather afraid of three days "on end" of my own society: that is, not on end, but sitting down. When I am tired of myself in common situations I can get up and walk away; so, in a word, I came in the train, and the train came in a tunnel—for it was almost all one—for five or six hours. I have been going to Venice—but it is so cold and blustering that I think to-morrow, when I depart from this place, the idea of reaching the southernmost point will get the better of me, and I shall make straight for Rome. I will write you from there—where I first beheld you: that is, familiarity (if I may be allowed the expression). Enough meanwhile about myself, my intentions and delays: let me hear, or at least let me ask, about your own circumstances and propensities.... You must have felt *spattered*, like all the world, with the blood of the poor Russian Czar! Aren't you glad you are not an Empress? But you are. God save your Majesty!—Mrs. Greville sent me Swinburne's complicated dirge upon her poor simple mother, and I thought it wanting in all the qualities that one liked in Mrs T. I should like very much to send a tender message to Mrs Gordon: indefinite—but *very* tender! To you I am both tender and definite (save when I cross).

Ever very faithfully yours,

H. JAMES jr.

III. THE MIDDLE YEARS(1882-1888)

AFTER his long absence Henry James had a few crowded months of American impressions, during the winter of 1881-2, in Boston, New York, and Washington. He was as sociable as usual, where-ever he went, and he used to the full the opportunity of reviving old memories and creating new. It will be seen that he confesses to having enjoyed "a certain success"; since the publication of Daisy Miller, three years before, he had known what it was to be a well-known author in London, but it was a fresh sensation on his native ground. Unhappily this interesting episode was cut short by the first great sorrow that had fallen upon his house. His mother died suddenly, in February 1882. To the end of his life Henry James was to remember this loss as the deepest stroke he had ever received; though she appears but little in his reminiscences there is no doubt that her presence, her completely selfless devotion to her husband and children, had been the greatest of all facts in their lives. Her care, her pride in them, the surrender of her whole nature and will to her love for them, had accompanied and supported all their doings; her husband, during the long years in which he poured out the strange fruits of his thought to a steadily indifferent world, had rested unreservedly on her true and gentle companionship. Her second son's letters to her from Europe will already have shewn the easy and delightful relation that existed between her and her children; they confided in her and leaned on her and rallied her, with an intimacy deepened by the almost unbroken union of the whole household throughout their youth. Henry James stayed by his father for some months after her death, and would have stayed longer; but his father was anxious that he should return to his own work and life. He sailed for England accordingly in May 1882.

A summer in London was followed by the autumn excursion to Touraine and Provence portrayed in *A Little Tour in France*. At Tours he had the company of Mrs. Fanny Kemble and her daughter; and as usual he spent a few weeks in Paris before going home. He arrived in London in December to receive almost at once a message announcing that his father was seriously ill.

He started immediately for America, but it was already too late; his father had died, so they felt, from mere cessation of the will to live bereft of their mother. "Nothing—he had enabled himself to make perfectly sure—was in the least worth while without her; this attested, he passed away or went out, with entire simplicity, promptness and ease, for the definite reason that his support had failed." So Henry James wrote, thirty years later, in the *Notes of a Son and Brother*, and his letters of the time confirm the impression. "There passes away with him," he says in one of them, "a certain sense of inspiration and protection which had, I think, accompanied each of us even to middle life." Thenceforward it was to his elder brother that Henry James always looked for something of the same kind of support, and many letters will shew how close the bond remained. In the mere prose of business William took complete charge of his brother's share in the family affairs, for which the younger never claimed the smallest aptitude. But during the months that followed their father's death William was in Europe, and it fell to Henry to be occupied with the details of their property, for perhaps the first and last time. The patrimony consisted mainly of certain houses in the town of Syracuse, N. Y., where their grandfather had had interests, and where "James Street" is still one of the principal thoroughfares. Henry was kept in America by the necessity of taking part in some rather complicated dispositions arising out of the terms of their father's will; and also by his care for the future of his sister Alice, the youngest of the family. Her health was very insecure, and he proposed that she should join him in Europe; but for the present she preferred to settle in Boston, where he helped her to instal herself. He did not finally return to London until the following August, 1883.

This was his last visit to America for more than twenty years. He now subsided once more into the life of London, with its incessant round of sociability and its equally incessant accompaniment of creative work. Gradually his tone in regard to his English setting is modified and deepened. In the correspondence of these middle years it is no longer the interested but slightly rebellious immigrant who speaks; it is rather the old-established colonist, now identified with his surroundings, a sharer in the general fortunes and responsibilities of the place. If he still regards himself as an observer from without and is still capable, as he once says, of "raging against British density in hours of irritation and disgust," it is none the less noticeable that English difficulties, English wars and politics and social troubles, of all of which these years were very full, begin to affect him as matters that concern his pride and solicitude for the country. There mingles with his exasperation an ardent desire that the English race may continue to stand high in the world, in spite of the many voices prophesying decadence and disaster. He writes as one who now has a stake in an old and honourable institution, and who feels a personal interest in its well-being and its good fame. Not indeed that he took, or ever for a moment wished to take, any share in the common life of the place but that of the most private fellowship; he resolutely avoided the least appearance of publicity, always refused to be drawn into popular functions, organisations, associations of any sort, and clung more and more, in the midst of all distractions, to the secrecy and seclusion of his work. And for that inner life these years were a very important turning-point. He now reached a period of his development when an immensely enlarged world of art seemed to open before him; and at the same time he made the discovery—one that had a deep and special effect upon him—that he was not the kind of writer who is rewarded with a big audience. Both these matters are heard of in the letters of this time, but their consequences do not appear fully until somewhat later. They were various and far-reaching, and some of them can hardly be called fortunate.

Meanwhile the outward incidents of his life were as few and simple as ever. The stream of social engagements remained indeed at its height, notwithstanding his protests of withdrawal from the world; but otherwise there is little to chronicle but the publication of his books and his yearly journeys abroad. Early in 1884 he spent some weeks in Paris, where the death of Turgenev had made a gap that he greatly felt. For the rest of the year he was occupied in writing The Bostonians, and went no further from London than to carry his manuscript into lodgings at Dover for August and September. A little later his sister Alice arrived from America, to make the experiment of life in Europe for the benefit of her now confirmed ill-health. Her presence near at hand, for the few years that remained to her, was a source of much pleasure, and also of constant anxiety, to her brother. She was a woman of rare talent and of strongly marked character; but the life of an invalid, which proved to be all she was capable of, prevented her from using her opportunities and from taking the place that would have been open to her. She lived in great retirement, at first in London, afterwards chiefly at Bournemouth and Leamington. Henry James was unwearied in his care for her; he visited her constantly, and never without keen delight in her company and her vigorous talk. His brotherly attention had yet a further reward in the summer of 1885, when she was at Bournemouth. To be near her he spent several weeks there, and was able at the same time to cultivate the society of another imprisoned invalid, close by, with whom he had already had some acquaintance. This was Robert Louis Stevenson, and the intimacy that thus arose very fortunately still survives in many admirable letters of each to the other. Stevenson's side of the correspondence, edited by Sir Sidney Colvin, is well known, and Henry James's can now be added to it; there could be no more illuminating interchange between two fine artists, so unlike in everything but their common passion.

By this time The Bostonians was beginning to appear in an American magazine, and a little later, again at Dover, The Princess Casamassima was finished. For two years Henry James now wrote nothing but shorter pieces (among them The Aspern Papers, The Lesson of the Master, The Reverberator,) with growing disconcertment as he found how tardily they seemed to appeal to editors, American or English. In the autumn of 1885 he spent his accustomed month in Paris, after which he scarcely stirred from London for another year. Early in 1886 he at last accomplished a move from his Bolton Street lodging, never a very cheerful or convenient abode, to a flat in Kensington (13 De Vere Mansions, presently known as 34 De Vere Gardens), close to the palace and the park, where he had much more agreeable conditions of light and air and quiet. He was planning, however, for another long absence in Italy, away from the interruptions of London, and this he secured during the first seven months of 1887. For most of the time he was at Florence, where he took rooms in a villa overhanging the view from Bellosguardo; and he paid two lengthy visits to Venice, staying first with Mrs. Bronson, in the apartment so often occupied by Browning, and later with Mr. and Mrs. Daniel Curtis in the splendid old Palazzo Barbaro, where years afterwards he placed the exquisite and stricken heroine of The Wings of the Dove, for the climax of her story. He returned to England, late in the summer, to settle down to the writing of The Tragic Muse—the first time, as he mentions, that he had attacked a purely English subject on a large scale. "I am getting to know English life better than American," he writes in September 1888, when he was still working upon the book, " ...and to understand the English character, or at least the mind, as well as if I had invented it—which indeed," he adds lightly, "I think I could have done without any very extraordinary expenditure of ingenuity." The end of the summer of 1888 was spent in an hotel at Torquay, which became one of his favourite retreats; and later in the autumn he was for a short while abroad, at Geneva and Paris, with a flying dip into Northern Italy. The letter to his brother, written from Geneva, with which this section closes, lucidly sums up the conclusions he had by now drawn from the experience of a dozen years of England. At the age of forty-five he could feel that he had exhausted the study of the old international distinctions, English and American, that had engaged him for so long. He was indeed to return to them again, later on, and to devote to them the final elaboration of his art; but that lay far ahead, and now for many years he faced in other directions.

A vivid glimpse of Henry James at this time is given in the following note of reminiscence, kindly written for this page by Mr. Edmund Gosse:

In the late summer of 1886 an experience, more often imagined than enjoyed, actually took place in the shape of a party of friends independently dispersed in the hotel or in lodgings through the Worcestershire village of Broadway, but with the home of Frank Millet, the American painter, as their centre. Edwin Abbey, John S. Sargent, Alfred Parsons, Fred Barnard and I, and others, lived through five bright weeks of perfect weather, in boisterous intimacy. Early in September Henry James joined us for a short visit. The Millets possessed, on their domain, a medieval ruin, a small ecclesiastical edifice, which was very roughly repaired so as to make a kind of refuge for us, and there, in the mornings, Henry James and I would write, while Abbey and Millet painted on the floor below, and Sargent and Parsons tilted their easels just outside. We were all within shouting distance, and not much serious work was done, for we were in towering spirits and everything was food for laughter. Henry James was the only sedate one of us all—benign, indulgent, but grave, and not often unbending beyond a genial chuckle. We all treated him with some involuntary respect, though he asked for none. It is remembered with what affability he wore a garland of flowers at a birthday feast, and even, nobly descending, took part one night in a cake-walk. But mostly, though not much our senior, he was serious, mildly avuncular, but very happy and un-upbraiding.

In those days Henry James wore a beard of vague darkish brown, matching his hair, which had not yet withdrawn from his temples, and these bushy ornaments had the effect of making him in a sense shadowy. Almost every afternoon he took a walk with me, rarely with Sargent, never with the sedentary rest; these walks were long in time but not in distance, for Henry was inclined to saunter. He had not wholly recovered from that weakness of the muscles of his back which had so long troubled him, and I suppose that this was the cause of a curious stiffness in his progress, which proceeded rather slowly. He had certain preferences, in particular for the level road through the green landscape to the ancient grey village of Aston Somerville. He always made the same remark, as if he had never noticed it before, that Aston was "so Italian, so Tuscan."

His talk, which flowed best with one of us alone, was enchanting; with me largely it concerned the craft of letters. I remember little definitely, but recall how most of us, with the ladies, spent one long rollicking day in rowing down the winding Avon from Evesham to Pershore. There was much "singing in the English boat," as Marvell says, and Edwin Abbey "obliged" profusely on the banjo. Henry James I can still see sitting like a beneficent deity, a sort of bearded Buddha, at the prow, manifestly a little afraid that some of us would tumble into the river.

TO MISS HENRIETTA REUBELL.

Metropolitan Club,

Washington, D. C.

Jan. 9th, 1882.

My dear Miss Reubell,

I have never yet thanked you for the amiable note in which you kindly invited me to write to you from the Americas; and the best way I can do so now is to simply respond to your invitation. I am in the Americas indeed, and behold I write. These countries are extremely pleasant, and I recommend you to come and see them au plus tôt. You would have a great career here, and would return—if you should return at all—with a multitude of scalps at your slim girdle. There is a great demand for brilliant women, and I can promise you that you would be intimately appreciated. I shall return about the first of May—but without any blond scalps, though with a great many happy impressions. Though I should perhaps not linger upon the point myself, I believe I have had a certain success. As for ces gens-ci, they have had great success with me, and have been delightfully genial and hospitable. It is here that people treat you well; venez-y voir. You have had a great many things, I know; but you have not had a winter in the Americas. The people are extremely nice and humane. I didn't care for it much at first—but it improves immensely on acquaintance, and after you have got the right point of view and *diapason* it is a wonderfully entertaining and amusing country. The skies are as blue as the blotting paper (as yet unspotted) on which this scrawl reposes, and the sunshine, which is deliciously warm, has always an air de fête. I have seen multitudes of people, and no one has been disagreeable. That is different from your pretentious Old World. Of Washington I can speak as yet but little, having come but four days ago; but it is like nothing else in the old world or the new. Enormous spaces, hundreds of miles of asphalte, a charming climate and the most entertaining society in America. I spent a month in Boston and another in New York, and have paid three or four visits in the country. All this was very jolly, and it is pleasant to be in one's native land, where one is someone and something. If I were to abide by my vanity only I should never return to that Europe which ignores me. Unfortunately I love my Europe better than my vanity, and I appreciate you, if I may say so, better than either! Therefore I shall return—about the month of May. I am thinking tremendously about writing to Mrs. Boit—kindly tell her so. My very friendly regards to your dear Mother, and your Brother.

A word to *Cambridge, Mass.* (my father's) will always reach me. It would be very *charming* of you to address one to yours very faithfully,

H. JAMES.

TO CHARLES ELIOT NORTON.

20 Quincy Street,

Cambridge, Mass.

Feb. 7th, 1882.

My dear Charles,

Only a word to thank you very heartily for your little note of friendship, and to send you a grateful message, as well, from my father and sister. My mother's death is the greatest change that could befall us, but our lives are so full of her still that we scarcely yet seem to have lost her. The long beneficence of her own life remains and survives.

I shall see you after your return to Shady Hill, as I am to be for a good while in these regions. I wish to remain near my father, who is infirm and rather tottering; and I shall settle myself in Boston for the next four or five months. In other words I shall be constantly in Cambridge and will often look in at you. I hope you have enjoyed your pilgrimage.

Ever faithfully yours,

H. JAMES jr.

To Mrs. John L. Gardner.

The play referred to in this letter is doubtless the dramatic version of *Daisy Miller*; it remained unacted, but was published in America in 1883.

3 Bolton St., Piccadilly.

June 5th [1882].

My dear Mrs. Gardner,

A little greeting across the sea! I meant to send it as soon as I touched the shore; but the huge grey mass of London has interposed. I experience the need of proving to you that I missed seeing you before I left America—though I tried one day—the one before I quitted Boston; but you were still in New York, contributing the harmony of your presence and the melodies of your toilet, to the din of Wagnerian fiddles and the crash of Teutonic cymbals. You must have passed me in the train that last Saturday; but you have never done anything but pass me—and *dépasser* me; so it doesn't so much matter. That final interview—that supreme farewell—will however always be one of the most fascinating incidents of life—the incidents that *didn't* occur, and leave me to muse on what they might have done for us. I think with extraordinary tenderness of those two pretty little evenings when I read you my play. They make a charming picture—a perfect picture—in my mind, and the memory of them appeals to all that is most *raffiné* in my constitution. Drop a tear—a diminutive tear (as *your* tears must be—small but beautifully-shaped pearls) upon the fact that my drama is not after all to be brought out in New York (at least for the present).... It is possible it may see the light here. I am to read it to the people of the St. James's Theatre next week. *Please don't speak of this.* London seems big and black and horrible and delightful—Boston seems only the last named. You indeed could make it horrible for me if you chose, and you could also make it big; but I doubt if you could make it black. It would be a fair and glittering horror, suggestive of icicles and white fur. I wonder if you are capable of writing me three words? Let one of them tell me you are well. The second—what you please! The third that you sometimes bestow a friendly thought upon yours very faithfully,

H. JAMES jr.

TO MISS GRACE NORTON.

Hôtel du Midi,

Toulouse.

Oct. 17th [1882].

My dear Grace,

You *shall* have a letter this morning, whatever happens! I am waiting for the train to Carcassonne, and you will perhaps ask yourself why you are thus sandwiched between these two mouldy antiquities. It is precisely because they are mouldy that I invoke your genial presence. Toulouse is dreary and not interesting, and I am afraid that Carcassonne will answer to the same description I heard given a couple of weeks ago by an English lady in Touraine, of the charming Château d'Amboise: "rather curious, you know, but very, very dirty." Therefore my spirit turns for comfort to what I have known best in life. I got your last excellent letter an abominable number of weeks ago; and I hereby propose, as a rule of our future correspondence, that I be graciously absolved from ever specifying the time that has elapsed since the arrival of the letter I am supposed to be answering. This custom will ease me off immensely. Your last, however, is not so remote but that the scolding you gave me for sending your previous letter to Mrs. Kemble is fearfully fresh in my mind. My dear Grace, I regret extremely having irritated you; but I would fain wrestle with you on this subject. I think you have a false code about the showing of letters—and in calling it a breach of confidence you surely confound the limits of things. Of course there is always a particular discretion for the particular case; but what are letters but talk, and what is the showing them but the repetition of talk? The same rules that govern that of course govern the other; but I don't see why they should be more stringent. It is indeed, I think, of the very essence of a good letter to be shown—it is wasted if it is kept for *one*. Was not Mme. de Sévigné's last always handed about to a hundred people—was not Horace Walpole's? What was right for them is, it seems to me, right for you. However, I make this little protest simply for the theory's sake, and promise you solemnly that in practice, in future, you shall be my own exclusive and peculiar Sévigné! Yet I don't at all insist on being your exclusive Walpole! I have indeed the sweet security of the conviction that you will never "want," as they say (*you* don't) in Cambridge, to exhibit my epistles. Only I give you full leave to read them aloud at your soirées! Have your soirées recommenced by the way? Where are you, my dear Grace, and how are you? The question about your whereabouts will perhaps make you smile, if anything in this letter can, as I make no doubt you are enjoying the gorgeous charm (I speak without irony) of a Cambridge October. For myself, as you see, I am "doing" the south of France—for literary purposes, into which I won't pretend to enter, as they are not of a very elevated character. (I am trying to write some articles about these regions for an American "illustrated"—*Harper*—but I don't foresee, as yet, any very brilliant results.) I left England some five weeks ago, and after a few days in Paris came down into Touraine—for the sake of the châteaux of the Loire. At the hotel at Tours, where I spent 12 days, I had the advantage of the society of Mrs. Kemble, and her daughter Mrs. Wister, with the son of the latter. We made some excursions together—that is, *minus* Mrs. K. (a large void,) who was too infirm to junket about, and then the ladies returned to Paris and I took my way further afield. Touraine is charming, Chenonceaux, Chambord, Blois, etc., very interesting, and that episode was on the whole a success—enlivened too by my exciting company. But the rest of France (that is those parts I have been through) [is] rather disappointing, though I suppose when I recite my itinerary you will feel that I ought to have found a world of picturesqueness—I mean at Bourges, Le Mans, Angers, Nantes, La Rochelle, Poitiers, etc. The cathedral of Bourges is worth a long pilgrimage to see; but for the rest France has preserved the physiognomy of the past much less than England and than Italy. Besides, when I come into the south, I don't console myself for not being in the latter country. I don't care for these people, and in fine I rather hate it. I return to Paris on November 1st, and spend a month there. Then I return to England for the winter. When I am in that country I want to get out of it, and when I am out of it I languish for its heavy air. England is just now in a rather "cocky" mood, and disposed to carry it high with her little Egyptian victories. It is such a satisfaction to me to see her again counting for something in Europe that I would give her *carte blanche* to go as far as she chooses—or dares; but at the same time I hope she won't exhibit a vulgar greed. It has a really dramatic interest for me to see how the great Gladstone will acquit himself of a situation in which all his high principles will be subjected to an extraordinary strain. He will be, I suspect, neither very lofty, nor very base, but will compromise. I don't suppose, however, you care much about these far-away matters. I hope, my dear Grace, that your life is taking more and more a possible shape—that your summer has left you some pleasant memories, and your winter brings some cheerful hopes. I don't *think* I shall be so long again—at any rate my letters are no proof of my sentiments—by which I mean that my silence is no *dis*proof; for after all I wish to be believed when I tell you that I am most affectionately yours,

HENRY JAMES jr.

TO WILLIAM JAMES.

131 Mt. Vernon St.,

Boston.

Dec. 26th, '82.

My dear William—

You will already have heard the circumstances under which I arrived at New York on Thursday 21st, at noon, after a very rapid and prosperous, but painful passage. Letters from Alice and Katherine L. were awaiting me at the dock, telling me that dear father was to be buried that morning. I reached Boston at 11 that night; there was so much delay in getting up-town. I found Bob at the station here. He had come on for the funeral only, and returned to Milwaukee the next morning. Alice, who was in bed, was very quiet and A. K. was perfect. They told me everything—or at least they told me a great deal—before we parted that night, and what they told me was deeply touching, and yet not at all literally painful. Father had been so tranquil, so painless, had died so easily and, as it were, deliberately, and there had been none—not the least—of that anguish and confusion which we imagined in London.... He simply, after the "improvement" of which, we were written before I sailed, had a sudden relapse—a series of swoons—after which he took to his bed not to rise again. He had no visible malady—strange as it may seem. The "softening of the brain" was simply a gradual refusal of food, because he *wished* to die. There was no dementia except a sort of exaltation of his belief that he had entered into "the spiritual life." Nothing could persuade him to eat, and yet he never suffered, or gave the least sign of suffering, from inanition. All this will seem strange and incredible to you, but told with all the details, as Aunt Kate has told it to me, it becomes real—taking father as he was—almost natural. He prayed and longed to die. He ebbed and faded away, though in spite of his strength becoming continually less, he was able to see people and talk. He wished to see as many people as he could, and he talked with them without effort. He saw F. Boott and talked much two or three days before he died. Alice says he said the most picturesque and humorous things. He knew I was coming and was glad, but not impatient. He was delighted when he was told that you would stay in my rooms in my absence, and seemed much interested in the idea. He had no belief apparently that he should live to see me, but was perfectly cheerful about it. He slept a great deal, and as A. K. says there was "so little of the sick-room" about him. He lay facing the windows, which he would never have darkened—never pained by the light.... 27th a.m. Will send this now and write again tonight. All our wish here is that you should remain abroad the next six months.

Ever your

H. JAMES.

TO GEORGE DU MAURIER.

The article on George du Maurier was that reprinted in *Partial Portraits* (1888).

115 East 25th Street,

New York.

April 17th, 1883.

My dear Du Maurier,

I send you by this post the sheets of that little tribute to your genius which I spoke of to you so many months ago and which appears in the *Century* for May. The magazine is not yet out, or I would send you that, and the long delay makes my article so slight in itself, rather an impotent conclusion. Let me hasten to assure you that the "London Society", tacked to the title, is none of my doing, but that of the editors of the Magazine, who put in an urgent plea for it. Such as my poor remarks are, I hope you will find in them nothing disagreeable, but only the expression of an exceeding friendliness. May my blessing go with them and a multitude of good wishes!

I should have been to see you again long ago if I had not suddenly been called to America (by the death of my father) in December last. The autumn, before that, I spent altogether abroad, and have scarcely been in England since I bade you good-bye, after that very delightful walk and talk we had together last July—an episode of which I have the happiest, tenderest memory. Romantic Hampstead seems very far away from East 25th St; though East 25th St. has some good points. I have been spending the winter in Boston and am here only on a visit to a friend, and though I am "New Yorkais d'origine" I never return to this wonderful city without being entertained and impressed afresh. New York is full of types and figures and curious social idiosyncrasies, and I only wish we had some one here, to hold up the mirror, with a 15th part of your talent. It is altogether an extraordinary growing, swarming, glittering, pushing, chattering, good-natured, cosmopolitan place, and perhaps in some ways the best imitation of Paris that can be found (yet with a great originality of its own.) But I didn't mean to be so geographical; I only meant to shake hands, and to remind myself again that if my dear old London life is interrupted, it isn't, heaven be praised, finished, and that therefore there is a use—a delightful and superior use—in "keeping up" my relations. I am talking a good deal like Mrs. Ponsonby de Tomkyns, but when you reflect that you are not Sir Gorgius Midas, you will acquit me. I have a fair prospect of returning to England late in the summer, and that will be for a long day. I hope your winter has used you kindly and that Mrs. du Maurier is well, and also the other ornaments of your home, including the Great St. Bernard. I greet them all most kindly and am ever very faithfully yours,

HENRY JAMES.

TO MISS GRACE NORTON.

131 Mount Vernon St., Boston.

July 28th [1883].

My dear Grace,

Before the sufferings of others I am always utterly powerless, and your letter reveals such depths of suffering that I hardly know what to say to you. This indeed is not my last word—but it must be my first. You are not isolated, verily, in such states of feeling as this—that is, in the sense that you appear to make all the misery of all mankind your own; only I have a terrible sense that you give all and receive nothing—that there is no reciprocity in your sympathy—that you have all the affliction of it and none of the returns. However—I am determined not to speak to you except with the voice of stoicism. I don't know *why* we live—the gift of life comes to us from I don't know what source or for what purpose; but I believe we can go on living for the reason that (always of course up to a certain point) life is the most valuable thing we know anything about, and it is therefore presumptively a great mistake to surrender it while there is any yet left in the cup. In other words consciousness is an illimitable power, and though at times it may seem to be all consciousness of misery, yet in the way it propagates itself from wave to wave, so that we never cease to feel, and though at moments we appear to, try to, pray to, there is something that holds one in one's place, makes it a standpoint in the universe which it is probably good not to forsake. You are right in your consciousness that we are all echoes and reverberations of the *same*, and you are noble when your interest and pity as to everything that surrounds you, appears to have a sustaining and harmonizing power. Only don't, I beseech you, *generalize* too much in these sympathies and tendernesses—remember that every life is a special problem which is not yours but another's, and content yourself with the terrible algebra of your own. Don't melt too much into the universe, but be as solid and dense and fixed as you can. We all live together, and those of us who love and know, live so most. We help each other—even unconsciously, each in our own effort, we lighten the effort of others, we contribute to the sum of success, make it possible for others to live. Sorrow comes in great waves—no one can know that better than you—but it rolls over us, and though it may almost smother us it leaves us on the spot, and we know that if it is strong we are stronger, inasmuch as it passes and we remain. It wears us, uses us, but we wear it and use it in return; and it is blind, whereas we after a manner see. My dear Grace, you are passing through a darkness in which I myself in my ignorance see nothing but that you have been made wretchedly ill by it; but it is only a darkness, it is not an end, or *the* end. Don't think, don't feel, any more than you can help, don't conclude or decide—don't do anything but *wait.* Everything will pass, and serenity and *accepted* mysteries and disillusionments, and the tenderness of a few good people, and new opportunities and ever so much of life, in a word, will remain. You will do all sorts of things yet, and I will help you. The only thing is not to *melt* in the meanwhile. I insist upon the necessity of a sort of mechanical condensation—so that however fast the horse may run away there will, when he pulls up, be a somewhat agitated but perfectly identical G. N. left in the saddle. Try not to be ill—that is all; for in that there is a failure. You are marked out for success, and you must not fail. You have my tenderest affection and all my confidence. Ever your faithful friend—

HENRY JAMES.

TO WILLIAM JAMES.

Hôtel de Hollande, Paris.

Feb. 20th, '84.

My dear William—

I owe you an answer to two letters—especially to the one in which you announce to me the birth of your little Israelite. I bid him the most affectionate welcome into this world of care and I hope that by this time he has begun to get used to it. I am too delighted to hear of Alice's well-being, and trust it has now merged into complete recovery. Apropos of the Babe, allow me to express an earnest hope that you will give him some handsome and pictorial name (within discreet limits). Most of our names are rather colourless—collez-lui dessus, therefore, a little patch of brightness—and don't call him *after* any one—give him a name quite to himself. And let it be only one.... I have seen several times the gifted Sargent, whose work I admire exceedingly and who is a remarkably artistic nature and charming fellow. I have also spent an evening with A. Daudet and a morning at Auteuil with Ed. de Goncourt. Seeing these people does me a world of good, and this intellectual vivacity and *raffinement* make an English mind seem like a sort of glue-pot. But their ignorance, corruption and complacency are strange, full strange. I wish I had time to give you more of my impressions of them. They are at any rate very interesting and Daudet, who has a remarkable personal charm and is as beautiful as the day, was extremely nice to me. I saw also Zola at his house, and the whole group are of course intense pessimists. Daudet justified this to me (as regards himself) by the general sadness of life and his fear, for instance, whenever he comes in, that his wife and children may have died while he was out! I hope *you* manage to keep free from this apprehension.... I return to London on the 27th, to stick fast there till the summer. I embrace Alice and the little Jew and am ever your affectionate

HENRY.

TO W. D. HOWELLS.

Paris.

Feb. 21st, 1884.

My dear Howells,

Your letter of the 2d last gives me great pleasure. A frozen Atlantic seemed to stretch between us, and I had had no news of you to speak of save an allusion, in a late letter of T. B. A., to your having infant-disease in your house. You give me a good account of this, and I hope your tax is paid this year at least. These are not things to make a hardened bachelor mend his ways.— Hardened as I am, however, I am not proof against being delighted to hear that my Barberina tale entertained you. I am not prepared even to resent the malignity of your remark that the last third is not the best. It isn't; the [last] part is squeezed together and écourté! It is always the fault of my things that the head and trunk are too big and the legs too short. I spread myself, always, at first, from a nervous fear that I shall not have enough of my peculiar tap to "go round." But I always (or generally) have, and therefore, at the end, have to fill one of the cups to overflowing. My tendency to this disproportion remains incorrigible. I begin short tales as if they were to be long novels. Apropos of which, ask Osgood to show you also the sheets of another thing I lately sent him—"A New England Winter." It is not very good—on the contrary; but it will perhaps seem to you to put into form a certain impression of Boston.—What you tell me of the success of ——'s last novel sickens and almost paralyses me. It seems to me (the book) so contemptibly bad and ignoble that the idea of people reading it in such numbers makes one return upon one's self and ask what is the use of trying to write anything decent or serious for a public so absolutely idiotic. It must be totally wasted. I would rather have produced the basest experiment in the "naturalism" that is being practised here than such a piece of sixpenny humbug. Work so shamelessly bad seems to me to dishonour the novelist's art to a degree that is absolutely not to be forgiven; just as its success dishonours the people for whom one supposes one's self to write. Excuse my ferocities, which (more discreetly and philosophically) I think you must share; and don't mention it, please, to any one, as it will be set down to green-eyed jealousy.

I came to this place three weeks since—on the principle that anything is quieter than London; but I return to the British scramble in a few days. Paris speaks to me, always, for about such a time as this, with many voices; but at the end of a month I have learned all it has to say. I have been seeing something of Daudet, Goncourt and Zola; and there is nothing more interesting to me now than the effort and experiment of this little group, with its truly infernal intelligence of art, form, manner—its intense artistic life. They do the only kind of work, to-day, that I respect; and in spite of their ferocious pessimism and their handling of unclean things, they are at least serious and honest. The floods of tepid soap and water which under the name of novels are being vomited forth in England, seem to me, by contrast, to do little honour to our race. I say this to you, because I regard you as the great American naturalist. I don't think you go far enough, and you are haunted with romantic phantoms and a tendency to factitious glosses; but you are in the right path, and I wish you repeated triumphs there—beginning with your

Americo-Venetian—though I slightly fear, from what you tell me, that he will have a certain "gloss." It isn't for me to reproach you with that, however, the said gloss being a constant defect of *my* characters; they have too much of it—too damnably much. But I am a failure!—comparatively. Read Zola's last thing: *La Joie de Vivre*. This title of course has a desperate irony: but the work is admirably solid and serious.... Addio—stia bene. I wish you could send me anything *you* have in the way of advance-sheets. It is rather hard that as you are the only English novelist I read (except Miss Woolson), I should not have more comfort with you. Give my love to Winnie: I am sure she will dance herself well. Why doesn't Mrs. Howells try it too?

Tout à vous,

HENRY JAMES.

TO JOHN ADDINGTON SYMONDS.

(3 Bolton St., Piccadilly, W.)

Paris.

Feb. 22nd, 1884.

My dear J. A. Symonds,

Your good letter came to me just as I was leaving London (for a month in this place—to return there in a few days,) and the distractions and interruptions incidental to a short stay in Paris must account for my not having immediately answered it, as the spirit moved me to do. I thank you for it very kindly, and am much touched by your telling me that a communication from me should in any degree, and for a moment, have lighted up the horizon of the Alpine crevice, in which I can well believe you find it hard, and even cruel, to be condemned to pass life. To condole with you on a fate so stern must seem at the best but a hollow business; I will therefore only wish you a continuance of the courage of which your abundant and delightful work gives such evidence, and take pleasure in thinking that there may be entertainment for you in any of my small effusions.—I *did* send you the *Century* more than a year ago, with my paper on Venice, not having then the prevision of my reprinting it with some other things. I sent it you because it was a constructive way of expressing the good will I felt for you in consequence of what you have written about the land of Italy—and of intimating to you, somewhat dumbly, that I am an attentive and sympathetic reader. I nourish for the said Italy an unspeakably tender passion, and your pages always seemed to say to me that you were one of a small number of people who love it as much as I do—in addition to your knowing it immeasurably better. I wanted to recognize this (to your knowledge;) for it seemed to me that the victims of a common passion should sometimes exchange a look, and I sent you off the magazine at a venture.... I thank you very sincerely for the good-natured things you say of its companions. It is all very light work, indeed, and the only merit I should dream of anyone finding in it would be that it is "prettily turned." I thank you still further for your offer to send me the Tauchnitz volumes of your Italian local sketches. I know them already well, as I have said, and possess them in the English issue; but I shall welcome them warmly, directly from you—especially as I gather that they have occasional retouchings.

I lately spent a number of months in America, after a long absence, but I live in London and have put my constant address at the top of my letter. I imagine that it is scarcely ever in your power to come to England, but do take note of my whereabouts, for this happy (and possibly, to you, ideal) contingency. I should very much like to see you—but I go little, nowadays, to Switzerland in summer (though at one time I was there a good deal). I think it possible moreover that at that season you get out of your Alps. I certainly should, in your place, for the Alps are easily too many for me.—I can well imagine the innumerable things you miss at Davos—year after year—and (I will say it) I think of you with exceeding sympathy. As a sign of that I shall send you everything I publish.

I shake hands with [you], and am very truly yours,

HENRY JAMES.

TO ALPHONSE DAUDET.

3 Bolton St., Piccadilly, W.

London, 19 Juin [1884].

Mon cher Alphonse Daudet,

J'aurais dû déjà vous remercier de tout le plaisir que vous m'avez fait en m'envoyant *Sapho*. Je vous suis très-reconnaissant de cette bonne et amicale pensée, qui s'ajoutera désormais, pour moi, au souvenir du livre. Je n'avais pas attendu l'arrivée de votre volume pour le lire—mais cela m'a donné l'occasion de m'y remettre encore et de tirer un peu au clair les diverses impressions que tant d'admirables pages m'ont laissées. Je n'essaierai pas de vous rapporter ces impressions dans leur plénitude—dans la crainte de ne réussir qu'à déformer ma pensée—tout autant que la vôtre. Un nouveau livre de vous me fait passer par l'esprit une foule de belles idées, que je vous confierais de vive voix— et de grand cœur—si j'avais le bonheur de vous voir plus souvent. Pour le moment, je vous dirai seulement que tout ce qui vient de vous compte, pour moi, comme un grand évènement, une jouissance rare et fructueuse. Je vous aime mieux dans certaines pages que dans d'autres, mais vous me charmez, vous m'enlevez toujours, et votre manière me pénètre plus qu'aucune autre. Je trouve dans *Sapho* énormément de vérité et de vie. Ce n'est pas du roman, c'est de l'histoire, et de la plus complète et de la mieux éclairée. Lorsqu'on a fait un livre aussi solide et aussi sérieux que celui-là, on n'a besoin d'être rassuré par personne; ce n'est donc que pour m'encourager moi-même que je constate dans Sapho encore une preuve—à ajouter à celles que vous avez données—de tout ce que le roman peut accomplir comme révélation de la vie et du drôle de mélange que nous sommes. La fille est étudiée avec une patience merveilleuse—c'est un de ces portraits qui épuisent un type. Je vous avouerai que je trouve le jeune homme un peu sacrifié—comme étude et comme recherche—sa figure me paraissant moins éclairée—en comparaison de celle de la femme—qu'il ne le faudrait pour l'ntérêt moral la valeur tragique. J'aurais voulu que vous nous eussiez fait voir davantage par où il a passé—en matière d'expérience plus personnelle et plus intime encore que les coucheries avec Fanny—en matière de rammollissement de volonté et de relâchement d'âme. En un mot, le drame ne se passe peut-être pas assez dans l'âme et dans la conscience de Jean. C'est à mesure que nous touchons à son caractère même que la situation devient intéressante—et ce caractère, vous me faites l'effet de l'avoir un peu négligé. Vous me direz que voilà un jugement bien anglais, et que nous inventons des abstractions, comme nous disons, afin de nous dispenser de toucher aux grosses réalités. J'estime pourtant qu'il n'y a rien de plus réel, de plus positif, de plus à peindre, qu'un caractère; c'est là qu'on trouve bien la couleur et la forme. Vous l'avez bien prouvé, du reste, dans chacun de vos livres, et en vous disant que vous avez laissé l'amant de Sapho un peu trop en blanc, ce n'est qu'avec vous-même que je vous compare. Mais je ne voulais que vous remercier et répondre à votre envoi. Je vous souhaite tout le repos qu'il vous faudra pour recommencer encore! Je garde de cette soirée que j'ai passée chez vous au mois de février une impression toute colorée. Je vous prie de me rappeler au souvenir bienveillant de Madame Daudet, je vous serre la main et suis votre bien dévoué confrère,

HENRY JAMES.

TO ROBERT LOUIS STEVENSON.

H. J.'s article on "The Art of Fiction" was reprinted in *Partial Portraits*. Stevenson's "rejoinder" was the essay called "A Humble Remonstrance," included in *Memories and Portraits*.

3 Bolton St., W.

Dec. 5th [1884].

My dear Robert Louis Stevenson,

I read only last night your paper in the December *Longman's* in genial rejoinder to my article in the same periodical on Besant's lecture, and the result of that charming half-hour is a friendly desire to send you three words. Not words of discussion, dissent, retort or remonstrance, but of hearty sympathy, charged with the assurance of my enjoyment of everything you write. It's a luxury, in this immoral age, to encounter some one who *does* write—who is really acquainted with that lovely art. It wouldn't be fair to contend with you here; besides, we agree, I think, much more than we disagree, and though there are points as to which a more irrepressible spirit than mine would like to try a fall, that is not what I want to say—but on the contrary, to thank you for so much that is suggestive and felicitous in your remarks—justly felt and brilliantly said. They are full of these things, and the current of your admirable style floats pearls and diamonds. Excellent are your closing words, and no one can assent more than I to your proposition that all art is a simplification. It is a pleasure to see that truth so neatly uttered. My pages, in Longman, were simply a plea for liberty: they were only half of what I had to say, and some day I shall try and express the remainder. Then I shall tickle you a little affectionately as I pass. You will say that my "liberty" is an obese divinity, requiring extra measures; but after one more go I shall hold my tongue. The native *gaiety* of all that you write is delightful to me, and when I reflect that it proceeds from a man whom life has laid much of the time on his back (as I understand it), I find you a genius indeed. There must be pleasure in it for you too. I ask Colvin about you whenever I see him, and I shall have to send him this to forward to you. I am with innumerable good wishes yours very faithfully,

HENRY JAMES.

TO WILLIAM JAMES.

The Literary Remains of the late Henry James, with an introduction by William James, had just been published in America.

3 Bolton Street, W.

Jan. 2d, 1885.

Dear William—

I must give some response, however brief, to your letter of Dec. 21st, enclosing the project of your house and a long letter from R. Temple. Three days ago, too, came the two copies of Father's (and your) book, which have [given] me great filial and fraternal joy. All I have had time to read as yet is the introduction—your part of which seems to me admirable, perfect. It must have been very difficult to do, and you couldn't have done it better. And how beautiful and extraordinarily individual (some of them magnificent) all the extracts from Father's writings which you have selected so happily. It comes over me as I read them (more than ever before,) how intensely original and personal his whole system was, and how indispensable it is that those who go in for religion should take some heed of it. I can't enter into it (much) myself—I can't be so theological nor grant his extraordinary premises, nor throw myself into conceptions of heavens and hells, nor be sure that the keynote of nature is humanity, etc. But I can enjoy greatly the spirit, the feeling, and the manner of the whole thing (full as this last is of things that displease me too,) and feel really that poor Father, struggling so alone all his life, and so destitute of every worldly or literary ambition, was yet a great writer. At any rate your task is beautifully and honourably done—may it be as great or even half as great a service as it deserves to be, to his memory! The book came at a bad time for Alice, as she has had an upset which I will tell you of; but though she has been able to have it in her hand but for a moment it evidently gives her great pleasure. She burst into tears when I gave it to her, exclaiming "How beautiful it is that William should have done it! Isn't it, isn't it beautiful? And how good William is, how good, how good!" And we talked of poor Father's fading away into silence and darkness, the waves of the world closing over this system which he tried to offer it, and of how we were touched by this act of yours which will (I am sure) do so much to rescue him from oblivion. I have received no notice from Scribner of the arrival of the other volumes, and shall write to him in a day or two if I don't hear. But I am rather embarrassed as to what to do with so many—wishing only to dispose of them in a manner which will entail some prospect of decent consideration and courtesy. I can give away five or six copies to persons who will probably have some attention and care for them (e.g. Fredk. Harrison, Stopford Brooke, Burne-Jones, Mrs. Orr, etc.) But the newspapers and reviews are so grim and philistine and impenetrable and stupid, that I can scarcely think of any to which it isn't almost an act of untenderness to send it. But I will go into the matter with Scribner.... The project for your house is charming—very big it looks, and of a most pleasant type. Love to all.

Ever your

HENRY.

TO MISS GRACE NORTON.

3 Bolton St., W.

Jan. 24th [1885].

My dear Grace,

.   .   .   .

It is a feature of life in this place that the longer it lasts the more one's liabilities of every kind accumulate—the more things there are to be done, every hour of the day. I have so many to do that I am thinking of inventing some new day with 40 or 50 hours—or else some newer one still, with only half a dozen, as that would simplify a large proportion of one's diurnal duties out of existence.... I am having a "quieter" winter than I have had for some years (in London) and have seen very few new people and not even many old friends. My quietness (comparative of course) is my solemn choice, and means that I have been dining out much less than at most former times, for the sacred purpose of getting my evenings to myself. I have been sitting at the festive British board for so many years now that I feel as if I had earned the right to give it up save in really seductive cases. You can guess the proportion of these! It is the only way to find any time to read—and my reading was going to the dogs. Therefore I propose to become henceforth an occasional and not a regular diner, with the well-founded hope that my mind, body, spirits, temper and general view of the human understanding and of the conversational powers of the English race, will be the gainers by it. Moreover, there is very little "going on"—the country is gloomy, anxious, and London reflects its gloom. Westminster Hall and the Tower were half blown up two days ago by Irish Dynamiters, there is a catastrophe to the little British force in the Soudan in the air (rather an ominous want of news since Gen. Stewart's victory at Aboukir a week ago,) and a general sense of rocks ahead in the foreign relations of the country—combined with an exceeding

119

want of confidence—indeed a deep disgust—with the present ministry in regard to such relations. I find such a situation as this extremely interesting and it makes me feel how much I am attached to this country and, on the whole, to its sometimes exasperating people. The possible *malheurs*—reverses, dangers, embarrassments, the "decline," in a word, of old England, go to my heart, and I can imagine no spectacle more touching, more thrilling and even dramatic, than to see this great precarious, artificial empire, on behalf of which, nevertheless, so much of the strongest and finest stuff of the greatest race (for such they are) has been expended, struggling with forces which perhaps, in the long run, will prove too many for it. If she only will struggle, and not collapse and surrender and give up a part which, looking at Europe as it is to-day, still may be great, the drama will be well worth watching from [such] a good, near standpoint as I have here. But I didn't mean to be so beastly political! Another drama interesting me is the question of poor dear J. R. Lowell's possible recall after Cleveland mounts the throne. This, to me, is tragic, pathetic. His position here is in the highest degree honourable, useful, agreeable—in short perfect; and to give it all up to return, from one day to another, to John Holmes and the Brattle Street horsecar (which is very much what it amounts to—save when he goes to see you) seems to me to be the sport of a cruel, a barbaric, fortune.... I haven't asked you about yourself—the complexion of your winter, etc. But there are some things I know sufficiently without asking. So do you—as that I am always praying for you (though I don't pray, in general, and don't understand it, I make this brilliant exception for *you*!)

Your very faithful friend,

HENRY JAMES.

TO WILLIAM JAMES.

The first number of *The Bostonians* appeared this month in the *Century Magazine*, containing scenes in which the veteran philanthropist "Miss Birdseye" figured.

3 Bolton St., W.

Feb. 14th [1885].

Dear William,

I am quite appalled by your note of the 2nd, in which you assault me on the subject of my having painted a "portrait from life" of Miss Peabody! I was in some measure prepared for it by Lowell's (as I found the other day) taking for granted that she had been my model, and an allusion to the same effect in a note from Aunt Kate. Still, I didn't expect the charge to come from you. I hold, that I have done nothing to deserve it.... I should be very sorry—in fact deadly sick, or fatally ill—if I thought Miss Peabody *herself* supposed I intended to represent her. I absolutely had no shadow of such an intention. I have not seen Miss P. for twenty years, I never had but the most casual observation of her, I didn't know whether she was alive or dead, and she was not in the smallest degree my starting-point or example. Miss Birdseye was evolved entirely from my moral consciousness, like every other person I have ever drawn, and originated in my desire to make a figure who should embody in a sympathetic, pathetic, picturesque, and at the same time grotesque way, the humanitary and ci-devant transcendental tendencies which I thought it highly probable I should be accused of treating in a contemptuous manner in so far as they were otherwise represented in the tale. I wished to make this figure a woman, because so it would be more touching, and an old, weary, battered, and simple-minded woman because that deepened the same effect. I elaborated her in my mind's eye—and after I had got going reminded myself that my creation would perhaps be identified with Miss Peabody—*that* I freely admit. So I have in mind the sense of being careful, at the same time that I didn't see what I could do but go my way, according to my own fancy, and make my image as living as I saw it. The one definite thing about which I had a scruple was some touch about Miss Birdseye's spectacles—I remembered that Miss Peabody's were always in the wrong place; but I didn't see, really, why I should deprive myself of an effect (as regards this point) which is common to a thousand old people. So I thought no more about Miss P. *at all*, but simply strove to realize my vision. If I have made my old woman *live* it is my misfortune, and the thing is doubtless a rendering, a vivid rendering, of my idea. If it is at the same time a rendering of Miss P. I am absolutely irresponsible—and extremely sorry for the accident. If there is any chance of its being represented to *her* that I have undertaken to reproduce her in a novel I will immediately write to her, in the most respectful manner, to say that I have done nothing of the kind, that an old survivor of the New England Reform period was an indispensable personage in my story, that my paucity of data and not my repletion is the faulty side of the whole picture, that, as I went, I had no sight or thought of her, but only of an imaginary figure which was much nearer to me, and that in short I have the vanity to claim that Miss Birdseye is a creation. You may think I protest too much: but I am alarmed by the sentence in your letter—"It is really a pretty bad business," and haunted by the idea that this may apply to some rumour you have heard of Miss Peabody's feeling *atteinte*. I can imagine no other reason why you should call the picture of Miss Birdseye a "bad business," or indeed any business at all. I would write to Miss P. on this chance—only I don't like to *assume* that she feels touched, when it is possible that she may not, and knows nothing about the matter. If you can ascertain whether or no she does and will let me know, I will, should there be need or fitness, immediately write to her. Miss Birdseye is a subordinate figure in the *Bostonians*, and after appearing in the first and second numbers vanishes till toward the end, where she re-enters, briefly, and pathetically and honourably dies. But though subordinate, she is, I think, the best figure in the book; she is treated with respect throughout, and every virtue of heroism and disinterestedness is attributed to her. She is represented as the embodiment of pure, the purest philanthropy. The story is, I think, the best fiction I have written, and I expected you, if you said anything about it, would intimate that you thought as much—so that I find this charge on the subject of Miss Peabody a very cold douche indeed....

Ever yours,

H. JAMES.

TO JAMES RUSSELL LOWELL.

Lowell was now leaving London after having held the post of American Minister there since 1880.

St. Alban's Cliff,

Bournemouth.

May 29th [1885].

My dear Lowell,

My hope of coming up to town again has been defeated, and it comes over me that your departure is terribly near. Therefore I write you a line of hearty and affectionate farewell—mitigated by the sense that after all it is only for a few months that we are to lose you. I trust, serenely, to your own conviction of this fact, but for extra safety just remark that if you don't return to London next winter I shall hurl myself across the ocean at you like a lasso. As I look back upon the years of your mission my heart swells and almost breaks again (as it did when I heard you were superseded) at the thought that anything so perfect should be gratuitously destroyed. But there is a part of your function which can go on again, indefinitely, whenever you take it up—and that, I repeat, I hope you will do soon rather than late. I think with the tenderest pleasure of the many fire-side talks I have had with you, from the first—and with a pleasure dimmed with sadness of so many of our more recent ones. You are tied to London now by innumerable cords and fibres, and I should be glad to think that you ever felt me, ever so lightly, pulling at one of them. It is a great disappointment to me not to see you again, but I am kept here fast and shall not be in town till the end of June. I give you my blessing and every good wish for a happy voyage. I wish I could receive you over there—and assist at your arrival and impressions—little as I want you to go back. Don't forget that you have produced a relation between England and the U.S. which is really a gain to civilization and that you must come back to look after your work. You can't look after it there: that is the function of an Englishman—and if *you* do it there they will call you one. The only way you can be a good American is to return to our dear old stupid, satisfactory London, and to yours ever affectionately and faithfully,

HENRY JAMES.

TO WILLIAM JAMES.

To prevent confusion of names it should be mentioned that the "Alice" referred to at the end of this letter is H. J.'s sister-in-law, Mrs. William James. His sister, Miss Alice James, remained in England till her death six years later.

13 De Vere Mansions, W.

March 9th [1886].

My dear William,

Long before getting your most excellent letter of Feb. 21st I had been pricked with shame and remorse at my long silence; you may imagine then how this pang sharpened when, three or four days ago, that letter arrived. There were all sorts of reasons for my silence which I won't take up time now with narrating—further than to say that they were not reasons of misfortune or discomfort—but only of other-engagement-and-occupation pressure—connected with arrears of writing, consumption of time in furnishing and preparing my new habitation, and the constant old story of London interruptions and distractions. Thank God I am out of them far more now than I have ever been before—in my chaste and secluded Kensington quatrième. I moved in here definitely only three days ago, and am still rather upside down. The place is excellent in every respect, improves on acquaintance every hour and is, in particular, flooded with light like a photographer's studio. I commune with the unobstructed sky and have an immense bird's-eye view of housetops and streets. My rooms are very pretty as well as very convenient, and will be more so when little by little I have got more things. When I have time I will make you a diagram, and later, when the drawing-room (or library: meantime I have a smaller sitting-room in order) is furnished (I have nothing for it yet), I shall have the place photographed. I shall do far better work here than I have ever done before.

Alice is going on the same very good way, and receiving visits almost daily. A great many people come to see her; she is highly appreciated, and might easily, if she were to stay here, getting sufficiently better to exert herself more &c., become a great success and queen of society. Her vigour of mind, decision of character &c., wax daily, and her conversation is brilliant and sémillant. She could easily, if she were to stay, beat the British female all round. She is also looking very well.... The weather continues bitterly cold, and there will be no question of her going out for a long time to come.

The two great public matters here have been the riot, and the everlasting and most odious ——— scandal. (I mean, of course, putting the all-overshadowing Irish question aside.) I was at Bournemouth (seeing R. L. Stevenson) the day of the émeute, and lost the spectacle, to my infinite chagrin. I should have seen it well from my balcony, as I should have been at home when it passed, and it smashed the windows in the houses (three doors from mine) on the corner of Bolton St. and Piccadilly. Alice was all unconscious of it till the morrow, and was not at all agitated. The wreck and ruin in Piccadilly and some other places (I mean of windows) was, on my return from Bournemouth, sufficiently startling, as was also the manner in which the carriages of a number of ladies were stopped, and the occupants hustled, rifled, slapped or kissed, as the case might be, and turned out. The real unemployed, I believe, had very little share in all this: it was the work of the great army of roughs and thieves, who seized, owing to the very favourable nature of their opportunity, a day of licence. It is difficult to know whether the real want of work is now, or not, so very much greater than usual—in face of positive affirmations and negations; there is, at any rate, immense destitution. Every one here is growing poorer—from causes which, I fear, will continue. All the same, what took place the other day is, I feel pretty sure, the worst that for a long time to come, the British populace is likely to attempt.... I can't talk about the Irish matter—partly because one is sick of it—partly because I *know* too little about it, and one is still more sick of all the vain words on the subject, without knowledge or thought, that fill the air here. I don't believe much in the Irish, and I believe still less [in] (consider with less complacency) the disruption of the British Empire, but I don't see how the management of their own affairs can be kept away from them—or why it should. I can't but think that, as they are a poor lot, with great intrinsic sources of weakness, their power to injure and annoy England (if they were to get their own parliament) would be considerably less than is assumed.

The "Bostonians" must be out, in America, by this time; I told them, of course, to send you a copy. It appears to be having a goodish success there. All your tidings about your own life, Bob, &c., were of the deepest interest.... I wish I could assist at your researches and see the children, and commune with Alice—to whom I send much brotherly love.

Ever your

HENRY.

TO CHARLES ELIOT NORTON.

Professor Norton had sent H. J. the first instalment of his edition of Carlyle's correspondence.

Milan, December 6th [1886].

My dear Charles,

I ought long ago to have thanked you for your very substantial present of Carlyle—but I waited in the first place till I should have read the book (which business was considerably delayed,) and then till I had wound up a variety of little matters, mainly matters of writing which pressed upon me in anticipation of my leaving England for two or three months. Now when at last I seize the moment, I *have* left England, but you will be as glad of a letter from here as from out of the dense grey medium in which we had been living for a month before I quitted London. I came hither straight from Dover last night through the hideous but convenient hole in the dear old St. Gotthard, and I have been strolling about Milan all the morning, drinking in the delicious Italian sun, which fortunately shines, and giving myself up to the sweet sense of living once more—after an interval of several years—in the adorable country it illumines. It is Sunday and all the world is in the streets and squares, and the Italian type greets me in all its handsomeness and friendliness, and also, I fear I must add, not a little in its vulgarity. But its vulgarity is the exaggeration of a merit and not, as in England and the U.S., of a defect. Churches and galleries have such a fatal chill that being sore-throatish and neuralgic I have had to keep out of them, but the Duomo lifts all its pinnacles and statues into the far away light, and looks across at the other white needles and spires of the Alps in the same bewildering cluster. I go to spend the remainder of this month in Florence and afterwards to—I hope—take a month between Rome, Naples and Venice—but it will be as it will turn out. Once I am in Italy it is about the same to me to be in one place as in another.

All this takes me away from Carlyle and from the Annandale view of life. I read the two volumes with exceeding interest; for my admiration of Carlyle as a letter writer is boundless, and it is curious to watch the first step and gradual amplification of his afterwards extraordinary style. Those addressed to his own family are most remarkable as dedicated to a household of peasants, by one of themselves, and in short for the *amateur* of Carlyle the book has a high value. But I doubt whether the general public will bite at it very eagerly. I don't know why I allude to this, though—for the general public has small sense and less taste, and its likes and dislikes, I think, must mostly make the judicious grieve. You seem to me a most perfect and ideal editor—and it is a great pleasure to me that so excellent and faultless a piece of editorial work should proceed from our rough and ready country—but at the same time your demolitions of the unspeakable Froude don't persuade me that Carlyle was *amiable*. It seems to me he remains the most disagreeable in character of men of genius of equal magnificence. In these youthful letters it appears to me even striking how his disagreeableness comes out more and more in proportion as his talent develops. This doesn't prevent him, however, from being in my opinion—and doubtless in yours—one of the very greatest— perhaps the very greatest of letter writers; only when one thinks of the other most distinguished masters of expression the image evoked has (though sometimes it may be sad enough) a serenity, a general *pleasantness*. When the vision of Carlyle comes to us there comes with it the idea of harshness and discord. The difference between the man and the genius seems to me, in other words, greater than in any other case—for if Voltaire was a rascal he was eminently a social one—and Rousseau (to think of a great intellectual swell who must have been odious) hadn't anything like Carlyle's "parts." All the same, I shall devour the volumes I am delighted to see you are still to publish.

I ought to have plenty of London news for you—but somehow I feel as if I had not brought it to Italy with me. Much of it, in these days, is such as there must be little profit in carrying about with one. The subject of the moment, as I came away, was the hideous —— divorce case, which will besmirch exceedingly the already very damaged prestige of the English upper class. The condition of that body seems to me to be in many ways very much the same rotten and *collapsible* one as that of the French aristocracy before the revolution—minus cleverness and conversation; or perhaps it's more like the heavy, congested and depraved Roman world upon which the barbarians came down. In England the Huns and Vandals will have to come *up*—from the black depths of the (in the people) enormous misery, though I don't think the Attila is quite yet found—in the person of Mr. Hyndman. At all events, much of English life is grossly materialistic and wants blood-letting. I had not been absent from London for a year before this—save for two or three days at a time. I remained in town all summer and autumn—only paying an occasional, or indeed a rather frequent, country visit—a business, however, which I endeavour more and more to keep, if possible, within the compass of *hours*. The gilded bondage of the country house becomes onerous as one grows older, and then the waste of time in vain sitting and strolling about is a gruesome thought in the face of what one still wants to do with one's remnant of existence. I saw Matt Arnold the other night, and he spoke very genially of you and of his visit to Ashfield—very *affectionately*, too, of George Curtis—which I loudly echoed. M. A. said of Stockbridge and the summer life thereabouts, etc. (with his chin in the air)—"Yes, yes—it's a proof that it's attaching that one thinks of it again—one thinks of it again." This was amiably sublime and amiably characteristic.—I see Burne-Jones from time to time, but not as often as I should like. I am always so afraid of breaking in on his work. Whenever he is at home he is working and when he isn't working he's not at home. When I *do* see him, it is one of the best human pleasures that London has for me. But I don't understand his life—that is the manner and tenor of his production—a complete *studio* existence, with doors and windows closed, and no search for impressions outside—no open air, no real daylight and no looking out for it. The things he does in these conditions have exceeding beauty—but they seem to me to grow colder and colder—pictured abstractions, less and less observed. Such as he is, however, he is certainly the most distinguished artistic figure among Englishmen to-day—the only one who has escaped vulgarization and on whom claptrap has no hold. Moreover he is, as you know, exquisite in mind and talk—and we fraternize greatly....

TO MISS GRACE NORTON.

34 De Vere Gardens, W.

July 23rd, 1887.

My dear Grace,

I am ashamed to find myself back in England without having fulfilled the inward vow I took when I received your last good and generous letter— that of writing to you before my long stay on the continent was over. But I *almost* don't fail of that vow—inasmuch as I returned only day before yesterday. My eight months escape into the happy immunities of foreign life is over and the stern realities of London surround me, in the shape of stuffy midsummer heat (that of this metropolis has a truly British ponderosity— it's as dull as an article in a Quarterly,) smoke, circulars, invitations, *bills*, the one sauce that Talleyrand commemorated, and reverberations of the grotesque Jubilee. On the other hand my small house seems most pleasant and peculiar (in the sense of being my own,) and my servants are as punctual as they are prim—which is saying much. But I enjoyed my absence, and I shall endeavour to repeat it every year, for the future, on a smaller scale; that is, to leave London, not at the beginning of the winter but at the end, by the mid-April, and take the period of the insufferable Season regularly in Italy. It was a great satisfaction to me to find that I am as fond of that dear country as I ever was—and that its infinite charm and interest are one of the things in life to be most relied upon. I was afraid that the dryness of age—which drains us of so many sentiments—had reduced my old *tendresse* to a mere memory. But no—it is really so much in my pocket, as it were, to feel that Italy is always there. It is rather rude, my dear Grace, to say all this to you—for whom it is there to so little purpose. But if I should observe this scruple about all the places that you don't go to, or are not in, when I write to you, my writing would go very much on one leg. I was back again in Venice—where I paid a second visit late in the season (from the middle of May to July 1st)—when I got your last letter. I was staying at the Palazzo Barbaro, with the Daniel Curtises—the happy owners, to-day, of that magnificent house—a place of which the full charm only sinks into your spirit as you go on living there, seeing it in all its hours and phases. I went for ten days, and they clinging to me, I stayed five weeks: the longest visit I ever paid a "private family." ... In the interval between my two visits to Venice I took again some rooms at the Villa Bricchieri at Bellosguardo—the one just below your old Ombrellino—where I had stayed for three December weeks on my arrival in Florence. The springtime there was enchanting, and you know what a thing that incomparable view is to live with. I really *did* live with it, and rejoiced in it every minute, holding it to be (to my sensibilities) positively the most beautiful and interesting in the world. Florence was given over to fêtes during most of those weeks—the fêtes of the completion of the façade of the Duomo—which by the way (the new façade) isn't "half bad." It is of a very splendouriferous effect, and there is doubtless too much of it. But it does great honour to the contemporary (as well as to the departed) Italian—and I don't believe such work could have been produced elsewhere than in that country of the delicate hand and the insinuating chisel. I stepped down into the fêtes from my hill top—and even put on a crimson *lucco* and a beautiful black velvet headgear and disported myself at the great *ballo storico* that was given at the Palazzo Vecchio to the King and Queen. This had the defect of its class—a profusion of magnificent costumes but a want of *entrain*; and the success of the whole episode was much more a certain really splendid procession of the old time, with all the Strozzis, Guicciardinis, Rucellais, etc., mounted on magnificent horses and wearing admirable dresses with the childlike gallantry and glee with which only Italians can wear them, riding through the brown old streets and followed by an immense train of citizens all in the carefullest quattro-cento garb. This was really a noble picture and testified to the latent love of splendour which is still in those dear people and which only asks for a favouring chance to shine out, even at the cost of ruining them. Before leaving Italy I spent a week with Mrs. Kemble at Lago Maggiore—she having dipped over there, in spite of torrid heat. She is a very (or at least a partly) extinct volcano to-day, and very easy and delightful to dwell with, in her aged resignation and *adoucissements*. But she did suggest to me, on seeing her again after so long an interval, that it is rather a melancholy mistake, in this uncertain life of ours, to have founded oneself on so many rigidities and rules—so many siftings and sortings. Mrs. Kemble is *toute d'une pièce*, more than any one, probably, that ever lived; she moves in a mass, and if she does so little as to button her glove it is the whole of her "personality" that does it. Let us be flexible, dear Grace; let us be flexible! and even if we don't reach the sun we shall at least have been up in a balloon.—I left Stresa on the 15th of this month, had a glorious day on the Simplon amid mountain streams and mountain flowers, and came quickly home.... I shall be here for the rest of the summer—save for little blotches of absence—and I look forward to some quiet months of work. I am trying, not without success, to get out of society—as hard as some people try to get in. I want to be dropped and cut and consummately ignored. This only demands a little patience, and I hope eventually to elbow my way down to the bottom of the wave—to achieve an obscurity. This would sound fatuous if I didn't add that success is easily within my grasp. I know it all—all that one sees by "going out"—to-day, as if I had made it. But if I had, I would have made it better! I think of you on your porch—amid all your creepers and tendrils; and wherever you are, dear Grace, I am your very faithful and much remembering friend,

HENRY JAMES.

TO EDMUND GOSSE.

Stevenson and his family sailed for America a few days after the date of this letter. Mr. Gosse has described the episode in his recollections of R. L. S.

(*Critical Kit-kats*). Stevenson's life in the South Seas began in the following year, and his friends in England saw him no more.

34 De Vere Gardens, W.

August 17th [1887].

Dear Gosse,

I went to-day to R. L. S.'s ship, which is at the Albert Dock, about 20 minutes in the train from Fenchurch Street. Its sailing has been put off till Monday forenoon, so there is more time to do something. I couldn't, after all, get *on* the ship—as she stood off from the dock, without a convenient approach, and both the captain and the steward (whom I wanted to see) were not there, as I was told by a man on the dock who was seeing some things being put on by a crane in which I couldn't be transferred. The appearance of the vessel was the reverse of attractive, though she is rather large than small. I write to-night to Mrs. Stevenson, to ask if they are really coming up to sail—that is if nothing has interfered at the last moment. If they are, there is nothing to be done to deter them, that I see. I shall ask her to *telegraph* me an answer. I shall feel that I must go again (to the ship), as I don't very well see how things are to be sent there. I will telegraph you what she telegraphs me and what I decide to do.

Ever yours,

HENRY JAMES.

TO ROBERT LOUIS STEVENSON.

H. J.'s article on R. L. S. appeared in the *Century Magazine*, April, 1888, and was reprinted in *Partial Portraits*.

34 De Vere Gardens, W.

October 30th, 1887.

My dear Louis,

It is really a delight to get your charming letter (from the undecipherable lake) just this very blessed minute. Long alienation has made my American geography vague, and not knowing *what* your lake is I know still less *where* it is. Nevertheless I roughly suspect it of being in the Adirondacks; if it isn't, may it excuse the injury. Let me tell you, quickly and crudely, that I am quite exhilarated that you like the Article. I thought—or rather I hoped—that you would, and yet I feared you wouldn't—i.e. mightn't—and altogether I was not so convinced but that your expression of pleasure is a reassurance to me as well a gratification. I felt, while I wrote, that you served me well; you were really, my dear fellow, a capital subject—I will modestly grant you that, though it takes the bloom from my merit. To be not only witty one's self but the cause in others of a wit that is not at one's expense—that is a rare and high character, and altogether yours. I devoutly hope that it's in the November Century that the thing appears, and also that it was not too apparent to you in it that I hadn't seen a proof—a privation I detest. I wrote to you some three weeks or so ago—c/o Scribners. Wondrous seems to me the fate that leads you to the prospect of wintering at—well, wherever you are. The succession of incidents and places in your career is ever romantic. May you find what you need—white, sunny Winter hours, not too stove-heated nor too pork-fed, with a crisp dry air and a frequent leisure and no desperation of inanition. And may much good prose flow from it all. I wish I could see you—in my mind's eye: but que dis-je? I do—and the minutest particularities of your wooden bower rise before me. I see the clapboards and the piazza and the door-step and the door-handle, and the road in front and the yard behind. Don't yearn to extinction for the trim little personality of Skerryvore. I have great satisfaction in hearing (from Mrs. Procter, of course) that that sweet house is let—to those Canadians. May they be punctual with their rent. Do tell your wife, on her return from the wild West, that I *supplicate* her to write to me, with items, details, specifications, and insistences. I am now collecting some papers into a volume; and the Article, par excellence, in the midst. May the American air rest lightly on you, my dear friend: I wish it were mine to turn it on!

Ever faithfully yours,

HENRY JAMES.

P.S. My love to your wife goes without saying—but I send a very explicit friendliness to your mother. I hope she returns the liking of America. And I bless the ticking Lloyd.

TO ROBERT LOUIS STEVENSON.

Stevenson's letter (answered by the following) of admiration of *Roderick Hudson* and *execration* of *The Portrait of a Lady* is included in the *Letters to his Family and Friends*, edited by Sir Sidney Colvin.

34 De Vere Gardens, W.

December 5th [1887].

My dear Louis,

I could almost hate poor Roderick H. (in whom, at best, as in all my past and shuffled off emanations and efforts, my interest is of the slenderest,) for making you write so much more about him than about a still more fascinating hero. If you had only given me a small instalment of that romantic serial, The Mundane Situation of R. L. S.! My dear fellow, you skip whole numbers at a time. Your correspondent wouldn't. I am really delighted you can find something at this late day in that work in which my diminutive muse first tried to elongate her little legs. It is a book of considerable good faith, but I think of limited skill. Besides, directly my productions are finished, or at least thrust out to earn their living, they seem to *me* dead. They dwindle when weaned—removed from the parental breast, and only flourish, a little, while imbibing the milk of my plastic care. None the less am I touched by your excellent and friendly words. Perhaps I am touched even more by those you dedicate to the less favoured *Portrait*. My dear Louis, I don't think I follow you here—why does that work move you to such scorn—since you can put up with Roderick, or with any of the others? As they are, so it is, and as it is, so they are. Upon my word you are unfair to it—and I scratch my head bewildered. 'Tis surely a graceful, ingenious, elaborate work—with too many pages, but with (I think) an interesting subject, and a good deal of life and style. There! *All* my works may be damnable—but I don't perceive the particular damnability of that one. However I feel as if it were almost gross to defend myself—for even your censure pleases and your restrictions refresh. I have this very day received from Mr. Bain your *Memories and Portraits*, and I lick my chops in advance. It is very delectable, I can see, and it has the prettiest coat and face of any of your volumes.—London is settling to its winter pace, and the cool rich fogs curtain us in. I see Colvin once in a while *dans le monde*, which however I frequent less and less. I miss you too sensibly. My love to your wife and mother—my greeting to the brave Lloyd.

Ever yours very faithfully,

H. JAMES.

P.S. I am unspeakably vexed at the Century's long delay in printing my paper on you—it is quite sickening. But I am helpless—and they tell me it won't come out till *March*—d——n 'em all. I am also sorry—very—not to have any other prose specimens of my own genius to send you. I have really written a good deal lately—but the beastly periodicals hold them back: I can't make out why. But I trust the dance will begin before long, and that then you may glean some pleasure. I pray you, do write something yourself for one who *knows* and yet is famished: for there isn't a morsel here that will keep one alive. I won't question you—'twere vain—but I wish I knew more about you. I want to *see* you—where you live and *how*—and the complexion of your days. But I don't know even the name of your habitat nor the date of your letter: neither were on the page. I bless you all the same.

TO W. D. HOWELLS.

34 De Vere Gardens, W.

January 2nd, 1888.

My dear Howells,

Your pretty read book (that is a misprint for *red*, but it looks well, better than it deserves, so I let it stand,) the neat and attractive volume, with its coquettish inscription over its mystifying date, came in to me exactly as a new year's gift. I was delighted to get it, for I had not perused it in the pages of Harper, for reasons that you will understand—knowing as you must how little the habit of writing in the serial form encourages one to read in that odious way, which so many simple folk, thank heaven, think the best. I was on the point of getting *April Hopes* to add to the brave array of its predecessors (mine by purchase, almost all of them,) when your graceful act saved me the almost equally graceful sacrifice. I can make out why you are at Buffalo almost as little as I believe that you believe that I have "long forgotten" you. The intimation is worthy of the most tortuous feminine mind that you have represented—say this wondrous lady, with the daughter, in the very first pages of April Hopes, with whom I shall make immediate and marvelling acquaintance. Your literary prowess takes my breath away—you write so much and so well. I seem to myself a small brown snail crawling after a glossy antelope. Let me hope that you *enjoy* your work as much as you ought to—that the grind isn't greater than the inevitable (from the moment one really tries to *do* anything). Certainly one would never guess it, from your abounding page. How much I wish I could keep this lovely new year by a long personal talk with you. I am troubled about many things, about many of which you could give me, I think (or rather I am sure,) advice and direction. I have entered upon evil days—but this is for your most private ear. It sounds portentous, but it only means that I am still staggering a good deal under the mysterious and (to me) inexplicable injury wrought—apparently—upon my situation by my two last novels, the *Bostonians* and the *Princess*, from which I expected so much and derived so little. They have reduced the desire, and the demand, for my productions to zero—as I judge from the fact that though I have for a good while past been writing a number of good short things, I remain irremediably unpublished. Editors keep them back, for months and years, as if they were ashamed of them, and I am condemned apparently to eternal silence. You must be so widely versed in all the reasons of things (of this sort, to-day) in the U.S. that if I could discourse with you awhile by the fireside I should endeavour to draw from you some secret to break the spell.

However, I don't despair, for I think I am now really in better form than I have ever been in my life, and I propose yet to do many things. Very likely too, some day, all my buried prose will kick off its various tombstones at once. Therefore don't betray me till I myself have given up. That won't be for a long time yet. If we could have that rich conversation I should speak to you too of your monthly polemics in *Harper* and tell you (I think I should go as far as that) of certain parts of the business in which I am less with you than in others. It seems to me that on occasions you mix things up that don't go together, sometimes make mistakes of proportion, and in general incline to insist more upon the restrictions and limitations, the *a priori* formulas and interdictions, of our common art, than upon that priceless freedom which is to me the thing that makes it worth practising. But at this distance, my dear Howells, such things are too delicate and complicated—they won't stand so long a journey. Therefore I won't attempt them—but only say how much I am struck with your energy, ingenuity, and courage, and your delightful interest in the charming questions. I don't care how much you dispute about them if you will only remember that a grain of example is worth a ton of precept, and that with the imbecility of babyish critics the serious writer need absolutely not concern himself. I am surprised, sometimes, at the things you notice and seem to care about. One should move in a diviner air.... I even confess that since the *Bostonians*, I find myself holding the "critical world" at large in a singular contempt. I go so far as to think that the literary sense is a distinctly waning quality. I can speak of your wife and children only interrogatively—which will tell you little—and me, I fear, less. But let me at least be affirmative to the extent of wishing them all, very affectionately, and to Mrs. H. in particular, the happiest New Year. Go on, my dear Howells, and send me your books always—as I *think* I send you mine. Continue to write only as your admirable ability moves you and believe me

Ever faithfully yours,

HENRY JAMES.

TO ROBERT LOUIS STEVENSON.

The novel, just begun, was *The Tragic Muse*.

34 De Vere Gardens, W.

July 31st [1888].

My dear Louis,

You are too far away—you are too absent—too invisible, inaudible, inconceivable. Life is too short a business and friendship too delicate a matter for such tricks—for cutting great gory masses out of 'em by the year at a time. Therefore come back. Hang it all—sink it all and come back. A little more and I shall cease to believe in you: I don't mean (in the usual implied phrase) in your veracity, but literally and more fatally in your relevancy—your objective reality. You have become a beautiful myth—a kind of unnatural uncomfortable unburied *mort*. You put forth a beautiful monthly voice, with such happy notes in it—but it comes from too far away, from the other side of the globe, while I vaguely know that you are crawling like a fly on the nether surface of my chair. Your adventures, no doubt, are wonderful; but I don't successfully evoke them, understand them, believe in them. I do in those you write, heaven knows—but I don't in those you perform, though the latter, I know, are to lead to new revelations of the former and your capacity for them is certainly wonderful enough. This is a selfish personal cry: I wish you back; for literature is lonely and Bournemouth is barren without you. Your place in my affection has not been usurped by another—for there is not the least little scrap of another to usurp it. If there were I would perversely try to care for him. But there isn't—I repeat, and I literally care for nothing but your return. I haven't even your novel to stay my stomach withal. The wan wet months elapse and I see no sign of it. The beautiful portrait of your wife shimmers at me from my chimney-piece—brought some months ago by the natural McClure—but seems to refer to one as dim and distant and delightful as a "toast" of the last century. I wish I could make you homesick—I wish I could spoil your fun. It is a very featureless time. The summer is rank with rheumatism—a dark, drowned, unprecedented season. The town is empty but I am not going away. I have no money, but I have a little work. I have lately written several short fictions—but you may not see them unless you come home. I have just begun a novel which is to run through the *Atlantic* from January 1st and which I aspire to finish by the end of this year. In reality I suppose I shall not be fully delivered of it before the middle of next. After that, with God's help, I propose, for a longish period, to do nothing but short lengths. I want to leave a multitude of pictures of my time, projecting my small circular frame upon as many different spots as possible and going in for number as well as quality, so that the number may constitute a total having a certain value as observation and testimony. But there isn't so much as a creature here even to whisper such an intention to. Nothing lifts its hand in these islands save blackguard party politics. Criticism is of an abject density and puerility—it doesn't exist—it writes the intellect of our race too low. Lang, in the D.N., every morning, and I believe in a hundred other places, uses his beautiful thin facility to write everything down to the lowest level of Philistine twaddle—the view of the old lady round the corner or the clever person at the dinner party. The incorporated society of authors (I belong to it, and so do you, I think, but I don't know what it is) gave a dinner the other night to American literati to thank them for praying for international copyright. I carefully forbore to go, thinking the gratulation premature, and I see by this morning's *Times* that the banquetted boon is further off than ever. Edmund Gosse has sent me his clever little life of Congreve, just out, and I have read it—but it isn't so good as his Raleigh. But no more was the insufferable subject.... Come, my dear Louis, grow not too thin. I can't question you—because, as I say, I don't conjure you up. You have killed the imagination in me—that part of it which formed your element and in which you sat vivid and near. Your wife and Mother and Mr. Lloyd suffer also—I must confess it—by this failure of breath, of faith. Of course I have your letter—from Manasquan (is that the idiotic name?) of the—ingenuous me, to think there was a date! It was terribly impersonal—it did me little good. A little more and I shan't believe in you enough to bless you. Take this, therefore, as your last chance. I follow all with an aching wing, an inadequate geography and an ineradicable hope. Ever, my dear Louis, yours, to the last snub—

HENRY JAMES.

TO WILLIAM JAMES.

Hôtel de l'Ecu, Geneva.

October 29th, 1888.

My dear William,

Your beautiful and delightful letter of the 14th, from your country home, descended upon me two days ago, and after penetrating myself with it for 24 hours I sent it back to England, to Alice, on whom it will confer equal beatitude: not only because so copious, but because so "cheerful in tone" and appearing to show that the essentials of health and happiness are with you. I wish to delay no hour longer to write to you, though I am at this moment rather exhausted with the effort of a long letter, completed five minutes since, to Louis Stevenson, in answer to one I lately received from his wife, from some undecipherable cannibal-island in the Pacific. They are such far-away, fantastic, bewildering people that there is a certain fatigue in the achievement of putting one's self in relation with them. I may mention in this connection that I have had in my hands the earlier sheets of the *Master of Ballantrae*, the new novel he is about to contribute to Scribner, and have been reading them with breathless admiration. They are wonderfully fine and perfect—he is a rare, delightful genius.

I am sitting in our old family *salon* in this place, and have sat here much of the time for the last fortnight in sociable converse with family ghosts—Father and Mother and Aunt Kate and our juvenile selves. I became conscious, suddenly, about Oct. 10th, that I wanted very much to get away from the stale dingy London, which I had not quitted, to speak of, for 15 months, and notably not all summer—a detestable summer in England, of wet and cold. Alice, whom I went to see, on arriving at this conclusion, assured me she could perfectly dispense for a few weeks with my presence on English soil; so I came straight here, where I have a sufficient, though not importunate sense of being in a foreign country, with a desired quietness for getting on with work. I have had 16 days of extraordinarily beautiful weather, full of autumn colour as vivid as yours at Chocorua, and with the Mt. Blanc range, perpetually visible, literally hanging, day after day, over the blue lake. I have treated myself, as I say, to the apartments, or a portion of them, in which we spent the winter of '59-'60, and in which nothing is changed save that the hotel seems to have gone down in the world a little, before the multiplication of rivals—a descent, however, which has the *agrément* of unimpaired cleanliness and applies apparently to the prices as well. It is very good and not at all dear. Geneva seems both duller and smarter—a good deal bigger, yet emptier too. The Academy is now the University—a large, winged building in the old public garden below the Treille. But all the old smells and tastes are here, and the sensation is pleasant. I expect in three or four days to go to Paris for about three weeks—and back to London after that. I shall be very busy for the next three or four months with the long thing I am doing for the *Atlantic* and which is to run no less than 15—though in shorter instalments than my previous fictions; so that I have no time for wanton travelling. But I enjoy the easier, lighter feeling of being out of England. I suppose if one lived in one of these countries one would take its problems to one's self, also, or be oppressed and darkened by them—even as I am, more or less, by those which hang over me in London. But as it is, the Continent gives one a refreshing sense of getting *away*—away from Whitechapel and Parnell and a hundred other constantly thickening heavinesses.... It is always a great misfortune, I think, when one has reached a certain age, that if one is living in a country not one's own and one is of anything of an ironic or critical disposition, one mistakes the inevitable reflections and criticisms that one makes, more and more as one grows older, upon life and human nature etc., for a judgment of that particular country, its natives, peculiarities, etc., to which, really, one has grown exceedingly accustomed. For myself, at any rate, I am deadly weary of the whole "international" state of mind—so that I *ache*, at times, with fatigue at the way it is constantly forced upon me as a sort of virtue or obligation. I can't look at the English-American world, or feel about them, any more, save as a big Anglo-Saxon total, destined to such an amount of melting together that an insistence on their differences becomes more and more idle and pedantic; and that melting together will come the faster the more one takes it for granted and treats the life of the two countries as continuous or more or less convertible, or at any rate as simply different chapters of the same general subject. Literature, fiction in particular, affords a magnificent arm for such taking for granted, and one may so do an excellent work with it. I have not the least hesitation in saying that I aspire to write in such a way that it would be impossible to an outsider to say whether I am at a given moment an American writing about England or an Englishman writing about America (dealing as I do with both countries,) and so far from being ashamed of such an ambiguity I should be exceedingly proud of it, for it would be highly civilized. You are right in surmising that it must often be a grief to me not to get more time for reading—though not in supposing that I am "hollowed out inside" by the limitations my existence has too obstinately attached to that exercise, combined with the fact that I produce a great deal. At times I do read almost as much as my wretched little *stomach* for it literally will allow, and on the whole I get much more time for it as the months and years go by. I touched bottom, in the way of missing time, during the first half of my long residence in London—and traversed then a sandy desert, in that respect—where, however, I took on board such an amount of human and social information that if the same necessary alternatives were presented to me again I should make the same choice. One can read when one is middle-aged or old; but one can mingle in the world with fresh perceptions only when one is young. The great thing is to be *saturated* with something—that is, in one way or another, with life; and I chose the form of my saturation. Moreover you exaggerate the degree to which my writing takes it out of my mind, for I try to spend only the interest of my capital.

I haven't told you how I found Alice when I last saw her. She is now in very good form—still going out, I hear from her, in the mild moments, and feeling very easy and even jolly about her Leamington winter. My being away is a sign of her really good symptoms. She was *wüthend* after the London police, in connection with the Whitechapel murders, to a degree that almost constituted robust health. I have seen a great many (that is, more than usual) Frenchmen in London this year: they bring me notes of introduction—and the other day, the night before coming away, I entertained at dinner (at a club,) the French Ambassador at Madrid (Paul Cambon), Xavier Charmes of the French Foreign Office, G. du Maurier, and the wonderful little Jusserand, the chargé d'affaires in London, who is a great friend of mine, and to oblige and relieve whom it was that I invited the two other diplomatists, his friends, whom he had rather helplessly on his hands. THERE is the *real* difference—a gulf from the English (or the American) to the Frenchman, and vice versâ (still more); and not from the Englishman to the American. The Frenchmen I see all seem to me wonderful the first time—but not so much, at all, the second.— But I must finish this without having touched any of the sympathetic things I meant to say to you about your place, your work on it, Alice's prowesses as a country lady, the children's vie champêtre, etc. Aunt Kate, after her visit to you, praised all these things to us with profusion and evident sincerity. I wish I could see them—but the day seems far.—I haven't lain on the ground for so many years that I feel as if I had spent them up in a balloon. Next summer I shall come here—I mean to Switzerland, for which my taste has revived. I am full of gratulation on your enlarged classes, chances of reading, etc., and on your prospect of keeping the invalid child this winter. Give my tender love to Alice. You are entering the period of keen suspense about Cleveland, and I share it even here. I have lately begun to receive and read the *Nation* after a long interval—and it seems to me very rough. Was it *ever* so?... Ever your affectionate

HENRY JAMES.

IV. LATER LONDON YEARS(1889-1897)

For the next five years, when once The Tragic Muse was off his hands, Henry James gave himself up with persevering determination to the writing of plays. He speaks very plainly, in his letters of the time, concerning the motives which urged him to the theatre, and there is no doubt that the chief of them was the desire for a kind of success which his fiction failed to achieve. He puts it simply that he wished to make money, that his books did not sell, and that he regarded the theatre solely as a much-needed pecuniary resource. But such belittling of his own motives—out of a feeling that was partly pride and partly shyness—was not unusual with him; and it seems impossible to take this language quite literally. For a man of letters with moderate tastes and no family, Henry James's circumstances were more than easy, even if his writings should earn him nothing at all; and he had no reason to doubt that his future was sufficiently assured. Moreover, though his work might have no great popular vogue—it had had a measure of that too, at the time of Daisy Miller—it still never wanted its own attentive circle; so that he had not to complain of the utter indifference that may wear upon the nerves of even the most disinterested artist. The sense of solitude that began to weigh upon him was perhaps more a matter of temperament than of fact; it never for a moment meant that he had lost faith in himself and his powers, but there mingled with it his inveterate habit of forecasting the future in the most ominous light. As he looked forward, he saw the undoubted decline of his popularity carrying him further and further away from recognition and its rewards; and the prospect, once the thought of it had taken root in his imagination, distressed and dismayed him. All would be righted, he felt, by the successful conquest of the theatre; there lay the way, not only to solid gains, but to the reassurance of vaguer, less formulated anxieties. With such a tangible gage of having made his impression he would be relieved for ever from the fear of working in vain and alone.

But from the moment when he began to write plays instead of novels, the task laid hold upon him with other attractions; and it was these, no doubt, which kept him at it through so many troubles and disappointments.

The dramatic form itself, in the first place, delighted and tormented him with its difficulty; the artistic riddle of lucidity in extreme compression, what he once characteristically described as the "passionate economy" of the play as he wrote it, appealed to him and drew him on to constantly renewed attempts. He admits that, but for this perpetual challenge to his ingenuity, he could never have supported the annoyances and irritations entailed by practical commerce with the theatre. And yet it is easy to see that these too had a certain fascination for him. He could not have been so eloquent in his denunciation of all theatrical conditions, the "saw-dust and orange-peel" of the trade, if he had not been enjoyably stimulated by them; and indeed from his earliest youth his interest in the stage had been keenly professional. The Tragic Muse herself, outcome of innumerable sessions at the Théâtre Français, shews how intently he had studied the art of acting—not as a spectacle only, but as a business and a life. The world behind the theatrical scene, though in the end he broke away from it with relief, closely occupied his mind during these few years; and with his gift for turning all experience to imaginative account he could scarcely look back on it afterwards as time wasted, little as his heavy expenditure of spirit and toil had to shew for it. His hope of finding fame and fortune in this direction failed utterly—and failed, which was much to the good, with clearness and precision at a given moment, so that he was able to make a clean cut and return at once to his right line. But he took with him treasures of observation lodged in a memory that to the end of his life always dwelt upon the theatre with a curious mixture of exasperation and delight.

Of all the plays, seven or eight in number, that he wrote between 1889 and 1894, only two were actually seen upon the stage. The first of these was a dramatic version of The American, produced by Edward Compton (who played the principal part) at Southport in January 1891. The piece had a fairly successful provincial life, but it failed to make good its hold upon London, where it was given for the first time on September 26, 1891, at the Opéra Comique, by the same company. It ran for about two months, after which it was seen no more in London, though it continued for some while longer to figure in Compton's provincial repertory. In its later life it was played with a re-written last act, in which, much against his will, Henry James conceded to popular taste a "happy ending" for his hero and heroine. The other and much more elaborate production was that of *Guy Domville* at the St. James's Theatre on January 5, 1895, with George Alexander and Miss Marion Terry in the chief parts. The story of this unfortunate venture is to be read in the letters that follow. The play (which has never been published) was enthusiastically received by the few and roughly rejected by the many; it ran for exactly a month and then disappeared for good. It was the most ambitious, and no doubt the best, piece of dramatic work that Henry James had produced, and he immediately accepted its failure as the end, for the present, of his play-writing. The first night of Guy Domville had been marked by an incident which wounded him so deeply that he could never afterwards bear the least reference to it; after the fall of the curtain he had been exposed, apparently by a misunderstanding, to the hostility of the grosser part of the audience, and the affront, the shock to his sensitive taste, was extreme and enduring. There had been various plans and projects in connection with his other plays, but by this time they had all come to nothing. To the relief of those friends who knew what an intolerable strain the whole agitated time had thrown upon his nerves, he went back to the work and the life which were so evidently the right scope for his genius. But before doing so he published four of his plays in two volumes of *Theatricals* (1894, 1895,) to the second of which he prefixed an introduction which sums up, with great candour and dignity, a part of the lesson he had learnt from his discouraging experience.

Outside the theatre his life proceeded as usual, and his yearly visits to Paris or Italy are almost the only events to be recorded. He was in Paris in the autumn of 1889 and in Italy, chiefly at Florence and Venice, for the following summer. But both these centres of attraction were beginning to lose their hold on him a little, though for different reasons: Paris for something in its artistic self-sufficiency that he found increasingly unsympathetic—and Italy as it became more and more a field of social claims, English and American, irresistible on the spot but destructive of quiet work. He began to feel the need of some settled country-home of his own in England, though for some years yet he took no practical steps to find one. He was in Paris again, early in 1891. At the end of the same year he was called to Dresden by the sudden death in hospital there of a gifted young American friend with whom he had latterly been much associated—Wolcott Balestier, whose short but remarkable career, as a writer and still more as a "literary agent" for other writers (including Henry James), has been commemorated by Mr. Gosse in his *Portraits and Sketches*. From this distressing excursion Henry James returned home to face another and greater sorrow which had begun to threaten him for some time past. For two years his sister had been growing steadily weaker; she had moved to London, and lived near her brother in Kensington, but her seclusion was so rigid that only those who knew him well understood how great a part she played in his life. Her vigour of mind and imagination was as keen as ever, and though the number of people she was able to see and know in England was very small she lived ardently in the interest, highly critical for the most part, that she took in public affairs. Her death in March 1892 meant for Henry James not only the end of a companionship that was very dear to him, but the breaking of the only family tie that he had had or was ever to have in England. So long as his sister was near him there was one person who shared his old memories and with whom he was in his own home; and when it is recalled how intensely he always clung to his distant kindred, and what a sense of support he drew from them even in his long separation, it is possible to measure the loss that befell him now—exactly at a time when such familiar and natural sympathy was most precious to him.

He spent the summer of 1892 again in Italy, avoiding the tourist-stream by settling at Siena, after it had subsided, in the company of M. and Mme. Paul Bourget, by this time his intimate friends. William James and his family were now in Europe for a year of Switzerland and Italy, and Henry joined them at Lausanne on his way home. The next two years of London were given up, almost without intermission, to the hopes and anxieties of his theatrical affairs, in which he was now completely immersed—so much so, indeed, as to test his very remarkable powers of physical endurance, which seem in middle life to have thrown off the early troubles of his health. When this time of fevered agitation was over he was able to compose himself at once to happier work, without apparently feeling even the need of a day's holiday. In 1893 he was in Paris in the spring, and again for a short while in Switzerland with his brother; but these excursions were never real holidays— he was quickly uneasy if he had not work of some kind on hand. He projected another summer in Italy for the following year, and spent it chiefly in Venice and Rome. This was the last of Italy, however, for some time; there were too many friends everywhere—"the most disastrous attempt I have ever made," he writes, "to come abroad for privacy and quiet." Still the only alternative seemed to be sea-side lodgings in England; and for the summer of 1895, escaping from the London season as usual, he went to Torquay. By this time Guy Domville had failed and he was free again; he had the happiest winter of work in London that he had known for five years. After finishing some short stories he began The Spoils of Poynton, and with it the series of his works that belong definitely to his "later manner." At last, in 1896, instead of his usual esplanade, he settled for a while upon an English country-side, making an accidental choice that was to prove momentous. He took a small house for the summer on the hill of Playden, in Sussex, where for the first time in his life, and after twenty years of England, he enjoyed a solitude of his own among trees and fields. From his terrace, where he sat under an ash-tree working at his novel, he looked across a wide valley to the beautiful old red-roofed town of Rye, climbing the opposite hill and crowned with its church-tower. The charm and tranquillity of the place were perfect, and when he had to give up the house at Playden he moved for the autumn into the old Rye vicarage. Exploring the steep cobbled streets round the church he came upon a singularly delightful old house, of the early eighteenth century, with a large walled garden behind it, which attracted him to the point of enquiring whether he might hope to possess it. There appeared to be no prospect of this; but he went back to London with a vivid sense that Lamb House was exactly the place he needed, if it should ever fall to him.

He had already finished The Spoils of Poynton and had immediately set to work on What Maisie Knew, deeply reconciled now to the indifference of the general public, which indeed became more and more confirmed. The only question by this time was whether London was any longer the right place for the determined concentration upon fiction that he decided was to fill the rest of his life. The country would hardly have drawn him thither for its own sake; there could not have been such a lack of it in his existence, for more than fifty years, if it had strongly appealed to him in itself. But London had long ago given him all it could, and his great desire now was for peace and quiet and freedom from interruption. In 1897, after a summer of the usual kind, at Bournemouth and Dunwich, he suddenly learned that a tenant was being sought for Lamb House, and he signed the lease within a few days. It was the most punctual and appropriate stroke of fortune that could have been devised.

TO ROBERT LOUIS STEVENSON.

34 De Vere Gardens, W.

April 29th, 1889.

This is really dreadful news, my dear Louis, odious news to one who had neatly arranged that his coming August should be spent gobbling down your yarns—by some garden-window of Skerryvore—as the Neapolitan lazzarone puts away the lubricating filaments of the vermicelli. And yet, with my hideous capacity to understand it, I am strong enough, superior enough, to say *anything*, for conversation, later. It's in the light of unlimited conversation that I see the future years, and my honoured chair by the ingleside will require a succession of new cushions. I miss you shockingly—for, my dear fellow, there is no one—literally no one; and I don't in the least follow you—I can't go with you (I mean in conceptive faculty and the "realising sense,") and you are for the time absolutely as if you were dead to me—I mean to my imagination of course—not to my affection or my prayers. And so I shall keep humble that you may pump into me—and make me stare and sigh and look simple and be quite out of it—for ever and ever. It's the best thing that can happen to one to see it written in your very hand that you have been so uplifted in health and cheer, and if another year will screw you up so tight that you won't "come undone" again, I will try and hold on through the barren months. I will go to Mrs. Sitwell, to hear what has made you blush—it must be something very radical. Your chieftains are dim to me—why shouldn't they be when you yourself are? *Va* for another year—but don't stay away longer, for we should really, for self-defence, have to outlive [?] you.... I myself do little but sit at home and write little tales—and even long ones—you shall see them when you come back. Nothing would induce me, by sending them to you, to expose myself to damaging Polynesian comparisons. For the rest, there is nothing in this land but the eternal Irish strife—the place is all gashed and gory with it. I can't tell you of it—I am too sick of it—more than to say that two or three of the most interesting days I ever passed were lately in the crowded, throbbing, thrilling little court of the Special Commission, over the astounding drama of the forged *Times* letters.

I have a hope, a dream, that your mother may be coming home and that one may go and drink deep of her narrations. But it's idle and improbable. A wonderful, beautiful letter from your wife to Colvin seemed, a few months ago, to make it clear that *she* has no quarrel with your wild and wayward life. I hope it agrees with her a little too—I mean that it renews her youth and strength. It is a woeful time to wait—for your prose as for your person—especially as the prose can't be better though the person may.

> Your very faithful
>
> HENRY JAMES.

TO WILLIAM JAMES.

> Hôtel de Hollande, Paris.
>
> Nov. 28th, '89.

My dear William,

...I send you this from Paris, where I have been for the last five weeks. Toward the end I relented in regard to the exhibition and came over in time for the last fortnight of it. It was despoiled of its freshness and invaded by hordes of furious Franks and fiery Huns—but it was a great impression and I'm glad I sacrificed to it. So I've remained on. I go back Dec. 1st. It happens that I have been working very hard all this month—almost harder than ever in my life before—having on top of other pressing and unfinished tasks undertaken, for the bribe of large lucre, to translate Daudet's new *Tartarin* novel for the Harpers.... I had a talk of one hour and a half with him the other day—about "our work" (!!) and his own queer, deplorable condition, which he intensely converts into art, profession, success, copy, etc.—taking perpetual notes about his constant suffering (terrible in degree,) which are to make a book called *La Douleur*, the most detailed and pessimistic notation of pain *qui fut jamais*. He is doing, in the midst of this, his new, gay, lovely "Tartarin" for the Harpers *en premier lieu*; that is, they are to publish it serially with wonderfully "processed" drawings before it comes out as a book in France—and I am to represent him, in English (a difficult, but with ingenuity a pleasant and amusing task,) while this serial period lasts. I have seen a good deal of Bourget, and as I have breakfasted with Coppée and twice dined in company with Meilhac, Sarcey, Albert Wolff, Goncourt, Ganderax, Blowitz, etc., you will judge that I am pretty well saturated and ought to have the last word about ces gens-ci. That last word hasn't a grain of subjection or of mystery left in it: it is simply, "Chinese, Chinese, Chinese!" They are finished, besotted mandarins, and their Paris is their celestial Empire. With that, such a Paris as it sometimes seems! Nevertheless I've enjoyed it, and though I am very tired, too tired to write to you properly, I shall have been much refreshed by my stay here, and have taken aboard some light and heat for the black London winter.... I hope that above house and college and life and everything you still hold up an undemented head, and are not in a seedy way.

Ever your affectionate

HENRY.

TO ROBERT LOUIS STEVENSON.

Stevenson was now beginning to break to his friends at home the possibility that he might settle permanently in the South Seas; but he still projected a preliminary visit to England, or at least to Europe.

34 De Vere Gardens, W.

March 21st, 1890.

My dear Louis and my dear Mrs. Louis,

It comes over me with horror and shame that, within the next very few months, your return to England may become such a reality that I shall before long stand face to face with you branded with the almost blood-guilt of my long silence. Let me break that silence then, before the bliss of meeting you again (heaven speed the day) is qualified, in prospect, by the apprehension of your disdain. I despatch these incoherent words to Sydney, in the hope they may catch you before you embark for our palpitating England. My despicable dumbness has been a vile accident—I needn't assure you that it doesn't pretend to the smallest backbone of system or sense. I have simply had the busiest year of my life and have been so drained of the fluid of expression—so tapped into the public pitcher—that my whole correspondence has dried up and died of thirst. Then, somehow, you had become inaccessible to the mind as well as to the body, and I had the feeling that, in the midst of such desperate larks, any news of mine would be mere irrelevant drivel to you. Now, however, you *must* take it, such as it is. It won't, of course, be news to you at all that the idea of your return has become altogether the question of the day. The other two questions (the eternal Irish and Rudyard Kipling) aren't in it. (We'll tell you all about Rudyard Kipling—your nascent rival; he has killed one immortal—Rider Haggard; the star of the hour, aged 24 and author of remarkable Anglo-Indian and extraordinarily observed barrack life—Tommy Atkins—tales.) What I am pledged to do at the present moment (pledged to Colvin) is to plead with you passionately on the question of Samoa and expatriation. But somehow, when it comes to the point, I can't do it—partly because I can't really believe in anything so dreadful (a long howl of horror has gone up from all your friends), and partly because before any step so fatal is irretrievably taken we are to have a chance to see you and bind you with flowery chains. When you tell me with your own melodious lips that you're committed, I'll see what's to be done; but I won't take a single plank of the house or a single hour of the flight for granted. Colvin has given me instantly all your recent unspeakable news—I mean the voyage to Samoa and everything preceding, and your mother has kindly communicated to me her own wonderful documents. Therefore my silence has been filled with sound—sound infinitely fearful sometimes. But the joy of your health, my dear Louis, has been to me as an imparted sensation—making me far more glad than anything that I could originate with myself. I shall never be as well as I am glad that you are well. We are poor tame, terrified products of the tailor and the parlour-maid; but we have a fine sentiment or two, all the same.... I, thank God, am in better form than when you first took ship. I have lately finished the longest and most careful novel I have ever written (it has gone 16 months in a periodical) and the last, in that form, I shall ever do—it will come out as a book in May. Also other things too flat to be bawled through an Australasian tube. But the intensest throb of my literary life, as of that of many others, has been the Master of Ballantrae—a pure hard crystal, my boy, a work of ineffable and exquisite art. It makes us all as proud of you as you can possibly be of *it*. Lead him on blushing, lead him back blooming, by the hand, dear Mrs. Louis, and we will talk over everything, as we used to lang syne at Skerryvore. When we *have* talked over everything and when all your tales are told, then you may paddle back to Samoa. But we shall call time. My heartiest greeting to the young Lloyd—grizzled, I fear, before his day. I have been very sorry to hear of your son-in-law's bad case. May all that tension be over now. *Do* receive this before you sail—*don't* sail till you get it. But then bound straight across. I send a volume of the Rising Star to goad you all hither with jealousy. He has quite done for your neglected even though neglectful friend,

HENRY JAMES.

TO ROBERT LOUIS STEVENSON.

34 De Vere Gardens, W.

April 28th, '90.

My dear Louis,

I didn't, for two reasons, answer your delightful letter, or rather exquisite note, from the Sydney Club, but I must thank you for it now, before the gulfs have washed you down, or at least have washed away from you all after-tastes of brineless things—the stay-at-home works of lubberly friends. One of the reasons just mentioned was that I had written to you at Sydney (c/o the mystic Towns,) only a few days before your note arrived; the other is that until a few days ago I hugged the soft illusion that by the time anything else would reach you, you would already have started for England. This fondest of hopes of all of us has been shattered in a manner to which history furnishes a parallel only in the behaviour of its most famous coquettes and courtesans. You are indeed the male Cleopatra or buccaneering Pompadour of the Deep—the wandering Wanton of the Pacific. You swim into our ken with every provocation and prospect—and we have only time to open our arms to receive you when your immortal back is turned to us in the act of still more provoking flight. The moral is that we have to be virtuous whether we like it or no. Seriously, it was a real heart-break to have September substituted for June; but I have a general faith in the fascinated providence who watches over you, to the neglect of all other human affairs—I believe that even *He* has an idea that you know what you are about, and even what *He* is, though He by this time doesn't in the least know himself. Moreover I have selfish grounds of resignation in the fact that I shall be in England in September, whereas, to my almost intolerable torment, I should probably not have been in June. Therefore when you come, if you ever do, which in my heart of hearts I doubt, I shall see you in all your strange exotic bloom, in all your paint and beads and feathers. May you grow a magnificent extra crop of all such things (as they will bring you a fortune here,) in this much grudged extra summer. Charming and delightful to me to see you with a palate for *my* plain domestic pudding, after all the wild cannibal smacks that you have learned to know. I think the better of the poor little study in the painfully-familiar, since hearing that it could bear such voyages and resist such tests. You have fed a presumption that vaguely stirs within me—that of trying to get at you in June or July with a fearfully long-winded but very highly-finished novel which I am putting forth in (probably) the last days of May. If I were sure it would overtake you on some coral strand I shouldn't hesitate; for, seriously and selfishly speaking, I can't (spiritually) afford *not* to put the book under the eye of the sole and single Anglo-saxon capable of perceiving—though he may care for little else in it—how well it is written. So I shall probably cast it upon the waters and pray for it; as I suppose you are coming back to Sydney, it may meet you there, and you can read it on the voyage home. In that box you'll *have* to. I don't say it to bribe you in advance to unnatural tolerance—but I have an impression that I didn't make copious or clear to you in my last what a grand literary life your Master of B. has been leading here. Somehow, a miracle has been wrought for you (for you they are,) and the fine old feather-bed of English taste *has* thrilled with preternatural recognitions. The most unlikely number of people *have* discerned that the Master is "well written." It has had the highest success of honour that the English-reading public can now confer; where it has failed (the success, save that it hasn't failed at all!) it has done so through the constitutional incapacity of the umpire—infected, by vulgar intercourses, as with some unnameable disease. We have lost our status—*nous n'avons plus qualité*—to confer degrees. Nevertheless, last year you woke us up at night, for an hour—and we scrambled down in our shirt and climbed a garden-wall and stole a laurel, which we have been brandishing ever since over your absent head. I tell you this because I think Colvin (at least it was probably he—he is visibly better—or else Mrs. Sitwell) mentioned to me the other day that you had asked in touching virginal ignorance for news of the fate of the book. Its "fate," my dear fellow, has been glittering glory—simply: and I ween—that is I hope—you will find the glitter has chinked as well. I sent you a new Zola the other day—at a venture: but I have no confidence that I gratified a curiosity. I haven't read The Human Beast—one knows him without that—and I am told Zola's account of him is dull and imperfect. I would read anything new about him—but this is old, old, old. I hope your pen, this summer, will cleave the deeps of art even as your prow, or your keel, or whatever's the knowing name for it, furrows the Pacific flood. Into what strange and wondrous dyes you must be now qualified to dip it! Roast yourself, I beseech you, on the sharp spit of perfection, that you may give out your aromas and essences! Tell your wife, please, to read between the lines of this, and between the words and the letters, all that I miss the occasion to write directly to *her*. I hope she has continued to distil, to your mother, the honey of those impressions of which a few months ago the latter lent me for a day or two a taste—on its long yellow foolscap combs. They would make, they *will* make, of course, a deliciously sweet book. I hope Lloyd, whom I greet and bless, is living up to the height of his young privilege—and secreting honey too, according to the mild discipline of the hive. There are lots of things more to tell you, no doubt, but if I go on they will all take the shape of questions, and that won't be fair. The supreme thing to say is

Don't, oh *don't*, simply ruin our nerves and our tempers for the rest of life by *not* throwing the rope in September, to him who will, for once in his life, not muff his catch:

H.J.

TO WILLIAM JAMES.

The project guardedly referred to in this letter was that of writing a series of plays. He had already finished the dramatisation of *The American*.

Hôtel de la Ville, Milan.

May 16th, 1890.

My dear William,

...I have been both very busy and very bent on getting away this year without fail, for a miracle, from the oppressive London season. I have just accomplished it; I passed the St. Gotthard day before yesterday, and I hope to find it possible to remain absent till August 1st. After that I am ready to pay cheerfully and cheaply for my journey by staying quietly in town for August and September, in the conditions in which you saw me last year. I shall take as much as possible of a holiday, for I have been working carefully, consecutively and unbrokenly for a very long time past—turning out one thing (always "highly finished") after another. However, I *like* to work, thank heaven, and at the end of a month's privation of it I sink into gloom and discomfort—so that I shall probably not wholly "neglect my pen".... I hope you will have received promptly a copy of *The Tragic Muse*, though I am afraid I sent my list to the publishers a little late. I don't in the least know, however, when the book is supposed to come out. I have no opinion or feeling about it now—though I took long and patient and careful trouble (which no creature will recognise) with it at the time: too much, no doubt: for my mind is now a muddled, wearied blank on the subject. I have shed and ejected it—it's void and dead—and my feeling as to what may become of it is reduced to the sordid hope it will make a little money—which it won't.... The matter you expressed a friendly hope about the success of, and which for all sorts of reasons I desire to be extremely secret, silent and mysterious about—I mean the enterprise I covertly mentioned to you as conceived by me with a religious and deliberate view of gain over a greater scale than the Book (my Books at least) can ever approach bringing in to me: this matter is on a good and promising footing, but it is too soon to say anything about it, save that I am embarked in it seriously and with rather remarkably good omens. By which I mean that it is not to depend on a single attempt, but on half a dozen of the most resolute and scientific character, which I find I am abundantly capable of making, but which, alas, in the light of this discovery, I become conscious that I ought to have made ten years ago. I was then discouraged all round, while a single word of encouragement would have made the difference. Now it is late. But on the other hand the thing would have been then only an experiment more or less like another—whereas now it's an absolute necessity, imposing itself without choice if I wish a loaf on the shelf for my old age. Fortunately as far as it's gone it announces itself well—but I can't tell you yet how far that is. The only thing is to do a great lot.

By the time this reaches you I suppose your wife and children will have gone to recline under the greenwood tree. I hope their gentle outlawry will be full of comfort for them. It's poor work to me writing about them without ever seeing them. But my interest in them is deep and large, and please never omit to give my great love to them: to Alice first in the lump, to be broken up and distributed by her. May you squeeze with a whole skin through the tight weeks of the last of the term—may you live to rest and may you rest to live. I shall not, I think, soon again write to you so rarely as for the last year. This will be partly because *The Tragic Muse* is to be my last long novel. For the rest of my life I hope to do lots of short things with irresponsible spaces between. I see even a great future (ten years) of such. But they won't make money. Excuse (you probably rather will esteem) the sordid tone of your affectionate

HENRY JAMES.

TO W. D. HOWELLS.

Hôtel de la Ville, Milan.

May 17th, 1890.

My dear Howells,

I have been not writing to you at a tremendous, an infamous rate, for a long time past; but I should indeed be sunk in baseness if I were to keep this pace after what has just happened. For what has just happened is that I have been reading the *Hazard of New Fortunes* (I confess I should have liked to change the name for you,) and that it has filled me with communicable rapture. I remember that the last time I came to Italy (or almost,) I brought your Lemuel Barker, which had just come out, to read in the train, and let it divert an intense professional eye from the most clamourous beauties of the way—writing to you afternoons from this very place, I think, all the good and all the wonder I thought of it. So I have a decent precedent for insisting to you, now, under circumstances exactly similar (save that the present book is a much bigger feat,) that, to my charmed and gratified sense, the *Hazard* is simply prodigious.... I should think it would make you as happy as poor happiness will let us be, to turn off from one year to the other, and from a reservoir in daily domestic use, such a free, full, rich flood. In fact your reservoir deluges me, altogether, with surprise as well as other sorts of effusion; by which I mean that though you do much to empty it you keep it remarkably full. I seem to myself, in comparison, to fill mine with a teaspoon and obtain but a trickle. However, I don't mean to compare myself with you or to compare you, in the particular case, with anything but life. When I do that—with the life you see and represent—your faculty for representing it seems to me extraordinary and to shave the truth—the general truth you aim at—several degrees closer than anyone else begins to do. You are less *big* than Zola, but you are ever so much less clumsy and more really various, and moreover you and he don't see the same things—you have a wholly different consciousness—*you* see a totally different side of a different race. Man isn't at all *one* after all—it takes so much of him to be American, to be French, &c. I won't even compare you with something I have a sort of dim stupid sense you might be and are not—for I don't in the least know that you might be it, after all, or whether, if you were, you wouldn't cease to be that something you are which makes me write to you thus. We don't know what people might give us that they don't—the only thing is to take them on what they do and to allow them absolutely and utterly their conditions. This alone, for the tastes, secures freedom of enjoyment. I apply the rule to you, and it represents a perfect triumph of appreciation; because it makes me accept, largely, all your material from you—an absolute gain when I consider that I should never take it from myself. I note certain things which make me wonder at your form and your fortune (e.g.—as I have told you before—the fatal colour in which they let *you*, because you live at home—is it?—paint American life; and the fact that there's a whole quarter of the heaven upon which, in the matter of composition, you seem consciously—*is* it consciously?—to have turned your back;) but these things have no relevancy whatever as grounds of dislike—simply because you communicate so completely *what* you undertake to communicate. The novelist is a particular *window*, absolutely—and of worth in so far as he is one; and it's because you open so well and are hung so close over the street that I could hang out of it all day long. Your very value is that you choose your own street—heaven forbid I should have to choose it for you. If I should say I mortally dislike the people who pass in it, I should seem to be taking on myself that intolerable responsibility of selection which it is exactly such a luxury to be relieved of. Indeed I'm convinced that no readers above the rank of an idiot—this number is moderate, I admit—really fail to take any view that is really *shown* them—any gift (of subject) that's really given. The usual imbecility of the novel is that the showing and giving simply don't come off—the reader never touches the subject and the subject never touches the reader; the window is no window at all—but only childish *finta*, like the ornaments of our beloved Italy. This is why, as a triumph of *communication*, I hold the *Hazard* so rare and strong. You communicate in touches so close, so fine, so true, so droll, so frequent. I am writing too much (you will think me demented with chatter;) so that I can't go into specifications of success....

I continue to scribble, though with relaxed continuity while abroad; but I can't talk to you about it. One thing only is clear, that henceforth I must do, or half do, England in fiction—as the place I see most today, and, in a sort of way, know best. I have at last more acquired notions of it, on the whole, than of any other world, and it will serve as well as any other. It has been growing distincter that America fades from me, and as she never trusted me at best, I can trust *her*, for effect, no longer. Besides I can't be doing *de chic*, from here, when you, on the spot, are doing so brilliantly the *vécu*....

TO MISS ALICE JAMES.

The play which H. J. had given his sister to read was the dramatic version of *The American*. It had now been accepted for production by Edward Compton, who was to play the part of Christopher Newman. Some intentional and humorous exaggeration, it ought perhaps to be mentioned, enters into H. J.'s constant appeal for discreet silence in these matters. As for the projected excursion with Mr. and Mrs. Curtis, he eventually went with them the whole way, and saw the Passion Play at Oberammergau.

Palazzo Barbaro, Venice.

June 6th [1890].

Dearest Sister,

I am ravished by your letter after reading the play (keep it locked up, safe and secret, though there are three or four copies in existence) which makes me feel as if there had been a triumphant première and I had received overtures from every managerial quarter and had only to count my gold. At any rate I am delighted that you have been struck with it exactly as I have tried to strike, and that the pure practical character of the effort has worked its calculated spell upon you. For what encourages me in the whole business is that, as the piece stands, there is not, in its felicitous form, the ghost of a "fluke" or a mere chance: it is all "art" and an absolute address of means to the end—the end, viz., of meeting exactly the immediate, actual, intense British conditions, both subjective and objective, and of acting in (to a minute, including entr'actes) 2 hours and 3/4. Ergo, I can do a dozen more infinitely better; and I am excited to think how much, since the writing of this one piece has been an education to me, a little further experience will do for me. Also I am sustained by the sense, on the whole, that though really superior acting would help it immensely, yet mediocrity of handling (which is all, at the best, I am pretty sure, that it will get) won't and can't kill it, and that there may be even something sufficiently general and human about it, to make it (given its eminent actability) "keep the stage," even after any first vogue it may have had has passed away. That fate—in the poverty-stricken condition of the English repertory—would mean profit indeed, and an income to my descendants. But one mustn't talk of this kind of thing yet. However, since you have been already so deeply initiated, I think I will enclose (keep it sacredly for me) an admirable letter I have just received from the precious Balestier in whose hands, as I wrote you, I placed the settlement of the money-question, the terms of the writing agreement with Compton. Compton saw him on Monday last—and I send the letter mainly to illustrate the capital intelligence and competence of Balestier and show you in what good hands I am. He will probably strike you, as he strikes me, as the perfection of an "agent"—especially when you consider that he has undertaken this particular job out of pure friendship. Everything, evidently, will be well settled—on the basis, of course, which can't be helped, of production in London only about the middle of next year. But by that time I hope to have done a good bit more work—and I shall be beguiled by beginning to follow, in the autumn, the rehearsals for the country production. Keep Balestier's letter till I come back—I shall get another one from him in a day or two with the agreement to sign.... These castles in Spain are at least exhilarating: in a certain sense I should like you very much to communicate to William your good impression of the drama—but on the whole I think you had better not, for the simple reason that it is very important it shouldn't be talked about (especially so long) in advance—and it wouldn't be safe, inasmuch as every whisper gets into the papers—and in some fearfully vulgarized and perverted form. You might hint to William that you have read the piece under seal of secresy to me and think so-and-so of it—but are so bound (to me) not to give a sign that he must bury what you tell him in tenfold mystery. But I doubt if even this would be secure—it would be in the *Transcript* the next week.

Venice continues adorable and the Curtises the soul of benevolence. Their upstairs apartment (empty and still unoffered—at forty pounds a year—to any one but me) beckons me so, as a foot-on-the-water here, that if my dramatic ship had begun to come in, I should probably be tempted to take it at a venture—for all it would matter. But for the present I resist perfectly—especially as Venice isn't all advantageous. The great charm of such an idea is the having, in Italy, a little cheap and private refuge independent of hotels etc., which every year grow more disagreeable and German and tiresome to face—not to say dearer too. But it won't be for this year—and the Curtises won't let it. What Pen Browning has done here ... with the splendid Palazzo Rezzonico, transcends description for the beauty, and, as Ruskin would say, "wisdom and rightness" of it. It is altogether royal and imperial—but "Pen" isn't kingly and the *train de vie* remains to be seen. Gondoliers ushering in friends from pensions won't fill it out.... I am thinking, after all, of joining the Curtises in the evidently most beautiful drive (of upwards of a week, with rests) they are starting upon on the 14th, from a place called Vittorio, in the Venetian Alps, two hours rail from here, through Cadore, Titian's country, the Dolomites etc., toward Oberammergau. They offer me pressingly the fourth seat in the carriage that awaits them when they leave the train—and also an extra ticket they have taken for the play at Oberammergau, if I choose to go so far. This I shall scarcely do, but I shall probably leave with them, drive 4 or 5 days and come back, via Verona, by rail—leaving my luggage here. Continue to address here—unless, before that, I give you one other address while I am gone. I shall find all letters here, on my return, if I do go, in the keeping of the excellent *maestro di casa*—the Venetian Smith. I should be back, at the latest, by the 25th—probably by the 20th. In this case I shall presumably go back to Florence to spend 4 or 5 days with Baldwin (going to Siena or Perugia;) after which I have a dream of going to Vallombrosa (nearly 4000 feet above the sea—but of a softness!) for 2 or 3 weeks—till I have to leave Italy on my way home. I am writing to Edith Peruzzi, who has got a summer-lodge there, and is already there, for information about the inn. If I don't go there I shall perhaps try Camaldoli or San Marcello—all high in the violet Apennines, within 3 or 4 hours, and mainly by a little carriage, of Florence. But I want to compass Vallombrosa, which I have never seen and have always dreamed of and which I am assured is divine—infinitely salubrious and softly cool. The idea of lingering in Italy a few weeks longer on these terms is very delightful to me—it does me, as yet, nothing but good. But I shall see. I put B.'s letter in another envelope. I rejoiced in your eight gallops; they may be the dozen now.

Ever your HENRY.

TO WILLIAM JAMES.

Paradisino, Vallombrosa, Tuscany.

July 23rd, 1890.

My dear Brother,

I had from you some ten days ago a most delightful letter written just after the heroic perusal of my interminable novel—which, according to your request, I sent off almost too precipitately to Alice, so that I haven't it here to refer to. But I don't need to "refer" to it, inasmuch as it has plunged me into a glow of satisfaction which is far, as yet, from having faded. I can only thank you tenderly for seeing so much good in the clumsy thing—as I thanked your Alice, who wrote me a most lovely letter, a week or two ago. I have no illusions of any kind about the book, and least of all about its circulation and "popularity." From these things I am quite divorced and never was happier than since the dissolution has been consecrated by (what seems to me) the highest authorities. One must go one's way and know what one's about and have a general plan and a private religion—in short have made up one's mind as to *ce qui en est* with a public the draggling after which simply leads one in the gutter. One has always a "public" enough if one has an audible vibration—even if it should only come from one's self. I shall never make my fortune—nor anything like it; but—I know what I shall do, and it won't be bad.—I am lingering on late in Italy, as you see, so as to keep away from London till August 1st or thereabouts. (I stay in this exquisite spot till that date.) I shall then, returning to my normal occupations, have had the best and clearest and pleasantest holiday of three months, that I have had for many a day. I have been accompanied on this occasion by a literary irresponsibility which has caused me to enjoy Italy perhaps more than ever before;—let alone that I have never before been perched (more than three thousand feet in the air) in so perfect a paradise as this unspeakable Vallombrosa. It is Milton's Vallombrosa, the original of his famous line, the site of the old mountain monastery which he visited and which stands still a few hundred feet below me as I write, "suppressed" and appropriated some time ago by the Italian Government, who have converted it to the State school of "Forestry." This little inn—the Paradisino, as it is called, on a pedestal of rock overhanging the violet abysses like the prow of a ship, is the Hermitage (a very comfortable one) of the old convent. The place is extraordinarily beautiful and "sympathetic," the most romantic mountains and most admirable woods—chestnut and beech and magnificent pine-forests, the densest, coolest shade, the freshest, sweetest air and the most enchanting views. It is full 20 years since I have done anything like so much wandering through dusky woods and lying with a book on warm, breezy hillsides. It has given me a sense of summer which I had lost in so many London Julys; given me almost the summer of one's childhood back again. I shall certainly come back here for other Julys and other Augusts—and I hate to go away now. May you, and all of you, these weeks, have as sweet, or half as sweet, an impression of the natural universe as yours affectionately,

HENRY JAMES.

TO EDMUND GOSSE.

The "ordeal" was the first night of *The American*, produced by Edward Compton and his company at Southport in anticipation of its eventual appearance in London.

Prince of Wales Hotel,

Southport.

Jan. 3rd [1891].

My dear Gosse,

I am touched by your *petit mot*. De gros mots seem to me to be so much more applicable to my fallen state. The only thing that can be said for it is that it is not so low as it may perhaps be to-morrow—after the vulgar ordeal of to-night. Let me therefore profit by the few remaining hours of a recognizable *status* to pretend to an affectionate reciprocity. I am yours and your wife's while yet I *may* be. After 11 o'clock to-night I *may* be the world's—

164

you know—and I may be the undertaker's. I count upon you both to spend this evening in fasting, silence and supplication. I will send you a word in the morning—wire you if I can—if there is anything at all to boast of. My hopes rest solely on intrinsic charms—the adventitious graces of art are not "in it." I am so nervous that I miswrite and misspell. Pity your infatuated but not presumptuous friend,

HENRY JAMES.

P.S. It would have been delightful—and terrible—if you had been able to come. I believe Archer is to come.

P.P.S. I don't return straight to London—don't get there till Tuesday or Wednesday. I shall have to wait and telegraph you which evening I can come in.

TO MRS. HUGH BELL.

34 De Vere Gardens, W.

Jan. 8th [1891].

Dear Mrs. Bell,

Your most kind gratulatory note deserved an answer more gratefully prompt than this. But I extended my absence from town to a short visit at Cheltenham, and the whole thing was virtually, till yesterday, a complete extinction of leisure. Delightful of you to want "details." I think, if I were to inflict them on you, they would all be illustrative of the cheering and rewarding side of our feverish profession. The passage from knock-kneed nervousness (the night of the *première*, as one clings, in the wing, to the curtain rod, as to the *pied des autels*) to a simmering serenity is especially life-saving in its effect. I flung myself upon Compton after the 1st act: "In heaven's name, is it *going*?" "Going?—Rather! You could hear a pin drop!" Then, after that, one felt it—one *heard* it—one blessed it—and, at the end of all, one (after a decent and discreet delay) simpered and gave oneself up to *courbettes* before the curtain, while the applausive house emitted agreeable sounds from a kind of gas-flaring indistinguishable dimness and the gratified Compton publicly pressed one's hand and one felt that, really, as far as Southport could testify to the circumstance, the stake was won. Of course it's only Southport—but I have larger hopes, inasmuch as it was just the meagre provincial conditions and the limited provincial interpretation that deprived the performance of all adventitious aid. And when my hero and heroine and another friend supped with me at the inn after the battle, I felt that they were really as radiant as if we were carousing among the slain. They *seem* indeed wondrous content. The great feature of the evening was the way Compton "came out" beyond what he had done or promised at rehearsal, and acted really most interestingly and admirably—if not a "revelation" at any rate a very jolly surprise. His part is one in which I surmise he really counts upon making a large success—and though I say it who shouldn't, it is one of incontestable opportunities. However, all this is to come—and we stumble in judgment. Amen. Voilà, ma chère amie. You have been through all this, and more, and will tolerate my ingenuities....

All merriment to *your* "full house."

Yours most truly,

HENRY JAMES.

TO ROBERT LOUIS STEVENSON.

34 De Vere Gardens, W.

January 12th, 1891.

My dear Louis,

I have owed you a letter too shamefully long—and now that I have taken my pen in hand, as we used to say, I feel how much I burn to communicate with you. As your magnanimity will probably have forgotten how long ago it was that you addressed me, from Sydney, the tragic statement of your permanent secession I won't remind you of so detested a date. That statement, indeed, smote me to the silence I have so long preserved: I couldn't—I didn't protest; I even mechanically and grimly assented; but I couldn't *talk* about it—even to you and your wife. Missing you is always a perpetual ache—and aches are disqualifying for gymnastic feats. In short we forgive you (the Muses and the soft Passions forgive *us*!) but we can't quite *treat* you as if we did. However, all this while I have many things to thank you for. In the first place for Lloyd. He was delightful, we loved him—nous nous l'arrachâmes. He is a most sympathetic youth, and we revelled in his rich conversation and exclaimed on his courtly manners. How vulgar you'll think us all when you come back (there is malice in that "when.") Then for the beautiful strange things you sent me and which make for ever in my sky-parlour a sort of dim rumble as of the Pacific surf. My heart beats over them—my imagination throbs—my eyes fill. I have covered a blank wall of my bedroom with an acre of painted cloth and feel as if I lived in a Samoan tent—and I have placed the sad sepia-drawing just where, 50 times a day, it most transports and reminds me. To-day what I am grateful for is your new ballad-book, which has just reached me by your command. I have had time only to read the first few things—but I shall absorb the rest and give you my impression of them before I close this. As I turn the pages I seem to see that they are full of charm and of your "Protean" imaginative life—but above all of your terrible far-off-ness. My state of mind about that is of the strangest—a sort of delight at having you poised there in the inconceivable; and a miserable feeling, at the same time, that I am in too wretched a back seat to assist properly at the performance. I don't want to lose *any* of your vibrations; and, as it is, I feel that I only catch a few of them—and that is a constant woe. I read with unrestrictive relish the first chapters of your prose volume (kindly vouchsafed me in the little copyright-catching red volume,) and I loved 'em and blessed them quite. But I *did* make one restriction—I missed the *visible* in them—I mean as regards people, things, objects, faces, bodies, costumes, features, gestures, manners, the introductory, the *personal* painter-touch. It struck me that you either didn't feel—through some accident—your responsibility on this article quite enough; or, on some theory of your own, had declined it. No theory is kind to us that cheats us of *seeing*. However, no doubt we shall rub our eyes for satiety before we have done. Of course the pictures—Lloyd's blessed photographs—y sont pour beaucoup; but I wanted more the note of portraiture. Doubtless I am greedy—but one *is* when one dines at the Maison d'or. I have an idea you take but a qualified interest in "Beau Austin"—or I should tell you how religiously I was present at that memorable première. Lloyd and your wonderful and delightful mother will have given you the agreeable facts of the occasion. I found it—not the occasion, so much, but the work—full of *quality*, and stamped with a charm; but on the other hand seeming to shrug its shoulders a little too much at scenic precautions. I have an idea, however, you don't care about the matter, and I won't bore you with it further than to say that the piece has been repeatedly played, that it has been the only honourable affair transacted dans notre sale tripot for many a day— and that Wm. Archer *en raffole* periodically in the "World." Don't despise me too much if I confess that *anch' io son pittore*. Je fais aussi du théâtre, moi; and am doing it, to begin with, for reasons too numerous to burden you with, but all excellent and practical. In the provinces I had the other night, at Southport, Lancashire, with the dramatization of an early novel— *The American*—a success dont je rougis encore. This thing is to be played in London only after several months—and to make the tour of the British Islands first. Don't be hard on me—simplifying and chastening necessity has laid its brutal hand on me and I have had to try to make somehow or other the money I don't make by literature. My books don't sell, and it looks as if my plays might. Therefore I am going with a brazen front to write half a dozen. I have, in fact, already written two others than the one just performed; and the success of the latter pronounced—really *pronounced*—will probably precipitate them. I am glad for all this that you are not here. Literature is out of it. I miss no occasion of talking of you. Colvin I tolerably often see: I expect to do so for instance to-night, at a decidedly too starched dining-club to which we both belong, of which Lord Coleridge is president and too many persons of the type of Sir Theodore Martin are members. Happy islanders— with no Sir Theodore Martin. On Mrs. Sitwell I called the other day, in a charming new habitat: all clean paint and fresh chintz. We always go on at a great rate about you—celebrate rites as faithful as the early Christians in the catacombs....

January 13th.—I met Colvin last night, after writing the above—in the company of Sir James Stephen, Sir Theo. Martin, Sir Douglas Galton, Sir

James Paget, Sir Alfred Lyall, Canon Ainger, and George du Maurier. How this will make you lick your chops over Ori and Rahiro and Tamatia and Taheia—or whatever ces messieurs et ces dames, your present visiting list, are called. He told me of a copious diary-letter he has just got from you, bless you, and we are discussing a day on which I shall soon come to meat or drink with him and listen to the same. Since yesterday I have also read the ballad book—with the admiration that I always feel as a helplessly verseless creature (it's a sentiment worth nothing as a testimony) for all performances in rhyme and metre—especially on the part of producers of fine prose.

January 19th.—I stopped this more than a week ago, and since then I have lacked time to go on with it—having been out of town for several days on a base theatrical errand—to see my tribute to the vulgarest of the muses a little further on its way over the provincial circuit and re-rehearse two or three portions of it that want more effective playing. Thank heaven I shall have now no more direct contact with it till it is produced in London next October.—I broke off in the act of speaking to you about your ballad-book. The production of ringing and lilting verse (by a superior proser) always does *bribe* me a little—and I envy you in that degree yours; but apart from this I grudge your writing the like of these ballads. They show your "cleverness," but they don't show your genius. I should say more if it were not odious to a man of my refinement to write to you—so expectantly far away—in remonstrance. I don't find, either, that the cannibalism, the savagery *se prête*, as it were—one wants either less of it, on the ground of suggestion—or more, on the ground of statement; and one wants more of the high impeccable (as distinguished from the awfully jolly,) on the ground of poetry. Behold I *am* launching across the black seas a page that may turn nasty—but my dear Louis, it's only because I love so your divine prose and want the comfort of it. Things are various because we do 'em. We mustn't do 'em because they're various. The only news in literature here—such is the virtuous vacancy of our consciousness—continues to be the infant monster of a Kipling. I enclose, in this, for your entertainment a few pages I have lately written about him, to serve as the preface to an (of course authorized) American *recueil* of some of his tales. I may add that he has just put forth his longest story yet—a thing in Lippincott which I also send you herewith—which cuts the ground somewhat from under my feet, inasmuch as I find it the most youthfully infirm of his productions (in spite of great "life,") much wanting in composition and in narrative and explicative, or even implicative, art.

Please tell your wife, with my love, that all this is constantly addressed to her also. I try to see you all, in what I fear is your absence of habits, as you live, grouped around what I also fear is in no sense the domestic hearth. Where do you go when you want to be "cosy"?—or what at least do you *do*? You think a little, I hope, of the faithful forsaken on whose powers of evocation, as well as of attachment, you impose such a strain. I wish I could send a man from Fortnum and Mason's out to you with a chunk of *mortadella*. I am trying to do a series of "short things" and will send you the least bad. I mean to write to Lloyd. Please congratulate your heroic mother for me very cordially when she leaps upon your strand, and believe that I hold you all in the tenderest remembrance of yours ever, my dear Louis,

HENRY JAMES.

TO WILLIAM JAMES.

34 De Vere Gardens, W.

Feb. 6th, 1891.

My dear William,

Bear with me that I haven't written to you, since my last, in which I promised you a better immediate sequel, till the receipt of your note of the 21st, this a.m., recalls me to decency. Bear with me indeed, in this and other ways, so long as I am in the fever of dramatic production with which I am, very sanely and practically, trying to make up for my late start and all the years during which I have *not* dramatically produced, and, further, to get well ahead with the "demand" which I—and others for me—judge (still very sanely and sensibly) to be *certain* to be made upon me from the moment I have a *London*, as distinguished from a provincial success. (You can form no idea— outside—of how a provincial success is confined to the provinces.) Now that I have tasted blood, c'est une rage (of determination to *do*, and triumph, on my part,) for I feel at last as if I had found my *real* form, which I am capable of carrying far, and for which the pale little art of fiction, as I have practised it, has been, for me, but a limited and restricted substitute. The strange thing is that I always, universally, knew *this* was my more characteristic form—but was kept away from it by a half-modest, half-exaggerated sense of the difficulty (that is, I mean the practical odiousness) of the conditions. But now that I have accepted them and met them, I see that one isn't at all, needfully, their victim, but is, from the moment one is anything, one's self, worth speaking of, their *master*; and may use them, command them, squeeze them, lift them up and better them. As for the form *itself*, its honour and inspiration are (à défaut d'autres) in its difficulty. If it were easy to write a good play I couldn't and wouldn't think of it; but it is in fact damnably hard (to this truth the paucity of the article—in the English-speaking world—testifies,) and that constitutes a solid respectability—guarantees one's *intellectual* self-respect. At any rate I am working hard and constantly—and am just attacking my 4th!...

No. 4 has a destination which it would be premature to disclose; and, in general, please breathe no word of these confidences, as publicity blows on such matters in an injurious and deflowering way, and interests too great to be hurt are at stake. I make them, the confidences, because it isn't fair to myself not to let you know that I may be absorbed for some months to come—as long as my present fit of the "rage" lasts—to a degree which may be apparent in my correspondence—I mean in its intermittence and in my apparent lapse of attention to, or appreciation of, other things. For instance, I blush to say that I haven't had freedom of mind or cerebral freshness (I find the drama much more *obsédant* than the novel) to tackle—more than dipping in just here and there—your mighty and magnificent book, which requires a stretch of leisure and an absence of "crisis" in one's own egotistical little existence. As this is essentially a year of crisis, or of epoch-making, for me, I shall probably save up the great volumes till I can recline upon roses, the fruits of my production fever, and imbibe them like sips of sherbet, giving meanwhile all my cerebration to the condensation of masterpieces....

Farewell, dear William, and bear with my saw-dust and orange-peel phase till the returns begin to flow in. The only hitch in the prospect is that it takes so long to "realise." *The American*, in the country, played only on Friday nights, with the very low country prices, gives me nothing as yet to speak of—my royalty making only about £5-0-0 for each performance. Later all this may be thoroughly counted upon to be different.

Ever your

HENRY.

TO ROBERT LOUIS STEVENSON.

34 De Vere Gardens, W.

Feb. 18th, 1891.

My dear Louis,

Your letter of December 29th is a most touching appeal; I am glad my own last had been posted to you 2 or 3 weeks before it reached me. Whether mine has—or will have been—guided to your coral strand is a matter as to which your disclosures touching the state of the Samoan post inspire me with the worst apprehensions. At any rate I did despatch you—supposedly via San Francisco—a really pretty long screed about a month ago. I ought to write to you all the while; but though I seem to myself to live with my pen in my hand I achieve nothing capable of connecting me so with glory. I am going to Paris to-morrow morning for a month, but I have vowed that I will miss my train sooner than depart without scrawling you and your wife a few words to-night. I shall probably see little or nothing there that will interest you much (or even interest myself hugely—) but having neither a yacht, an island, an heroic nature, a gallant wife, mother and son, nor a sea-stomach, I have to seek adventure in the humblest forms. In writing the other day I told you more or less what I was doing—*am* doing—in these elderly days; and the same general description will serve. I am doing what I can to launch myself in the dramatic direction—and the strange part of the matter is that

I am doing it more or less seriously, as if we *had* the Scène Anglaise which we haven't. And I secretly dream of supplying the vile want? Pas même—and my zeal in the affair is only matched by my indifference. What is serious in it is that having begun to work in this sense some months ago, to give my little ones bread—I find the *form* opens out before me as if there were a kingdom to conquer—a kingdom forsooth of ignorant brutes of managers and dense cabotins of actors. All the same, I feel as if I had at last *found* my form—my real one—that for which pale fiction is an ineffectual substitute. God grant this unholy truth may not abide with me more than two or three years—time to dig out eight or ten rounded masterpieces and make withal enough money to enable me to retire in peace and plenty for the unmolested business of a *little* supreme writing, as distinguished from gouging—which is the Form above-mentioned. Your loneliness and your foodlessness, my dear Louis, bring tears to my eyes. If there were only a parcels' post to Samoa I would set Fortnum and Mason to work at you at this end of the line. But if they intercept the hieroglyphics at Sydney, what would they do to the sausage? Surely there is some cure for your emptiness; if nothing else, why not coming away? Don't eat up Mrs. Louis, whatever you do. You are precious to literature—but she is precious to the affections, which are larger, yet in a still worse way.... I shall certainly do my utmost to get to Egypt to see you, if, as is hinted to me by dear Colvin, you turn up there after the fitful fever of Samoa. Your being there would give me wings—especially if plays should give me gold. This is an exquisitely blissful dream. Don't fail to do your part of it. I almost joy in your lack of the *Tragic Muse*; as proving to me, I mean, that you are curious enough to have missed it. Nevertheless I have just posted to you, registered, the first copy I have received of the 1 vol. edition; but this moment out. I wanted to send you the three volumes by Lloyd, but he seemed clear you would have received it, and I didn't insist, as I knew he was charged with innumerable parcels and bales. I will presently send another *Muse*, and one, at least, must reach you.... Colvin is really better, I think—if any one can be better who is so absolutely good. I hope to God my last long letter will have reached you. I promise to write soon again. I enfold you all in my sympathy and am ever your faithfullest

HENRY JAMES.

TO CHARLES ELIOT NORTON.

34 De Vere Gardens, W.

Aug. 28th, 1891.

My dear Charles,

It is only the conspiracy of hindrances so perpetually characteristic of life in this place, even when it is theoretically not alive, as in the mid-August, that has stayed my hand, for days past, when it has most longed to write to you. Dear Lowell's death—the words are almost as difficult as they are odious to write—has made me think almost as much of you as of him. I imagine that you are the person in the world to whom it makes the most complete and constant difference that he is no longer here; just as you must have been the one most closely associated with the too vain watching of his last struggle with the monster. It is a dim satisfaction to me, therefore, to say to you how fond I was of him and how I shall miss him and miss him and miss him. During these last strange English years of his life (it would take me long to tell you why I call them strange,) I had seen a great deal of him, and all with the effect of confirming my affection for him. London is bestrewn, to my sense, with reminders of his happy career here, and his company and his talk. He was kind and delightful and gratifying to me, and all sorts of occasions in which he will ever be vivid swarm before me as I think of him.... Strange was his double existence—the American and the English sides of his medal, which had yet so much in common. That is, I don't know how English he was at home, but he was conspicuously American here. However, I am not trying to characterize him, to you least of all who had known him well so much longer and seen all, or most, of the chapters of his history; but only letting you see how much I wish we might talk of him together. Some day we will, though it's a date that seems unfixable now. I am taking for granted ... that you inherit the greatest of literary responsibilities to his memory. I think of this as a very high interest, but also a very arduous labour. It's a blessing, however, to feel that such an office is in such hands as yours. The posthumous vulgarities of our day add another grimness to death. Here again is another matter as to which I really miss not having the opportunity to talk with you. This is a brief communication, my dear Charles, for I am literally catching a train. I go down to the Isle of Wight half an hour hence....

TO EDMUND GOSSE.

This refers to the recent production of *The American* in London.

34 De Vere Gardens, W.

October 2nd [1891].

My dear Gosse,

Your good and charming letter should have been answered on the spot—but my days are abnormal and perspective and relation are blurred. I shall come to see you the moment you return, and then I shall be able to tell you more in five minutes than in fifteen of such hurried scrawls as this. Meanwhile many thanks for your sympathy and curiosity and suspense—*all* thanks, indeed—and, in return, all eagerness for your rentrée here. My own suspense has been and still is great—though the voices of the air, rightly heard, seem to whisper *prosperity*. The papers have been on the whole quite awful—but the audiences are altogether different. The only thing is that these first three or four weeks *must* be up-hill: London is still empty, the whole enterprise is wholly new—the elements must assemble. The strain, the anxiety, the peculiar form and colour of such an ordeal (not to be divined the least in advance) have sickened me *to death*—but I am getting better. I forecast nothing, however—I only wait. Come back and wait with me—it will be easier. Your picture of your existence and circumstance is like the flicker of the open door of heaven to those recumbent in the purgatory of yours not *yet* damned—ah no!—

HENRY JAMES.

TO MRS. MAHLON SANDS.

Hôtel de l'Europe,

Dresden.

Dec. 12th [1891].

Dear Mrs. Sands,

Just a word—in answer to your note of sympathy—to say that I am working through my dreary errand and service here as smoothly as three stricken women—a mother and two sisters—permit. They are however very temperate and discreet—and one of the sisters a little person of extraordinary capacity—who will float them all successfully home. Wolcott Balestier, the young American friend beside whose grave I stood with but three or four others here on Thursday, was a very remarkable creature who had been living in London for some three years—he had an intimate *business*-relation with literature and was on the way to have a really artistic and creative one. He had made himself a peculiar international place—which it would take long to describe, and was full of capacities, possibilities and really big inventions and ideas. He had rendered me admirable services, become in a manner a part of my life, and I was exceedingly attached to him. And now, at 30, he dies— in a week—in a far-away German hospital—his mother and sisters were in Paris—of a damnable vicious typhoid, contracted in his London office, the "picturesqueness" of which he loved, as it was in Dean's Yard, Westminster, just under the Abbey towers, and in a corner like that of a peaceful Cathedral close. Many things, many enterprises, interests, visions, originalities perish with him. Oh, the "ironies of fate," the ugly tricks, the hideous practical jokes of life! I start for London some time next week and shall very soon come and see you. I hope all is well with you.

Yours always,

HENRY JAMES.

TO MRS. HUMPHRY WARD.

The following was written a few days after the death of Miss Alice James.

34 De Vere Gardens, W.

March 10th [1892].

Dear Mrs. Ward,

Many, many thanks for your friendly remembrance of me—the flowers are full of spring and life and the universe, as it were, and, besides this, are very close and charming company to me as I sit scribbling—writing many notes among other things—in still, indoor days that are grateful to me. You were one of the very few persons in England who had seen my sister even a little—and I am very glad of that. She was a rare and remarkable being, and her death makes a great difference in my existence. But for her it is only blessed. I hope you are happy in the good reasons you have for being so—if one *is* happy strictly (certainly one isn't the reverse) for "reasons."

Believe me yours always,

HENRY JAMES.

TO ROBERT LOUIS STEVENSON.

Stevenson, it will be recalled, dedicated *Across the Plains* to M. Paul Bourget, as an expression of his delight in that author's *Sensations d'Italie*, sent him by H. J. Mr. Kipling did not, as it turned out, pay his projected visit to Samoa, referred to in this letter.

34 De Vere Gardens, W.

March 19th, 1892.

My dear Louis,

I send you to-day by book-post, registered, a little volume of tales which I lately put forth—most of which however you may have seen in magazines. Please accept at any rate the modest offering. Accept, too, my thanks for your sweet and dateless letter which I received a month ago—the one in which you speak with such charming appreciation and felicity of Paul Bourget. I echo your admiration—I think the Italian book one of the most exquisite things of our time. I am in only very occasional correspondence with him—and have not written since I heard from you; but I shall have an early chance, now probably, to repeat your words to him, and they will touch him in a tender place. He is living much, now, in Italy, and I may go there for May or June—though indeed I fear it is little probable. Colvin tells me of the volume of some of your *inédites* beauties that is on the point of appearing, and the news is a bright spot in a vulgar world. The vulgarity of literature in these islands at the present time is not to be said, and I shall clutch at you as one turns one's ear to music in the clatter of the market-place. Yet, paradoxical as it may appear, oh Louis, I have still had the refinement not to read the *Wrecker* in the periodical page. This is an enlightened and judicious heroism, and I do as I would be done by. Trust me, however, to taste you in long draughts as soon as I can hold the book. Then will I write to you again. You tell me nothing of yourself—so I have nothing to take up or take hold of, save indeed the cherished superstition that you enjoy some measure of health and cheer. You are, however, too far away for my imagination, and were it not for dear Colvin's friendly magic, which puts in a pin here and there, I shouldn't be able to catch and arrest at all the opaline iridescence of your legend. Yet even when he speaks of intending wars and the clash of arms, it all passes over me like an old-time song. You see how much I need you close at hand to stand successfully on the tiptoe of emulation. You fatigue, in short, my credulity, though not my affection. We lately clubbed together, all, to despatch to you an eye-witness in the person of the genius or the *genus*, in himself, Rudyard, for the concussion of whose extraordinary personality with your own we are beginning soon to strain the listening ear. We devoutly hope that this time he will really be washed upon your shore. With him goes a new little wife—whose brother—Wolcott Balestier, lately dead, in much youthful promise and performance (I don't allude, in saying that, especially to the literary part of it,) was a very valued young friend of mine.... The main thing that has lately happened to myself is the death of my dear sister a fortnight ago—after years of suffering, which, however, had not made her any less rare and remarkable a person or diminished the effect of the event (when it should occur) in making an extreme difference in my life. Of my occupation what shall I tell you? I have of late years left London less and less—but I am thinking sooner or later (in a near present) of making a long foreign, though not distant, absence. I am busy with the *short*—I have forsworn the long. I hammer at the horrid little theatrical problem, with delays and intermissions, but, horrible to relate, no failure of purpose. I shall soon publish another small story-book which I will incontinently send you. I have done many brief fictions within the last year.... The good little Thomas Hardy has scored a great success with *Tess of the d'Urbervilles*, which is chock-full of faults and falsity and yet has a singular beauty and charm....

What we most talk of here, however, is the day when it may be believed that you will come to meet us on some attainable southern shore. We will *all* go to the Mediterranean for you—let that not nail you to Samoa. I send every greeting to your play-fellows—your fellow-phantoms. The wife-phantom knows my sentiments. The ghost of a mother has my heartiest regard. The long Lloyd-spectre laughs an eerie laugh, doubtless, at my [word illegible] embrace. Yet I feel, my dear Louis, that I *do* hold you just long enough to press you to the heart of your very faithful old friend,

HENRY JAMES.

TO ROBERT LOUIS STEVENSON.

34 De Vere Gardens, W.

April 15th, 1892.

My dear Louis,

I send you by this post the magnificent Mémoires de Marbot, which should have gone to you sooner by my hand if I had sooner read them and sooner, thereby, grasped the idea of how much they would probably beguile for you the shimmering tropical noon. The three volumes go to you in three separate registered book-post parcels and all my prayers for an escape from the queer perils of the way attend and hover about them. Some people, I believe, consider this fascinating warrior a bien-conditionné Munchausen—but perish the injurious thought. Me he not only charms but convinces. I can't manage a letter, my dear Louis, to-day—I wrote you a longish one, via San Francisco (like this,) just about a month ago. But I mustn't fail to tell you that I have just read the last page of the sweet collection of some of your happiest lucubrations put forth by the care of dear Colvin. They make a most desirable, and moreover a very honourable, volume. It was indispensable to bring them together and they altogether justify it. The first one, and the Lantern-Bearers and two last, are of course the best—these last are all made up of high and admirable pages and do you the greatest credit. You have never felt, thought, said, more finely and happily than in many a passage here, and are in them altogether at your best. I don't see reviews or meet newspapers now (beside which the work is scarcely in the market,) so I don't know what fortune the book encounters—but it is enough for me—I admit it can hardly be enough for you—that I love it. I pant for the completion of The Wrecker—of which Colvin unwove the other night, to my rapturous ear, the weird and wondrous tangle. I hope I don't give him away if I tell you he even read me a very interesting letter from you—though studded with critical stardust in which I a little lost my way—telling of a project of a dashing roman de mœurs all about a wicked woman. For this you may imagine how I yearn—though not to the point of wanting it before the sequel of Kidnapped. For God's sake let me have them both. I marvel at the liberality of your production and rejoice in this high meridian of your genius. I leave London presently for 3 or 4 months—I wish it were with everything required for leaping on your strand. Sometimes I think I have got through the worst of missing you and then I find I haven't. I pine for you as I pen these words, for I am more and more companionless in my old age—more and more shut up to the solitude inevitably the portion, in these islands, of him who would really try, even in so small a way as mine, to *do* it. I'm often on the point of taking the train down to Skerryvore, to serenade your ghosts, get them to throw a fellow a word. Consider this, at any rate, a plaintive invocation. Again, again I greet your wife, that lady of the closed lips, and I am yours, my dear Louis, and Lloyd's and your mother's undiscourageably,

HENRY JAMES.

TO THE COUNTESS OF JERSEY.

The "little story" is *The Lesson of the Master*, the opening scenes of which take place at "Summersoft." Lord Jersey was at this time Governor of New South Wales.

Hôtel de Sienne, Siena.

June 11th [1892].

Dear Lady Jersey,

Your kind letter finds me in a foreign land—the land in the world, I suppose, least like New South Wales—and gives me very great pleasure. It is charming to hear your voice so distinctly round so many corners of the globe. Yes, "Summersoft" *did* venture in a timorous and hesitating manner to be an affectionate and yet respectful reminiscence of Osterley the exquisite—of whose folded and deserted charms I can't bear to think. But I beg you to believe—as indeed you will have perceived if you were so good as to look at the little story—that the attempted resemblance was only a matter of the dear old cubic sofa-cushions and objects of the same delightful order, and not of the human furniture of the house. I take the liberty of being, in your absence, so homesick for Osterley that I can scarcely conceive of the pangs by which you and your children and Lord Jersey—with your much greater right to indulge in them—must sometimes be visited. I am delighted, however, to gather from your letter that you have occupations and interests which drop a kindly veil over that dreamland. It must indeed, I can imagine, be a satisfaction to be really lending a hand in such a great young growing world—doing something in it and with it and for it. May the sense of all this make the years roll smoothly—till they roll you back into our ken.... Please give my very friendliest remembrance to Lord Jersey—to whom I wish—as to all of you—and indeed to myself, that you may serve your term with an appearance of rapidity. And please believe, dear Lady Jersey, that when it is over, no one will more heartily rejoice than yours most faithfully,

HENRY JAMES.

TO CHARLES ELIOT NORTON.

Hôtel de Sienne, Siena.

July 4th, 1892.

My dear Charles,

Too long have I owed you a letter and too many times have your generosities made me blush for my silence. I have received beautiful books from you and they have given me almost more pleasure as signs of your remembrance than as symbols of your wisdom and worth. The Purgatorio reached me just before I came abroad—or a short time—and I was delighted to know that you continue to find time and strength for labours so various and so arduous. Great glory is yours—for making something else come out of America than railway-smashes and young ladies for lords. During a singularly charming month that I have been spending in this most loveable old city I have often thought of you and wished I had a small fraction of your power to put the soul of history into Italian things. But I believe I shouldn't love Siena any better even if I knew it better. I am very happy indeed to feel that—as I grow older—many things come and go, but Italy remains. I have been here many times—regularly every year or almost, for many years now, but the spell, the charm, the magic is still in the air. I always try, between May and August, to give London a wide berth, and I find these parts far and away most pleasant when the summer has begun and the barbarians have fled. As one stays and stays on here—I mean on *this* spot—one feels how untouched Siena really is by the modern hand. Yesterday was the Palio of the ten contrade, and though I believe it is not so intense a festival as the second one—of Aug. 15th (you have probably—or certainly—seen them both)—it was a most curious and characteristic (of an uninterrupted tradition) spectacle. The Marchese Chigi asked me and a couple of friends—or rather asked *them*, and me with them—to see it from the balcony of his extraordinarily fine old palace, where by the way he has a large collection of Etruscan and Tarentine treasures—a collection to break the heart of envy. My friends were Paul Bourget, the

French essayist and novelist (some of whose work you probably know,) and his very remarkably charming, cultivated and interesting young wife. They have been living in Italy these two years—ever since their marriage, and I have been living much *with* them here. Bourget is a very interesting mind—and figure altogether—and the first—easily, to my sense—of all the talkers I have ever encountered. But it would take me much too far to *begin* to give you a portrait of such a complicated cosmopolitan Frenchman as he! But they departed, alas, this morning, for the Piedmontese Alps, and I take my way, in a couple of hours, to Venice, where I spend but a few days—with perhaps a few more at Asolo—before joining my brother William and his wife for a month in Switzerland. After that I expect to return to London for the last of the summer and the early autumn—the season I prefer there above all others. But before I do this I wish I could talk to you more about this sweet old Siena. I have been talking for a month about it with Bourget—but how much better it would have been for both of us if you could have broken in and taken up the tale! But you did, sometimes, very happily—for Mme. Paul knows you by heart (she is the Madonna of cosmopolitan culture) and cites you with great effect. Have you read P. B.'s *Sensations d'Italie*? If you haven't, do—it is one of the most exquisite of books. Have you read any of his novels? If you haven't, *don't*, though they have remarkable parts. Make an exception, however, for *Terre Promise*, which is to appear a few months hence, and which I have been reading in proof, here—if on trial, indeed, you find you can stand so suffocating an analysis. It is perhaps "psychology" gone mad—but it is an extraordinary production. A fortnight ago, on a singularly lovely Sunday, we drove to San Gimignano and back. I had never been there before, and the whole day was a delight. There are of course four Americans living at San G.—one of whom proved afterwards to have been an American "lady-newspaper-correspondent" furious at having missed two such birds as Bourget and me—whom a single stone from that rugged old quarry would have brought down. But she didn't know us until we had departed and we fortunately didn't suspect her till a suppliant card reached us two days later at Siena. We were in the hands of the good old Canonico—the proposito, as they call him—and he put us gently through. You remember well enough of course—though to such a far-away world your Siena summer must seem to belong—the rich loveliness, at this moment, of this exquisite old Tuscany. One can't say enough about it, and the way the great sea of growing things—the corn and the vines and the olives—breaks in green surges at the very foot of the old golden-brown ramparts, is one of the most enchanting features of Siena. There is still never a suburb to speak of save in the quarter of the railway-station, and everywhere you look out of back-windows and back-doors and off terraces and over parapets straight down into the golden grain and the tangled poderi. Every evening we have gone to walk in the Lizza and hang over the bastions of the Castello; where the near views and the far, and the late afternoons and the sunsets and the mountains have made us say again and again that we could never, never go away. But we are coming back, and I greatly wish *you* were. We went the other day to the archivio, which I had never seen before, and where I was amazed and fascinated. (It is a great luxury to be in Italy with a French celebrity—he is so tremendously known and well treated, as the "likes" of *us* can never be, and one comes in for some of his privileges.) You of course probably know, however, what the fullness, detail, continuity and curiosity of the records of this place are—filling with their visible, palpable medievalism the great upper chamber of Pal. Piccolomini.

Basta—I have my trunk to pack and my reckoning to pay. I am very glad to have shaken hands with you before I go. I saw dear Burne-Jones tolerably often this spring—often unwell, but almost always stippling away. He is the most loveable of men and the most disinterested of artists, but sometimes I wish that he set himself a different order of tasks. *Painting*—as I feel it most—it is true I have ceased to feel it very much—is, with him, more and more "out of it." There remains, however, a beautiful poetry.... I want to ask you 20 questions about [Lowell's] papers—but I feel it isn't fair—and I must wait and see. I hope this work—and your masses of other work—don't take all your holiday.... I shall send this to Ashfield, and if you are there will you give, for me, a very cordial greeting to that mythical man George Curtis? I embrace all your house and am, my dear Charles, very affectionately yours,

HENRY JAMES.

TO W. D. HOWELLS.

34 De Vere Gardens, W.

Jan. 29th [1893].

My dear Howells,

Two beneficent notes have I had from you since last I wrote you a word: one in regard to looking, effectively, after some *Cosmopolitan* business in the autumn; the other a heavenly remark or two (still further sublimated by Mildred's lovely photograph) in lately forwarding me—with a courtesy worthy of a better cause—a particularly shameless autograph-seeker's letter. For such and all of these good gifts I am more thankful than the hurrying, days have left me much of a chance to tell you. Most especially am I grateful for the portrait of the beautiful, beautiful maiden. Please thank her from me, if not for sending it, at least for so felicitously sitting for it. It makes me jump the torrent of the years and reconstruct from her fine features the mythological past—a still tenderer youth than her present youth. (I ought to be able to mean my *own*; but I can't manage it—her profile won't help me to *that*.) I envy you and your wife her company and I rejoice for you in her presence. I rejoice for myself, my dear Howells, about your so delicate words to me in regard to a bit of recent work. They go to my heart—they go perhaps still straighter to my head! I am so utterly lonely here—on the "literary plane"—that it is the strangest as well as the sweetest sensation to be conscious in the boundless void—the dim desert sands—of any human approach at all or any kindly speech. Therefore please be very affectionately thanked.—All this while I never see anything that you yourself have lately flowered with—I mean the volumes that you freehandedly scatter. I console myself with believing that one or two of your last serial fictions are not volumes yet. Please hold them not back from soon becoming so. I see you are drawing a longish bow in the *Cosmopolitan*—but I only read you when I can sit down to a continuous feast and all the courses. You asked me in your penultimate—I am talking now of your early-in-the-winter letter—if I should object to being made a feature of your composed reminiscences. To which I reply that I only wish that I could enrich them better. I won't pretend that I like being written about—the sight of my own name on a printed page makes me as ill (and the sensibility increases strangely with time) as that of one of my creations makes me well. I have a morbid passion for personal privacy and a standing quarrel with the blundering publicities of the age. I wince even at eulogy, and I wither (for exactly 2 minutes and 1/2) at any qualification of adulation. But on the other hand I like, I love, to be remembered by you and I surrender myself to your discretion. I hope your winter, and Mrs. Howells' and the fairest of daughters's, is rich and full and sane. How you must miss the Boy. I go abroad soon and hope to see him in Paris. When do you do the same? Yours always, my dear Howells,

HENRY JAMES.

TO ROBERT LOUIS STEVENSON.

34 De Vere Gardens, W.

Feb. 17th, 1893.

My dear distant Louis,

The charmingest thing that had happened to me for a year was the advent of your reassuring note of Dec. 5th (not 189*1*—my dear time-deluded islander: it is enviable to see you so luxuriously "out." When you indulge in the eccentricity of a date you make it eccentric indeed.) I call your good letter reassuring simply on the general ground of its making you credible for an hour. You are otherwise wholly of the stuff that dreams are made of. I think this is why I don't keep writing to you, don't talk to you, as it were, in my sleep. Please don't think I forget you or am indifferent to anything that concerns you. The mere thought of you is better company than almost any that is tangible to me here, and London is more peopled to me by your living in Samoa than by the residence of almost anybody else in Kensington or Chelsea. I fix my curiosity on you all the while and try to understand your politics and your perils and your public life. If in these efforts I make a poor figure it is only because you are so wantonly away. Then I think I envy you too much—your climate, your thrill of life, your magnificent facility. You judge well that I have far too little of this last—though you *can't* judge how much more and more difficult I find it every day to write. None the less I am presently putting forth, almost with exact simultaneity, three little (distinct) books—2 volumes of penny fiction and one of little essays, all material gathered, no doubt, from sources in which you may already have encountered some of it. However this may be, the matter shall again be (D.V.) deposited on your coral strand. Most refreshing, even while not wholly convincing, was the cool trade-wind (is the trade-wind cool?) of your criticism of some of *ces messieurs*. I grant you Hardy with all my heart.... I am meek and ashamed where the public clatter is deafening—so I bowed my head and let "Tess of the D.'s" pass. But oh yes, dear Louis, she is vile. The pretence of "sexuality" is only equalled by the absence of it, and the abomination of the language by the author's reputation for style. There are indeed some pretty smells and sights and sounds. But you have better ones in Polynesia. On the other hand I can't go with you three yards in your toleration either of —— or of ——. Let me add that I can't read them, so I don't know anything about them. All the same I make no bones to pronounce them shameless *industriels* and their works only glories of Birmingham. You will have gathered that I delight in your year of literary prowess. None the less I haven't read a word of you since the brave and beautiful *Wrecker*. I won't *touch* you till I can feel that I embrace you in the embracing cover. So it is that I languish till the things now announced appear. Colvin makes me impatient for *David Balfour*—but doesn't yet stay my stomach with the *Beach of Falesà*.... Mrs. Sitwell *me fait part* of every savoury scrap she gets from you. I know what you all magnificently eat, and what dear Mrs. Louis splendidly (but not somewhat transparently—no?) wears. Please assure that intensely-remembered lady of my dumb fidelity. I am told your mother nears our shores and I promise myself joy on seeing her and pumping her. I don't know, however, alas, how long this ceremony may be delayed, as I go to Italy, for all the blessed spring, next week. I have been in London without an hour's absence since the middle of Aug. last. I hear you utter some island objurgation, and go splashing, to banish the stuffy image, into the sapphire sea. Is it all a fable that you will come some month to the Mediterranean? I would go to the Pillars of Hercules to greet you. Give my love to the lusty and literary Lloyd. I am very glad to observe him spreading his wings. There is absolutely nothing to send you. The Muses are dumb, and in France as well. Of Bourget's big 7 franc *Cosmopolis* I have, alas, purchased three copies—and given them away; but even if I were to send you one you would find it too round and round the subject—which heaven knows it is—for your taste. I will try and despatch you the charming little "Etui de Nacre" of Anatole France—a real master. Vale—age. Yours, my dear Louis, in a kind of hopeful despair and a clinging alienation,

HENRY JAMES.

TO MRS. EDMUND GOSSE.

Hôtel Westminster, Paris.

March 21st [1893].

Dear Mrs. Gosse,

Many thanks for your better news—and especially for the good news that Gosse is coming to Paris. I shall be very glad to see him and shall rejoice to take him gently by that injured—but I trust soon to be reanimated—member. Please express this to him, with all my sympathy and impatience. Won't he—or won't you (though indeed I shall cull the precious date from Harland,) give me a hint, in advance of the particular moment at which one may look for him? Please tell him confidently to expect that Paris will create within him afresh all the finest pulses of life. It is mild, sunny, splendid—blond and fair, all in order for his approach. I allude of course to the specious allurements of its exterior. The state is odorously rotten—but everything else is charming. And then it's such a blessing, after long grief and pain, to find the arms of a *climate* around us once again! Hasten, my dear Edmund, to be healed.

Thank heaven, my allusion to my own manual distress was mainly a florid figure. My hand *is* infirm—but I am not yet thinking of the knife. Mille choses to the Terrace.

Yours and Gosse's always,

HENRY JAMES.

TO EDMUND GOSSE.

The seductive "Queen of the Golconda," and of the Boulevard St. Michel, appears in Mr. Gosse's anecdote of Paul Verlaine (*French Profiles*.) The passage of Loti's *Matelot*, to which H. J. refers, is the following: "Donc, ils en venaient à s'aimer d'une également pure tendresse, tous les deux. Elle, ignorante des choses d'amour et lisant chaque soir sa bible; elle, destinée à rester inutilement fraîche et jeune encore pendant quelques printemps pâles comme celui-ci, puis à vieillir et se faner dans l'enserrement monotone de ces mêmes rues et de ces mêmes murs. Lui, gâté déjà par les baisers et les étreintes, ayant le monde pour habitation changeante, appelé à partir, peut-être demain, pour ne revenir jamais et laisser son corps aux mers lointaines."

Hôtel Westminster, Paris.

Monday [May 1st, 1893].

My dear Gosse,

I have delayed too long to thank you for your genial last: which please attribute to the misery of my Boulevard-baffled aspirations. Paris n'est plus possible—from any point of view—and I leave it tomorrow or next day, when my address will become: *Hotel National, Lucerne.* I join my brother there for a short time. This place continues to *rengorger* with sunshine and sauces, not to mention other appeals to the senses and pitfalls to the pocket. I am not alluding in particular to the Queen of Golconda! I have read *Matelot* more or less over again; for the extreme penury of the *idea* in Loti, and the almost puerile thinness of this particular donnée, wean me not a jot from the irresistible charm the rascal's very limitations have for me. I drink him down as he *is*—like a philtre or a *baiser*, and the coloration of his *moindre mots* has a peculiar magic for me. Read *aloud* to yourself the passage ending section XXXV—the upper part of page 165, and perhaps you will find in it something of the same strange *eloquence* of suggestion and rhythm as I do: which is what literature gives when it is most exquisite and which constitutes its sovereign value and its resistance to devouring time. And yet what *niaiseries*! Paris continues gorgeous and rainless, but less torrid. I have become inured to fear as careless of penalties. There are no new books but old papiers de famille et d'arrière-boutique dished up. Poor Harland came and spent 2 or 3 hours with me the other afternoon—at a café-front and on chairs in the Champs-Elysées. He looked better than the time previous, but not well; and I am afraid things are not too well *with* him. One would like to help him—and I try to—in talk; but he is not too helpable, for there is a chasm too deep to bridge, I fear, in the pitfall of his literary longings unaccompanied by the *faculty*. Apropos of such things I am very glad to see *your* faculty is reflowering. I shall return to England for the volume. Are you writing about Symonds? Vale—especially in the manual part. And valeat your *dame compagne*.

Yours, my dear Gosse, always,

HENRY JAMES.

TO ROBERT LOUIS STEVENSON.

Stevenson, writing to H. J. from Vailima, June 17, 1893, announced that he was sending a photograph of his wife. "It reminds me of a friend of my grandmother's who used to say when talking to younger women, 'Aweel, when I was young, I wasnae just exactly what ye wad call *bonny*, but I was pale, penetratin', and interestin'.'" (*Letters to his Family and Friends.*)

34 De Vere Gardens, W.

August 5th, 1893.

My dear Louis,

I have a most charming and interesting letter, and a photographic representation of your fine head which I cannot so unrestrictedly commend, to thank you for. The portrait has its points as a memento, but they are not fine points as a likeness. I remember you, I think of you, I evoke you, much more plastically. But it was none the less liberal and faithful of you to include me in the list of fond recipients. Your letter contained all sorts of good things, but best of all the happy news of your wife's better condition. I rejoice in that almost obstreperously and beg you to tell her so with my love. The Sydney photograph that you kindly announce (of her) hasn't come, but I impatiently desire it. Meanwhile its place is gracefully occupied by your delightful anecdote of your mother's retrospective Scotch friend—the pale, penetratin' and interestin' one. Perhaps you will permit me to say that it is exquisitely Scotch; at any rate it moves altogether in the highest walks of anecdote.

I get, habitually, the sympathetic infection, from Colvin, of so much general uneasiness and even alarm about you, that it is reassuring to find you apparently incommoded by nothing worse than the privation of liquor and tobacco. "Nothing worse?" I hear you echo, while you ask to what more refined savagery of torture I can imagine you subjected. You would rather perhaps—and small blame to you—perish by the sword than by famine. But you won't perish, my dear Louis, and I am here to tell you so. *I* should have perished—long ago—if it were mortal. No liquor—to speak of—passes my wasted lips, and yet they are capable of the hypocrisy of the sigh of resignation. I am very, very sorry for you—for I remember the genial tray which in the far-off, fabulous time used to be placed, as the evening waxed, under the social lamp at Skerryvore. The evenings wax at Vailima, but the tray, I gather, has waned. May this heavy trial be lightened, and, as you missionaries say, be even blessed to you. It wounds, I repeat, but it doesn't kill—more's the pity. The tobacco's another question. I have smoked a cigarette—at Skerryvore; and I shall probably smoke one again. But I don't look forward to it. However, you will think me objectionably destitute of temperament. What depresses me much more is the sad sense that you receive scarcely anything I send you. This, however, doesn't deter me from posting you to-day, registered, via San Francisco (it is post-day,) a volume of thin trifles lately put forth by me and entitled *Essays in London and Elsewhere*. It contains some pretty writing—not addressed to the fishes. My last letter to you, to which yours of June 17th [was a reply]—the only dated one, dear Louis, I ever got from you!—was intended to accompany two other volumes of mine, which were despatched to you, registered, via San F., at the same moment (*The Real Thing* and *The*

Private Life.) Yet neither of these works, evidently, had reached you when you ask me not to send you the former (though my letter mentioned that it had started,) as you had ordered it. It is all a mystery which the fishes only will have sounded. I also post to you herewith Paul Bourget's last little tale (*Un Scruple*,) as to which nothing will induce me to utter the faintest rudiments of an opinion. It is full of talent (I don't call *that* a rudiment,) but the French are passing strange. I am very glad to be able to send you herewith enclosed a *petit mot* from the said Paul Bourget, in response to your sense of outrage at his too-continuous silence.... His intentions, I can answer for it, had been the best; but he leads so migratory a life that I don't see how *any* intention can ever well fructify. He has spent the winter in the Holy Land and jumps thence in three weeks (from Beyrout) to his queer American expedition. A year ago—more—he earnestly asked me (at Siena) for your address. I as eagerly gave it to him—par écrit—but the acknowledgment that he was then full of the desire to make to you succumbed to complex frustrations. Now that, at last, here it is, I wish you to be able to *read* it! But you won't. My hand is the hand of Apollo to it.

I have been at the sea-side for six weeks, and am back in the empty town mainly because it is empty. *My* sea-side is the sordid sands of Ramsgate—I see your coral-reefs blush pink at the vulgarity of the name. The place has for me an unutterable advantage (in the press of working-weeks) which the beach of Falesà would, fortunately, *not* have—that of being full of every one I don't know. The beach of Falesà would enthrall but sterilize me—I mean the social muse would disjoint the classic nose of the other. You will certainly think me barren enough as I am. I am really less desiccated than I seem, however, for I am working with patient subterraneity at a trade which it is dishonour enough to practise, without talking about it: a trade supremely dangerous and heroically difficult—*that* credit at least belongs to it. The case is simplified for me by the direst necessity: the *book*, as my limitations compel me to produce it, doesn't bring me in a penny. Tell it not in Samoa—or at least not in Tahiti; but I *don't* sell ten copies!—and neither editors nor publishers will have anything whatever to say to me. But I never mention it—nearer home. "Politics," dear politician—I rejoice that you are getting over them. When you say that you always "believed" them beastly I am tempted to become superior and say that I always knew them so. At least I don't see how one can have glanced, however cursorily, at the contemporary newspapers (I mean the journal of one's whole time,) and had any doubt of it. The morals, the manners, the materials of all those gentlemen are writ there more large than any record is elsewhere writ, and the impudence of their airs and pretensions in the presence of it revolts even the meekness of a spirit as resigned to everything as mine. The sordid fight in the House of Commons the other night seemed to me only a momentary intermission of hypocrisy. The hypocrisy comes back with the pretended confusion over it. The Lives of the Stevensons (with every respect to them) isn't what I want you most to write, but I would rather you should publish ten volumes of them than another letter to the *Times*. Meanwhile I am languishing for *Catriona*—and the weeks follow and I must live without you. It isn't life. But I am still amicably yours and your wife's and the insidious Lloyd's,

HENRY JAMES.

TO ROBERT LOUIS STEVENSON.

34 De Vere Gardens, W.

October 21st [1893.]

My dear Louis,

The postal guide tells me, disobligingly, that there is no mail to you via San Francisco this month and that I must confide my few lines to the precarious and perfidious Hamburg. I do so, then, for the plain reason that I can no longer repress the enthusiasm that has surged within me ever since I read *Catriona*. I missed, just after doing so, last month's post, and I was infinitely vexed that it should not have conveyed to you the freshness of my rapture. For the said *Catriona* so reeks and hums with genius that there is no refuge for the desperate reader but in straightforward prostration. I'm not sure that it's magnanimous of you to succeed so inconsiderately— there is a modesty in easy triumph which your flushed muse perhaps a little neglects.—But forgive that lumbering image—I won't attempt to carry it out. Let me only say that I don't despatch these ineffectual words on their too watery way to do anything but thank you for an exquisite pleasure. I hold that when a book has the high beauty of that one there's a poor indelicacy in what simple folk call criticism. The work lives by so absolute a law that it's grotesque to prattle about what *might* have been! I shall express to you the one point in which my sense was conscious of an unsatisfied desire, but only after saying first how rare an achievement I think the whole personality and tone of David and with how supremely happy a hand you have coloured the palpable women. They are quite too lovely and everyone is running after them. In David not an error, not a false note ever; he is all of an exasperating truth and rightness. The one thing I miss in the book is the note of *visibility*—it subjects my visual sense, my *seeing* imagination, to an almost painful underfeeding. The *hearing* imagination, as it were, is nourished like an alderman, and the loud audibility seems a slight the more on the baffled lust of the eyes—so that I seem to myself (I am speaking of course only from the point of view of the way, as I read, *my* impression longs to complete itself) in the presence of voices in the darkness—voices the more distinct and vivid, the more brave and sonorous, as voices always are—but also the more tormenting and confounding—by reason of these bandaged eyes. I utter a pleading moan when you, e.g., transport your characters, toward the end, in a line or two from Leyden to Dunkirk without the glint of a hint of all the ambient picture of the 18th century road. However, stick to your own system of evocation so long as what you positively achieve is so big. Life and letters and art all take joy in you.

I am rejoiced to hear that your wife is less disturbed in health and that your anxieties are somewhat appeased. I don't know how sufficiently to renew, to both of you, the assurance of all my friendliest sympathy. You live in conditions so unimaginable and to the tune of experience so great and so strange that you must forgive me if I am altogether out of step with your events. I know you're surrounded with the din of battle, and yet the beauty you produce has the Goethean calm, even like the beauty distilled at Weimar when the smoke was over Jena. Let me touch you at least on your bookish side and the others may bristle with heroics. I pray you be made accessible some day in a talkative armchair by the fire. If it hadn't been for *Catriona* we couldn't, this year, have held up our head. It had been long, before that, since any decent sentence was turned in English. We grow systematically vulgarer and baser. The only blur of light is that your books are tasted. I shall try to see Colvin before I post this—otherwise I haven't seen him for three months. I've had a summer of the British seaside, the bathing machine and the German band. I met Zola at luncheon the day before he left London and found him very sane and common and inexperienced. Nothing, literally nothing, has ever happened to him but to write the Rougon-Macquart. It makes that series, I admit, still more curious. Your tour de force is of the opposite kind. Renew the miracle, my dear Louis, and believe me yours already gaping,

HENRY JAMES.

P.S. I have had to keep my poor note several days—finding that after all there *is*, thank heaven, a near post by San Francisco. Meanwhile I have seen Colvin and made discreetly, though so eagerly, free of some of your projects—and gyrations! Trapezist in the Pacific void!

..."Catriona" is more and more BEAUTIFUL. There's the rub!

H.J.

TO WILLIAM JAMES.

The incident referred to in the following letter was the unexpected miscarriage of one of H. J.'s theatrical schemes. Meanwhile *Guy Domville* had been accepted for future production at the St. James's Theatre.

34 De Vere Gardens, W.

Dec. 29th, 1893.

...I rejoice greatly in Alice's announcement (which you, William, coyly don't mention) of the presidency of the [Society for Psychical Research]. I hope it's all honour and kudos and pleasantness, without a tax of botherations.

I wish I could give you some correspondingly good tidings of my own ascensory movement; but I had a fall—or rather took a jump—the other day (a month ago) of which the direction was not vulgarly—I mean theatrically and financially—upward. You are so sympathetic about the whole sordid development that I make a point of mentioning the incident.... It was none the less for a while a lively disgust and disappointment—a waste of patient and ingenious labour and a sacrifice of coin much counted on. But à la guerre comme à la guerre. I mean to wage this war ferociously for one year more—1894—and then (unless the victory and the spoils have by that become more proportionate than hitherto to the humiliations and vulgarities and disgusts, all the dishonour and chronic insult incurred) to "chuck" the whole intolerable experiment and return to more elevated and more independent courses. The whole odiousness of the thing lies in the connection between the drama and the theatre. The one is admirable in its interest and difficulty, the other loathsome in its conditions. If the drama could only be theoretically or hypothetically acted, the fascination resident in its all but unconquerable (*circumspice!*) form would be unimpaired, and one would be able to have the exquisite exercise without the horrid sacrifice. However, Alexander's preparations of my play are going on sedulously, as to which situation and circumstances are all essentially different. He will produce me at no distant date, infallibly.... But meanwhile I am working heroically, though it every month becomes more difficult to give time to things of which the pecuniary fruit is remote. Excuse these vulgar confidences. I *have* come to *hate* the whole theatrical subject.... Don't write to condole with me about the business. I don't in the least "require" it. May the new year not have too many twists and turns for you, but lie straight and smooth before you.

Evermore your

HENRY.

TO JULIAN R. STURGIS.

34 De Vere Gardens, W.

Sunday [1893].

My dear Julian,

I wish I had your gift of facile and fascinating rhyme: I would turn it to account to thank you for your note and your sympathy. Yes, Ibsen is ugly, common, hard, prosaic, bottomlessly bourgeois—and with his distinction so far *in*, as it were, so behind doors and beyond vestibules, that one is excusable for not pushing one's way to it. And yet of his art he's a master— and I feel in him, to the pitch of almost intolerable boredom, the presence and the insistence of life. On the other hand his mastery, so bare and lean as it is, wouldn't count nearly as much in any medium in which the genus was otherwise represented. In *our* sandy desert even this translated octopus (excuse my confusion of habitats!!) sits alone, and isn't kept in his place by relativity. "Thanks awfully" for having retained an impression from the few Tales. My intentions are mostly good. I hope to knock at your door this p.m.

Yours always,

HENRY JAMES.

TO GEORGE DU MAURIER.

An article by H. J. on George du Maurier had appeared in *Harper's Weekly*, April 14, 1894.

Casa Biondetti, San Vio 715,

Venice.

Thursday [May 1894].

Only see, my dear Kikaccio, to what my thick-and-thin espousal of your genius exposes me at the hands of an unknown American female. Guileless, stupid, muddled, distracted, well-meaning, but slightly hypocritical American female!—Don't return, of course, the letter. I haven't seen the little *cochonnerie* I wrote about you, bothered, preoccupied with other work, more and more incapable of writing *that* sort of thing gracefully and properly—in the muddle and confusion of my coming abroad; and I hope *you* haven't, by the trop bons soins of McIlvaine, seen it either. But I bless it in that through arousing the American female my clumsy 'critique' has given me the occasion to salutarvi tutti. Are you on the hill or in the vale? I give it up, only pressing you all to my bosom wherever you are. Trilby goes on with a life and charm and loveability that gild the whole day one reads her. It's most delightfully and vividly talked! And then drawn!—no, it isn't fair. Well, I'm in Venice and you're not—so you've not got quite everything. It has been cold and wet; but Italy is always Italy—and the only thing really to be depended on quand même. I hope you have not returned to Hampstead, if you *have* returned, without tying your legs somewhere or other to Bayswater. I hope that everything has been well with you all—you yourself most well. It makes me homesick to write to you—but it is the only thing that does. I trust fame and flattery and flowers flow in upon you with the revolving Harpers.... Write me a word—tell me you don't hate me. I seem to remember rather disagreeably what I wrote about you.

Yours, caro mio, always,

HENRY JAMES.

TO WILLIAM JAMES.

H. J. had just received from his brother the diary which their sister had kept during her last years in England.

Grand Hotel, Rome.

May 28th, 1894.

My dear William:—my dear Alice:—

I wrote you a scrabbly note from Ravenna a few days since—but I must follow it up, without delay, with something better. I came on here an hour afterwards, and shall remain till June 1st or 2nd. I find Rome deliriously cool and empty, and still very pleasing in spite of the "ruining" which has been going on so long and of which one has heard so much, i.e., the redemption and cockneyfication of the ruins. This "changes" immensely—as everyone says; but I find myself, I am afraid, so much *more* changed—since I first knew and rhapsodized over it, that I am bound in justice to hold Rome the less criminal of the two. I am thinking a little about going down—if the coolness lasts—for three or four days to Naples; but I haven't decided. I feel rather hard and heartless to be prattling about these touristries to you, with the sad picture I have had these last weeks of your—William's—state of suffering. But it is only a way of saying that that state makes one feel it to be the greater duty for me to be as well as I can. Absit omen! Your so interesting letter of the 6th dictated to Alice speaks of the possibility of your abscess continuing not to heal—but I trust the event has long ere this reassured, comforted and liberated you. Meanwhile may Alice have smoothed your pillow as even she has never smoothed it before.... As regards the life, the power, the temper, the humour and beauty and expressiveness of the Diary in itself—these things were partly "discounted" to me in advance by so much of Alice's talk during her last years—and my constant association with her—which led me often to reflect about her extraordinary force of mind and character, her whole way of taking life—and death—in very much the manner in which the book does. I find in its pages, for instance, many things I heard her say. None the less I have been immensely impressed with the thing as a revelation of a moral and personal picture. It is heroic in its individuality, its independence—its face-to-face with the universe for and by herself—and the beauty and eloquence with which she often expresses this, let alone the rich irony and humour, constitute (I wholly agree with you) a new claim for the family renown. This last element—her style, her power to write—are indeed to me a delight—for I have had many letters from her. Also it brings back to me all sorts of things I am glad to keep—I mean things that happened, hours, occasions, conversations—brings them back with a strange, living richness. But it also puts before me what I was tremendously conscious of in her life-time—that the extraordinary intensity of her will and personality really would have made the equal, the reciprocal, life of a "well" person—in the usual world—almost impossible to her—so that her disastrous, her tragic health was in a manner the only solution for her of the practical problem of life—as it suppressed the element of equality, reciprocity, etc. The violence of her reaction against her British *ambiente*, against everything English, engenders some of her most admirable and delightful passages—but I feel in reading them, as I always felt in talking with her, that inevitably she simplified too much, shut up in her sick room, exercised her wondrous vigour of judgment on too small a scrap of what really surrounded her. It would have been modified in many ways if she had *lived* with them (the English) more—seen more of the men, etc. But doubtless it is fortunate for the fun and humour of the thing that it wasn't modified—as surely the critical emotion (about them,) the essence of much of their nature, was never more beautifully expressed. As for her allusions to H.—they fill me with tears and cover me with blushes.... I find an immense eloquence in her passionate "radicalism"—her most distinguishing feature almost—which, in her, was absolutely direct and original (like everything that was in her,) unreflected, uncaught from entourage or example. It would really have made her, had she lived in the world, a feminine "political force." But had she lived in the world and seen things nearer she would have had disgusts and disillusions. However, what comes out in the book—as it came out to me in fact—is that she was really an Irishwoman; transplanted, transfigured—yet none the less fundamentally national—in spite of her so much larger and finer than Irish intelligence. She felt the Home Rule question absolutely as only an Irishwoman (not anglicised) could. It was a tremendous emotion with her— inexplicable in any other way—but perfectly explicable by "atavism." What a pity she wasn't born there—and had her health for it. She would have been (if, always, she had not fallen a victim to disgust—a large "if") a national glory! But I am writing too much and my late hindrances have left me with tremendous arrears of correspondence. I thank you, dear Alice, *caramente*, for your sweet letter received two or three weeks before William's. I crudely hope you won't let your house—so as to have it to go to in the summer. Otherwise what will become of you. I dig my nose into the fleshiest parts of the young Francis. Tell Peggy I cling to her—and to Harry too, and Billy not less.... I haven't sent you "The Yellow Book"—on purpose; and indeed I have been weeks and weeks receiving a copy of it myself. I say on purpose because although my little tale which ushers it in ("The Death of the Lion") appears to have had, for a thing of mine, an unusual success, I hate too much the horrid aspect and company of the whole publication. And yet I am again to be intimately, conspicuously associated with the 2d number. It is for gold and to oblige the worshipful Harland (the editor). Wait and read the two tales in a volume—with 2 or 3 others. Above all be *debout* and forgive the long reticence of your affectionate

HENRY.

TO EDMUND GOSSE.

Mr. Gosse and his family, with Mr. A. C. Benson, were at this time spending a holiday in Switzerland, apparently not without mischance. Stevenson's offending letter is to be found among his published correspondence, dated from Vailima, July 7, 1894. H. J. misrepresents the phrase he quotes. "I decline any longer to give you examples of how not to write" are Stevenson's words.

Tregenna Castle Hotel,

St. Ives.

August 22nd [1894].

My dear Gosse,

I should have been very glad to hear from you yesterday if only for the sweet opportunity it gives me of crying out that I told you so! It gives me more than this—and I *didn't* tell you so; but I wanted to awfully—and I only smothered my wisdom under my waistcoat. Tell Arthur Benson that I wanted to tell *him* so too—that guileless morning at Victoria: I knew so well, both then and at Delamere Terrace, with my half century of experience, straight into what a purgatory you were *all* running. The high Swiss mountain inn, the crowd, the cold, the heat, the rain, the Germans, the scramble, the impossible rooms and the still more impossible everything else—the hope deferred, the money misspent, the weather accurst: these things I saw written on your azure brows even while I perfidiously prattled with your prattle. The only thing was to let you do it—for one can no more come between a lady and her Swiss hotel than between a gentleman and his wife. Meanwhile I sit here looking out at *my* nice, domestic, inexpensive English rain, in *my* nice bad stuffy insular inn, and thanking God that I am not as Gosses and Bensons are. I am pretty bad, I recognise—but I am not so bad as you. I am so bad that I am fleeing in a day or two—as I hope you will have been doing if your ineluctable fate doesn't spare you. I stopped on my way down here to spend three days with W. E. Norris, which were rendered charming by the urbanity of my host and the peerless beauty of Torquay, with which I fell quite in love. Here I go out for long walks on wet moors with the silent Stephen, the almost speechless Leslie. In the morning I improve the alas not shining hours, in a little black sitting-room which looks out into the strange area—like unto that of the London milkman—with which this ci-devant castle is encompassed and which sends up strange scullery odours into my nose. I am very sorry to hear of any friends of yours suffering by the Saturday Review, but I know nothing whatever of the cataclysm. It's a journal which (in spite of the lustre you add to it) I haven't so much as seen for 15 years, and no echoes of its fortunes ever reach me.

23rd. I broke off yesterday to take a long walk over bogs and brambles, and this morning my windows are lashed by a wet hurricane. It makes me wish I could settle down to a luxurious irresponsible day with the *Lourdes* of your appreciation, which lies there on my table still uncut. But my "holiday" is no holiday and I must drive the mechanic pen. Moreover I have vowed not to open *Lourdes* till I shall have closed with a final furious bang the unspeakable *Lord Ormont*, which I have been reading at the maximum rate of ten pages—ten insufferable and unprofitable pages, a day. It fills me with a critical rage, an artistic fury, utterly blighting in me the indispensable principle of *respect*. I have finished, at this rate, but the first volume—whereof I am moved to declare that I doubt if any equal quantity of extravagant verbiage, of airs and graces, of phrases and attitudes, of obscurities and alembications, ever *started* less their subject, ever contributed less of a statement—told the reader less of what the reader needs to know. All elaborate predicates of exposition without the ghost of a nominative to hook themselves to; and not a difficulty met, not a figure presented, not a scene constituted—not a dim shadow condensing once either into audible or into visible reality—making you hear for an instant the tap of its feet on the earth. Of course there are pretty things, but for what they are they come so much too dear, and so many of the profundities and tortuosities prove when threshed out to be only pretentious statements of the very simplest propositions. Enough, and forgive me. Above all don't send this to the P.M.G. There is another side, of course, which one will utter another day. I have a dictated letter from R. L. S., sent me through Colvin, who is at Schwalbach with the horsey Duchess of Montrose, a disappointing letter in which the too apt pupil of Meredith tells me nothing that I want to know—nothing save that his spirits are low (which I would fain ignore,) and that he has been on an excursion on an English man-of-war. The devilish letter is wholly about the man-of-war, not a word else; and at the end he says "I decline to tell you any more about it!" as if I had prescribed the usurping subject. You shall see the rather melancholy pages when you return—I must keep them to answer them. Bourget and his wife are in England again—at Oxford: with Prévost at Buxton, H. Le Roux at Wimbledon etc., it is the Norman conquest beginning afresh. What will be the end, or the effect, of it? P. B. has sent me some of the sheets (100 pp.) of his *Outremer*, which are singularly agreeable and lively. It will be much the prettiest (and I should judge kindest) socio-psychological book written about the U.S. That is saying little. It is very living and interesting. Prévost's fetid étude (on the little girls) represents a perfect bound, from his earlier things, in the way of hard, firm, knowing ability. So clever—and so common; no ability to imagine his "queenly" girl, made to dominate the world, do anything finally by way of illustrating her superiority but become a professional cocotte, like a *fille de portier*.

Pity's akin to love—so I send that to Mrs Nellie and Tessa and to A. Benson.

Yours ever,

HENRY JAMES.

TO EDMUND GOSSE.

This refers to an essay by Mr. Gosse on the Norwegian novelist Björnson, prefixed to an English translation of his *Synnöve Solbakken*.

34 De Vere Gardens, W.

Nov. 9th, 1894.

My dear Gosse,

Many thanks for the study of the roaring Norseman, which I read attentively last night—without having time, claimed by more *intimes* perusals, for reading his lusty fable. Björnson has always been, I frankly confess, an untended prejudice—a hostile one—of mine, and the effect of your lively and interesting monograph has been, I fear, to validate the hardly more than instinctive mistrust. I don't think you justify him, *rank* him enough—hardly quite enough for the attention you give him. At any rate he sounds in your picture—to say nothing of looking, in his own!—like the sort of literary fountain from which I am ever least eager to drink: the big, splashing, blundering genius of the hit-or-miss, the *a peu près*, family—without perfection, or the effort toward it, without the exquisite, the love of selection: a big super-abundant and promiscuous democrat. On the other hand the impossibly-named *Novelle* would perhaps win me over. But the human subject-matter in these fellows is so rebarbatif—"Mrs. Bang-Tande!" What a Romeo and Juliet! Have you seen Maurice Barrès's last volume—"Du Sang, de la Volupté et de la Mort"? That is exquisite in its fearfully intelligent impertinence and its diabolical Renanisation. We will talk of these things—all thanks meanwhile for the book.

Yours ever,

HENRY JAMES.

TO EDMUND GOSSE.

Mr. Gosse's study of Walter Pater is included in his *Critical Kit-kats*.

34 De Vere Gardens, W.

[Dec. 13th, 1894.]

My dear Gosse,

I return with much appreciation the vivid pages on Pater. They fill up substantially the void of one's ignorance of his personal history, and they are of a manner graceful and luminous; though I should perhaps have relished a little more insistence on—a little more of an inside view of—the nature of his mind itself. Much as they tell, however, how curiously negative and faintly-grey he, after all telling, remains! I think he has had—will have had—the most exquisite literary fortune: i.e. to have taken it out all, wholly, exclusively, with the pen (the style, the genius,) and absolutely not at all with the person. He is the mask without the face, and there isn't in his total superficies a tiny point of vantage for the newspaper to flap his wings on. You have been lively about him—but about whom *wouldn't* you be lively? I think you'd be lively about *me*!—Well, faint, pale, embarrassed, exquisite Pater! He reminds me, in the disturbed midnight of our actual literature, of one of those lucent matchboxes which you place, on going to bed, near the candle, to show you, in the darkness, where you can strike a light: he shines in the uneasy gloom—vaguely, and has a phosphorescence, not a flame. But I quite agree with you that he is not of the little day—but of the longer time.

Will you kindly ask Tessa if I may *still* come, on Saturday? My visit to the country has been put off by a death—and if there is a little corner for me I'll appear. If there isn't—so late—no matter. I daresay I ought to write to Miss Wetton. Or will Tessa amiably inquire?

Yours always,

HENRY JAMES.

TO EDMUND GOSSE.

The news of Stevenson's death in Samoa reached London at this moment, when H. J. was deeply occupied with the rehearsals of *Guy Domville* at the St. James's Theatre. "Jan. 5th" was to be the first night of the play.

34 De Vere Gardens, W.

Dec. 17th, 1894.

My dear Gosse,

I meant to write you to-night on another matter—but of what can one think, or utter or dream, save of this ghastly extinction of the beloved R.L.S.? It is too miserable for cold words—it's an absolute desolation. It makes me cold and sick—and with the absolute, almost alarmed sense, of the visible material quenching of an indispensable light. That he's silent forever will be a fact hard, for a long time, to live with. To-day, at any rate, it's a cruel, wringing emotion. One feels how one cared for him—what a place he took; and as if suddenly *into* that place there had descended a great avalanche of ice. I'm not sure that it's not for *him* a great and happy fate; but for us the loss of charm, of suspense, of "fun" is unutterable. And how confusedly and pityingly one's thought turns to those far-away stricken women, with their whole principle of existence suddenly quenched and yet all the monstrosity of the rest of their situation left on their hands! I saw poor Colvin to-day—he is overwhelmed, he is touching: But I can't write of this—we must talk of it. Yet these words have been a relief.

And I can't write, either, of the matter I had intended to—viz. that you are to rest secure about the question of Jan. 5th—I will do everything for you. *That* business becomes for the hour tawdry and heartless to me.

Yours always,

HENRY JAMES.

TO SIDNEY COLVIN.

H. J. unexpectedly found himself named by Stevenson as one of his executors; but this charge he felt it impossible to undertake, on account of his complete inexperience in matters of business. The last paragraph of this letter refers to a suggestion that the cabled news of Stevenson's death might prove to be mistaken.

34 De Vere Gardens, W.

Dec. 20th, '94.

My dear Colvin,

I didn't come, as I threatened, to see you this a.m.; because up to the time I was forced (early) to absent myself from home for several hours no sign had come from Edinburgh. On coming home at 4 o'clock, however, I found both a telegram and a letter from Mr. Mitchell. The telegram asked for a telegraphic *Yea* or *Nay* that might instantly be cabled to Baxter at Port Said. I immediately wired a profoundly regretful, but unconditional and insurmountable refusal. The absolute necessity of doing this has gathered still more overwhelming force since I saw you yesterday—if indeed there could have been any "still more" when the maximum had been so promptly reached. To ease still more (at all events) my conscience—though God knows it was, and is, easy!—I conferred last p.m. with a sage friend about the matter, and if I had been in the smallest degree unsettled some words he dropped about the pecuniary liability of executors, under certain new regulations (in regard to the Revenue &c.,) would sufficiently have fixed me. But in truth the question was not even one to talk of at all—even to the extent of asking for confirmations. I wish the thing could have been otherwise. But that is idle. So I have answered Mr. Mitchell's letter, by this evening's post, in a manner that leaves no doubt either of my decision or my sorrow. There *may* be something legal for me to do to be exonerated: I have inquired.

And meanwhile comes the torture of such phenomena as Dr. Balfour's letter in to-day's *P.M.G.*—a torture doubtless only meant (by a perverse Providence) to deepen the final pain. At any rate it is unsettling to the point of nervous anguish—or à peu près. But to whom do I say this? I don't like to think of *your* horrible worry—your all but damnable suspense. *Don't answer this*—or write me unless you particularly want to: I ache, in sympathy, under the letters, telegrams, complications of every sort you have to meet: that you may find strength to bear which is the hearty wish of yours, my dear Colvin, more than ever,

HENRY JAMES.

TO MISS HENRIETTA REUBELL.

34 De Vere Gardens, W.

December 31st, 1894.

Dear Miss Etta,

This is to wish you a brand-New Year, and to wish it very affectionately—and to wish it of not more than usual length but of more than usual fulness. I have had an unacknowledged letter from you longer than is decorous. But I have shown you ere this that epistolary decorum is a virtue I have ceased to pretend to. And during the last month I have not pretended to any other virtue either—save an endless patience and an heroic resignation, as I have been, and still am, alas, in the sorry position of having in rehearsal a little play—3 acts—which is to be produced on Saturday next, at the St. James's Theatre, as to which I beg you heartily to indulge for me, about 8.30 o'clock on that evening, in very fervent prayer. It is a little "romantic" play of which the action is laid (in England) in the middle of the last century, and it will be exquisitely mounted, dressed &c., and very creditably acted, as things go here. But rehearsal is an *écœurment* is the right spelling] and one's need of heroic virtues infinite. I have been in the breach daily for 4 weeks, and am utterly exhausted. To-night (the theatre being closed for the week on purpose) is the first dress rehearsal—which is here of course not a public, as in Paris, but an intensely private function—all for me, *me prélassant dans mon fauteuil*, alone, like the King of Bavaria at the opera. There are to be three nights more of this, to give them ease in the wearing of their clothes of a past time, and that, after the grind of the earlier work, is rather amusing—as amusing as anything can be, for a man of taste and sensibility, in the odious process of practical dramatic production. I may have been meant for the Drama—God knows!—but I certainly wasn't meant for the Theatre. C'est pour vous dire that I am much pressed and am only sending you mes vœux très-sincères in a shabbily brief little letter. There are a number of interesting things in your last to which I want to respond. I send you also by post 3 or 4 miserable little (old) views of Tunbridge Wells, which I have picked up in looking, at rare leisure moments, for one good one for you. I haven't, alas, found that; but I think I am on the track of it, and you shall have it as soon as it turns up. Accept these meanwhile as a little stop-gap and a symbol of my New Year's greeting.... I hope you are in good case and good hope. We are having here an excellent winter, almost fogless and generally creditable. Write me a little word of hope and help for the 5th; I shall regard it as a happy influence for yours forever,

HENRY JAMES.

TO WILLIAM JAMES.

34 De Vere Gardens, W.

Jan. 9th, 1895.

My dear William,

I never cabled to you on Sunday 6th (about the first night of my play,) because, as I daresay you will have gathered from some despatches or newspapers (if there have been any, and you have seen them,) the case was too complicated. Even now it's a sore trial to me to have to write about it—weary, bruised, sickened, disgusted as one is left by the intense, the cruel ordeal of a first night that—after the immense labour of preparation and the unspeakable tension of suspense—has, in a few brutal moments, not gone well. In three words the delicate, picturesque, extremely human and extremely artistic little play was taken profanely by a brutal and ill-disposed gallery which had shown signs of malice prepense from the first and which, held in hand till the end, kicked up an infernal row at the fall of the curtain. There followed an abominable quarter of an hour during which all the forces of civilization in the house waged a battle of the most gallant, prolonged and sustained applause with the hoots and jeers and catcalls of the roughs, whose *roars* (like those of a cage of beasts at some infernal "zoo") were only exacerbated (as it were) by the conflict. It was a cheering scene, as you may imagine, for a nervous, sensitive, exhausted author to face—and you must spare my going over again the horrid hour, or those of disappointment and depression that have followed it; from which last, however, I am rapidly and resolutely, thank God, emerging. The "papers" have, into the bargain, been mainly ill-natured and densely stupid and vulgar; but the only two dramatic critics who count, W. Archer and Clement Scott, have done me more justice. Meanwhile all *private* opinion is apparently one of extreme admiration—I have been flooded with letters of the warmest protest and assurance.... Everyone who was there has either written to me or come to see me—I mean every one I know and many people I don't. Obviously the little play, which I strove to make as broad, as simple, as clear, as British, in a word, as possible, is over the heads of the *usual* vulgar theatre-going London public—and the chance of its going for a while (which it is too early to measure) will depend wholly on its holding on long enough to attract the *unusual*. I was there the second night (Monday, 7th) when, before a full house—a remarkably good "money" house Alexander told me—it went singularly well. But it's soon to see or to say, and I'm prepared for the worst. The thing fills me with horror for the abysmal vulgarity and brutality of the theatre and its regular public, which God knows I have had intensely even when working (from motives as "pure" as pecuniary motives *can* be) against it; and I feel as if the simple freedom of mind thus begotten to return to one's legitimate form would be simply by itself a divine solace for everything. Don't worry about me: I'm a Rock. If the play has no life on the stage I shall publish it; it's altogether the best thing I've done. You would understand better the elements of the case if you had seen the thing it followed (*The Masqueraders*) and the thing that is now succeeding at the Haymarket—the thing of Oscar Wilde's. On the basis of *their* being plays, or successes, my thing is necessarily neither. Doubtless, moreover, the want of a roaring actuality, simplified to a few big *familiar* effects, in my subject—an episode in the history of an old English Catholic family in the last century—militates against it, with all usual theatrical people, who don't want plays (from variety and nimbleness of fancy) of different *kinds*, like books and stories, but only of one kind, which their stiff, rudimentary, clumsily-working vision recognizes as the kind they've had before. And yet I had tried so to meet them! But you can't make a sow's ear out of a silk purse.—I can't write more—and don't ask for more details. This week will probably determine the fate of the piece. If there is increased advance-booking it will go on. If there isn't, it will be withdrawn, and with it all my little hope of profit. The time one has given to such an affair from the very first to the very last represents in all—so inconceivably great, to the uninitiated, is the amount—a pitiful, tragic bankruptcy of hours that might have been rendered retroactively golden. But I am not plangent—one must take the thick with the thin—and I have such possibilities of another and better sort before me. I am only sorry for your and Alice's having to be so sorry for yours forever,

HENRY.

TO GEORGE HENSCHEL.

Answering a suggestion that H. J. should write a libretto to be set to music by Sir George Henschel.

34 De Vere Gardens, W.

January 22d, 1895.

My dear Henschel,

Your flattering dream is beautiful—but, I fear, alas, delusive. When I say I 'fear' it, I mean I only too completely feel it. It is a charming idea, but the root of the libretto is not in me. We will talk of it—yes: because I will talk with you, with joy, of *anything*—will even play to myself that I have convictions I haven't, for that privilege. But I am unlyrical, unmusical, unrhythmical, unmanageable. And I hate "old New England stories"!—which are lean and pale and poor and ugly. But let us by all means talk—and the more the better. I am touched by your thinking so much good of me—and I embrace you, my dear Henschel, for such rich practical friendship and

211

confidence. I congratulate you afresh on your glorious wife, I await you with impatience, and I stretch out to you across the wintry wastes the very grateful hand of yours always,

HENRY JAMES.

TO W. D. HOWELLS.

34 De Vere Gardens, W.

January 22d, 1895.

My dear Howells,

...I am indebted to you for your most benignant letter of December last. It lies open before me and I read it again and am soothed and cheered and comforted again. You put your finger sympathetically on the place and spoke of what I wanted you to speak of. I *have* felt, for a long time past, that I have fallen upon evil days—every sign or symbol of one's being in the least *wanted*, anywhere or by any one, having so utterly failed. A new generation, that I know not, and mainly prize not, has taken universal possession. The sense of being utterly out of it weighed me down, and I asked myself what the future would be. All these melancholies were qualified indeed by one redeeming reflection—the sense of how little, for a good while past (for reasons very logical, but accidental and temporary,) I had been producing. I *did* say to myself "Produce again—produce; produce better than ever, and all will yet be well;" and there was sustenance in that so far as it went. But it has meant much more to me since *you* have said it—for it *is*, practically, what you admirably say. It is exactly, moreover, what I meant to admirably do—and have meant, all along, about this time to get into the motion of. The whole thing, however, represents a great change in my life, inasmuch as what is clear is that periodical publication is practically closed to me—I'm the last hand that the magazines, in this country or in the U.S., seem to want. I won't afflict you with the now accumulated (during all these past years) evidence on which this induction rests—and I have spoken of it to no creature till, at this late day, I speak of it to you.... All this, I needn't say, is for your segretissimo ear.

What it means is that "production" for me, as aforesaid, means production of the little *book*, pure and simple—independent of any antecedent appearance; and, truth to tell, now that I wholly *see* that, and have at last accepted it, I am, incongruously, not at all sorry. I am indeed very serene. I have always hated the magazine form, magazine conditions and manners, and much of the magazine company. I hate the hurried little subordinate part that one plays in the catchpenny picture-book—and the negation of all literature that the insolence of the picture-book imposes. The money-difference will be great—but not so great after a bit as at first; and the other differences will be so all to the good that even from the economic point of view they will tend to make up for that and perhaps finally even completely do so. It is about the distinctness of one's *book-position* that you have so substantially reassured me; and I mean to do far better work than ever I have done before. I have, potentially, improved immensely and am bursting with ideas and subjects—though the act of composition is with me more and more slow, painful and difficult. I shall never again write a *long* novel; but I hope to write six immortal short ones—and some tales of the same quality. Forgive, my dear Howells, the cynical egotism of these remarks—the fault of which is in your own sympathy. Don't fail me this summer. I shall probably not, as usual, absent myself from these islands—not be beyond the Alps as I was when you were here last. That way Boston lies, which is the deadliest form of madness. I sent you only last night messages of affection by dear little "Ned" Abbey, who presently sails for N.Y. laden with the beautiful work he has been doing for the new Boston public library. I hope you will see him—he will speak of me competently and kindly. I wish all power to your elbow. Let me hear as soon as there is a sound of packing. Tell Mildred I rejoice in the memory of her. Give my love to your wife, and believe me, my dear Howells, yours in all constancy,

HENRY JAMES.

TO WILLIAM JAMES.

34 De Vere Gardens, W.

February 2nd, 1895.

...The poor little play seems already, thank God, ancient history, though I have lived through, in its company, the horridest four weeks of my life. Produce a play and you will know, better than I can tell you, how such an ordeal—odious in its essence!—is only made tolerable and palatable by great success; and in how many ways accordingly non-success may be tormenting and tragic, a bitterness of every hour, ramifying into every throb of one's consciousness. Tonight the thing will have lived the whole of its troubled little life of 31 performances, and will be "taken off," to be followed, on Feb. 5th, by a piece by Oscar Wilde that will have probably a very different fate. On the night of the 5th, too nervous to do anything else, I had the ingenious thought of going to some other theatre and seeing some other play as a means of being coerced into quietness from 8 till 10.45. I went accordingly to the Haymarket, to a new piece by the said O.W. that had just been produced—"An Ideal Husband." I sat through it and saw it played with every appearance (so far as the crowded house was an appearance) of complete success, and *that* gave me the most fearful apprehension. The thing seemed to me so helpless, so crude, so bad, so clumsy, feeble and vulgar, that as I walked away across St. James's Square to learn my own fate, the prosperity of what I had seen seemed to me to constitute a dreadful presumption of the shipwreck of *G.D.*, and I stopped in the middle of the Square, paralyzed by the terror of this probability— afraid to go on and learn more. "How *can* my piece do anything with a public with whom *that* is a success?" It couldn't—but even then the full truth was, "mercifully," not revealed to me; the truth that in a short month my piece would be whisked away to make room for the triumphant Oscar. If, as I say, this episode has, by this time, become ancient history to me, it is, thank heaven, because when a thing, for me (a piece of work,) is done, it's done: I get quickly detached and away from it, and am wholly given up to the better and fresher life of the next thing to come. This is particularly the case now, with my literary way blocked so long and my production smothered by these theatrical lures: I have such arrears on hand and so many things seem to wait for me—that I want far more and that it will be nobler to do—that

I am looking in a very different direction than in that of the sacrificed little play. Partly for this reason, this receiving from you all the retarded echo of my reverse and having to live over it with you (you must excuse me if I don't do so much,) is the thing, in the whole business, that has been most of an anguish and that I dreaded most in advance. As for the play, in three words, it has been, I think I may say, a rare and distinguished private success and scarcely anything at all of a public one. By a private success, I mean with the even moderately cultivated, civilised and intelligent *individual*, with "people of taste" in short, of almost any kind, as distinguished from the vast English Philistine mob—the regular "theatrical public" of London, which, of all the vulgar publics London contains, is the most brutishly and densely vulgar. This congregation the things they do like sufficiently judge.... I no sooner found myself in the presence of those yelling barbarians of the first night and learned what could be the savagery of their disappointment that one wasn't perfectly the *same* as everything else they had ever seen, than the dream and delusion of my having made a successful appeal to the cosy, childlike, naïf, domestic British imagination (which was what I had calculated) dropped from me in the twinkling of an eye. I saw they couldn't care one straw for a damned young last-century English Catholic, who lived in an old-tune Catholic world and acted, with every one else in the play, from remote and romantic Catholic motives. The whole thing was, for them, remote, and all the intensity of one's ingenuity couldn't make it anything else. It has made it something else for the *few*—but that is all. Such is the bare history of poor G.D.—which, I beg you to believe, throws no light on my "technical skill" which isn't a light that that mystery ought to rejoice to have thrown. The newspaper people muddle things up with the most foredoomed crudity; and I am capable of analysing the whole thing far more scientifically and drawing from it lessons far more pertinent and practical than all of them put together. It is perfectly true that the novelist has a fearful long row to hoe to get into any practical relation to the grovelling stage, and his difficulty is precisely double: it bears, on one side, upon the question of method and, on the other, upon the question of subject. If he is really in earnest, as I have been, he surmounts the former difficulty before he surmounts the latter. I have worked like a horse—far harder than any one will ever know—over the whole stiff mystery of "technique"—I have run it to earth, and I don't in the least hesitate to say that, for the comparatively poor and meagre, the piteously simplified, purposes of the English stage, I have made it absolutely my own, put it into my pocket. The question of realising how different is the attitude of the theatre-goer toward the quality of thing which might be a story in a book from his attitude toward the quality of thing that is given to him as a story in a play is another matter altogether. *That* difficulty is portentous, for any writer who doesn't approach it naïvely, as only a very limited and simple-minded writer can. One has to *make* one's self so limited and simple to conceive a subject, see a subject, simply enough, and that, in a nutshell, is where I have stumbled. And yet if you were to have seen my play! I haven't been near the theatre since the second night, but I shall go down there late this evening to see it buried and bid good-bye to the actors.... I am very sorry for Marion Terry, who has delighted in her part and made the great hit of her career, I should suppose, in it, and who has to give it up thus untimely. Her charming acting has done much for the little run.... The money disappointment is of course keen—as it was wholly for money I adventured. But the poor four weeks have brought me $1,100—which shows what a tidy sum many times four weeks would have brought; without my lifting, as they say, after the first performance, a finger.

I have written you so long-windedly on this matter that I have left neither time nor space for anything else. I must catch the post and will write more sociably something by the next one. One's time, in the whole history, has gone like water, and still it pours out. *Please* don't send me anything out of newspapers.

Always your

HENRY.

TO SIDNEY COLVIN.

The first of Stevenson's letters to be published, it will be remembered, were the "Vailima Letters" to Sir Sidney Colvin.

34 De Vere Gardens, W.

Feb. 19th, 1895.

My dear Colvin,

I shall send you all the Vailima Letters back to-morrow or next day by hand. I have completely read them. I can't say, and I don't want to say, anything of them but "Publish them—they make the man so loveable." It's on *that* I should take my stand. I think your estimate of them as ranking high in their class (epistolary) is perhaps (if I remember what you seemed to express of it) a larger one than I should concur in; but I think still more that that makes little difference; for they will assuredly be *liked*—immensely, and that is mainly what one is concerned to ask for him. They are charming, living, touching, absolutely natural; and I think *better* toward the end than at the beginning. What they suffer from is: 1º Want of interest and want of clearness as to the subject-matter of much of them—the Samoan personalities, politics, &c; all to me almost squalid—and the irritating effect of one's sense of his clearing the very ground to be able to do his daily work. Want also to a certain extent of *generalization* about all these matters and some others—into the dreary specifics of which the reader perhaps finds himself plunged too much. 2º A certain tormenting effect in his literary confidences (to you,) glimpses, promises, revelations &c., arising from his so seldom telling the subject, the *idea* of the thing—what he sees, what he wants to do, &c—as against his pouring forth titles, chapters, divisions, names &c., in such magnificent abundance.—On the other hand the personality shines out so beautiful and there are so many charming things—passages, pages—that not to publish them would seem to me like the burial of something alive. I see but little in what you have left in these copies to excise on grounds of discretion, unless it be many of those reports of the state of public affairs and allusions to public personages which are *primarily* excisable by reason of obscurity, failure to appeal to reader's interest, &c. But I should like to see you and talk about the matter with you better than thus, and shall take the earliest occasion. The hideous sadness of them—to *us*! To readers at large—no. But I feel as though I had been sitting with him for hours.

Yours always,

HENRY JAMES.

TO MRS. JOHN L. GARDNER.

Royal Hospital, Dublin.

March 23d, 1895.

Dear Isabella Gardner,

Yes, I have delayed hideously to write to you, since receiving your note of many days ago. But I always delay hideously, and my shamelessness is rapidly becoming (in the matter of letter-writing) more disgraceful even than my procrastination. I brought your letter with me to Ireland more than a fortnight ago with every intention of answering it on the morrow of my arrival; but I have been leading here a strange and monstrous life of demoralisation and frivolity and the fleeting hour has mocked, till today, at my languid effort to stay it, to clutch it, in its passage. I have been paying three monstrous visits in a row; and if I needed any further demonstration of the havoc such things make in my life I should find it in this sense of infidelity to a charming friendship of so many years.

I return to England to enter a monastery for the rest of my days—and crave your forgiveness before I take this step. I have been staying in this queer, shabby, sinister, sordid place (I mean Dublin,) with the Lord Lieutenant (poor young Lord Houghton,) for what is called (a fragment, that is, of what is called) the "Castle Season," and now I am domesticated with very kind and valued old friends, the Wolseleys—Lord W. being commander of the forces here (that is, head of the little English army of occupation in Ireland—a five-years appointment) and domiciled in this delightfully quaint and picturesque old structure, of Charles II's time—a kind of Irish Invalides or Chelsea Hospital—a retreat for superannuated veterans, out of which a commodious and stately residence has been carved. We live side by side with the 140 old red-coated cocked-hatted pensioners—but with a splendid great rococo hall separating us, in which Lady Wolseley gave the other night the most beautiful ball I have ever seen—a fancy-ball in which all the ladies were Sir Joshuas, Gainsboroughs, or Romneys, and all the men in uniform, court dress or evening hunt dress. (*I* went as—guess what!—alas, nothing smarter than the one black coat in the room.) It is a world of generals, aide-de-camps and colonels, of military colour and sentinel-mounting, which amuses for the moment and makes one reflect afresh that in England those who *have* a good time have it with a vengeance. The episode at the tarnished and ghost-haunted Castle was little to my taste, and was a very queer episode indeed—thanks to the incongruity of a vice-regal "court" (for that's what it considers itself) utterly boycotted by Irish (landlord) society—the present viceroy being the nominee of a home-rule government, and reduced to dreary importation from England to fill its gilded halls. There was a ball every night, etc., but too much standing on one's hind-legs—too much pomp and state—for nothing and nobody. On my return (two days hence) to my humble fireside I get away again as quickly as possible into the country—to a cot beside a rill, the address of which no man knoweth. There I remain for the next six months to come; and nothing of any sort whatever is to happen to me (this is all arranged,) save that you are to come down and stay a day or two with me when you come to England. There is, alas, to be no "abroad" for me this year. I rejoice with you in *your* Rome—but my Rome is in the buried past. I spent, however, last June there, and was less excruciated than I feared. Have you seen my old friend Giuseppe Primoli—a great friend, in particular, of the Bourgets? I dare say you have breakfasted deep with him. May this find you perched on new conquests. It's vain to ask you to write me, or tell me, anything. Let me only ask you therefore to believe me your very affectionate old friend.

HENRY JAMES.

TO ARTHUR CHRISTOPHER BENSON.

The excursion to Windsor was one of several on which H. J. conducted Alphonse Daudet and his family during their visit to England this spring. The "adorable cottage" was the house then occupied by Mr. Benson as a master at Eton.

34 De Vere Gardens, W.

May 11th [1895].

My dear Arthur B.

A quelque chose malheur est bon: my very natural failure to find you brought me your engaging letter. Strike, but hear me. I knew but too well that it would not seem felicitous to you that I should leave a mere card at your ravishing bower: but please believe that I had no alternative. I weighed the question of notifying you in advance—weighed it anxiously; but the scale against it was pressed down by overwhelming considerations. Daudet is so unwell and fatigable and unable to walk or to mount steps or stairs (he could do Windsor Castle only from the carriage,) that I didn't know he would pull through the excursion at all—and I thought it unfair to inflict on you the awkward problem of his getting, or not getting, into your house—of his getting over to Eton at all—and of the five other members of his family being hurled upon you. We had, in fact, only just time to catch our return train. Still, I had a sneaking romantic *hope* of you. I should have liked them, hungry for the great show, to behold you! As I turned sadly from your "adorable cottage" and got back into the carriage A. D. said to me—having waited contemplatively during my conference with your domestic: "Ah, si vous saviez comme ces petits coins d'Angleterre m'amusent!" A. C. B. would have amused him still more. Content yourself, for the hour, my dear Arthur Benson, with "amusing" a humbler master of Dichtung—and an equal one, perhaps, of Wahrheit. I am delighted you have been thinking of me—and beg you to be sure that *whenever* you happen to do so, Telepathy, as you say, will happen to be in it! This time, e.g., it was intensely in it—for you had been peculiarly present to me all these last days in connection with my alternations of writing to you or not writing to you about the projected Thursday at Windsor. I wanted to confine myself to the pure feasible for Daudet, and yet I wanted (still more) to write to you "anyway," as they say in the U. S. And I *am* writing to you—q.e.d. So there we are. I rejoice in a certain air of happiness in your letter. Dine with you some day? De grand cœur—after a little—after the very lively practical pre-occupation of the presence of my helpless and bewildered Gauls has abated. There is a late train from Windsor that would put me back after dinner—unless I err. Your mother has kindly invited me to a party on the 16th and I shall certainly go—if I survive (and return from) the process of taking Daudet down to see G. Meredith at Box Hill—which has been fixed for that day. You won't be there (at Lambeth) I ween—but if you *were*, what possibilities (of the order hinted at above) we might discuss in a Gothic embrasure!

Respond—respond, if ever so briefly, to yours, my dear Arthur Benson, for ever,

HENRY JAMES.

TO W. E. NORRIS.

The "American outbreak" was the trouble over the question of the Venezuelan frontier. The articles in the *Times* by the late G. W. Smalley (correspondent for the journal in New York) did much, in H. J.'s view, to preserve the relations between England and the United States during this difficult time.

34 De Vere Gardens, W.

Feb. 4th [1896].

My dear Norris,

Your letter is as good as the chair by your study-table (betwixt it, as it were, and the tea-stand) used to be; and as that luxurious piece of furniture shall (D.V.) be again. Your news, your hand, your voice sprinkle me—most refreshingly—with the deep calm of Torquay. It is in short in every way good to hear from you, so that, behold, for your sweet sake, I perpetrate that intensest of my favourite immoralities—I snatch the epistolary, the disinterested pen before (at 10 a.m.) squaring my poor old shoulders over the painful instrument that I fondly try to believe to be lucrative. It *isn't*— but one must keep up the foolish fable to the end. I am having in these difficult conditions a very decent winter. It is mild, and it isn't wet—not here and now; and it is—for me—thanks to more than Machiavellian cunning, more dinnerless than it has, really, ever been. My fireside really knows me on some evenings. I forsake it too often—but a little less and less. So you bloom and smack your lips, while I shrivel and tighten my waistband. In spite of my gain of private quiet I have suffered acutely by my loss of public. The American outbreak has darkened all my sky—and made me feel, among many other things, how long I have lived away from my native land, how long I *shall* (D.V.!) live away from it and how little I understand it today. The explosion of jingoism there is the result of all sorts of more or less domestic and internal conditions—and what is most indicated, on the whole, as coming out of it, is a vast new split or cleavage in American national feeling—politics and parties—a split almost, roughly speaking, between the West and the East. There are really two civilisations there side by side—in one yoke; or rather one civilisation and a barbarism. All the expressions of feeling *I* have received from the U.S. (since this hideous row) have been, intensely, of course, from the former. It is, on the whole, the stronger force; but only on condition of its fighting hard. But I think it *will* fight hard. Meanwhile, the whole thing sickens me. That unfortunately, however, is not a reason for its not being obviously there. It's there all the while. But let it not be any more *here*: I mean in this scribblement. My admiration of Smalley is boundless, and my appreciation and comfort and gratitude. He has really *done* something—and will do more—for peace and decency.

I went yesterday to Leighton's funeral—a wonderful and slightly curious public demonstration—the streets all cleared and lined with police, the day magnificent (his characteristic good fortune to the end;) and St. Paul's very fine to the eye and crammed with the *whole* London world.... The music was fine and severe, but I thought wanting in volume and force—thin and meagre for the vast space. But what do I know?

No, my dear Norris, I *don't* go abroad—I go on May 1st into the depths (somewhere) of old England. A response to that proposal I spoke to you of (from Rome) is utterly impossible to me now.... I've two novels to write before I can *dream* of anything else; and to go abroad is to plunge into the fiery furnace of people. So either Devonshire or some other place will be my six months' lot. I must take a house, this time—a small and cheap one—and I must (deride me not) be somewhere where I can, without disaster, bicycle. Also I must be a little nearer town than last year. I'm afraid these things rather menace Torquay. But it's soon to say—I must wait. I shall decide in April—or by mid-March—only. Meanwhile things will clear up. I'm intensely, thank heaven, busy. I will, I think, send you the little magazine tale over which (I mean over whose number of words—infinite and awful) I struggled so, in Sept. and Oct. last, under your pitying eye and with your sane and helpful advice. It comes in to me this a.m.

...I hope your daughter is laying up treasure corporeal in Ireland. I like *your* dinners—even I mean in the houses of the other hill-people; and I beg you to feel yourself clung to for ever by yours irrepressibly,

HENRY JAMES.

TO WILLIAM JAMES.

Point Hill,

Playden, Rye.

July 24th, 1896.

My dear William,

...I wrote you at some length not very long since, and my life has been, here, so peaceful that nothing has happened to me since save an incident terminated this a.m.—a charming little visit (of 24 hours) from Wendell Holmes, who was in admirable youth, spirits, health and "form," and whose presence I greatly enjoyed. He is—or has been—having his usual social triumphs in London, was as vivid and beautiful as ever about them—also seems to enjoy much *this* humble but picturesque little place and sails for the U.S. on Aug. 22nd. Save that he seems to see you rarely and precariously, he will carry you good news of me. I have only five days more of Point Hill, alas—but I have solved the problem of not returning on Aug. 1st to the stifling London (we are having a summer of transcendent droughts and

223

heat—like last, only more so,) and not on the other hand sacrificing precious days to hunting up another refuge—solved it by taking, for two months, the Vicarage at Rye, which is shabby, fusty—a sad drop from P.H., but close at hand to this (15 minutes walk,) and has much of the same picturesque view (from a small terrace garden behind—a garden to sit in, and more or less, as here, to *eat* in) and almost the same very moderate *loyer*. It has also more room, and more tumblers and saucepans, and above all, at a moment when I am intensely busy, saves me a wasteful research. So I shall be there from the 29th of this month till the last week in September. "*The Vicarage, Rye, Sussex*," is my address. The place, unfortunately, isn't quite up to the pretty suggestion of the name. But this little corner of the land endears itself to me—and the peace of the country is a balm. It is all, about here, most mild and mellow and loveable—too "relaxing," but that is partly the exceptional summer. I have been able, *every* evening, for three months, to dine, at *8*, on my little terrace. So the climate of England is, literally, not always to be sneezed at. But the absence of rain threatens a water-famine, and the "tub" is a short allowance. With Chocorua let, I am at a loss to place you all, and only hope you are succeeding better in placing yourselves. It would delight me to hear that Alice is "boarding" somewhere with Peggy and the afflicted infant whom I refuse to denominate "Tweedy." I hope, at any rate, she is getting rest and refreshment of some sort. There would be room for two or three of you at my Vicarage—I wish you were here to feel the repose of it. May your summer be merciful and your lectures *on ne peut plus suivies*. I say nothing about the political bear-garden—I fear I pusillanimously keep out of it. I am well (absit omen) and interested in what I *am* in—and I embrace you all. Ever your affectionate

HENRY.

TO EDMUMD GOSSE.

The Spoils of Poynton (under the title of *The Old Things*) had begun to appear in the *Atlantic Monthly* in April 1896.

The Vicarage,

Rye.

August 28th, 1896.

My dear Edmund,

Don't think me a finished brute or a heartless fiend or a soulless one, or any other unhappy thing with a happy name. I have pressed your letter to my bosom again and again, and if I've not sooner expressed to you how I've prized it, the reason has simply been that for the last month there has been no congruity between my nature and my manners—between my affections and my lame right hand. A crisis overtook me some three weeks ago from which I emerge only to hurl myself on this sheet of paper and consecrate it to *you*. I will reserve details—suffice it that in an evil hour I began to pay the penalty of having arranged to let a current serial begin when I was too little ahead of it, and when it proved a much slower and more difficult job than I expected. The printers and illustrators overtook and denounced me, the fear of breaking down paralysed me, the combination of rheumatism and fatigue rendered my hand and arm a torture—and the total situation made my existence a nightmare, in which I answered not a single note, letting correspondence go to smash in order barely to save my honour. I've finished (day before yesterday,) but I fear my honour—with *you*—lies buried in the ruin of all the rest. You will soon be coming home, and this will meet or reach you God only knows when. Let it take you the assurance that the most lurid thing in my dreams has been the glitter of your sarcastic spectacles. It was charming of you to write to me from dear little old devastated Vevey—as to which indeed you make me feel, in a few vivid touches, a faint nostalgic pang. I don't want to think of you as still in your horrid ice-world (for it is cold even here and I scribble by a morning fire;) and yet it's in my interest to suppose you still feeling so all abroad that these embarrassed lines will have for you some of the charm of the bloated English post. That makes me, at the same time, doubly conscious that I've nothing to tell you that you will most languish for—news of the world and the devil—no throbs nor thrills from the great beating heart of the thick of things. I went to town for a week on the 15th, to be nearer the devouring maw into which I had to pour belated copy; but I spent the whole time shut up in De Vere Gardens with an inkpot and a charwoman. The only thing that befell me was that I dined one night at the Savoy with F. Ortmans and the P. Bourgets—and that the said Bourgets—but two days in London—dined with me one night at the Grosvenor club. But these occasions were not as rich in incident and emotion as poetic justice demanded—and your veal-fed table d'hôte will have nourished your intelligence quite as much. The only other thing I did was to read in the Revue de Paris of the 15th Aug. the wonderful article of A. Daudet on Goncourt's death—a little miracle of art, adroitness, demoniac tact and skill, and taste so abysmal, judged by *our* fishlike sense, that there is no getting alongside of it at all. But I grieve to say I can't send you the magazine—I saw it only at a club. Doubtless you will have come across it. I have this ugly house till the end of September and don't expect to move from Rye even for a day till then. The date of your return is vague to me—but if it should be early in the month I wonder if you couldn't come down for another Sunday. I fear you will be too blasé, much. For comfort my Vicarage is distinctly superior to my eagle's nest—but, alas, beauty isn't in it. The peace and prettiness of the whole land, here, however, has been good to me, and I stay on with unabated relish. But I stay in solitude. I don't see a creature. That, too, dreadful to relate, I like. You will have been living in a crowd, and I expect you to return all garlanded and odorous with anecdote and reminiscence. Mrs Nelly's will all bear, I trust, on miraculous healings and feelings. I feel far from all access to the French volume you recommend. Are you crawling over the Dorn, or only standing at the bottom to catch Philip and Lady Edmund as they drop? Pardon my poverty and my paucity. It is your absence that makes them. Yours, my dear Edmund, not inconstantly,

HENRY JAMES.

TO JONATHAN STURGES.

34 De Vere Gardens, W.

Thursday [Nov. 5, 1896].

My dear Jonathan,

I spill over, this a.m., in a certain amount of jubilation—all the more that I have your little letter of the other day to thank you for. One breathes, I suppose—the alarmed, anxious, prudent part of one. But I don't feel that McKinley is the *end* of anything—least of all of big provincial iniquities and abuses and bloody billionaires. However he's more decent than the alternative—and your fortune will flow in, more regularly; and mine will permit me to say I'm delighted you "accept," and shall see that the cold mutton is not too much "snowed under" before you come. Only give me a few—three or four if possible—days' notice: then we will talk of many things—and among them of Rudyard Kipling's "Seven Seas," which he has just sent me and which I will send you tomorrow or next day (kindly guard it,) on the assumption that you won't have seen it. I am laid low by the absolutely uncanny talent—the prodigious special faculty of it. It's all *violent*, without a dream of a *nuance* or a hint of "distinction"; all prose trumpets and castanets and such—with never a touch of the fiddle-string or a note of the nightingale. But it's magnificent and masterly in its way, and full of the most insidious art. He's a rum 'un—and one of the very few first *talents* of the time. There's a vilely idiotic reference to his "coarseness" in this a.m.'s *Chronicle*. The coarseness of the *The Mary Gloster* is absolutely one of the most triumphant "values" of that triumphant thing. How lovely, in these sweet days, your Haslemere hermitage must be! I hope you've still the society of your young friend—it eases the mind of your old one. What you said about Howells most true—he is very touching. And I feel so *remote* from him! The little red book is extremely charming. Write to me. Tout à vous,

HENRY JAMES.

TO W. E. NORRIS.

34 De Vere Gardens, W.

Dec. 23rd, 1896.

My dear Norris,

I respond with joy to your suggestion in your beautiful letter of two days ago—that I shall enable you to find a word from me on your table on the darkest a. m. of the year; in the first place because I am much touched by your attaching to any word of mine any power to comfort or charm; and in the second because I can well measure—by my own—your sense of a melancholy from which you must appeal. It is indeed a lugubrious feast and a miserable merriment. But it is something to spend the evil season by one's own poor hearthstone (save that yours is opulent), crouching over the embers and chuckling low over all the dreadful places where one is not! I've been literally pressed to go to two or three—one of them in Northumberland! (the cheek of some people!) and the reflection that I *might* be there and yet by heaven's mercy am not, does give a faint blush as of the rose to my otherwise deep depression. It is a mild, gray, rainless, sunless inoffensive sort of Xmas here—and the shop fronts look rather prettily pink and green and golden in the dear dirty old London streets—and I have ventured into three or four— but *I* do it, bless you, for nine and sevenpence half-penny, all told! No wonder you want epistolary balm if you're already in the fifties! Do you give them diamond necklaces and Arab horses all round?—But Torquay, I too intensely felt, has gorgeous ways of its own. Really it isn't bad here, for almost every one has left town. I have yet had nothing worse to suffer than a first night at the Lyceum—the too great Irvingism of which—mainly in Ellen Terry's box— had been, the same day, pleasantly mitigated, in advance, by Tessa Gosse in Sheridan's *Critic*. Tessa had a play and acted Mr Puff better than any of her blushing fellow-nymphs acted anything else. And on New Year's eve I go to her parents for a carouse of some sort, and until then, thank God! I don't dine out save on Xmas day. Nor in 1897—by all that's holy! *ever* again! I have been quite smothered with it these two months—and it's getting far beyond a joke.... I see no literary fry, and languish in incorrigible obscurity. I had a fevered dream that *The Other House* might reach a second edition—but it declines to do anything of the sort, and the pauper's grave continues to yawn. Nevertheless—as it is assured any way—I *may* go to Italy on April 1st. Meanwhile, my dear Norris, I think of you with a degree of envy which even the manners of Topper scarce avail to diminish—I mean because you have a beautiful home and are so many miles nearer than I am to nature. You are also nearer to Miss Norris, and that is another advantage, even though it does make a hole in £50! I have nothing better to offer her on Xmas a.m. than the very friendly handshake of yours and hers, my dear Norris, affectionately and always,

HENRY JAMES.

TO ARTHUR CHRISTOPHER BENSON.

34 De Vere Gardens, W.

December 28th, 1896.

My dear Arthur,

Your generous letter has, this wild, mild, soft, sombre morning, made me feel as if I were standing beside you, with my hand on your shoulder, in an embrasure of one of the windows—at that fine old Farnham Castle that I have seen (years ago)—that look out on the noble things you speak of. And the communication in question is worthy, exactly, of the *things* in question; and grave and handsome and interesting and touching even as they are. "Burn" it, quotha!—it *wouldn't* have burnt, I would have you know: it would have flown straight up the chimney and taken, unscathed as marble, its invulnerable way to the individual for whom it had just been so admirably winged. You say to me exactly the right things, and you say them to exactly the right person. I can't tell you how glad I am for you that you have all that highest sanity and soundness (though it isn't as if I doubted it!) of emotion, full, frank and deep. If there be a wisdom in not feeling—to the last throb—the great things that happen to us, it is a wisdom I shall never either know or esteem. Let your soul live—it's the only life that isn't, on the whole, a sell. You have evidently been magnificent, and as I have my hand on your shoulder I take the opportunity of patting you very tenderly on the back. That back will evidently carry its load and be all the straighter for the—as it seems to me—really quite massive experience. I rejoice that the waters have held you up—they do, always, I think, when they are only deep *enough*. And all your missings and memories and contrasts and tendernesses are a part—the essence—of the very force that is in you to live, and to feel again—and yet again and again; when, at last, to *have* so felt will be the thing in the world you'll be gladdest to have done.

I don't know, in spite of your compliment, whether I *am* much like Gray, save in the devil of a time it takes me to do a thing. What keeps me incommunicative, however, is not indifference, but almost a kind of suspense, a fear to break—by speaking—the spell of some *other* spectacle—other than that of my own *fonctionnement*. But I respond to the lightest touch of a friendly hand, I think I may say; and I haven't the slightest fear of breaking any spell in saying—to you—that I seem to myself just now (absit omen!) to *fonctionner* pretty well. I am as occupied and preoccupied with work as even *my* technical temper can desire, and out of it something not irremediably nauseating will not improbably spring! I never had more intentions—what do I say?—more ferocities; I am sitting in my boat and my oars rhythmically creak. In short I propose to win my little battle—and even believe, more than hitherto, that I may annex my little province. It will be as small as the Grand Duchy of Pumpernickel—but there will be room to put up a friend. Therefore you must come and stay with me there; in fact I give you rendez-vous on the battlefield itself, the moment the day is declared. I mix my metaphors—but it all means that it's *all* a fight and that the only thing that changes is our fighting train. Let us then fight side by side, never too far out of sight.

How I congratulate you on the value of your friends; I mean the particular Davidsons. I don't know them, but I like them for liking you. I think I have a strong sense, too, of the beauty and charm of many of the conditions in which you are engaged and which have a really decorative effect—so that the aesthetic sense too is pleased—on everything that makes you minister to the confidence, my dear Arthur, of yours very constantly,

HENRY JAMES.

TO THE VISCOUNTESS WOLSELEY.

The reference in the following letter is to a visit paid by H. J., with Lady Wolseley, to the elaborately beautiful old house of the late C. E. Kempe, the well-known artist of church-decoration, at Lindfield, Sussex.

Dictated.

34 De Vere Gardens, W.

8th March, 1897.

Dear Lady Wolseley,

I was so deprived, yesterday, for all those beautiful hours, of a word with you away from our host that I felt as if I didn't say to you a tenth of what I wanted; which, however, will make it all the better for our next meeting—when I shall overflow like a river fed by melting snows. Let these few words, therefore, not anticipate the deluge—let them only express to you afresh my grateful sense of the interest and success of our excursion. The whole wonder of it was the greater through my wholly unprepared state, my antecedent inward blank—which blank is now overscored with images and emotions as thick as any page of any of your hospitable house-books ever was with visitors' names. The man himself made the place more wonderful and the place the man. I was greatly affected by his courtesy and charm; and I got afterwards, in the evening, a little of the light that I couldn't snatch from you under his nose. What struck me most about the whole thing was the consummate cleverness: *that* was the note it sounded for me more than any one of the notes more imposing, more deep, that an artistic creation *may* throw out. Don't for the world—and for my ruin—ever breathe to him I have said it; but the whole thing, and his taste, are far too Germanic, too Teutonic, a business to make a medium in which I could ever sink down in final peace or take as the domestic and decorative last word. The element of France and Italy are too much out of it—and they, to me, are the real secret of Style. But we will talk of these things—heaven speed the day. Do have a little of France and a great deal of Italy at South Wraxall; but do have also a great deal of the cunning Kempe and of the candid—too candid—companion of your pilgrimage. Don't imagine the companion didn't have a most sweet and glorious day—from which the light, even in London dusk again, has not yet wholly faded. I hope your security was complete to the end, and I am, in earnest hope also of a speedy reunion, yours, dear Lady Wolseley, more gratefully, if possible, than ever,

HENRY JAMES.

TO MISS FRANCES R. MORSE.

H. J.'s admiration for St. Gaudens's memorial to Col. R. G. Shaw, when he afterwards saw it at Boston, found expression, it will be remembered, in *The American Scene*.

Dictated.

34 De Vere Gardens, W.

June 7th, 1897.

My dear Fanny,

I have, as usual, endless unacknowledged benefits to thank you for after too many days. The last is your letter of the end of March, full of interesting substance as always and of things that no one else has the imagination or the inspiration to tell me. (My allusion to the imagination there is not, believe me, an imputation on your exactitude. The light of truth, of good solid vivid Boston truth, shines in each of your pages.) Especially are you interesting and welcome, as I have told you before, I think, on the young generations and full-blown, though new, existences, that are in possession of a scene I knew as otherwise occupied. All the old names—or most of them—appear to be represented by the remote posterity of my old acquaintance. In this remote posterity, however, I take an interest—and scraps and specimens of it, even here, occasionally flash past me....

I have stayed on in town later than for some years past, and though I had, at the end of March, all my plans made to go to Italy, have put it off till so late that, in a few days, I shall have to be content with simply crossing to Paris and seeing then what is to be further done. London is given up to carpenters and seat-mongers—being prepared, on an enormous scale and a rather unsightly way, for the "circus" of the 22nd. The circus is already, amid the bare benches and the mere *bousculade* of the preparations, a thing to fly from—in spite of the good young George Vanderbilt's having offered me an ample share of a beautiful balcony in Pall Mall to see it from. I shall spend the next few weeks in some place or places, north of the Alps, as yet utterly undefined, and be back in England before the summer is over. The voice of Venice, all this time, has called very loud. But it has been drowned a good deal in the click of the typewriter to which I dictate and which, some months ago, crept into my existence through the crevice of a lame hand and now occupies in it a place too big to be left vacant for long periods of hotel and railway life. All this time I am not coming to the great point, which is my hope that you may have been able to be present (I believe with all my heart of course you were) at the revelation of the Shaw Memorial. In charity, my dear Fanny, if this be the case, do write me a frank word about it. I heard from William and Alice more or less on the eve, but I fear they will have afterwards—just now be having—too much to do to be able to send me many echoes. I daresay that you will, for that matter, already have sent me one. I receive, as it happens, only this morning, a copy of Harper's Weekly with a big reproduction of St. Gaudens's bas-relief, which strikes me as extraordinarily beautiful and noble. How I rejoice that something really fine is to stand there forever for R. G. S.—and for all the rest of them. This thing of St. G.'s strikes me as a real perfection, and I have appealed to William to send me the finest and biggest photograph of it that can be found—for such surely have been taken. How your spiritual lungs must, over it all, have filled themselves with the air of the old wartime. Even here—I mean simply in the depths of one's own being—I myself, for an hour, seem to breathe it again. But the strange thing is that however much, in memory and imagination, it may live for one again, with all its dim figures and ghosts and reverberations and emotions, it appears to belong yet to some far away *other* world and state of being. I talked of this the other day with Sara Darwin, whose memories are so much identical with my own, and it was a relief to do so—in the absence of all other communications: that absence produced by the up-growth, since, of a whole generation, which began after the end and for which the whole history is as alien as the battles of Alexander. But I am writing you a long letter when I only meant to wave you a hand of greeting and gratitude. Correspondence is rather heavy to me, for I can tackle it only in the margin of time left over after the other matters that my machine has to grind. I hope your summer promises, and in the midst of a peculiar degree, at the present moment, of smoky London stuffiness, I envy you—for I see you in the mind's eye at Beverly—the element of wide verandahs, cut peaches—I mean peaches and cream, you know—white frocks and Atlantic airs. You make me, my dear Fanny, in these high lights, quite incredibly homesick.... Yours very constantly,

HENRY JAMES.

TO MRS. GEORGE HUNTER.

Instead of going abroad for the summer, as he had proposed, H. J. went first to Bournemouth, and from there to join his cousin, Mrs. George Hunter, and her daughters at Dunwich, near Saxmundham.

Bath Hotel, Bournemouth.

Saturday [July 3, 1897].

Dearest Elly,

It is an immense satisfaction to get your news—and no figure of speech to say that it has found me literally on the point of reaching out, for it, into the thick twilight of your whereabouts. I have had my general silence much on my conscience—and especially my dumbness and darkness to Rosina and Bay, for whom my movements must have been enveloped in a perfidious mystery that has caused me, I fear, to forfeit all their esteem. But let me tell you first of all how I rejoice in your good conditions and in your having found your feet. It was "borne in" upon me, on general grounds, that Southwold would never do for long, and it is charming that you have found so near and so nice a substitute. I especially delight (without wanting to sacrifice the rest of you) in such a letting-down-easy of the Art-Daughters. Please give them my tender love and tell them that, preposterous as it sounds, I have never, all this time, and in spite of the rosiest asseverations, crossed the channel at all. The nearest I have come to it is to have, early last month, come down here to the edge of the sea and collapsed into the peace and obscurity of this convenient corner (long familiar to me,) which, having a winter season, is practically empty at present. I will tell R. and B. when I see them just how it was that I happened to be so false—it is too long a story now. Suffice it that my reasons (for continuing to hug this fat country) were overwhelming, and my regrets (at not tasting of their brave Bohemia) of the sharpest. Moreover all's well that ends well. If I *had* gone abroad I should be abroad now and the rest of the summer; and therefore unable to join you on your Suffolk shore—or at least alight upon you there—which is what I shall be enchanted to do. You describe a little Paradise—houris and all; and I beseech you to keep a divan for me there. The only thing is that I fear I shan't be able to come till toward the end—or *by* the end—of the month. I have more or less engaged myself (to a pair of friends who are coming down here next week for my—strange as it may seem—sweet sake) to remain on this spot till toward the 25th. But I will come then, and stay as long as you will let me. If you can *bespeak* any quarters for me at the inn, in advance, I will take it very kindly of you. Can they give me a little *sitting-room* as well as a bed-room? If you can achieve any effective [word illegible] at them to do so I shall be very grateful. I always *need* some small literary bower other than the British bed-room—and in this case I would of course "meal" there, as that makes them always more zealous. I don't know the East Coast to speak of at all—and I can imagine no more winsome introduction to it. I quite yearn to commune with the young Parisians. Bravo, McMonnies. Bravo everybody—especially Grenville. How I shall joy to frolic with him in the sand! Have they seen—the art-daughters—the image of the St. Gaudens Shaw? It is altogether great. William's oration was a first-class success. I encircle you all and will write again!

Ever, my dear Elly, so constantly yours,

HENRY JAMES.

P.S. The oddest trio of coincidences yesterday afternoon. I was reading the delightful Letters of that peculiarly Suffolk genius (of Woodbridge) Edward FitzGerald ("Omar Khayyam") and, just finishing a story in one of them about his relations with a boatman of Saxmundham (a name—seen for the first time—that struck me—by its strangeness and handsomeness,) laid down the book and went a long walk—five miles along this coast, to where, in a very picturesque and lonely spot, I met a sea-faring man with whom I fraternised.

"Do you belong to this place?"

"Oh no. I've been here five years; but I come from the Suffolk coast—Saxmundham."

"Did you know Mr. FitzGerald?"

"Know him? My brother was his boatman!"—and he tells me the story! Then I walk home and coming in, find your letter on my table. I tear it open and the first word I see in it—in your date—is *Saxmundham*! Tableau!!! It never rains but it pours!—

TO EDWARD WARREN.

On returning from Dunwich—it was there that he had been bicycling with Mr. Warren—H. J. heard that Lamb House, which he had seen and admired at Rye the year before, was unexpectedly vacant. He at once appealed to Mr. Warren for professional advice with regard to the condition of the house, and as this proved satisfactory, secured it without delay.

Dictated.

34 De Vere Gardens, W.

15th September, 1897.

My dear Edward,

Very kindly read, for me, the enclosed—which throws an odd coincidental light on the very house we talked of, day before yesterday (or was it yesterday?) as we bumped and bounced and vainly shifted sides. The place in question is none other than the mansion with the garden-house perched on the wall; and though to be fairly confronted with the possibility and so brought to the point is a little like a blow in the stomach, what I am minded to say to you is that perhaps you may have a chance to tell me, on Friday, that you will be able to take some day next week to give me the pleasure of going down there with me for a look. I feel as if I couldn't *think* on the subject at all without seeing it—the subject—again; and there would be no such seeing it as seeing it in your company. Perhaps I shall have speech of you long enough on Friday to enable us to settle a day. *I* should be capable of Monday. I hope you slid gently home and are fairly on all fours—that is on hands and feet—again. What a day we should have had again also—I mean this one—if we had kept it up! But basta così!—it does beautifully for your journey. A thousand friendships to Margaret. Always yours,

HENRY JAMES.

TO ARTHUR CHRISTOPHER BENSON.

The following refers to a manuscript diary of Mr. Benson's and to the privately printed *Letters and Journals* of William Cory, author of *Ionica*.

34 De Vere Gardens, W.

September 25th, 1897.

My dear Arthur,

Send me by all means the Diary to which you so kindly allude—nothing could give me greater pleasure than to feel I might freely—and yet so responsibly—handle it. I hope it contains a record of your Hawarden talk—of which you speak.

I shall be very glad indeed of a talk with you about W. Cory—my impression of whom, on the book, you deepen—whenever anything so utterly unlikely as articulate speech between us miraculously comes to pass.—I am just drawing a long breath from having signed—a few moments since—a most portentous parchment: the lease of a smallish, charming, cheap old house in the country—down at Rye—for *21* years! (One would think I was *your* age!) But it is exactly what I want and secretly and hopelessly coveted (since knowing it) without dreaming it would ever fall. But it *has* fallen—and has a beautiful room for you (the "King's Room"—George II's—who slept there;) together with every promise of yielding me an indispensable retreat from May to October. I hope you are not more sorry to take up the load of

237

life that awaits, these days, the hunch of one's shoulders than *I* am. You'll ask me what I mean by "life." Come down to Lamb House and I'll tell you. And open the private page, my dear Arthur, to yours very eagerly,

HENRY JAMES.

TO MRS. WILLIAM JAMES.

Dictated.

34 De Vere Gardens, W.

1st December, 1897.

Dearest Alice,

It's too hideous and horrible, this long time that I have not written you and that your last beautiful letter, placed, for reminder, well within sight, has converted all my emotion on the subject into a constant, chronic blush. The reason has been that I have been driving very hard for another purpose this inestimable aid to expression, and that, as I have a greater loathing than ever for the mere manual act, I haven't, on the one side, seen my way to inflict on you a written letter, or on the other had the virtue to divert, till I should have finished my little book, to another stream any of the valued and expensive industry of my amanuensis. I *have*, at last, finished my little book—that is *a* little book, and so have two or three mornings of breathing-time before I begin another. Le plus clair of this small interval "I consecrate to thee!"

I am settled in London these several weeks and making the most of that part of the London year—the mild, quiet, grey stretch from the mid-October to Christmas—that I always find the pleasantest, with the single defect of its only not being long enough. We are having, moreover, a most creditable autumn; no cold to speak of and almost no rain, and a morning-room window at which, this December 1st, I sit with my scribe, admitting a radiance as adequate as that in which you must be actually bathed, and probably more mildly golden. I have no positive plan save that of just ticking the winter swiftly away on this most secure basis. There are, however, little doors ajar into a possible brief absence. I fear I have just closed one of them rather ungraciously indeed, in pleading a "non possumus" to a most genial invitation from John Hay to accompany him and his family, shortly after the new year, upon a run to Egypt and a month up the Nile; he having a boat for that same—I mean for the Nile part—in which he offers me the said month's entertainment. It is a very charming opportunity, and I almost blush at not coming up to the scratch; especially as I shall probably never have the like again. But it isn't so simple as it sounds; one has on one's hands the journey to Cairo and back, with whatever seeing and doing by the way two or three irresistible other things, to which one would feel one might never again be so near, would amount to. (I mean, of course, then or never, on the return, Athens, Corfu, Sicily the never-seen, etc., etc.) It would all "amount" to too much this year, by reason of a particular little complication—most pleasant in itself, I hasten to add—that I haven't, all this time, mentioned to you. Don't be scared—I haven't accepted an "offer." I have only taken, a couple of months ago, a little old house in the country—for the rest of my days!—on which, this winter, though it is, for such a commodity, in exceptionally good condition, I shall have to spend money enough to make me quite concentrate my resources. The little old house you will at no distant day, I hope, see for yourself and inhabit and even, I trust, temporarily and gratuitously possess— for half the fun of it, in the coming years, will be occasionally to lend it to you. I marked it for my own two years ago at Rye—so perfectly did it, the first instant I beheld it, offer the solution of my long-unassuaged desire for a calm retreat between May and November. It is the very calmest and yet cheerfullest that I could have dreamed—*in* the little old, cobble-stoned, grass-grown, red-roofed town, on the summit of its mildly pyramidal hill and close to its noble old church—the chimes of which will sound sweet in my goodly old red-walled garden.

The little place is so rural and tranquil, and yet discreetly animated, that its being within the town is, for convenience and immediate accessibility, purely to the good; and the house itself, though modest and unelaborate, full of a charming little stamp and dignity of its period (about 1705) without as well as within. The next time I go down to see to its "doing up," I will try to have a photograph taken of the pleasant little old-world town-angle into which its nice old red-bricked front, its high old Georgian doorway and a most delightful little old architectural garden-house, perched alongside of it on its high brick garden-wall—into which all these pleasant features together so happily "compose." Two years ago, after I had lost my heart to it—walking over from Point Hill to make sheep's eyes at it (the more so that it is called Lamb House!)—there was no appearance whatever that one could ever have it; either that its fond proprietor would give it up or that if he did it would come at all within one's means. So I simply sighed and renounced; tried to think no more about it; till at last, out of the blue, a note from the good local ironmonger, to whom I had whispered at the time my hopeless passion, informed me that by the sudden death of the owner and the preference (literal) of his son for Klondyke, it might perhaps drop into my lap. Well, to make a long story short, it *did* immediately drop and, more miraculous still to say, on terms, for a long lease, well within one's means—terms quite deliciously moderate. The result of these is, naturally, that they will "do" nothing to it: but, on the other hand, it has been so well lived in and taken care of that the doing—off one's own bat—is reduced mainly to sanitation and furnishing—which latter includes the peeling off of old papers from several roomfuls of pleasant old top-to-toe wood panelling. There are two rooms of complete old oak—one of them a delightful little parlour, opening by one side into the little vista, church-ward, of the small old-world street, where not one of the half-dozen wheeled vehicles of Rye ever passes; and on the other straight into the garden and the approach, from that quarter, to the garden-house aforesaid, which is simply the making of a most commodious and picturesque detached study and workroom. Ten days ago Alfred Parsons, best of men as well as best of landscape-painters-and-gardeners, went down with me and revealed to me the most charming possibilities for the treatment of the tiny out-of-door part—it amounts to about an acre of garden and lawn, all shut in by the peaceful old red wall aforesaid, on which the most flourishing old espaliers, apricots, pears, plums and figs, assiduously grow. It appears that it's a glorious little growing exposure, air, and soil—and all the things that were still flourishing out of doors (November 20th) were a joy to behold. There went with me also a good friend of mine, Edward Warren, a very distingué architect and loyal spirit, who is taking charge of whatever is to be done. So I hope to get in, comfortably enough, early in May. In the meantime one must "pick up" a sufficient quantity of ancient mahogany-and-brass odds and ends—a task really the more amusing, here, where the resources are great, for having to be thriftily and cannily performed. The house is really quite charming enough in its particular character, and as to the stamp of its period, not to do violence to by rash modernities; and I am developing, under its influence and its inspiration, the most avid and gluttonous eye and most infernal watching patience, in respect of lurking "occasions" in not too-delusive Chippendale and Sheraton. The "King's Room" will be especially treated with a preoccupation of the comfort and aesthetic sense of cherished sisters-in-law; King's Room so-called by reason of George Second having passed a couple of nights there and so stamped it for ever. (He was forced ashore, at Rye, on a progress somewhere with some of his ships, by a tempest, and accommodated at Lamb House as at the place in the town then most consonant with his grandeur. It would, for that matter, quite correspond to this description still. Likewise the Mayors of Rye have usually lived there! Or the persons usually living there have usually *become* mayors! That was conspicuously the case with the late handsome old Mr. Bellingham, whose son is my landlord. So you see the ineluctable dignity in store for me.) But enough of this swagger. I have been copious to copiously amuse you.

Your beautiful letter, which I have just read over again, is full of interest about you all; causing me special joy as to what it says of William's present and prospective easier conditions of work, relinquishment of laboratory, refusal of outside lectures, etc., and of the general fine performance, and promise, all round, of the children. What you say of each makes me want to see that particular one most.... I had a very great pleasure the other day in a visit, far too short—only six hours—from dear old Howells, who did me a lot of good in an illuminating professional (i.e. commercial) way, and came, in fact, at quite a psychological moment. I hope you may happen to see him soon enough to get from him also some echo of *me*—such as it may be. But, my dear Alice, I must be less interminable. Please tell William that I have two Syracuse "advices," as yet gracelessly unacknowledged—I mean to him—to thank him for. It's a joy to find these particular months less barren than they used to be. I embrace you tenderly all round and am yours very constantly,

HENRY JAMES.

TO MISS GRACE NORTON.

Dictated.

34 De Vere Gardens, W.

Christmas Day, 1897.

My dear Grace,

Is it really a year? I have been acutely conscious of its getting to be a horrible time, but it hadn't come home to me that it was taking on quite that insolence. Well, you see what the years—since years *il y a*—are making of me: I don't write to you for a hideous age, and then, when at last I do, I take the romantic occasion of this particular day to write in this *un*sympathetic ink. But that is exactly what, as I say, the horrid time has made of me. The use of my hand, always difficult, has become impossible to me; and since I am reduced to dictation, this form of dictation is the best. May its distinctness make up for its indirectness....

I dare say that, from time to time, you hear something of me from William; and you know, by that flickering light, that my life has had, for a long time past, a very jog-trot sort of rhythm. I have ceased completely to "travel." It is going on into four years since I have crossed the Channel; and the day is not yet. This will give you a ghastly sense of the insular object that I must have become; however, I shall break out yet, perhaps, and surprise you. Meanwhile, none the less, I was unable, these last days, to break the spell of immobility even to the extent of going over to Paris to poor Daudet's funeral. I felt that, là-bas—by which I mean in the immediate house—a certain expectation rested on me, but I looked it straight in the face and cynically budged not. I dislike, more and more, the terrific organized exploitation, in Paris, on the occasion of death and burial, of every kind of personal privacy and every kind of personal hysterics. It is newspaperism and professionalism gone mad—in a way all its own; and I felt as if *I* should go mad if I even once more, let alone twenty times more, heard Daudet personally compared (more especially *facially* compared, eyeglass and all) to Jesus Christ. Not a French notice of him that I have seen but has plumped it coquettishly out. I had not seen him, thanks to my extreme recalcitrance, since the month he spent more than two years ago in London. His death was not unhappy—was indeed too long delayed, for all his later time has been sadly (by disease, borne with wonderful patience and subtlety) blighted and sterilized. Yet it is a wonderful proof of what a success his life had been that it had remained a success in spite of that. It was the most *worked* thing that ever was—I mean his whole career. His talent was so great that I feel, as to his work, that the best of it will quite intensely remain. But he was a queer combination of a great talent with an absence of the greater mind, as it were—the greater feeling.

...Well, my dear Grace, I can't tell you the comfort and charm it is to be talking with you even by this horrid machinery, and to squeeze the little round golden orange of your note dry of every testimony to your honoured tranquillity that I can gouge out of it. My metaphors are mixed, but my fidelity is pure. How is the mighty Montaigne? I don't read him a millionth part as much as I ought, for of all the horrors of London almost the worst horror is the way it conspires against the evening book under the evening lamp. I don't "go out"—and yet, far too much of the time, I *am* out. The main part of the rest I devote to wondering how I got there. A propos of which, as much as anything, do you read Maurice Barrès? If you do, his last thing, Les Déracinés, is very curious and serious, but a gruesome picture of young France. If it didn't sound British and Pharisaic I would almost risk saying that, on all the more and more showing, young and old France both seem to me to be in a strange state of moral and intellectual decomposition. But this isn't worth saying without going into the detail of the evidence—and that would take me too far. Then there is Leslie Stephen and the little Kiplings. Leslie seems to be out-weathering his woes in the most extraordinary way. His health is literally better than it was in his wife's lifetime, and is perhaps, more almost than anything else, a proof of what a life-preserver in even the wildest waves is the perfect possession of a *métier*. His admirable habit and knowledge of work have saved him.... Rudyard and his wife and offspring depart presently for South Africa. They have settled upon a small propriété at Rottingdean near the [Burne-Jones's], and the South Africa is but a parenthetic family picnic. It would do as well as anything else, perhaps, if one still felt, as one used to, that everything is grist to his mill. I don't, however, think that everything is, as the affair is turning out, at all; I mean as to the general complexity of life. His *Ballad* future may still be big. But my view of his prose future has much shrunken in the light of one's increasingly observing how little of life he can make use of. Almost nothing civilised save steam and patriotism—and the latter only in verse, where I *hate* it so, especially mixed up with God and goodness, that that half spoils my enjoyment of his great talent. Almost nothing of the complicated soul or of the female form or of any question of *shades*—which latter constitute, to my sense, the real formative literary discipline. In his earliest time I thought he perhaps contained the seeds of an English Balzac; but I have quite given that up in proportion as he has come steadily from the less simple in subject to the more simple—from the Anglo-Indians to the natives, from the natives to the Tommies, from the Tommies to the quadrupeds, from the quadrupeds to the fish, and from the fish to the engines and screws....

Goodbye, my dear Grace. Believe that through all fallacious appearances of ebb and flow, of sound and silence, of presence and absence, I am always constantly yours,

HENRY JAMES.

V. RYE(1898-1903)

The first five years that Henry James spent at Rye were the least eventful and the most serenely occupied of his life. Even at the height of his London activities he had always clung fast to his daily work; and now that his whole time was his own, free from all interruptions save those invited by his own hospitality, he lived in his writing with a greater concentration than ever before. His letters shew indeed that he could still be haunted occasionally by the thought of the silence with which his books were received by the public at large—an indifference, it must be said, which he was always inclined to exaggerate; but these misgivings were superficial in comparison with the deep joy of surrender to his own genius, now at the climax of its power. He was satisfied at length with his mastery of his instrument; he knew perfectly what he wished to do and knew that he could do it; and the long mornings of summer in the pleasant old garden-room of Lamb House, or of winter in his small southern study indoors, were perhaps the best, the most intimately contenting hours he had ever passed. He was now confirmed in the habit of dictation, and never again wrote his books with his own hand except under special stress. At Rye or in London his secretary would be installed at the typewriter by ten o'clock in the morning, and for three or four hours he would pace the room, pausing, hesitating, gradually massing and controlling the stream of his imagination, till at a favouring moment it rolled forward without a check. So, in these five years, the most characteristic works of his later maturity were produced. They began with The Awkward Age, The Sacred Fount, and many short stories presently collected in The Soft Side and The Better Sort; and they culminated, still within the limit of this short period, with the great triad of novels that were to crown the long tale of his fiction—The Ambassadors, The Wings of the Dove, The Golden Bowl.

With his life at Rye, too, his correspondence with his family and his friends began to spread out in an amplitude of which the following selection can give at the best a very imperfect idea. The rich apologies for silence and backwardness that preface so many of his letters must be interpreted in the light, partly indeed of his natural luxuriance of phraseology, but much more of his generous conception of the humblest correspondent's claim on him for response. He could not answer a brief note of friendliness but with pages of abounding eloquence. He never dealt in the mere small change of intercourse; the post-card and the half-sheet did not exist for him; a few lines of enquiry would bring from him a bulging packet of manuscript, overwhelming in its disproportion. No wonder that with this standard of the meaning of a letter he often groaned under his postal burden. He discharged himself of it, in general, very late at night; the morning's work left him too much exhausted for more composition until then. At midnight he would sit down to his letter-writing and cover sheet after sheet, sometimes for hours, with his dashing and not very readable script. Occasionally he would give up a day to the working off of arrears by dictation, seldom omitting to excuse himself to each correspondent in turn for the infliction of the "fierce legibility" of type. The number of his letters was in fact enormous, and even within the limits of the present selection they form a picture of his life at Rye to which there is little to add.

He had intended Lamb House to be a retreat from the pressure of the world, but it need hardly be said that from the first it was thrown open to his friends with hospitable freedom. In the matter of entertainment his standard again was munificently high, and the consequences it entailed were sometimes weightier than he found to his liking. But once more it is necessary to read his laments over his violated hermitage with many reserves. Lonely as he was in his work, he was not made for any other kind of solitude; he needed companionship, and soon missed it when it was withdrawn. After a few experiments he discovered that the isolation of the winter at Rye by no means agreed with him; for the short days and long evenings he preferred Pall Mall, where (after letting his flat in Kensington) he engaged a permanent lodging at the Reform Club. He could thus divide the year as he chose between London and Rye, and the arrangement was so much to his liking that in five years he made only one long absence from home. In 1899 he returned again to Italy for the summer, paying a visit on the way to M. and Mme. Bourget at Hyères. At Rome many associations were recalled for him by a suggestion that he should write the life of William Wetmore Story, his friend and host of twenty years before—a suggestion carried out somewhat later in a book filled, as he said, with the old Roman gold-dust of the seventies. He brought back new impressions also from a visit to Mrs. Humphry Ward at Castel Gandolfo—where she and her family were spending some weeks at the Villa Barberini, on the ridge between the Roman Campagna and the Alban lake—and another to Marion Crawford at Sorrento. He stayed briefly at Florence and Venice, and returned home to find a special reason awaiting him for renewed application to work. He had taken Lamb House on a lease, but the death of its owner now made it necessary to decide whether he should purchase it outright. He paid the price without hesitation; he was by this time deeply attached to the place and he seized the chance of making it his own. The earnings of his work would not go far towards paying for it, but he felt it all the more urgent to concentrate upon production for some time to come. He did not leave England again till four years later, nor his own roof for more than a few days now and then.

By far the greatest of all his interests, outside his work, was the opportunity he now had of seeing more than hitherto of his elder brother and his household. In the autumn of 1899 Professor and Mrs. William James came to Europe for a visit of two years, and during that time the brothers were together in London or at Lamb House as often as possible. Unfortunately it was the state of his health that had made a long holiday desirable for William James, and most of the time had to be spent by him in a southern climate, in Italy or on the Riviera. Nevertheless it was a deep delight to the younger brother to feel able to share the life of the elder at nearer range. They were curiously unlike in their whole cast of mind; nothing could have been further from Henry James's massive and ruminatory imagination than his brother's quick-footed, freely-ranging, experimental genius. But their devotion to each other grew only the closer as their intellectual lives diverged; and as they approached old age together, there was still something protective in William James's attitude, and in Henry something that appealed to his brother, and to his brother only, for moral support and reassurance. The next generation, moreover, were by this time growing up and were beginning to take a place in

Henry James's life that was a source of ever-increasing pride and pleasure to him. From now onward there was nothing he so welcomed as the recurring visits to Lamb House of one or other of his elder brother's children. William James was again in Europe in 1902, delivering at Edinburgh the lectures that presently appeared as The Varieties of Religious Experience.

It was now all but twenty years since Henry had last seen America, and the desire once more to visit his country began to stir obscurely in his mind. The idea was long pondered and circuitously approached, but it will be seen from one of the following letters that it had become definite in 1903. Long absence had made a return seem a formidable adventure, and it was not in his nature to undertake it without many scruples and debates. In the midst of these his mind was gradually made up and the journey determined upon for 1904.

TO W. D. HOWELLS.

34 De Vere Gardens, W.

January 28th, 1898.

My dear Howells,

Too long, too long have I delayed to thank you for your last good letter; yet if I've been thus guilty the fault—as it were! the deep responsibility— is largely your own. It all comes from that wonderful (and still-in-my-ears reverberating) little talk we had that morning here in the soft lap, and under the motherly apron, of the dear old muffling fog—which will have kept every one else from hearing *ever*—and only let me hear, and have been heard! I mean that the effect of your admirable counsel and comfort was from that moment to give me the sense of being, somehow, suddenly, preposterously, renewingly and refreshingly, at a kind of practical high pressure which has— well, which has simply, my dear Howells, made all the difference! There it is. It is the absurd, dizzy consciousness of this difference that has constituted (failing other things!) an exciting, absorbing feeling of occupation and preoccupation—and thereby paralysed the mere personal activity of my pen....

I hope you have by this time roared—and not *wholly* with rage and despair!—through the tunnel of your dark consciousness of return. I dare say you are now quite out on the flowery meads of almost doubting of having been away. This makes me fear your promise to come back—right soon—next summer—may even now have developed an element of base alloy. I rushed off to see Mrs. Harland the instant I heard *she* was back, and got hold of you—and of Mildred—for five minutes (and of all the handsomest parts of both of you) in her talk. She had left a dying mother, however, and her general situation has, I fear, its pressure and pinch. What an interest indeed your boy's outlook must be to you! But, as you say—seeing them *commence*—! Well, they never commenced before; and the pain is all in *us*—not out of us. The thing is to keep it in. But this scrawl—or sprawl—is about all my poor hand can now sustainedly perpetrate; if I continue I shall have to clamour for a mount—a lift—my brave boy of the alphabetic hoofs. But I spare you those caracoles. I greet you each again, affectionately, and am yours, my dear Howells, intensely,

HENRY JAMES.

TO ARTHUR CHRISTOPHER BENSON.

The origin of *The Turn of the Screw* in an anecdote told him by Archbishop Benson is described in the preface that H. J. wrote for it when it appeared in the collected edition of his works.

34 De Vere Gardens, W.

March 11th, 1898.

My dear Arthur,

I suppose that in the mysterious scheme of providence and fate such an inspiration as your charming note—out of the blue!—of a couple of days ago, is intended somehow to make up to me for the terror with which my earlier—in fact *all* my past—productions inspire me, and for the insurmountable aversion I feel to looking at them again or to considering them in any way. This morbid state of mind is really a blessing in disguise— for it has for happy consequences that such an incident as your letter becomes thereby extravagantly pleasant and gives me a genial glow. All thanks and benedictions—I shake your hand very hard—or *would* do so if I could attribute to you anything so palpable, personal and actual *as* a hand. Yet I shall never write a sequel to the *P. of an L.*—admire my euphonic indefinite article. It's all too faint and far away—too ghostly and ghastly—and I have bloodier things *en tête*. I can do better than that!

But à propos, precisely, of the ghostly and ghastly, I have a little confession to make to you that has been on my conscience these three months and that I hope will excite in your generous breast nothing but tender memories and friendly sympathies.

On one of those two memorable—never to be obliterated—winter nights that I spent at the sweet Addington, your father, in the drawing-room by the fire, where we were talking a little, in the spirit of recreation, of such things, repeated to me the few meagre elements of a small and gruesome spectral story that had been told *him* years before and that he could only give the dimmest account of—partly because he had forgotten details and partly—and much more—because there had *been* no details and no coherency in the tale as he received it, from a person who also but half knew it. The vaguest essence only was there—some dead servants and some children. This essence *struck* me and I made a note of it (of a most scrappy kind) on going home. There the note remained till this autumn, when, struck with it afresh, I wrought it into a fantastic fiction which, first intended to be of the briefest, finally became a thing of some length and is now being "serialised" in an American periodical. It will appear late in the spring (chez Heinemann) in a volume with *one* other story, and then I will send it to you. In the meanwhile please think of the *doing* of the thing on my part as having sprung from that kind old evening at Addington—quite gruesomely as my unbridled imagination caused me to see the inevitable development of the subject. It was all worth mentioning to you. I am very busy and very decently fit and very much yours, always, my dear Arthur,

HENRY JAMES.

TO WILLIAM JAMES.

The following letter was written immediately before the outbreak of war between Spain and the United States.

Dictated.

34 De Vere Gardens, W.

20 April, 1898.

My dear William,

There are all sorts of *intimes* and confidential things I want to say to you in acknowledgment of your so deeply interesting letter—of April 10th—received yesterday; but I must break the back of my response at least with this mechanical energy; not having much of any other—by which I mean simply too many odd moments—at my disposal just now. I do answer you, alas, almost to the foul music of the cannon. It is this morning precisely that one feels the fat to be at last fairly in the fire. I confess that the blaze about to come leaves me woefully cold, thrilling with no glorious thrill or holy blood-thirst whatever. I see nothing but the madness, the passion, the hideous clumsiness of rage, of mechanical reverberation; and I echo with all my heart your denouncement of the foul criminality of the screeching newspapers. They have long since become, for me, the danger that overtops all others. That became clear to one, even here, two years ago, in the Venezuela time; when one felt that with a week of simple, enforced silence everything could be saved. If things *were* then saved without it, it is simply that they hadn't at that time got so bad as they are now in the U.S. My sympathy with you all is intense—the whole horror must so mix itself with all your consciousness. I am near enough to hate it, without being, as you are, near enough in some degree, perhaps, to understand. I am leading at present so quiet a life that I don't measure much the sentiment, the general attitude around me. Much of it can't possibly help being Spanish—and from the "European" standpoint in general Spain *must* appear savagely assaulted. She is so quiet—publicly and politically—so decent and picturesque and harmless a member of the European family that I am bound to say it argues an extraordinary illumination and a very predetermined radicalism not to admire her pluck and pride. But publicly, of course, England will do nothing whatever that is not more or less—negatively—for our benefit. I scarcely know what the newspapers say—beyond the Times, which I look at all for Smalley's cables: so systematic is my moral and intellectual need of ignoring them. One must save one's life if one can. The next weeks will, however, in this particular, probably not a little break me down. I must at least read the Bombardment of Boston. May you but scantly suffer from it!...

I rejoice with intense rejoicing in everything you tell me of your own situation, plans, arrangements, honours, prospects—into all of which I enter with an intimacy of participation. Your election to the *Institut* has, for me, a surpassing charm—I simply revel and, as it were, wallow in it. Je m'y vautre. But oh, if it could only have come soon enough for poor Alice to have known it—such a happy little nip as it would have given her; or for the dear old susceptible Dad! But things come as they can—and I am, in general, lost in the daily miracle of their coming at all: I mean so many of them—few as that many may be: and I speak above all for myself. I am lost, moreover, just now, in the wonder of what effect on American affairs, of every kind, the shock of battle will have. Luckily it's of my nature—though not of my pocket—always to be prepared for the worst and to expect the least. Like you, with all my heart, I have "finance on the brain." At least I try to have it—with a woeful lack of natural talent for the same. It is none too soon. But one arrives at dates, periods, corners of one's life: great changes, deep operations are begotten. This has more portée than I can fully go into. I shall certainly do my best to let my flat when I am ready to leave town; the difficulty, this year, however, will be that the time for "season" letting begins now, and that I can't depart for at least another month. Things are not ready at Rye, and won't be till then, with the limited local energy at work that I have very wisely contented myself with turning on there. It has been the right and much the best way in the long run, and for one's good little relations there; only the run has been a little longer. The remnant of the season here may be difficult to dispose of—to a sub-lessee; and my books—only a part of which I can house at Rye—are a complication. However, I shall do what I can this year; and for subsequent absences, so long as my present lease of De Vere Gardens runs, I shall have the matter on a smooth, organised, working basis. I mean to arrange myself always to let—being, as such places go, distinctly lettable. And for my declining years I have already put my name down for one of the invaluable south-looking, Carlton-Gardens-sweeping bedrooms at the Reform Club, which are let by the year and are of admirable and convenient (with all the other resources of the place at one's elbow) *general* habitability. The only thing is they are so in demand that one has sometimes a long time to await one's turn. On the other hand there are accidents—"occasions." ... I embrace you all—Alice longer than the rest—and am—with much actuality of emotion, ever your

HENRY.

TO MISS MUIR MACKENZIE.

Miss Muir Mackenzie, who was staying at Winchelsea, had reported on the progress of the preparations at Lamb House.

34 De Vere Gardens, W.

Thursday [May 19, 1898].

Dear Miss Muir Mackenzie,

Forgive the constant pressure which has delayed the expression of my gratitude for your charming, vivid, pictorial report of—well, of everything. It was most kind of you to paddle again over to Rye to minister to my anxieties. You both assuage and encourage them—but with the right thing for each. I am content enough with the bathroom—but hopeless about the garden, which I don't know what to do with, and shall never, *never* know.

I am *densely* ignorant—only just barely know dahlias from mignonette—and shall never be able to work it in any way. So I shan't try—but remain gardenless—only go in for a lawn; which requires mere brute force—no intellect! For the rest I shall do decently, perhaps—so far as one can do for two-and-ninepence. I shall have nothing really "good"—only the humblest old fifth-hand, 50th hand, mahogany and brass. I have collected a handful of feeble relics—but I fear the small desert will too cruelly interspace them. Well, *speriamo*. I'm very sorry to say that getting down before Saturday has proved only the fondest of many delusions. The whole place has to be mattinged before the rickety mahogany can go in, and the end of that—or, for aught I know, the beginning—is not yet. I have but just received the "estimate" for the (humblest) window-curtains (two tiers, *on* the windows, instead of blinds: white for downstairs etc., greeny-blue for *up*, if you like details,) and the "figure" leaves me prostrate. Oh, what a tangled web we weave!—Still, I hope *you*, dear lady, have a nice tangled one of some sort to occupy you such a day as this. I think of you, on the high style of your castled steep, with tender compassion. I scarce flatter myself you will in the hereafter again haunt the neighbourhood; but if you ever do, I gloat over the idea of making up for the shame of your having gone forth tea-less and toast-less from any door of mine. I wish that, within it—my door—we might discuss still weightier things. Of an ordinary—a normal—year, I hope always to be there in May.

Deeply interesting your Winchelsea touches—especially so the portrait of my future colleague—confrère—the Mayor—for the inhabitants of Lamb House have always been Mayors of Rye. When I reach this dignity I will appoint you my own Sketcher-in-Chief and replace for you by Château Ypres (the old Rye stronghold) the limitations of Château Noakes. I express to you fresh gratitude and sympathy, and am yours, dear Miss Muir Mackenzie, most cordially,

HENRY JAMES.

TO GAILLARD T. LAPSLEY.

Dictated.

34 De Vere Gardens, W.

17th June, 1898.

My dear G. T. L.

I am very unhappy and humiliated at not having succeeded in again putting my hand on you, and the fear that you may possibly have departed altogether is a fearful aggravation of my misery. Therefore I am verily stricken—so stricken as to be incapable of holding a pen and to be reduced to this ugly—by which I mean this thoroughly beautiful—substitute. If I wait for a pen, God knows when or where I shall overtake you. Accordingly, in my effort to catch up, I let Remington shamelessly loose. I lash his sides—I damn his eyes. Be found by him, my dear man, somehow or somewhere—before the burden of my shame crushes me to the earth and I sink beneath it into a frequently desired grave. The worst of it all is that I saw E. Fawcett yesterday and he told me he really believed you *had* gone. I hammer away, but I don't in the least know where to send this. Fawcett gave me a sort of a tip—at which I think I shall clutch. A day or two after I last saw you I went out of town till the following Monday, and then, coming back, had but the Tuesday here, crammed with a frenzy and fury of conflicting duties. On Wednesday I was obliged to dash away again—to go down to Rye, where domestic complications of the gravest order held me fast the rest of the week, or at least till the Saturday, when I rushed up to town only in time to rush off again and spend, at Cobham, two days with the Godkins, to whose ensconcement there it had been, for a long time before, one of the features of a devouring activity that I had responsibly helped to contribute. But now that I am at home again till, as soon as possible, I succeed in breaking away for the rest of the summer, I have lost you beyond recall, and my affliction is deep and true. But we know what it is better to have done even as an accompaniment of losing than never to have done at all. And I didn't do nothing at all—on the contrary, I did *that*:

that which is better. This is but a flurried and feverish word—hurried off in the hope of keeping your inevitable hating me from becoming a settled habit. I follow you with much sympathy, and with still more interest, attention and hope. I follow you, in short, with a great many sentiments. May the great globe whirl round before long some such holiday for you as will convert—for *me*—the pursuit I so inadequately allude to into something in the nature of an encounter. Only write to me. Do write to me. I mean when you begin to see your way. I know you will have lots to do first—and I am very patient, as befits one who is so constantly yours,

HENRY JAMES.

TO PAUL BOURGET.

Dictated.

Lamb House, Rye.

19th August, 1898.

Mon cher Ami,

I have hideously delayed to acknowledge your so interesting letter from Paris, and now the manner of my response does little to repair the missing grace of my silence. I trust, however, to your general confidence not to exact of me the detail of the reasons why I am more and more *asservi* to this benevolent legibility, which I so delight in on the part of others that I find it difficult to understand their occasional resentment of the same on my own—a resentment that I know indeed, from generous licence already given, you do not share. I have promised myself each day to attack you pen in hand, but the overpowering heat which, I grieve to say, has reigned even on my balmy hilltop, has, by really sickening me, taken the colour out of all my Gallo-latin, leaving very blanched as well the paler idiom in which I at last perforce address you.

I have been entering much more than my silly silence represents into the sequel of your return to London, and not less into the sequel of *that*.

Please believe in my affectionate participation as regards the Bezly Thorne consultation and whatever emotion it may have excited in either of you. To that emotion I hope the healing waters have already applied the most cooling, soothing, softening douche—or administered a not less beneficent draught if the enjoyment of them has had in fact to be more inward. I congratulate you on the decision you so speedily took and, with your usual Napoleonic celerity when the surface of the globe is in question, so energetically acted upon. I trust you are, in short, really settled for a while among rustling German woods and plashing German waters. (Those are really, for the most part, my own main impressions of Germany—the memory of ancient summers there at more or less bosky Bäder, or other Kur-orten, involving a great deal of open air strolling in the shade and sitting under trees.) This particular dose of Deutschland will, I feel, really have been more favourable to you than your having had to swallow the Teuton-element in the form of the cookery, or of any other of the manifold attributes, of the robust fausse anglaise whom I here so confoundingly revealed to you. Let it console you also a little that you would have had to bear, as well, with that burden, a temperature that the particular conditions of the house I showed you would not have done much to minimise. I have been grilled, but I have borne it better for not feeling that I had put you also on the stove. Rye goes on baking, this amazing summer, but, though I suppose the heat is everywhere, you have a more refreshing regimen. I pray for the happiest and most marked results from it.

I have received the *Duchesse Bleue*, and also the Land of Cockaigne from Madame Paul, whom I thank very kindly for her inscription. I had just read the Duchess, but haven't yet had leisure to attack the great Matilda. The Duchess inspires me with lively admiration—so close and firm, and with an interest so nourished straight from the core of the subject, have you succeeded in keeping her. I never read you sans vouloir me colleter with you on what I can't help feeling to be the detrimental parti-pris (unless it be wholly involuntary) of some of your narrative, and other technical, processes. These questions of art and form, as well as of much else, interest me deeply—really much more than any other; and so, not less, do they interest you: yet, though they frequently come up between us, as it were, when I read you, I nowadays never seem to see you long enough at once to thresh them comfortably out with you. Moreover, after all, what does threshing-out avail?—that conviction is doubtless at the bottom of my disposition, half the time, to let discussion go. Each of us, from the moment we are worth our salt, writes as he can and only as he can, and his writing at all is conditioned upon the very things that from the standpoint of another method most lend themselves to criticism. And we each know much better than anyone else can what the defect of our inevitable form may appear. So, though it does strike me that your excess of anticipatory analysis undermines too often the reader's curiosity—which is a gross, loose way of expressing one of the things I mean—so, probably, I really understand better than anyone except yourself why, to do the thing at all, you must use your own, and nobody's else, trick of presentation. No two men in the world have the same idea, image and measure of presentation. All the same, I must some day read one of your books with you, so interesting would it be to me—if not to *you*!—to put, from page to page and chapter to chapter, your finger on certain places, showing you just where and why (selon moi!) you are too prophetic, too exposedly constructive, too disposed yourself to swim in the thick reflective element in which you set your figures afloat. All this is a clumsy notation of what I mean, and, on the whole, mal àpropos into the bargain, inasmuch as I find in the Duchess plenty of the art I most like and the realisation of an admirable subject. Beautifully done the whole episode of the actress's intervention in the rue Nouvelle, in which I noted no end of superior touches. I doubt if any of your readers lose less than I do—to the fiftieth part of an intention. All this part of the book seems to me thoroughly handled—except that, I think, I should have given Molan a different behaviour after he gets into the cab with the girl—not have made him act so *immediately* "in character." He takes there no line—I mean no deeper one—which is what I think he would have done. In fact I think I see, myself, positively what he would have done; and in general he is, to my imagination, as you give him, too much in character, too little mysterious. So is Mme. de Bonnivet—so too, even, is the actress. Your love of intellectual daylight, absolutely your pursuit of complexities, is an injury to the patches of ambiguity and the abysses of shadow which really are the clothing—or much of it—of the *effects* that constitute the material of our trade. Basta!

I ordered my year-old "Maisie" the other day to be sent to you, and I trust she will by this time have safely arrived—in spite of some ambiguity in the literation of the name of your villa as, with your letter in my hand, I earnestly meditate upon it. I have also despatched to Madame Paul myself a little volume just published—a poor little pot-boiling study of nothing at all, qui ne tire pas à conséquence. It is but a monument to my fatal technical passion, which prevents my ever giving up anything I have begun. So that when something that I have supposed to be a subject turns out on trial really to be none, je m'y acharne d'autant plus, for mere superstition—superstitious fear, I mean, of the consequences and omens of weakness. The small book in question is really but an exercise in the art of not appearing to one's self to fail. You will say it is rather cruel that for such exercises the public also should have to pay. Well, Madame Paul and you get your exemplaire for nothing.

I have not seen La Femme et le Pantin—I see nothing in the way of books here; but what you tell me disposes me to send for it—as well as my impression of the only other thing that I have read by the same hand. Only, on the question of talent and of effect produced, don't you forget, too much, with such people, that talent and effect are comparatively easy things with the licence of such gros moyens? They are a great short-cut—the extremities to which all these people proceed, and anyone can—no matter who—be more or less striking with them. But I am writing you an interminable letter. Do let me know—sans m'en vouloir for the quantity and quality of it—how Nauheim turns out, and receive my heartiest wishes for all sorts of comfortable results. Yours both always constantly,

HENRY JAMES.

TO W. D. HOWELLS.

Dictated.

Lamb House, Rye.

19th August, 1898.

259

My dear Howells,

I throw myself without hesitation into this familiar convenience, for the simple reason that I can thus thank you to-day for your blessed letter from York Harbour, whereas if I were to wait to be merely romantic and illegible, I should perhaps have, thanks to many things, to put off *la douce affaire* till week after next. If I strike, moreover, while the iron is hot, I strike also while the weather is—so unprecedentedly hot for this lukewarm land that even the very moderate cerebral performance to which I am treating you requires [*sic*] no manual extension. It has been delicious to hear from you, and, even though I be here domiciled in some gentility, in a little old quasi-historic wainscotted house, with a real lawn and a real mulberry-tree of my own to kick my heels on and under, I draw from the folds of your page a faint, far sense of the old and remembered breath of New England woods and New England waters—such as there is still somewhere on my jaded palate the power to taste and even a little, over-built and over-planted as I at the best am, to languish for....

I can't speak to you of the war very much further than to admire the wit of your closing epigram about it, which, however, at the rate you throw out these things, you must long since have forgotten. But my silence isn't in the least indifference; it is a deep embarrassment of thought—of imagination. I have hated, I have almost loathed it; and yet I can't help plucking some food for fancy out of its results—some vision of how much the bigger complexity we are landed in, the bigger world-contacts, may help to educate us and force us to produce people of capacity greater than a less pressure demands. Capacity for *what?* you will naturally ask—whereupon I scramble out of our colloquy by saying that I should perhaps tell you beautifully if you were here and sitting with me on the darkening lawn of my quaint old garden at the end of this barely endurable August day. I will make more things than that clear to you if you will only turn up there. Each of you, Mrs. Howells, Mildred, and John all included—for I have four spare rooms, tell it not anywhere—has been individually considered, as to what you would most like, in my domestic arrangements. Good-bye, good-bye. It is getting so dark that I can't see to dictate—which represents to you sufficiently the skill of my secretary. I am deeply impatient for your novel. But I fear a painful wait.... Yours, my dear Howells, evermore,

HENRY JAMES.

TO MADAME PAUL BOURGET.

The Awkward Age began to appear in *Harper's Weekly* on October 1, 1898. Madame Bourget had sent H. J. her translation into French of Mathilde Serao's *Paese di Cuccagna*.

Lamb House, Rye.

August 22nd, 1898.

Dear Madame Paul,

I rejoice in your charming letter and find it most kind. I wrote to Bourget four or five days ago, so that you are not without my news (unless my misconstruction of the name of your villa has deprived you,) and meanwhile it is an immense satisfaction to have something of the detail of yours. It rather sounds, indeed, as if it were summed up in the one word (con rispetto parlando) perspiration—but I doubt if the difference between Rye and Nauheim has been other than that of the frying-pan and the fire. Here we have very sufficiently fried, and I have been moved to see the finger of Providence in the large, fat, dirty *index* of the bouncing dame who, to your vision, pointed away from Watchbell St. I have said to myself on the torrid afternoons: "Les malheureux—boxed up with that staircase in that stuffiness—comment y eussent-ils survécu!" Such reflections are what has principally happened to me—except, thank heaven, to get on more or less with my novel, the serial publication of which begins, in New York, on October 1st. I hope with all my heart that, in spite of everything, you feel your cure to be deep-based and wide-striking.... I am distressed that "Maisie" hasn't yet reached you, and will immediately write to London to see how my publishers have *envisagé* the address I sent them. But I trust she may perhaps be in the act of arriving— now. It is a volume the merit of which is that the subject—and there is a subject—is, I think, exhaustively treated—over-treated, I dare say. But I feel it—suppose it—to be probably what I have done, in the way of meeting the artistic problem, of best. The elements, however, are none of the largest. Let me thank you more directly for the solid *cadeau* of your so accomplished translation. I am only waiting for the first cool day to begin it: I shrink a little, otherwise, under the dog-star, from Naples and the ardent Matilda. But you will neither of you lose by it.... My affectionate greeting to Bourget. Believe me, dear Madame Paul, yours very constantly,

HENRY JAMES.

TO MISS FRANCES R. MORSE.

Dictated.

Lamb House, Rye.

October 19th, 1898.

My dear Fanny,

I have received, month after month, the most touching and admirable signs of your remembrance, and yet haven't—visibly to yourself—so much as waved a hat at you in return: a brutality which, however, is all on the surface only and no measure of the deep appreciation I have really felt. Your letters, from the moment the war began, were a real waft of the real thing, penetrating all the more deeply on account of all the old memories stirred by the particular things, the names and persons and kind of anxiety, they were full of—so many echoes of the far-away time it makes one, in the presence of the *un*-knowing generation, feel so horribly old to recall. I can thank you, affectionately, for all these things now very much better than I can explain in detail why you have not heard from me sooner. The best explanation is simply the general truth that I've had a summer in which my correspondence has very much gone to the wall. I moved down here rather early, but that operated not quite—or really not at all—as a simplification. You know for yourself what it means to start a new home, on however humble a basis—from the moment one has to do it mainly single-handed and with a great deal else to do at the same tune. Here I am at last on somewhat quieter days—though even this does happen to be a week of such small hospitalities as I am restricted to, and I have, if only from the still large arrears of my correspondence, which reduce me to this ugly process, the sense of the shining hour at best unimproved.

I won't attempt to take up in detail your innumerable bits of news and all your evocations of the Boston picture. I move through *that*, always, as through a company of ghosts, so completely have sound and sight of individuals and presences faded away from me. Still, I *have* had some close reminders. Wendell Holmes was here, still beautiful and charming, for a day or two, and above all, off and on, for a couple of months my nephew Harry, whom you well know, and in whom I took no end of comfort and pleasure. His being here was a great satisfaction to me—and doubled by the fact of my so getting more news of William and Alice than I have had for many a year. She sent to the boy all his father's letters from California and elsewhere—the consequence of which, for me, was a wonderful participation and interest. William appears to have had a magnificent sort of summer and no end of success on the Pacific slope—besides innumerable impressions by the way and an excellent series of weeks in the Adirondacks before going forth. But after all, all these things have flashed by. The very war, now that it's over, seems merely to have flashed—the dreadful marks of the flash, in so many a case, being beyond my ken. Well, I won't attempt to go into it—it's all beyond me. It only, I'm afraid, makes me want to curl up more closely in this little old-world corner, where I can successfully beg such questions. They become a spectacle merely—a drama of great interest, but as to which judgment and prophecy are withered in me, or at all events absolutely checked.

I am very sorry you and your mother have ceased coming out just at the time I've something to show you. My little old house is really pretty enough for that, and has given me, all this wonderful, hot, rainless, radiant summer, a peace that would pass understanding if I had only got through the first botherations a little earlier in the season. However, I've done very well—have only not been quite such an anchorite as I had planned. The bump of luggage has been frequent on my stair, and the conference with the cook proved a greater strain than, in that particular way, I have ever before had to meet. But it's doubtless my own fault. I should have sought a drearier refuge. I am staying here late—as far on into the autumn as wind and weather may permit. I hope this will find you in the very heart of the American October crystal.... I congratulate you, my dear Fanny, on all the warm personal, local life that surrounds you, and that you touch at so many points very much more the normal state for one's afternoon of existence, after all, than my expatriated one. But we go on as we may. I don't feel as if I had thanked you half enough for your so many beautiful bulletins—and can only ask you to believe that each, in its order, more or less brought tears to my eyes. Recall me, please, to your mother's kindest remembrance, and believe me

Yours evermore,

HENRY JAMES.

TO DR. LOUIS WALDSTEIN.

Lamb House, Rye.

Oct. 21st, 1898.

Dear Sir,

Forgive my neglect, under great pressure of occupation, of your so interesting letter of the 12th. I have since receiving it had complicated calls on my time. That the *Turn of the Screw* has been suggestive and significant to you—in any degree—it gives me great pleasure to hear; and I can only thank you very kindly for the impulse of sympathy that made you write. I am only afraid, perhaps, that my conscious intention strikes you as having been larger than I deserve it should be thought. It is the intention so primarily, with me, always, of the artist, the *painter*, that *that* is what I most, myself, feel in it—and the lesson, the idea—ever—conveyed is only the one that deeply lurks in any vision prompted by life. And as regards a presentation of things so fantastic as in that wanton little Tale, I can only rather blush to see real substance read into them—I mean for the generosity of the reader. *But*, of course, where there *is* life, there's truth, and the truth was at the back of my head. The poet is always justified when he is not a humbug; always grateful to the justifying commentator. My bogey-tale dealt with things so hideous that I felt that to save it at all it needed some infusion of beauty or prettiness, and the beauty of the pathetic was the only attainable—was indeed inevitable. But ah, the exposure indeed, the helpless plasticity of childhood that isn't dear or sacred to *some*body! That *was* my little tragedy—over which you show a wisdom for which I thank you again. Believe me, thus, my dear Sir, yours most truly,

HENRY JAMES.

TO H. G. WELLS.

The reference in the second paragraph of this letter is to *Covering End*, the second story of *The Two Magics*. Mr. Wells was at this time living near Folkestone, distant from Rye by the breadth of Romney Marsh.

Lamb House, Rye.

Dec. 9th, 1898.

My dear H. G. Wells,

Your so liberal and graceful letter is to my head like coals of fire—so repeatedly for all these weeks have I had feebly to suffer frustrations in the matter of trundling over the marsh to ask for your news and wish for your continued amendment. The shortening days and the deepening mud have been at the bottom of this affair. I never get out of the house till 3 o'clock, when night is quickly at one's heels. I would have taken a regular day—I mean started in the a.m.—but have been so ridden, myself, by the black care of an unfinished and *running* (galloping, leaping and bounding,) serial that parting with a day has been like parting with a pound of flesh. I am still a neck ahead, however, and *this* week will see me through; I accordingly hope very much to be able to turn up on one of the ensuing days. I will sound a horn, so that you yourself be not absent on the chase. Then I will express more articulately my appreciation of your various signs of critical interest, as well as assure you of my sympathy in your own martyrdom. What will you have? It's all a grind and a bloody battle—as well as a considerable lark, and the difficulty itself is the refuge from the vulgarity. Bless your heart, I think I could easily say worse of the T. of the S., the young woman, the spooks, the style, the everything, than the worst any one else could manage. One knows the most damning things about one's self. Of course I had, about my young woman, to take a very sharp line. The grotesque business I had to make her picture and the childish psychology I had to make her trace and present, were, for me at least, a very difficult job, in which absolute lucidity and logic, a singleness of effect, were imperative. Therefore I had to rule out subjective complications of her own—play of tone etc.; and keep her impersonal save for the most obvious and indispensable little note of neatness, firmness and courage—without which she wouldn't have had her data. But the thing is essentially a pot-boiler and a *jeu d'esprit*.

With the little play, the absolute creature of its conditions, I had simply to make up a deficit and take a small *revanche*. For three mortal years had the actress for whom it was written (utterly to try to *fit*) persistently failed to produce it, and I couldn't wholly waste my labour. The B.P. won't read a play with the mere names of the speakers—so I simply paraphrased these and added such indications as might be the equivalent of decent acting—a history and an evolution that seem to me moreover explicatively and sufficiently smeared all over the thing. The moral is of course: Don't write one-act plays. But I didn't mean thus to sprawl. I envy your hand your needle-pointed fingers. As you don't say that you're *not* better I prepare myself to be greatly struck with the same, and with kind regards to your wife,

Believe me yours ever,

HENRY JAMES.

P.S. What's this about something in some newspaper?—I read least of all—from long and deep experience—what my friends write about me, and haven't read the things you mention. I suppose it's because they know I don't that they dare!

TO F. W. H. MYERS.

Lamb House, Rye.

Dec. 19, 1898.

My dear Myers,

I don't know what you will think of my unconscionable delay to acknowledge your letter of so many, so very many days ago, nor exactly how I can make vivid to you the nature of my hindrances and excuses. I have, in truth, been (until some few days since) intensely and anxiously busy, finishing, under pressure, a long job that had from almost the first—I mean from long before I had reached the end—begun to be (loathsome name and fact!) "serialized"—so that the printers were at my heels and I had to make a sacrifice of my correspondence *utterly*—to keep the sort of cerebral freshness required for not losing my head or otherwise collapsing. But I won't expatiate. Please believe my silence has been wholly involuntary. And yet, now that I *am* writing I scarce know what to say to you on the subject on which you wrote, especially as I'm afraid I don't quite *understand* the principal question you put to me about "The Turn of the Screw." However, that scantily matters; for in truth I am afraid I have on some former occasions rather awkwardly signified to you that I somehow can't pretend to give any coherent account of my small inventions "after the fact." There they are—the fruit, at best, of a very imperfect ingenuity and with all the imperfections thereof on their heads. The one thing and another that are questionable and ambiguous in them I mostly take to be conditions of their having got themselves pushed through at all. The *T. of the S.* is a very mechanical matter, I honestly think— an inferior, a merely *pictorial*, subject and rather a shameless pot-boiler. The thing that, as I recall it, I most wanted not to fail of doing, under penalty of extreme platitude, was to give the impression of the communication to the children of the most infernal imaginable evil and danger—the condition, on their part, of being as *exposed* as we can humanly conceive children to be. This was my artistic knot to untie, to put any sense or logic into the thing, and if I had known any way of producing *more* the image of their contact and condition I should assuredly have been proportionately eager to resort to it. I evoked the worst I could, and only feel tempted to say, as in French: "Excusez du peu!"

I am living so much down here that I fear I am losing hold of some of my few chances of occasionally seeing you. The charming old humble-minded "quaintness" and quietness of this little brown hilltop city lays a spell upon me. I send you and your wife and all your house all the greetings of the season and am, my dear Myers, yours very constantly,

HENRY JAMES.

TO MRS. WILLIAM JAMES.

Dictated.

Lamb House, Rye.

19th December, 1898.

Dearest Alice,

I have gone on and on most abominably and inexorably owing you a letter since a date so distant that I associate the time intimately with the admirable summer, here, that we so long ago left behind and of which Harry will—at a period by this time quite prehistoric—have given you something of the pleasant little story. But the sense always abides with me that when I am for weeks and months together dumb—as I know I more than once *have* been—you and William are quite *de force* to read into it all the kindly extenuations I require. I have in fact, for many weeks, down here, been taking the general line of saving up all the cerebration not imperatively drained off from day to day for a long job that I have had to carry through under the nightmare of belatedness—a belatedness so great (produced by time lost originally in arranging this place, moving down, taking possession, etc.) as to leave me no margin whatever for accident, indisposition or languor. My capacity for the distillation of prose of decent quality remains, alas, with all the amendments time has brought it, still, each day, so limited that I get awfully nervous under a very continuous task unless I by certain flagrant sacrifices keep up to myself the fiction of freshness—of not getting simply *sick*, in other words, by adding any writing that I haven't absolutely to do to the quantity that *is* each morning imposed. So the sacrifices, for a long time past, have been, as usual, my correspondence, and as the most tender morsels for the Moloch you and William naturally *en première ligne*. The Moloch at last, however—since these four or five days, has been temporarily appeased; and I have instantly begun to transfer my attention from one form of belatement to another. I am working off arrears of letters, and if I take you, dearest Alice, in the heap, I at least pay you the sweet tribute of taking you *first*. You have been without sign or sound of me so long that I daresay you may have even wild imaginings about my "location" and other conditions. I am located only just where Harry left me and where I have stuck fast since July last without the excision of twenty-four hours. The autumn and the early winter have followed the ardent summer here only to multiply my points of contact with my environment and to saturate me more deeply with the grateful sense of it. This contentment has defied all winds and weathers—in plenty of which we have for the last two months rejoiced. I like to send all our little news of such matters in the form of news to Harry in particular, whose mind is furnished with the proper little hooks for it to hold on by. Tell him then, since I won't attempt to burden him individually with acknowledgements that will overload him, that everything he fancied and fondled here only kept growing, all the autumn long, more adapted to such a relation, and that in short both the little brown city and the so amiable countryside were not in July and August a "patch," for charm, colour, "subtlety" and every kind of daily grace, to what they became, in an uninterrupted crescendo, all through October and November. All the good that I hoped of the place has, in fine, profusely bloomed and flourished here. It was really at about the end of September, when the various summer supernumeraries had quite faded away, that the special note of Rye, the feeling of the little hilltop community, bound together like a very modest, obscure and impecunious, but virtuous and amiable family, began most unmistakably to come out. This is the present note of life here, and it has floated me (excuse mixture of metaphor) very placidly along. Nothing would induce me now *not* to be here for Christmas and nothing will induce me not to do my best at least to be here for the protrusion of the bulbs—the hyacinths and tulips and crocuses—that, in return for expended shillings, George Gammon promises me for the earliest peep of spring. As he has broken no word with me yet, I trust him implicitly for this. Meantime too I have trusted him, all the autumn, for all sorts of other things as well: we have committed to the earth together innumerable unsightly roots and sprigs that I am instructed to depend upon as the fixed foundation of a future herbaceous and perennial paradise. Little by little, even with other cares, the slowly but surely working poison of the garden-mania begins to stir in my long-sluggish veins. Tell Harry, as an intimate instance, that by a masterly inspiration I have at one bold stroke swept away all the complications in the quarter on which the studio looks down, uprooting the wilderness of shrubs, relaying paths, extending borders, etc., and made arrangements to throw the lawn, in one lordly sweep, straight up into that angle—a proceeding that greatly increases our apparent extent and dignity: an improvement, in short, quite unspeakable. But the great charm is the simply *being* here, and in particular the beginning of the day no longer with the London blackness and foulness, the curtain of fog and smoke that one has each morning muscularly to lift and fasten back; but with the pleasant, sunny garden outlook, the grass all haunted with starlings and chaffinches, and the in-and-out relation with it that in a manner gilds and refreshes the day. This indeed—with work and a few, a very few, people—is the *all*. But that is just the beauty. I've missed nothing that I haven't been more than resigned to. There have been a few individuals from Saturday to Monday, and one—Jonathan Sturges, whose identity, if it is too dim for you, it would take me too long to explain—ever since mid-October. He remains till over Christmas; but save as making against pure intensity of concentration, he is altogether a boon. I go to town the last of the month, but only for two or three weeks and in a pure picnicking way. I have a plan and a desire really to achieve this winter after an intermission of five years, ten or twelve weeks in Italy; and it now seems probable I shall do so. I shall not know with absolute definiteness till I go to London; but the omens and portents are favourable. On my return I shall come straight down here, and I already foresee how the thought of the spring here will draw me from almost wherever I may at that time be. I shall write you again, however, about this; so that you shall definitely know what becomes of me. You see this is a pure outpouring of the ego. I am after all without fresh news of yourselves to rebound from. The latest and best is William's kind dispatch to me of his "Immortality" lecture, for which I heartily thank him, and which I have read with great appreciation of the art and interest of it. I am afraid I don't very consciously come in to either of the classes it is designed to pacify—either that of the yearners, I mean, or that of the objectors. It isn't the difficulties that keep me from the yearning—it is somehow the lack of the principle of the same. However, I go not now into this. I only acknowledge, till after the turn of the year I write to him, William's communication of the book. Every illustration of his magnificent activity—at the spectacle of which I am condemned to such a woefully back seat—gives me more joy than I will now pretend to express. For the rest, dearest Alice, take from me all my "hopes"; the inevitable vain ones about your household health and happiness and the complexion and outlook of the season for all of you. I try to see you all as cheerfully and gregariously—yet not, for the dignity of each, too much of the latter—fire-lighted and eke furnace-heated. Strange things contend with this image—wild newspaper blizzards and other public bewilderments. Are you individually expanding?—I mean even to the islands of the sea. I myself have no policy. I have no judgment. I am too far and too unadvised and too out of it and too "subtle," also, to see gospel truth in all the so genial encouragement that our swelling state finds, naturally and very logically, in this country. That the two countries should swell together offers material convenience—and that is for much. But I only meant to ask if William and you and the children are definitely in or out of the swell. I will be myself wherever you are.... Yours dearest Alice, always constantly,

HENRY JAMES.

TO CHARLES ELIOT NORTON.

Dictated.

Lamb House, Rye.

26th December, 1898.

My dear Charles,

...Let me say at once that a great part of the secret of my horrid prolonged dumbness has been just this ugly fact of my finding myself reduced, in my declining years, like a banker or a cabinet minister, altogether to *dictating* my letters. The effect of this, in turn, has been to give me a great shyness about them—which has indeed stricken me with silence just in proportion as the help so rendered has seemed to myself really to minister to speech. Many people, I find, in these conservative climes, take it extremely ill to be addressed in Remingtonese.... Forgive, however, this long descant on my delays, my doubts and fears, my final jump, rendered thus clumsy by my nervousness....

The worst of such predicaments is, my dear Charles, that when one does write, everything one has, at a thousand scattered moments, previously wanted to say, seems to have dried up with desuetude and neglect. Oh, all the things that should have been said on the spot if they were ever to be said at all! This applies, you will immediately recognise—though it's a stern truth by which I suffer most—very poignantly to all the utterance I feel myself to have so odiously failed of at the time of the death of dear Burne-Jones. I can only give you a very partially lucid account of why on *that* occasion at least no word from me reached you. I saw myself, heard myself, felt myself, not write—and yet even then knew perfectly both that I should be writing now and that I should now be sorrier than ever for not writing then. It came, the miserable event, at the very moment I was achieving, very single-handed and unassisted, a complicated transfer of residence from London to this place, with all sorts of bewildering material detail (consequent on renovation, complete preparation of every kind, of old house and garden) adding its distraction to the acute sense of pressing work fatally retarded and blighted; so that a postponement which has finally grown to this monstrous length began with being a thing only of moments and hours. Then, moreover, it was simply so wretched and odious to feel him, by a turn of the wheel of fate that had taken but an instant, gone for ever from sight and sound and touch. I was tenderly attached to him, with abundant reason for being, and there was something that choked and angered me beyond what words could trust themselves to express, in the mere blind bêtise of the business. So the days and the weeks went. I went up from here to town, and thence to Rottingdean, for the committal of his ashes, there, to the earth of the little grey-towered churchyard, in sight of the sea, that was at the moment all smothered in lovely spring flowers. It was a day of extraordinary beauty, and in every way a quite indescribably sincere—I remember I could find at the time no other word for the impression—little funeral and demonstration. The people from London were those, almost all, in whose presence there was a kind of harmony.... I had seen the dear man, to my great joy, only a few hours before his death: meeting him at a kind of blighted and abortive wedding-feast (that is a dinner before a marriage that was to take place on the morrow) from which we were both glad to disembroil ourselves: so that we drove together home, intimately moralising and talking nonsense, and he put me, in the grey London midnight, down at my corner to go on by himself to the Grange. It was the last time I saw him, and, as one always does, I have taken ever since a pale comfort in the thought that our parting was explicitly affectionate and such, almost, as one would have wished it even had one known. I miss him even here and now. He was one of the most loveable of men and most charming of friends—altogether and absolutely distinguished. I think his career, as an artistic one, and speaking quite apart from the degree of one's sympathy with his work, one of the greatest of boons to our most vulgar of ages. There was no false note in him, nothing to dilute the strain; he knew his direction and held it hard—wrought with passion and went as straight as he could. He was for all this always, to me, a great comfort. For the rest death came to him, I think, at none so bad a moment. He had, essentially, to my vision, really *done*. And he was very tired, and his cup was, with all the mingled things, about as full as it would hold. It was so good a moment, in short, that I think his memory is already feeling the benefit of it in a sort of rounded finished way. I was not at the sale of his pictures and drawings which took place after his death—I have not stirred from this spot since I came to it at the end of June; but though I should immensely have cherished some small scrap, everything went at prices—magnificent for his estate—that made acquisition a vain dream.... I have had—and little wonder—scant news of you. I know you've renounced your professorship. I know you felt strongly on public events. But I am in a depressed twilight—of discrimination, I mean—that enables me to make less of these things than I should like to do. So much has come and gone, these six months, that how can I talk about it? It's strange, the consciousness possible to an American here to-day, of being in a country in which the drift of desire—so far as it concerns itself with the matter—is that we *shall* swell and swell, and acquire and *re*quire, to the top of our opportunity. My own feeling, roughly stated, is that we have not been good enough for our opportunity—vulgar, in a manner, as that was and is; but it may be the real message of the whole business to make us as much better as the great grabbed-up British Empire has, unmistakeably, made the English. But over these abysses—into them rather—I peer with averted eye. I fear I am too lost in the mere spectacle for any decent morality. Good-bye, my dear Charles, and forgive my mechanic volubility. Isn't it better to have ticked and shocked than never to have ticked at all? I send my love to all your house....

Your ever, my dear Charles, affectionate old friend,

HENRY JAMES.

TO HENRY JAMES, JUNIOR.

Lamb House, Rye.

Feb. 24, 1899.

Dearest Harry,

I have a good letter from you too long unanswered—but you will easily condone my offence of not too soon loading you with the burdensome sense that it is I—not your virtuous self—who have last written. And you must now let that sense sit on you very lightly. Don't trouble about me till all college pressure is completely over—by which I mean till some as yet comparatively remote summer-day.... We've had of late a good lot of wondrous, sunny, balmy days—to-day is splendid—in which I have kept saying to myself

"What a climate—dear old much-abused thing—after all!" and feeling quite balmily and baskingly southern. I've been "sitting" all the last month in the green upstairs south-west room, whose manifest destiny is clearly to become a second-story boudoir. Whenever my books arrive in their plenitude from De Vere Gardens it will be absolutely required to help to house them. It has been, at any rate, constantly flooded with sun, and has opened out its view toward Winchelsea and down the valley in the most charming way. The garden is beginning to smile and shimmer almost as if it were already May. Half the crocuses and hyacinths are up, the primrose and the jonquil abound, the tulips are daily expected, and the lawn is of a rich and vivid green that covers with shame the state in which you saw it. George Gammon proves as regular as a set of false teeth and improves each shining hour. In short the quite essential amiability of L.H. only deepens with experience. Therefore see what a house I'm keeping for you....

But I am writing you a letter that *will* burden you. I won't break ground on the greater questions—though I think them—think *it*, at least, in the U.S., the main one, extraordinarily interesting. To live in England is, inevitably, to feel the "imperial" question in a different way and take it at a different angle from what one might, with the same mind even, do in America. Expansion has so made the English what they are—for good or for ill, but on the whole for good—that one doesn't quite feel one's way to say for one's country "No—I'll have *none* of it!" It has educated the English. Will it only demoralize *us*? I suppose the answer to that is that we can get at home a bigger education than they—in short as big a one as we require. Thank God, however, I've no *opinions*—not even on the Dreyfus case. I'm more and more only aware of things as a more or less mad panorama, phantasmagoria and dime museum. It would take me longer than to finish this paper to send you all the fond incitement or solicitation that I have on hand for you or to work off my stored-up messages to your *Eltern* and brethren. There is time to talk of it, but I count on as many of you as possible for next summer.... I hope you are conscious of a little tethering string of attachment to the old mulberry in the garden, and am ever your affectionate

HENRY JAMES.

P.S. Am just up again from such a sweet sunny spacious after-luncheon stroll in the garden. You'll think it very vulgar of me, but I continue to find it ravishing.

TO A. F. DE NAVARRO.

Lamb House,

Rye.

Monday—Small hours—1.30 a.m.

[Feb. 27. 1899].

My dear Don Tony,

You can't say I overwhelm you with acknowledgments, din my gratitude into your ear or make you curse the day you suffered a kindly impulse to an intensely susceptible friend to get the better of your appreciation of a quiet life. No—you can do none of these things. On the other hand you can perhaps complete your graceful generosity by remembering that your admirable little Xmas memento was accompanied with a "Now hold your tongue!" almost as admirable in its distinguished consideration as the felicitous object itself. It was, clearly, that you felt: "Oh yes, *of course* you're charmed: à qui le dites-vous? But for heaven's sake, thanked to satiety as I am on all sides, don't set your ponderous machinery in motion to drop the last straw!" So I've put out the fires and stopped the wheels and paid off the stokers till now. I've held my tongue like an angel, but I've thought of you—and of your matchless mate—like—well, if not *a*, at least, *the* devil, and at last the whole shop insists on beginning again to hum. I cherish your so periodical and so munificent thoughts of me as one of the good things of this world of worries. Nothing ever touches me more. I am finally going abroad for three months—on Tuesday or Wednesday, and the little sensitive blank record, in its little green sheath, accompanies me—to drink in Impressions—in the usual itinerant shrine of your gifts: my left-hand upper waistcoat-pocket. There are vulgar things—a watch, an eyeglass, seven-and-sixpence—in the other pockets; but nothing but *you* in that one. Voilà. I go to Italy after more than 5 years interlude.

* * * * * * * * *

Drama—tableau! My dear Tony, you are literally my saviour. The above row of stars represents midnight emotions and palpitations of no mean order. As I finished the line just before the stars I became aware that a smell of smoke, a sense of burning that had worried me for the previous hour, had suddenly very much increased and that the room was full of it. *De fil en aiguille*, and in much anxiety, I presently discovered that the said smoke was coming up through the floor between the painted dark-green planks (*dark* green!) of the margin—outside of matting and rugs, and under a table near the fireplace. To assure myself that there was no source of flame in the room below, and then to go up and call my servant, do you see? (he long since snoring in bed—for it's now 2.15 a.m.) was the work of a moment. With such tools as we could command we hacked and pried and sawed and tore up a couple of planks—from which volumes of smoke issued!! Do you see the midnight little flurry? Bref, we got *at* it—a charred, smouldering—*long*-smouldering, I suppose—beam under, or almost under, the hearthstone and in process of time kindled—that is heated to smoking-point by its temperature (that of the hearth,) which was very high. We put him out, we made him stop, with soaked sponges—and then the relief: even while gazing at the hacked and smashed and disfigured floors. Now my man is gone to bed, and I, rather enlivened for immediate sleep, sit and watch by the scene of the small scare and finish my letter to you: really, you know, to grasp your hand, to hang upon your neck, in gratitude, you being at the bottom of the whole thing. I sat up late in the first instance to write to you, because I knew I shouldn't have time to-morrow: and it was because I did so that I was saved a much worse later alarm. Two or three hours hence the smoke would have penetrated to the rest of the house and we should have started up to "fly round" to a much livelier tune.

Bravo, then, again, dear indispensable man! How I feel with magnificent Mrs Tony—for if you're such an "A no. 1" guardian-angel to my house, what are you to your own? The only thing is that I was going to write to you of two or three other things and this stupid little accident has smoked them all out. I've lent this really most amiable little old house to Jonathan Sturges while I'm away—and he's to come as soon as he can. He has been wretched, as you know, with poisonous influenza, but I went up to town to see him a few days since, and he seemed really mending. He was here a long time in the autumn and the early winter and our conversation hung and hovered about you. Good night—it's 2.45 and all's well. I *must* turn in. I grovel before your wife—and take endless liberties with your son—and am yours—after all this—more than ever—much as *that* was—

HENRY JAMES.

P.S. *Tuesday night.* This, my dear Tony, is a sorrier postscript than I expected. I had just—on Sunday night, in the small hours—signed my name as above when my fond delusion of the cessation of my scare dropped from me and I became aware that I had, really, a fire "on." The rest was sad—and I can't detail it—but I've got off wondrous easy. We got the brave pumpers with creditable promptitude—they were thoroughly up to the mark—above all without trop de zèle—and the damage is limited wholly to one side of two rooms—especially the room I was writing to you in so blandly. The pumpers were here till 5—and I slept not till the following (last) night. Still more, therefore, I repeat, it was you preserved me. *Finishing* my letter to you kept me on the spot and being on the spot was all. If I had had my head under the bed-clothes I wouldn't—*couldn't* have sniffed till two or three hours later, when headway would have been gained—and headway would have doubled, quadrupled damage, and perhaps even deprived you of this missive—and its author—altogether. Aussi je vous embrasse—and am your startled but re-quieted and fully insured H. J.

P.P.S. But look out for insidious *under*-fireplace-and-hearth tricks and traps in old houses!

P.S. Will you very kindly tell Frank Millet that I think of him with pride and joy and want so excruciatingly to see him and turn him on, that if I were stopping at home these next months I should extend toward him a long persuasive, somehow ingeniously alluring arm.

TO EDWARD WARREN.

(Telegram.)

(Rye, 9.38 a.m., Feb. 27, 1899.)

Am asking very great favour of your coming down for inside of day or for night if possible house took fire last night but only Green Room and Dining Room affected hot hearth in former igniting old beam beneath with tiresome consequences but excellent local brigade's help am now helpless in face of reconstructions of injured portions and will bless you mightily if you come departure of course put off Henry James.

TO WILLIAM JAMES.

Le Plantier,

Costebelle,

Hyères.

April 22nd, 1899.

Dearest William,

I greatly appreciate the lucidity and liberality of your so interesting letter of the 19th, telling me of your views and prospects for next summer &c—of all of which I am now able to make the most intimate profit. I enter fully into your reasons for wanting to put in the summer quietly and concentratedly in Cambridge—so much that with work unfinished and a spacious house and library of your "very own" to contain you, I ask myself how you can be expected to do anything less. Only it all seems to mean that I shall see you all but scantly and remotely. However, I shall wring from it when the time comes every concession that can be snatched, and shall meanwhile watch your signs and symptoms with my biggest opera-glass (the beautiful one, one of the treasures of my life: que je vous dois.)

Nothing you tell me gives me greater pleasure than what you say of the arrangements made for Harry and Billy in the forest primeval and the vision of their drawing therefrom experiences of a sort that I too miserably lacked (poor Father!) in my own too casual youth. What I most of all feel, and in the light of it conjure you to keep doing for them, is their being *à même* to contract local saturations and attachments in respect to their *own* great and glorious country, to learn, and strike roots into, its infinite beauty, as I suppose, and variety. Then they won't, as I do now, have to assimilate, but half-heartedly, the alien splendours—inferior ones too, as I believe—of the indigestible midi of Bourget and the Vicomte Melchior de Vogüé, kindest of hosts and most brilliant of *commensaux* as I am in the act of finding both these personages. The beauty here is, after my long stop at home, admirable and exquisite; but make the boys, none the less, stick fast and sink up to their necks in everything their *own* countries and climates can give de pareil et de supérieur. Its being that "own" will double their *use* of it.... This little estate (two houses—near together—in a 25-acre walled "parc" of dense pine and cedar, along a terraced mountain-side, with exquisite views inland and to the sea) is a precious and enviable acquisition. The walks are innumerable, the pleasant "wildness" of the land (universally accessible) only another form of sweetness, and the light, the air, the noble, graceful lines &c., all of the first order. It's classic—Claude—Virgil....

I expect to get to Genoa on the 4th or 5th April, and there to make up my mind as to how I can best spend the following eight weeks, in Italy, in evasion and seclusion. Unhappily I *must* go to Rome, and Rome is infernal. But I shall make short work of it. My nostalgia for Lamb House is already such as to make me capable de tout. *Never* again will I leave it. I don't take you up on the Philippines—I admire you and agree with you too much. You have an admirable eloquence. But the age is *all* to the vulgar!... Farewell with a wide embrace.

Ever your

HENRY.

TO HOWARD STURGIS.

Hôtel de l'Europe, Rome.

May 19, 1899.

My dear Howard,

It's a great pleasure to hear from you in this far country—though I greatly wish it weren't from the bed of anguish—or at any rate of delicacy: if delicacy may be connected, that is, with anything so indelicate as a bed! But I'm very glad to gather that it's the couch of convalescence. Only, if you have a Back, for heaven's sake take care of it. When I was about your age—in 1862!—I did a bad damage (by a strain subsequently—through crazy juvenility—neglected) to mine; the consequence of which is that, in spite of retarded attention, and years, really, of recumbency, later, I've been saddled with it for life, and that even now, my dear Howard, I verily write you *with* it. I even wrote *The Awkward Age* with it: therefore look sharp! I wanted especially to send you that volume—as an "acknowledgment" of princely hospitalities received, and formed the intention of so doing even in the too scant moments we stood face to face among the Rembrandts. That's right—*be* one of the few! I greatly applaud the tact with which you tell me that scarce a human being will understand a word, or an intention, or an artistic element or glimmer of any sort, of my book. I tell *myself*—and the "reviews" tell me—such truths in much cruder fashion. But it's an old, old story—and if I "minded" now as much as I once did, I should be well beneath the sod. Face to face I should be able to say a bit how I saw—and why I *so* saw—my subject. But that will keep.

I'm here in a warmish, quietish, emptyish, pleasantish (but not maddeningly so,) altered and cockneyfied and scraped and all but annihilated Rome. I return to England some time next month (to the country—Lamb House, Rye—now my constant address—only.) ... However, this is only to greet and warn you—and to be, my dear Howard, your affectionate old friend,

HENRY JAMES.

TO MRS. HUMPHRY WARD.

The allusions at the end of this letter are to the visit paid by H. J. to Mr. and Mrs. Humphry Ward at the Villa Barberini, Castel Gandolfo, during his stay in Italy. Mrs. Ward has described the excursion to Nemi, "the strawberries and Aristodemo," in *A Writer's Recollections*, pp. 327-9.

Lamb House, Rye.

July 10th, 1899.

Dear Mrs. Ward,

I have a very bad conscience and a very heavy heart about my failure to communicate with you again before you left Rome—for I heard (afterwards—*much* afterwards) that you had had final trouble and inconvenience—that Miss Gertrude, brave being, tempted providence—by her very bravery—to renew its assaults—and that illness and complications encumbered your last steps. On the subject of all this I ought long since to have condoled with you, in default of having condoled at the time—yet lo, I have shamefully waited for the ignoble facility of my own table and inkstand, to which, after too prolonged a separation, I have but just been restored. I got home—from Turin—but three days ago—and very, very cool and green and wholesome (though only comparatively, I admit) does this little insular nook appear. After I last saw you I too was caught up, if not cast down, by the Fates—whirled, by irresistible Marion Crawfords—off to Sorrento, Capri, Naples—all of which had not been in the least in my programme—thence, afterwards, to live in heat and hurry and inconvenient submission and compromise—till Florence, in its turn, made a long arm and pocketed me (oh, so stuffily!) till but a few days ago. All this time I've been the slave of others—and I return to a perfect mountain of unforwarded (by a rash and delusive policy) postal matter. But I bore through the mountain straight at Stocks—or even, according to an intimation you gave me, at Grosvenor Place. I heartily hope all the crumples and stains of travel have by this time been washed and smoothed away—and that you have nothing but romantic recollections and regrets. I pray Miss Ward be wholly at her ease again and that, somehow or other, you may have woven a big piece of your tapestry. I should say, frankly, "Mayn't I come down and *see?*—or hear?" were it not that I return to fearful arrears myself, and restored to this small temple of application, from which I've so long been absent, feel absolutely obliged to sit tight for several weeks to come. Later in the summer, if you'll let me, I *shall* ask for an invitation. If all this while I've not sent you *The Awkward Age* it has been because I thought it not fair to make any such appeal to your attention while you were preoccupied and worried. Perhaps—absolutely, in fact—I wanted the book to reach you at a moment when the coast might be comparatively clear. Possibly it isn't clear even now. At all events I am writing to Heinemann to-day to despatch to you the volume. But *please* don't look at it till all the elements of leisure— margin—peace of mind—lend themselves. And don't answer *this*. You have far other business in hand.

My four months in Italy did more for me, I imagine, than I shall yet awhile know. One must draw on them a little to find out. Doubtless you are drawing hard on yours. For me (I am clear about that) the Nemi Lake, and the walk down and up (the latter perhaps most,) and the strawberries and Aristodemo were the cream. It will be a joy to have it all out again with you and to hear of your other adventures. I hope Miss Dorothy and Miss Janet (please tell them) are finding London, if you *are* still there, *come si deve.* Yours and theirs and Humphry's, dear Mrs. Ward, very constantly,

HENRY JAMES.

TO MRS. HUMPHRY WARD.

It will be understood that Mrs. Ward had consulted H. J. on certain details, relating in particular to the American background of one of the characters in her forthcoming novel *Eleanor,* the scene of which was partly laid at Castel Gandolfo.

Lamb House, Rye.

Sunday. [July 1899].

Dear Mrs. Ward,

I return the proofs of *Eleanor*, in a separate cover from this, and as I think it wise to *register* them I must wait till to-morrow a.m. to do that, and this, therefore, will reach you first. Let me immediately say that I don't light (and I've read carefully every word, and many two or three times, as Mr. Bellasis would say—and is Mr. B., by the way, naturally—as it were—H. J.???!!! on any peccant particular spots in the aspect of Lucy F. that the American reader would challenge. I do think he, or she, may be likely, at first, to think her more English than American—to say, I mean: "Why, this isn't *us*—it's English 'Dissent.'" For it's well—generally—to keep in mind how very different a thing that is (socially, aesthetically &c.) from the American free (and easy) multitudinous churches, that, practically, in any community, are like so many (almost) clubs or Philharmonics or amateur theatrical companies. I *don't* quite think the however obscure American girl I gather you to conceive would have any shockability about Rome, the Pope, St. Peter's, kneeling, or anything of that sort—least of all any girl whose concatenations *could*, by any possibility of social handing-on, land her in the milieu you present at Albano. She would probably be either a Unitarian or "Orthodox" (which is, I believe, "Congregational," though in New England always called "Orthodox") and in either case as Emersonized, Hawthornized, J. A. Symondsized, and as "frantic" to *feel* the Papacy &c., as one could well represent her. And this, I mean, even were she of any provincial New England circle whatever that one could conceive as ramifying, however indirectly, into Villa Barb. This particularly were her father a college professor. In that case I should say "The bad clothes &c., oh yes; as much as you like. The beauty &c., *scarcely*. The offishness to Rome—as a spectator &c.—almost not at all." All this, roughly and hastily speaking. But there is no false note of surface, beyond this, I think, that you need be uneasy about at all. Had I looked over your shoulder I should have said: "*Specify*, localise, a little more—give her a *definite* Massachusetts, or Maine, or whatever, habitation—imagine a country-college-town—invent, if need be, a name, and stick to that." This for smallish, but appreciable reasons that I haven't space to develop—but after all not imperative. For the rest the chapters you send me are, as a beginning, to my vision very charming and interesting and pleasing—full of promise of strong elements—as your beginnings always are.

And may I say (as I *can* read nothing, if I read it at all, save in the light of how one would *one's self* proceed in tackling the same *data*!) just two other things? One is that I think your material suffers a little from the fact that the reader feels you approach your subject too *immediately*, show him its elements, the cards in your hand, too bang off from the first page—so that a wait to begin to guess *what and whom the thing is going to be about* doesn't impose itself: the ante-chamber or two and the crooked corridor before he is already in the Presence. The other is that you don't give him a positive sense of dealing with your subject from its logical centre. This centre I gathered to be, from what you told me in Rome (and one gathers it also from the title,) the consciousness of Eleanor—to which all the rest (Manisty, Lucy, the whole phantasmagoria and drama) is presented by life. I should have urged you: "Make that consciousness full, rich, universally prehensile and *stick* to it— don't shift—and don't shift *arbitrarily*—how, otherwise, do you get your unity of subject or keep up your reader's sense of it?" To which, if you say: How then do I get *Lucy's* consciousness, I impudently retort: "By that magnificent and masterly *indirectness* which means the *only* dramatic straightness and intensity. You get it, in other words, by Eleanor." "And how does Eleanor get it?" "By *Everything*! By Lucy, by Manisty, by every pulse of the action in which she is engaged and of which she is the fullest—an exquisite—register. Go behind *her*—miles and miles; don't go behind the others, or the subject— *i.e.* the unity of impression—goes to smash." But I am going too far—and this is more than you will have bargained for. On these matters there is far too much to say. This makes me all the more sorry that, in answer to your kind invitation for the last of this month, I greatly fear I can't leave home for several weeks to come. I am in hideous backwardness with duties that after a long idleness (six full months!) have awaited me here—and I am cultivating "a unity of impression!" In *October* with joy.

Your history of your journey from V.B., your anxieties, complications, horrid tension and tribulation, draws hot tears from my eyes. I blush for the bleak inn at the bare Simplon. I only meant it for rude, recovered health. Poor Miss Gertrude—heroine partout et toujours—and so privately, modestly, exquisitely. Give her, please, all my present benediction. And forgive my horrid, fatigued hieroglyphics. Do let me have more of "Eleanor"—to re-write! And believe me, dear Mrs. Ward, ever constantly yours,

HENRY JAMES.

P.S. I've on reflection determined that as a *registered* letter may not, perhaps, reach Stocks till Tuesday a.m. and you wish to despatch for Wednesday's steamer, it is my "higher duty" to send the proofs off in ordinary form, apart from this, but to-night. May it be for the best!

H. J.

TO MRS. HUMPHRY WARD.

Lamb House, Rye.

July 26th, 1899.

Dear Mrs. Ward,

I beg you not to believe that if you elicit a reply from me—to your so interesting letter just received—you do so at any cost to any extreme or uncomfortable pressure that I'm just now under. I am always behind with everything—and it's no worse than usual. Besides I shall be very brief. [A] But I must say two or three words—not only because these are the noblest speculations that can engage the human mind, but because—to a degree that distresses me—you labour under two or three mistakes as to what, the other day, I at all wanted to express. I don't myself, for that matter, recognise what you mean by any "old difference" between us on *any* score—and least of all when you appear to glance at it as an opinion of mine (if I understand you, that is,) as to there being but *one general* "hard and fast rule of *presentation*." I protest that I have never had with you any difference—consciously—on any such point, and rather resent, frankly, your attributing to me a judgment so imbecile. I hold that there are five million such "rules" (or as many as there are subjects in all the world—I fear the subjects are *not* 5,000,000!) only each of them imposed, artistically, by the particular case—involved in the writer's responsibility to it; and each *then*—and then only—"hard and fast" with an immitigable hardness and fastness. I don't see, *without* this latter condition, where any work of art, any artistic *question* is, or any artistic probity. Of course, a 1000 times, there are as many magnificent and imperative cases as you like of presenting a thing by "going behind" as many forms of consciousness as you like—all Dickens, Balzac, Thackeray, Tolstoi (save when they use the autobiographic dodge,) are huge illustrations of it. But they are illustrations of extreme and calculated selection, or singleness, too, whenever that has been, by the case, imposed on them. My own immortal works, for that matter, if I may make bold, are recognizable instances of all the variation. I "go behind" right and left in "The Princess Casamassima," "The Bostonians," "The Tragic Muse," just as I do the same but singly in "The American" and "Maisie," and just as I do it consistently *never at all* (save for a false and limited *appearance*, here and there, of doing it a *little*, which I haven't time to explain) in "The Awkward Age." So far from not seeing what you mean in *Pêcheur d'Islande*, I see it as a most beautiful example—a crystal-clear one. It's a picture of a *relation* (a *single* relation) and that relation isn't given at all unless given on both sides, because, practically, there are no other relations to make *other* feet for the situation to walk withal. The logic jumps at the eyes. Therefore acquit me, please, *please*, of anything so abject as putting forward anything at once specific and *a priori*. "Then why," I hear you ask, "do you pronounce for *my book* a priori?" Only because of a mistake, doubtless, for which I do here humble penance—that of assuming too precipitately, and with the freedom of an inevitably too-foreshortened letter, that I was dealing with it *a posteriori*!—and *that* on the evidence of only those few pages and of a somewhat confused recollection of what, in Rome, you told me of your elements. Or rather—more correctly—I was giving way to my irresistible need of wondering how, *given* the subject, one could best work one's self into the presence of it. And, lo and behold, the subject isn't (of course, in so scant a show and brief a piece) "given" at all—I have doubtless simply, with violence and mutilation, *stolen* it. It is of the nature of that violence that I'm a wretched person to *read* a novel—I begin so quickly and concomitantly, *for myself*, to write it rather—even before I know clearly what it's about! The novel I can *only* read, I can't read at all! And I had, to be just with me, one attenuation—I thought I gathered from the pages already absorbed that your *parti pris* as to your process with "Eleanor" was already defined—and defined as "dramatic"—and that was a kind of *lead*: the people all, as it were, phenomenal to a particular imagination (hers) and that imagination, with all its contents, phenomenal to the reader. I, in fine, just rudely and egotistically thrust forward the beastly way *I* should have done it. But there is too much to say about these things—and I am writing too much—and yet haven't said half I want to—*and*, above all, there *being* so much, it is doubtless better not to attempt to say pen in hand what one can say but so partially. And yet I *must* still add one or two things more. What I said above about the "rule" of presentation being, in each case, hard and fast, *that* I will go to the stake and burn with slow fire for—the slowest that will burn at all. I hold the artist must (infinitely!) know how he is doing it, or he is not doing it at all. I hold he must have a perception of the interests of his subject that grasps him as in a vise, and that (the subject being of course formulated in his mind) he sees *as* sharply the way that most presents it, and presents most of it, as against the ways that comparatively give it away. And he must there choose and stick and be consistent—and that is the hard-and-fastness and the vise. I am afraid I *do* differ with you if you mean that the picture can get any *objective* unity from any other source than that; can get it from, e.g., the "personality of the author." From the personality of the author (which, however enchanting, is a thing for the reader only, and not for the author himself, without humiliating abdications, to my sense, to count in at all) it can get nothing but a unity of execution and of tone. There is no short cut for the subject, in other words, out of the process, which, having made out most what it (the subject) is, *treats* it most, handles it, in that relation, with the most consistent economy. May I say, to exonerate myself a little, that when, e.g., I see you make Lucy "phenomenal" to Eleanor (one has to express it briefly and somehow,) I find myself supposing completely that you "know how you're doing it," and enjoy, as critic, the sweet peace that comes with that sense. But I haven't the sense that you "know how you're doing it" when, at the point you've reached, I see you make Lucy phenomenal, even for one attempted stroke, to the little secretary of embassy. And the reason of this is that Eleanor counts as presented, and thereby *is* something to go behind. The secretary *doesn't* count as presented (and isn't he moreover engaged, at the very moment—*your* moment—in being phenomenal himself, to Lucy?) and is therefore, practically, *nothing* to go behind. The promiscuous shiftings of standpoint and centre of Tolstoi and Balzac for instance (which come, to my eye, from their being not so much big dramatists as big *painters*—as Loti is a painter,) are the inevitable result of the *quantity of presenting* their genius launches them in. With the complexity they pile up they *can* get no clearness without trying again and again for new centres. And they don't *always* get it. However, I don't mean to say they don't get enough. And I hasten to add that you have—I wholly recognise—every right to reply to me: "Cease your intolerable chatter and dry up your preposterous deluge. If you will have the decent civility to *wait*, you will see that *I* 'present' also—*anch' io!*—enough for *every* freedom I use with it!"—*And with my full assent to that, and my profuse* prostration in the dust for this extravagant discourse, with all faith, gratitude, appreciation and affection, I *do* cease, dear Mrs. Ward, I dry up! and am yours most breathlessly,

HENRY JAMES.

[A] Later!!!! Latest. Don't rejoin!—*don't!*

TO MRS. A. F. DE NAVARRO.

The "priceless volume" was an album belonging to Mrs. de Navarro (Miss Mary Anderson), in which she had asked H. J. to inscribe some words. His contribution, given below, recalls a memory of Miss Anderson before she left the stage.

Lamb House, Rye.

Oct. 13: 1899.

Dearest, greatest lady,

I've filled a page, with my horrid hieroglyphics, in the priceless volume—and my characters are the more unsightly for having to be squeezed in—for I found that to point my little moral I had to take more than 20 words. Forgive their sad futility. I hope I understood you right—that I was to do it *opposite* Watts—I obeyed your law to what I supposed to be the letter. If I'm not quite correct, I can assure you that it will be the only time I shall ever break it! Yours and Tony's very constantly,

HENRY JAMES.

P.S. The volume goes by *to-morrow* a.m.'s post; tenderly and stoutly wrapped, violently sealed, convulsively corded and rigorously registered. Bon voyage!

THE GOLDEN DREAM.

A LITTLE TALE.

It was in the days of his golden dreams that he first saw her, and she immediately became one of them—made them glow with a new rosy fire. The first night, on leaving the theatre in his breathless ecstasy, he could scarce compose himself to go home: he wandered over the town, murmuring to himself "I want, oh I want to write something for her!" He went again and again to see her—he was always there, and after each occasion, and even as the months and years rolled by, kept repeating to himself, and even to others, what he *did* want to. Now one of these others was his great friend, who irritated and probably jealous, coldly and cynically replied: "You may want to, but you won't. No, you will never write anything."

"I will!" he vehemently insisted. And he added in presumptuous confidence: "Just wait till she asks me!" And so they kept it up, and he said *that* too often for the G.F., who, exasperated, ended by retorting:

"She never will!"

"Well, you see if she doesn't!"

"You must think—" said the G.F. scathingly.

"Well, what?"

"Why, that she thinks you're somebody."

"She'll find out in time that I *am. Then* she'll ask me."

"Ask *who* you are?"

"No"—with majesty. "To write something."

"Then I shall be sorry for her. Because you won't."

"Why not?"

"Because you *can't*!"

"Oh!" But the months and years revolved and at last his dream came true; also it befell that, just at the same moment, the G.F. reappeared; to whom he broke out ecstatically: "I told you so! She *has* found out! She *has* asked me."

The G.F. was imperturbable. "What's the use? You can't."

"You'll see if I can't!" And he sat down and tried. Oh, he tried long—he tried hard. But the G.F. was right. It was too late. He couldn't.

HENRY JAMES.

Lamb House, Rye. Oct. 13, 1899.

TO SIDNEY COLVIN.

The following refers to R. L. Stevenson's *Letters to his Family and Friends*, edited by Sir Sidney Colvin. H. J.'s article appeared in the *North American Review*, January 1900, and was afterwards reprinted in *Notes on Novelists*.

Lamb House, Rye.

Wednesday night.

[October 1899.]

My dear Colvin,

Many things hindered my quietly and immediately reabsorbing the continuity of the two gathered volumes, and I have delayed till this the acknowledgment of your letter (sent a few days after them,) I having already written (hadn't I?) before the letter arrived. I have spent much of the last two days with them—beautifully and sadly enough. I think you need have no doubt as to the impression the constituted book will make—it will be one of extraordinarily rare, particular and individual beauty. I want to write about it really critically, if I can—i.e. intelligently and interpretatively—but I sigh before the difficulty. Still, I shall probably try. One thing it seems to me I foresee—i.e. a demand for *more* letters. There *are* more publishable?—aren't there? But you will tell me of this. How extraordinarily fine the long (almost last of all) one to his cousin Bob! If there were only more *de cette force*! But there couldn't be. "I *think* I think" the impression more *equal* than you do—indeed some of the early ones better than the earlier ones after expatriation. But the whole series reek with charm and hum with genius. It will serve as a *high* memorial—by which I mean as a large (comprehensive) one. Remember that I shall be delighted to see you on the 18th. I *may* be alone—or Jon Sturges may be here. Probably nessun' altro. Please communicate your decision as to this at your convenience. If not *then*, then on one of the next Saturdays, I hope!

What horridly overdarkening S. African news! One must sit close—but for too long.

Yours ever,

HENRY JAMES.

P.S. Re-reading your letter makes me feel I haven't perhaps answered enough your query about early vol. I. I don't, however, see what you need be uneasy about. The young flame of life and agitation of genius in them flickers and heaves only to make one regret whatever (more) is *not* there: *never* to make one feel your discretion has anywhere been at fault. I'm not sure I don't think it has erred a little on the side of over-suppression. One has the vague sense of omissions and truncations—one *smells* the things unprinted. However, that doubtless had to be. But I don't see *any* mistake you have made. With less, there would have been no history—and one wants what made, what makes for his history. It *all* does—and so would more. But you have given nothing that valuably doesn't. Be at peace.

H. J.

TO EDMUND GOSSE.

This refers to a suggestion that Stevenson's body should be removed from his place of burial, on the mountain-top above Vailima, and brought home.

Lamb House, Rye.

Sunday [Nov. 12, 1899].

My dear Gosse,

I wholly agree with you as to any motion toward the preposterous and unseemly deportation from their noble resting-place of those illustrious and helpless ashes. I find myself, somehow, unable to think of Louis in these days (much more to speak of him) without an emotion akin to tears; and such blatant busybody ineptitude causes the cup to overflow and sickens as well as enrages. But nothing but cheap newspaperism will come of it—it has in it the power, fortunately, to drop, utterly and abysmally, if not *touched*—if decently ignored. Don't write a protest—don't write *anything*: simply *hush*! The *lurid* asininity of the hour!

...I will write you about your best train Saturday—which heaven speed! It will probably be the 3.23 from Charing Cross—better, really, than the (new) 5.15 from St. Paul's. I find S. Africa a nightmare and need cheering. Arrive therefore primed for that office.

Ever yours,

HENRY JAMES.

TO MISS HENRIETTA REUBELL.

Lamb House, Rye.

Sunday midnight.

[Nov. 12th, 1899.]

Dear Miss Reubell,

I have had great pleasure of your last good letter and this is a word of fairly prompt reconnaissance. Your bewilderment over *The Awkward Age* doesn't on the whole surprise me—for that ingenious volume appears to have excited little *but* bewilderment—except indeed, *here*, thick-witted denunciation. A work of art that one has to *explain* fails in so far, I suppose, of its mission. I suppose I must at any rate mention that I had in view a certain special social (highly "modern" and actual) London group and type and tone, which seemed to me to se prêter à merveille to an ironic—lightly and simply ironic!—treatment, and that clever people at least would know who, in general, and what, one meant. But here, at least, it appears there are very few clever people! One must point with finger-posts—one must label with *pancartes*—one must explain with *conférences!* The *form*, doubtless, of my picture is against it—a form all dramatic and scenic—of presented episodes, architecturally combined and each making a piece of the building; with no going behind, no *telling about* the figures save by their own appearance and action and with explanations reduced to the explanation of everything by all the other things *in* the picture. Mais il parait qu'il ne faut pas faire comme ça: personne n'y comprend rien: j'en suis pour mes frais—qui avaient été considérables, très considérables! Yet I seem to make out you were interested—and that consoles me. I think Mrs. Brook the best thing I've ever done—and Nanda also much *done*. Voilà! Mitchy marries Aggie by a calculation—in consequence of a state of mind—delicate and deep, but that I meant to show on his part as highly conceivable. It's absolute to him that N. will never have him—and she *appeals* to him for another girl, whom she sees him as "saving" (from things—realities she sees). If he does it (and she shows how she values him by wanting it) it is still a way of getting and keeping near her—of making for *her*, to him, a tie of gratitude. She becomes, as it were, to him, responsible for his happiness—they can't (*especially if the marriage goes ill*) *not* be—given the girl that Nanda is—more, rather than less, together. And the *finale* of the picture *justifies* him: it leaves Nanda, precisely, with his case on her hands. Far-fetched? Well, I daresay: but so are diamonds and pearls and the beautiful Reubell turquoises! So I scribble to you, to be sociable, by my loud-ticking clock, in this sleeping little town, at my usual more than midnight hour.

...Well, also, I'm like you—I like growing (that is I like, for many reasons, *being*) old: 56! But I don't like growing *older*. I quite love my present age and the compensations, simplifications, freedom, independences, memories, advantages of it. But I don't keep it long enough—it passes too quickly. But it mustn't pass *all* (good as that is) in writing to *you*! There is nothing I shall like more to dream of than to be convoyed by you to the expositionist Kraals of the Savages and the haunts of the cannibals. I surrender myself to you de confiance—in vision and hope—for that purpose. Jonathan Sturges lives, year in, year out, at Long's Hotel, Bond St., and promises to come down here and see me, but never does. He knows hordes of people, every one extraordinarily likes him, and he has tea-parties for pretty ladies: one at a time. Alas, he is three quarters of the time ill; but his little spirit is colossal. Sargent grows in weight, honour and interest—to *my* view. He does one fine thing after another—and his crucifixion (that is big Crucifié with Adam and Eve under each arm of cross catching drops of blood) for Boston Library is a most noble, grave and admirable thing. But it's already to-morrow and I am yours always,

HENRY JAMES.

TO H. G. WELLS.

Lamb House, Rye.

November 20th, 1899.

My dear H. G. Wells,

You reduce me to mere gelatinous grovel. And the worst of it is that you know so well how. You, with a magnanimity already so marked as to be dazzling, sent me last summer a beautiful and discouraging volume which I never mastered the right combination of minutes and terms to thank you for as it deserved—and then, perfectly aware that this shameful consciousness had practically converted me to quivering pulp, you let fly the shaft that has finished me in the fashion to which I now so distressfully testify. It is really most kind and charming of you, and the incident will figure largely in all your eventual biographies: yet it is almost more than I can bear. Seriously, I am extremely touched by your great humanity in the face of my atrocious bad manners. I think the reason *why* I didn't write to thank you for the magnificent romance of three or four months ago was that I simply dreaded a new occasion for still more purple perjury on the subject of coming over to see you! I *was*—I *am*!—coming: and yet I couldn't—and I *can't*—say it without steeping myself afresh in apparent falsehood, to the eyes. It is a weird tale of the *acharnement* of fate against an innocent action—I mean the history of my now immemorial failure: which I must not attempt to tell you thus and now, but reserve for your convinced (from the moment it isn't averted) ear on the day, and at the very hour and moment, that failure is converted to victory. I AM coming. I was lately extremely sorry to hear that you have been somewhat unwell again—unless it be a gross exaggeration. Heaven send that same. I AM coming. I thank you very cordially for the two beautiful books. The new tales I have already absorbed and, to the best of my powers, assimilated. You fill me with wonder and admiration. I think you have too great an unawareness of difficulty—and (for instance) that the four big towns and nice blue foods and belching news-trumpets, etc., will be the *least* of the differences in the days to come.—But it's unfair to say that without saying a deal more: which I can't, and [which] isn't worth it—and is besides irrelevant and ungracious. Your spirit is huge, your fascination irresistible, your resources infinite. *That* is much more to the point. And I AM coming. I heartily hope that if you *have* been incommoded it is already over, and for a corrigible cause. I AM coming. Recall me, please, kindly to Mrs. Wells, and believe me (I AM coming,) very truly (*and* veraciously) yours,

HENRY JAMES.

TO CHARLES ELIOT NORTON.

Dictated.

Lamb House, Rye.

* *Please read postscript first.*

24 November 1899.

My dear Charles,

I heartily welcomed your typed letter of a couple of months ago, both for very obvious and for respectable subsidiary reasons. I am almost altogether reduced—I would much rather say promoted—to type myself, and to communicate with a friend who is in the same predicament only adds to the luxury of the business. I was never intended by nature to write—much less to be, without anguish, read; and I have recognised that perfectly patent law late in the day only, when I might so much better have recognised it early. It would have made a great difference in my life—made me a much more successful person. But "the New England conscience" interposed; suggesting that the sense of being so conveniently assisted could only proceed, somehow, from the abyss. So I floundered and fumbled and failed, through long years for the mere want of the small dose of cynical courage required for recognising frankly my congenital inaptitude. Another proof, or presumption, surely, of the immortality of the soul. It takes one whole life—for some persons, at least, *dont je suis*—to learn how to live at all; which is absurd if there is not to be another in which to apply the lesson. I feel that in *my* next career I shall start, in this particular at least, from the first, straight. Thank heaven I don't write such a hand as you! Then where would my conscience be?

You wrote me from Ashfield, and I can give you more than country for country, as I am still, thank heaven, out of town—which is more and more my predominant and natural state. I am only reacting, I suppose, against many, many long years of London, which has ended by giving me a deep sense of the quantity of "cry" in all that life compared to the almost total absence of "wool." By which I mean, simply, that acquaintances and relations there have a way of seeming at last to end in smoke—while having consumed a great deal of fuel and taken a great deal of time. I dare say I shall some day re-establish the balance, and I have kept my habitation there, though I let it whenever I can; but at present I am as conscious of the advantage of the Sussex winter as of that of the Sussex summer. But I've just returned from three days in London, mainly taken up with seeing my brother William as to whom your letter contained an anxious inquiry to which I ought before this to have done justice. The difficulty has been, these three months, that he has been working, with the most approved medical and "special" aid, for a change of condition, which one hoped would have been apparent by now—so that one might have good news to give. I am sorry to say the change remains, as yet, but imperfectly apparent—though I dare say it has, within the last month, really begun. His German cure—Nauheim—was a great disappointment; but he is at present in the hands of the best London man, who professes himself entirely content with results actually reached. The misfortune is that the regimen and treatment—the "last new" one—are superficially depressing and weakening even when they are doing the right work; and from that, now, I take William to be suffering. Ci vuol pazienza! He will probably spend the winter in England, whatever happens. Only, alas, his Edinburgh lectures are indefinitely postponed—and other renouncements, of an unenlivening sort, have had, as indispensable precautions and prudences, to follow. They have placed their little girl very happily at school, near Windsor; they are in convenient occupation, at present, of my London apartment; and luckily the autumn has been, as London autumns go, quite cheerfully—distinguishably—crepuscular. I am two hours and a half from town; which is far enough, thank heaven, not to be near, and yet near enough, from the point of view of shillings, invasions and other complications, not to be far; they have been with me for a while, and I am looking for them again for longer. William is able, fortunately, more or less to read, and strikes me as so richly prepared, by an immense quantity of this—to speak of that feature alone—for the Edinburgh lectures—that the pity of the frustration comes home the more. A truce, however, to this darksome picture—which may very well yet improve.

I went, a month ago, during a day or two in town, down to Rottingdean to lunch with the Kiplings (those Brighton trains are wondrous!) but failed, to my regret, to see Lady Burne-Jones, their immediate neighbor, as of course you know; who was perversely, though most accidentally, from home. But they told me—and it was the first I knew—of her big project of publishing the dear beautiful man's correspondence: copious, it appears, in a degree of which I had not a conception. Living, in London, near him, though not seeing him, thanks to the same odious London, half so often as I desired, I seldom heard from him on paper, and hadn't, at all, in short, the measure of his being, as the K.'s assured me he proves to have been, a "great letter-writer."

(28th Nov.)

I was interrupted, my dear Charles, the other day: difficulties then multiplied, and I only now catch on again. I see, on reading over your letter, that you are quite *au courant* of Lady B. J.'s plan; and I of course easily take in that she must have asked you, as one of his closest correspondents, for valuable material. Yet I don't know that I wholly echo your deprecation of these givings to the world. The best letters seem to me the most delightful of all written things—and those that are not the best the most negligible. If a correspondence, in other words, has not the real charm, I wouldn't have it published even privately; if it has, on the other hand, I would give it all the glory of the greatest literature. B. J.'s, I should say, must have it (the real charm)—since he did, as appears, surrender to it. Is this not so? At all events we shall indubitably see.... As for B. J., I miss him not less, but more, as year adds itself to year; and the hole he has left in the London horizon, the eclipse of the West Kensington oasis, is a thing much to help one to turn one's back on town: and this in spite of the fact that his work, alas, had long ceased to interest me, with its element of painful, niggling embroidery—the stitch-by-stitch process that had come at last to beg the *painter* question altogether. Even the poetry—the kind of it—that he tried for appeared to me to have wandered away from the real thing; and yet the being himself grew only more loveable, natural and wise. Too late, too late! I gather, à propos of him, that you have read Mackail's Morris; which seems to me quite beautifully and artistically done—wonderful to say for a contemporary English biography.

It is really composed, the effect really produced—an effect not altogether, I think, happy, or even endurable, as regards Morris himself—for whom the formula strikes me as being—being at least largely—that he was a boisterous, boyish, British man of action and practical faculty, launched indeed by his imagination, but really floundering and romping and roaring through the arts, both literary and plastic, very much as a bull through a china-shop. I felt much moved, after reading the book, to try to write, with the aid of some of my own recollections and impressions, something possibly vivid about it; but we are in a moment of such excruciating vulgarity that nothing worth doing about anything or anyone seems to be wanted or welcomed anywhere. The great little Rudyard—à propos of Rottingdean—struck me as quite on his feet again, and very sane and sound and happy. Yet I am afraid you'll think me a very disgusted person if I show my reserves, again, over *his* recent incarnations. I can't swallow his loud, brazen patriotic verse—an exploitation of the patriotic idea, for that matter, which seems to me not really much other than the exploitation of the name of one's mother or one's wife. Two or three times a century—yes; but not every month. He is, however, such an embodied little talent, so economically constructed for all use and no waste, that he will get again upon a good road—leading *not* into mere multitudinous noise. His talent I think quite diabolically great; and this in spite—here I am at it again!—of the misguided, the unfortunate "Stalky." Stalky gives him away, aesthetically, as a man in his really now, as regards our roaring race, bardic condition, should not have allowed himself to be given. That is not a thing, however, that, in our paradise of criticism, appears to occur to so much as three persons, and meanwhile the sale, I believe, is tremendous. Basta, basta.

We are living, of course, under the very black shadow of S. Africa, where the nut is proving a terribly hard one to crack, and where, alas, things will probably be worse before they are better. One ranges one's self, on the whole, to the belief not only that they *will* be better, but that they really had to be taken in hand to be made so; they wouldn't and couldn't do at all as they were. But the job is immense, complicated as it is by distance, transport, and many preliminary illusions and stupidities; friends moreover, right and left, have their young barbarians in the thick of it and are living so, from day to day, in suspense and darkness that, in certain cases, their images fairly haunt one. It reminds me strangely of some of the far-away phases and feelings of *our* big, dim war. What tremendously ancient history that now seems!— But I am launching at you, my dear Charles, a composition of magnitude— when I meant only to encumber you with a good, affectionate note. I have presently to take on myself a care that may make you smile; nothing less than to proceed, a few moments hence, to Dover, to meet our celebrated friend (I think she can't *not* be yours) Mrs. Jack Gardner, who arrives from Brussels, charged with the spoils of the Flemish school, and kindly pays me a fleeting visit on her way up to town. I must rush off, help her to disembark, see all her Van Eycks and Rubenses through the Customs and bring her hither, where three water-colours and four photographs of the "Rye school" will let her down easily. My little backwater is just off the highway from London to the Continent. I am really quite near Dover, and it's absurd how also quite near Italy that makes me feel. To get there without the interposition of the lumbering London, or even, if need be, of the bristling Paris, seems so to simplify the matter to the mind. And yet, I grieve to say that, in a residence here of a year and a half, I have only been to patria nostra once.... Good-bye, my dear Charles—I must catch my train. Fortunately I am but three minutes from the station. Fortunately, also, you are not to associate with this fact anything grimy or noisy or otherwise suggestive of fever and fret. At Rye even the railway is quaint—or at least its neighbours are.

Yours always affectionately,

HENRY JAMES.

January 13, 1900.

P.S. This should be a prescript rather than a postscript, my dear Charles, to prepare you properly for the monstrosity of my having dictated a letter to you so long ago and then kept it over unposted into the next century—if next century it be! (They are fighting like cats and dogs here as to where in our speck of time we are.) There has been a method in my madness—my delay has not quite been, not wholly been, an accident; though there *was* at first that intervention. What happened was that I had to dash off and catch a train before I had time to read this over and enclose it; and that on the close of that adventure, which lasted a couple of days and was full of distractions, I had in a still more belated and precipitate way to rush up to London. These sheets, meanwhile, languished in an unfrequented drawer into which, after hurrying off, I had at random thrust them; and there they remained till my return from London—which was not for nearly a fortnight. When I came back here I brought down William and his wife, the former, at the time, so off his balance as to give me almost nothing but *him* to think about; and it thereby befell that some days more elapsed before I rediscovered my letter. Reading it over then, I had the feeling that it gave a somewhat unduly emphasised account of W.; whereupon I said to myself: "Since it has waited so long, I will keep it a while longer; so as to be able to tell better things." That is just, then, what I have done; and I am very glad, in consequence, to be able to tell them. Only I am again (it seems a fate!—giving you a strangely false impression of my normally quiet life) on the point of catching a train. I go with W. and A., a short time hence, on—again!—to Dover—a very small and convenient journey from this—to see them so far on their way to the pursuit, for the rest of the winter, of southern sunshine. They will cross the Channel to-morrow or next day and proceed as they find convenient to Hyères—which, as he himself has written to you, you doubtless already know. I do, at any rate, feel much more at ease about him now. The sight of the good he can get even by sitting for a chance hour or two, all muffled and hot-watered, in such sun, pale and hindered sun, as a poor little English garden can give him in midwinter, quite makes me feel that a real climate, the real thing, will do much toward making him over. He needs it—though differently—even as a consumptive does. And moreover he has become, these last weeks, much more fit to go find it. Q.E.D. But this *shall* be posted. Yours more than ever before,

H. J.

TO EDMUND GOSSE.

Lamb House, Rye.

January 1st, 1900.

My dear Gosse,

I much welcome your note and feel the need of exonerations—as to my own notelessness. It was very good of you, staggering on this gruesome threshold and meeting only new burdens, I fear (of correspondence,) as its most immediate demonstration, to find a moment to waggle me so much as a little finger. I was painfully conscious of my long silence—after a charming book from you, never properly acknowledged, etc.; but I have been living with very few odd moments or off-hours of leisure, and my neglect of every one and everything is now past reparation. The presence with me of my brother, sister-in-law and little niece has, with a particular pressure of work, walled me in and condemned my communications. My brother, for whom this snug and secure little nook appears to have been soothing and sustaining, is better than when he came, and I am proportionately less depressed; but I still go on tiptoe and live from day to day. However, that way one does go on. They go, probably, by the middle of the month, to the South of France—and a right climate, a *real* one, has presumably much to give him....

I never thanked you—en connaissance de cause—for M. Hewlett's Italian *Novelle*: of so brilliant a cleverness and so much more developed a one than his former book. They are wonderful for "go" and grace and general ability, and would almost make me like the *genre*, if anything could. But I so hunger and thirst, in this deluge of cheap romanticism and chromolithographic archaics (babyish, puppyish, as evocation, all, it seems to me,) for a note, a gleam of reflection of the life *we* live, of artistic or plastic intelligence of it, something one can say yes or no to, as discrimination, perception, observation, rendering—that I am really not a judge of the particular commodity at all: I am out of patience with it and have it *par-dessus les oreilles*. What I don't doubt of is the agility with which Hewlett does it. But oh Italy—the Italy *of* Italy! Basta!

May the glowering year clear its dark face for all of us before it has done with us!... Vale. Good-night.

Yours always,

HENRY JAMES.

<u>TO MRS. EVERARD COTES.</u>

This refers to Mrs. Cotes's novel, *His Honor and a Lady*, and to a suggestion that its manner in some way resembled his own.

Lamb House, Rye.

January 26th, 1900.

Dear Mrs. Cotes,

I grovel in the dust—so ashamed am I to have made no response to your so generous bounty and to have left you unthanked and unhonoured. And all the while I was (at once) so admiring your consummately clever book, and so blushing to the heels and groaning to the skies over the daily paralysis of my daily intention to make you some at least (if not adequate) commonly courteous and approximately intelligible sign. And I have absolutely no valid, no sound, excuse to make but that *I am like that*!—I mean I am an abandonedly bad writer of letters and acknowledger of kindnesses. I throw myself simply on my confirmed (in old age) hatred of the unremunerated pen—from which one would think I have a remunerated one!

Your book is extraordinarily keen and delicate and able. How can I tell if it's "like me"? I don't know what "me" is like. I can't *see* my own tricks and arts, my own effect, from outside at all. I can only say that if it *is* like me, then I'm much more of a *gros monsieur* than I ever dreamed. We are neither of us dying of simplicity or common addition; that's all I can make out; and we are both very intelligent and observant and conscious that a work of art must make some small effort to *be* one; must sacrifice somehow and somewhere to the exquisite, or be an asininity altogether. So we open the door to the Devil himself—who is nothing but the sense of beauty, of mystery, of relations, of appearances, of abysses of the whole—*and* of EXPRESSION! That's *all* he is; and if he is our common parent I'm delighted to welcome you as a sister and to be your brother. One or two things my acute critical intelligence murmured to me as I read. I think your drama lacks a little, *line*—bony structure and palpable, as it were, tense cord—on which to string the pearls of detail. It's the frequent fault of women's work—and *I* like a rope (the rope of the *direction and march of the subject*, the action) pulled, like a taut cable between a steamer and a tug, from beginning to end. It lapses and lapses along a trifle too liquidly— and is too *much* conceived (I think) in dialogue—I mean considering that it isn't conceived like a play. Another reflection the Western idiot makes is that he is a little tormented by the modern mixture (maddening medley of our cosmopolite age) of your India (vast, pre-conceived and absently-present,) and your subject not of Indian essence. The two things—elements—don't somehow illustrate each other, and are juxtaposed only by the terrible globe-shrinkage. But that's not *your* fault—it's mine that I suffer from it. Go on and go on—you are full of talent; of the sense of life and the instinct of presentation; of wit and perception and resource. Voilà.

It would be much more to the point to *talk* of these things with you, and some day, again, this must indeed be. But just now I am talking with few—wintering, for many good reasons, in the excessive tranquillity of this tiny, inarticulate country town, in which I have a house really adapted to but the balmier half of the year. And there is nothing cheerful to talk of. South Africa darkens all our sky here, and I gloom and brood and have craven questions of "Finis Britanniae?" in solitude. Your Indian vision at least keeps *that* abjectness away from you. But good-night. It's past midnight; my little heavy-headed and heavy-hearted city sleeps; the stillness ministers to fresh flights of the morbid fancy; and I am yours, dear Mrs. Cotes, most constantly,

HENRY JAMES.

TO A. F. DE NAVARRO.

Lamb House, Rye.

April 1st, 1900.

My dear brave Don Tony and dear beautiful Doña Mary: (not that Tony isn't beautiful too or that Mary isn't brave!) You are awfully exclusive; you won't be written to if you can help it—or if *I* can; but wonderful as you individually and conjoinedly are, you must still taste of the common cup—you must recognise that, after all, you are, humanly, *exposed*—! Well, *this* is all, at the worst, you are exposed to: to my only scribbling at you, a little, for the pride of the thought of you. A fellow has feelings, hang it—and the feelings *will* overflow. I am a very sentient and affectionate, albeit out-of-the-way and out-of-the-fashion person. I *like* to add with my own clumsy fingers a small knot to the silken cord that, for the starved romance of my life, does, by God's blessing, happen to unite me to two or three of my really decorative contemporaries. Besides, if you *will* write such enchanting letters! The communication that (a few days ago in London) reached [me] from each of you, makes up for many grey things. Many things *are* grey, in a *blafard* English March and moist English club-chambers: (tell me not of the pains of Provence!) Without our gifted Jon. close at hand I should have parted forever with my sense of colour. However, I don't want simply to thank you for all the present, the past and the future—I want also to say, right distinctly, that if you *can* conveniently send me a copy of *L'Aiglon* you'll stick the biggest feather yet in your cap of grace. I believe the book isn't yet out—so I shall be as patient as I am attached. You couldn't do a more charming thing—and nobody *but* you could do as charming a one.—I hold you both fast and am your fond and faithful old friend,

HENRY JAMES.

P.S. I send this to C.F. as you may have shifted. How delightful your picture of the little time-beating boy! What a family!

TO W. D. HOWELLS.

The Sense of the Past, the first chapters of which were written at this time, was presently laid aside and not continued until the autumn of 1914. The other projected "tale of terror," referred to in this letter, was never carried out; there seems to be no indication of its subject.

Lamb House, Rye.

29th June, 1900.

My dear Howells,

I can't emulate your wonderful little cursive type on your delicate little sheets—the combination of which seems to suggest that you dictate, at so much an hour, to an Annisquam fairy; but I will do what I can and make out to be intelligible to you even, over the joy it is, ever and always, to hear from you. You say that had you not been writing me the particular thing you were, you fear you wouldn't have been writing at all; but it is a compliment I can better. I really believe that if I weren't writing you this, on my side, I *should* be writing you something else. For I've been, of late, reading you again as continuously as possible—the worst I mean by which is as continuously as the book-sellers consent: and the result of "Ragged Lady," the "Silver Journey," the "Pursuit of the Piano" and two or three other things (none wrested from your inexorable hand, but paid for from scant earnings) has been, ever so many times over, an impulse of reaction, of an intensely cordial sort, directly *at* you—all, alas, spending itself, for sad and sore want of you, in the heavy air of this alien clime and the solitude, here, of my unlettered life. I wrote to you to Kittery Point—I think it was—something like a year ago, and my chief occupation since then has been listening for the postman's knock. But let me quickly add that I understand overwhelmingly well what you say of the impossibility for you, at this time of day, of letters. God knows they *are* impossible—the great fatal, incurable, unpumpable leak of one's poor sinking bark. Non ragioniam di lor—I understand all about it; and it only adds to the pleasure with which, even on its personal side, I greet your present communication.

This communication, let me, without a shred of coyness, instantly declare, much interests and engages me—to the degree even that I think I find myself prepared to post you on the spot a round, or a square, Rather! I won't go through any simpering as to the goodness of your "having thought of me"—nor even through any frank gaping (though there might be, for my admiration and awe, plenty of that!) over the wonder of your multiform activity and dauntlessly universal life. Basta that I will write anything in life that anyone asks me in decency—and a fortiori that you so gracefully ask. I can only feel it to be enough for me that you have a hand in the affair, that you are giving a book yourself and engaging yourself otherwise, and that I am in short in your company. What I understand is that my little novel shall be of fifty thousand (50,000) words, neither more, I take it, nor less; and that I shall receive the sum mentioned in the prospectus "down," in advance of royalties, on such delivery. (I shall probably in point of fact, in my financial humility, prefer, when the time comes, to avail myself of the alternative right mentioned in the prospectus—that of taking, instead of a royalty, for the two years "lease," the larger sum formed by the so-much-a-word aggregation. But that I shall be clear about when the work is done; I only glance at this now as probable.) It so happens that I can get at the book, I think, almost immediately and do it within the next three or four months. You will therefore, unless you hear from me a short time hence to the contrary, probably receive it well before December. As for the absoluteness of the "order," I am willing to take it as, practically, sufficiently absolute. If you shouldn't like it, there is something else, definite enough, that I can do with it. What, however, concerns me more than anything else is to take care that you *shall* like it. I tell myself that I am not afraid!

I brood with mingled elation and depression on your ingenious, your really inspired, suggestion that I shall give you a ghost, and that my ghost shall be "international." I say inspired because, singularly enough, I set to work some months ago at an international ghost, and on just this scale, 50,000 words; entertaining for a little the highest hopes of him. He was to have been wonderful and beautiful; he was to have been called (perhaps too metaphysically) "The Sense of the Past"; and he was to have been supplied to a certain Mr —— who was then approaching me—had then approached me.... The outstretched arm, however, alas, was drawn in again, or lopped off, or otherwise paralysed and negatived, and I was left with my little project—intrinsically, I hasten to add, and most damnably difficult—on my hands.... It is very possible, however, it is indeed most probable, that I should have broken down in the attempt to do him this particular thing, and this particular thing (divine, sublime, if I *could* do it) is not, I think, what I shall now attempt to nurse myself into a fallacious faith that I shall be able to pull off for Howells and Clarke. The damnable *difficulty* is the reason; I have rarely been beaten by a subject, but I felt myself, after upwards of a month's work, destined to be beaten by that one. This will sufficiently hint to you how awfully good it is. But it would take too long for me to tell you here, more vividly, just how and why; it would, as well, to tell you, still more subtly and irresistibly, why it's difficult. There it lies, and probably will always lie.

I'm not even sure that the international ghost is what will most bear being worried out—though, again, in another particular, the circumstances, combining with your coincident thought, seemed pointed by the finger of providence. What —— wanted was two Tales—both tales of "terror" and making another duplex book like the "Two Magics." Accordingly I had had (dreadful deed!) to puzzle out more or less a second, a different piece of impudence of the same general type. But I had only, when the project collapsed, caught hold of the tip of the tail of this other monster—whom I now mention because his tail seemed to show him as necessarily still more interesting than No. 1. If I can at all recapture *him*, or anything like him, I will do my best to sit down to him and "mount" him with due neatness. In short, I will do what I can. If I can't be terrible, I shall nevertheless still try to be international. The difficulties are that it's difficult to be terrible save in the short piece and international save in the long. But trust me. I add little more. This by itself will begin by alarming you as a precipitate instalment of my responsive fury. I rejoice to think of you as basking on your Indian shore. *This* shore is as little Indian as possible, and we have hitherto—for the season—had to combat every form of inclemency. To-day, however, is so charming that, frankly, I wish you were all planted in a row in the little old garden into which I look as I write to you. Old as it is (a couple of hundred years) it wouldn't be too old even for Mildred. But these thoughts undermine. The "country scenes" in your books make me homesick for New England smells and even sounds. Annisquam, for instance, is a smell as well as a sound. May it continue sweet to you! Charles Norton and Sally were with me lately for a day or two, and you were one of the first persons mentioned between us. You were *the* person mentioned most tenderly. It was strange and pleasant and sad, and all sorts of other things, to see Charles again after so many years. I found him utterly unchanged and remarkably young. But I found myself, *with* him, Methusalesque and alien! I shall write you again when my subject condenses. I embrace you all and am yours, my dear Howells, always,

HENRY JAMES.

<u>TO W. D. HOWELLS.</u>

The book already begun, and now "the greatest obsession of all," is evidently *The Ambassadors*.

Dictated.

Read P.S. (Aug. 14th) first!

Lamb House, Rye,

August 9, 1900.

My dear Howells,

I duly received and much pondered your second letter, charming and vivid, from Annisquam; the one, I mean, in reply to mine dispatched immediately on the receipt of your first. If I haven't since its arrival written to you, this is because, precisely, I needed to work out my question somewhat further first. My impulse was immediately to say that I wanted to do my little stuff at any rate, and was willing therefore to take any attendant risk, however, measured as the little stuff would be, at the worst, a thing I should see my way to dispose of in another manner. But the problem of the little stuff itself intrinsically worried me—to the extent, I mean, of my not feeling thoroughly sure I might make of it what I wanted and above all what your conditions of space required. The thing was therefore to try and satisfy myself practically— by threshing out my subject to as near an approach to certainty as possible. This I have been doing with much intensity—but with the result, I am sorry to say, of being still in the air. Let the present accordingly pass for a provisional communication—not to leave your last encompassed with too much silence. Lending myself as much as possible to your suggestion of a little "tale of terror" that should be also international, I took straight up again the idea I

310

spoke to you of having already, some months ago, tackled and, for various reasons, laid aside. I have been attacking it again with intensity and on the basis of a simplification that would make it easier, and have done for it, thus, 110 pages of type. The upshot of this, alas, however, is that though this second start is, if I—or if *you*—like, magnificent, it seriously confronts me with the element of *length*; showing me, I fear, but too vividly, that, do what I will for compression, I shall not be able to squeeze my subject into 50,000 words. It will make, even if it doesn't, for difficulty, still beat me, 70,000 or 80,000— dreadful to say; and that faces me as an excessive addition to the ingredient of "risk" we speak of. On the other hand I am not sure that I can hope to substitute for this particular affair *another* affair of "terror" which will be expressible in the 50,000; and that for an especial reason. This reason is that, above all when one has done the thing, already, as I have rather repeatedly, it is not easy to concoct a "ghost" of any freshness. The want of ease is extremely marked, moreover, if the thing is to be done on a certain scale of length. One might still toss off a spook or two more if it were a question only of the "short-story" dimension; but prolongation and extension constitute a strain which the merely apparitional—discounted, also, as by my past dealings with it— doesn't do enough to mitigate. The beauty of this notion of "The Sense of the Past," of which I have again, as I tell you, been astride, is precisely that it involves without the stale effect of the mere bloated bugaboo, the presentation, for folk both in and out of the book, of such a sense of gruesome malaise as can only—success being assumed—make the fortune, in the "literary world," of every one concerned. I haven't, in it, really (that is save in one very partial preliminary and expository connection,) to make anything, or anybody, "appear" to anyone: what the case involves is, awfully interestingly and thrillingly, that the "central figure," the subject of the experience, has the terror of a particular ground for feeling and fearing that *he himself* is, or may at any moment become, a producer, an object, of this (for you and me) state of panic on the part of others. He lives in an air of *malaise* as to the malaise he may, woefully, more or less fatally, find himself creating—and that, roughly speaking, is the essence of what I have seen. It is less gross, much less *banal* and exploded, than the dear old familiar bugaboo; produces, I think, for the reader, an almost equal funk—or at any rate an equal suspense and unrest;

and carries with it, as I have "fixed" it, a more truly curious and interesting drama—especially a more human one. *But*, as I say, there are the necessities of space, as to which I have a dread of deluding myself only to find that by trying to blink them I shall be grossly "sold," or by giving way to them shall positively spoil my form for your purpose. The hitch is that the thing involves a devil of a sort of prologue or preliminary action—interesting itself and indispensable for lucidity—which impinges too considerably (for brevity) on the core of the subject. My one chance is yet, I admit, to try to attack the same (the subject) from still another quarter, at still another angle, that I make out as a possible one and which may keep it squeezable and short. If this experiment fails, I fear I shall have to "chuck" the supernatural and the high fantastic. I have just finished, as it happens, a fine flight (of eighty thousand words) *into* the high fantastic, which has rather depleted me, or at any rate affected me as discharging my obligations in that quarter. But I believe I mentioned to you in my last "The Sacred Fount"—this has been "sold" to Methuen here, and by this time, probably, to somebody else in the U.S.— but, alas, not to be serialized (as to which indeed it is inapt)—as to the title of which kindly preserve silence. The *vraie vérité*, the fundamental truth lurking behind all the rest, is furthermore, no doubt, that preoccupied with half a dozen things of the altogether human order now fermenting in my brain, I don't care for "terror" (terror, that is, without "pity") so much as I otherwise might. This would seem to make it simple for me to say to you: "Hang it, if I can't pull off my Monster on *any* terms, I'll just do for you a neat little *human*— and not the less international—fifty-thousander consummately addressed to your more cheerful department; do for you, in other words, an admirable short novel of manners, thrilling too in its degree, but definitely ignoring the bugaboo." Well, this I *don't* positively despair of still sufficiently overtaking myself to be able to think of. *That* card one has always, thank God, up one's sleeve, and the production of it is only a question of a little shake of the arm. At the same time, here, to be frank—and above all, you will say, in this communication, to be interminable—that alternative is just a trifle compromised by the fact that I've two or three things begun ever so beautifully in such a key (and only awaiting the rush of the avid bidder!)—each affecting me with its particular obsession, and one, the most started, affecting me with the greatest obsession, for the time (till I can do it, work it off, get it out of the way and fall with still-accumulated intensity upon the *others*,) of all. But alas, if I don't say, bang off, that *this* is then the thing I will risk for you, it is because "this," like its companions, isn't, any way I can fix it, workable as a fifty-thousander. The scheme to which I am *now* alluding is lovely—human, dramatic, international, exquisitely "pure," exquisitely everything; only absolutely condemned, from the germ up, to be workable in not less than 100,000 words. If 100,000 were what you had asked me for, I would fall back upon it ("terror" failing) like a flash; and even send you, without delay, a detailed Scenario of it that I drew up a year ago; beginning then—a year ago—to *do* the thing—immediately afterwards; and then again pausing for reasons extraneous and economic.... It really constitutes, at any rate, the work I intimately want actually to be getting on with; and—if you are not overdone with the profusion of my confidence—I dare say I best put my case by declaring that, if you don't in another month or two hear from me either as a Terrorist or as a Cheerful Internationalist, it will be that intrinsic difficulties will in each case have mastered me; the difficulty in the one having been to keep my Terror down by *any* ingenuity to the 50,000; and the difficulty in the *other* form of Cheer than the above-mentioned obsessive hundred-thousander. I only wish you wanted *him*. But I have now in all probability a decent outlet for him.

Forgive my pouring into your lap this torrent of mingled uncertainties and superfluities. The latter indeed they are properly not, if only as showing you how our question does occupy me. I shall write you again—however vividly I see you wince at the prospect of it. I have it at heart not to fail to let you know how my alternatives settle themselves. Please believe meanwhile in my very hearty thanks for your intimation of what you might perhaps, your own quandary straightening out, see your way to do for me. It is a kind of intimation that I find, I confess, even at the worst, dazzling. All this, however, trips up my response to your charming picture of your whereabouts and present conditions—still discernible, in spite of the chill of years and absence, to my eye, and eke to my ear, of memory. We have had here a torrid, but not a wholly horrid, July; but are making it up with a brave August, so far as we have got, of fires and floods and storms and overcoats. Through everything, none the less, my purpose holds—my genius, I may even say, absolutely thrives—and I am unbrokenly yours,

HENRY JAMES.

14th August.

P.S. The hand of Providence guided me, after finishing the preceding, to which the present is postscriptal, to keep it over a few days instead of posting it directly: so possible I thought it that I might have something more definite to add—and I was a little nervous about the way I had left our question. Behold then I *have* then to add that I have just received your letter of August 4—which so simplifies our situation that this accompanying stuff becomes almost superfluous. But I have let it go for the sake of the interest, the almost top-heavy mass of response that it embodies. Let us put it then that all is for the moment for the best in this worst of possible worlds; all the more that had I not just now been writing you exactly as I am, I should probably—and thanks, precisely, to the lapse of days—be stammering to you the ungraceful truth that, after I wrote you, my tale of terror did, as I was so more than half fearing, give way beneath me. It *has*, in short, broken down for the present. I am laying it away on the shelf for the sake of something that *is* in it, but that I am now too embarrassed and preoccupied to devote more time to pulling out. I really shouldn't wonder if it be not still, in time and place, to make the world sit up; but the curtain is dropped for the present. All thanks for your full and prompt statement of how the scene has shifted for you. There is no harm done, and I don't regard the three weeks spent on my renewed wrestle as wasted—I have, within three or four days, rebounded from them with such relief, vaulting into another saddle and counting, D.V., on a straighter run. I have *two* begun novels: which will give me plenty to do for the present—they being of the type of the "serious" which I am too delighted to see you speak of as lifting again ... its downtrodden head. I mean, at any rate, I assure you, to lift *mine*! Your extremely, touchingly kind offer to find moments of your precious time for "handling" something I might send you is altogether too momentous for me to let me fail of feeling almost ashamed that I haven't something—the ghost or t'other stuff—in form, already, to enable me to respond to your generosity "as meant." But heaven only knows what may happen yet! For the moment, I must peg away at what I have in hand—biggish stuff, I fear, in bulk and possible unserialisability, to saddle you withal. But thanks, thanks thanks. Delighted to hear of one of your cold waves—the newspapers here invidiously mentioning none but your hot. We have them all, moreover, *réchauffées*, as soon as you have done with them; and we are just sitting down to one now. I dictate you this in my shirtsleeves and in a draught which fails of strength—chilling none of the pulses of yours gratefully and affectionately,

HENRY JAMES.

TO W. E. NORRIS.

Lamb House, Rye,

September 26th, 1900.

My dear Norris,

Charming and "gracious" your letter, and welcome sign of your restoration in more senses than one. Though I see you, alas, nowadays, at such intervals, I feel this extremely individual little island to be appreciably less its characteristic self when you are away from it, and sensibly more so, and breathing the breath of relief, when it gets you back and plumps you down with a fond "There!" on your high hilltop, a beacon-like depository of traditions no one else so admirably embodies. Your invitation to come and share for a few days your paradise with you finds me, I am very sorry to say, in a hindered and helpless moment. I am obliged to recognise the stern fact that I *can't* leave home just now. I have had a complicated and quite overwhelmed summer—agreeably, interestingly, anxiously and worriedly, even; but inevitably and logically—waves of family history, a real deluge, having rolled over my bowed head and left me, as to the question of work, production, time, ease and other matters, quite high and dry. I went on Saturday last to Dover to see my sister-in-law off to the Continent—and as she took a night boat had to stop there over Sunday, at the too-familiar (and too other things) Lord Warden; after which I came back to bury (yes, bury!) my precious, my admirable little Peter, whom I think you had met. (He passed away on Sunday at St. Leonard's, fondly attended by the local "canine specialist"—after three days of dreadful little dysentery.) Thus is constituted the first moment of my being by myself for about four months. It may last none too long, and is, already, to be tempered by the palpable presence of Gosse from Saturday p.m. to Monday next. So, with arrears untold, in every direction, with preoccupations but just temporarily arranged, I feel that I absolutely *must* sit close for a good many weeks to come; in fact till the New Year—after which I depart. I don't quite know what becomes of me then, but I don't, distinctly, for a third year, hibernate here. My London rooms are as probably as sordidly let for 1901 (though not to a certainty,) and it will (my wretched fate—not *fat*—*fate*) depend more or less upon that. My brother, ill, but thank God, better, wants me to come to Egypt with him and his wife for 12 weeks—his health demanding it, but he only going if I will accompany him. So the pistol is at my head. Will it bring me down? I've a positive terror of it. The alternatives are Rome (of which I've a still greater terror than of Egypt, for it's an equal complication and less reward,) or De Vere Gardens, or a more squalid perch in town if De V.G. are closed to me. The latter, the last-named, doom is what I really want. If I should, clingingly, clutchingly, stick to these shores, I might *then*, were it agreeable to you, be able to put in three days of Underbank, which I've never seen in its tragic winter mood. But these things are in the lap of the gods.

Later, same night.

I broke off this a.m. to go over to Lydd, where I've had, all summer, a friend in camp, and promised to pay him a visit. My amanuensis, who has been taking at the Paris exhibition a week of joy refused to his employer (and indeed wholly undesired by him—did your "slow" return from Marienbad partly consist of the same?) comes back to-morrow, and my friend's battalion departs on Saturday—so it was my one chance to redeem my perpetually falsified vow. I went by train and bicycled back—in the teeth of a gale now fully developed here and howling in my old chimneys; which sounds the knell of this (to do it justice) incomparable September. I don't quite know what Drury Lane military drama effects I had counted on—but I trundled home with the depressed sense of something that hadn't wholly come off (in the way of a romantic appeal,) a dusty, scrubby plain in which dirty, baby soldiers pigged about with nothing particular to do. However, I've performed my promise, and I sit down to a pile of correspondence that, for many days past, has refused visibly to shrink.... You excite, with your Scandinavian and Austrian holidays and junketings, the envious amaze of poor motionless and shillingless me. I've been thinking of appealing to your "Suffrages," but I more and more feel that I could never afford you. My watering place is Hastings, and my round tour is rounded by the afternoon. But good-night; my servant has just deposited by my side the glass of boiling water which constitutes his nightly admonition that it's "high time" I went to bed—and constitutes my own inexpensive emulation of Marienbad and Copenhagen—where I am sure Gosse drinks the most exotic things. Please say to Miss Effie that I doubly regret having to be deaf to any kind urgency of hers, and that I hope she will find means to include me in some prayer for the conversion of the benighted. But my hot water is cooling, and it takes me so long to let it gouge its inward course that I will be first yours, my dear Norris, always—though I'm afraid you will say always impracticably—

HENRY JAMES.

TO A. F. DE NAVARRO.

"The Place of the Thirty Peacocks" was H. J.'s name for the old moated house of Groombridge Place, near Tunbridge Wells, which he had visited some years before with Mr. de Navarro.

Lamb House, Rye.

November 13, 1900.

Dear and exquisite Tony,

I would deal death, or à peu près, to the man who should have said that I would have delayed these too many days to acknowledge your beautiful little letter from—or about—the Place of the Thirty Peacocks. Yet he, low wretch, would have been, after all, in the secrets of Fate; he would have foreseen me a good deal accablé with arrears, interruptions, a deluge of proofsheets, a complexity of duties and distractions; he would have heard in advance my ineffectual groans and even have pitied my baffled efforts. These things have eventuated to-night in the irresistible desire to chat with you by the fire before turning in. The fire burns low, and the clock marks midnight: everything but the quantity of combustion reminds me of those small nocturnal hours, two years ago, when I was communing with you thus and the fire *didn't* burn low. You saved my life then, and my house, and all that was mine; and for aught I know you are now saving us all again—from some other deadly element. To-night it's *water*—or the absense of it; I don't quite understand which. Something has happened to my water supply, through a pulling-up of the street, though it doesn't yet quite appear whether I'm to perish by thirst or by submersion. Here I sit as usual, at any rate, holding on to you—also as usual—while the clock ticks in the stillness.—I can't tell you how happily inspired I feel it to have been of you to remember our erstwhile pilgrimage to the Maeterlinck house and moat and peacocks and ladies—for that's how—as a moated Maeterlinck matter—the whole impression of our old visit, yours and mine and Miss Reubell's comes back to me. I rejoice that they are still *en place*, and how glad they must have been to see *you*! Willingly would I too taste again the sweet old impression—which your letter charmingly expresses. But I seem to travel, to peregrinate, less and less—and I am reduced to living on my past accumulations. I wish they were larger. But I make the most of them. They include very closely you and *Mrs*. You. To *them* I do seem reduced with you. What with our so far separated country settlements and present absence of a London common centre (save the Bond St. corner of which J. S. is the pivot!) memories and sighs, echoes and ghosts are our terms of intercourse. You oughtn't, you know, to have driven in stakes in your merciless Midland. This southern shore, twinkling and twittering, with a semi-foreign light, a kind of familiar *wink* in the air, would have favoured your health, your spirits, and heaven knows your being here would have favoured mine. I breakfast all these weeks, mostly, with my window open to the garden and a flood of sunshine pouring in. It's really meridional. It would—Rye would—remind you of Granada—more or less. But I hope, after Xmas, to be in town for three or four months. You will surely pass and repass there. When I, at intervals, go up, on some practical urgency, for three or four hours, I always see the abysmal Jon. He usually has some news of you to give; and when he hasn't it's not for want of—on my part—solemn invocation. However, I must now solemnly invoke slumber. Good-night—good-morning. I bless your house, its glorious mistress and its innocent heir.

Yours always and ever,

HENRY JAMES.

TO W. E. NORRIS.

Lamb House, Rye.

December 23rd, 1900.

My dear Norris,

I greatly desire that this shall not fail to convey you my sentiments on this solemn Xmas morn; so I sit here planning and plotting, and making well-meant *pattes de mouche*, to that genial end. A white sea-fog closes us in (in which I've walked healthily, with my young niece, out to the links—with the sense of being less of a golfist than ever;) the clock ticks and the fire crackles during the period between tea and dinner; the young niece aforesaid (my only companion this season of mirth, with her parents abroad and a scant snatch of school holidays to spend with me) sits near me immersed in *Redgauntlet*; so the moment seems to lend itself to my letting off this signal in such a manner as *may*, even in these troublous times (when my nerves are all gone and I feel as if *anything* shall easily happen,) catch your indulgent eye. I feel as if I hadn't caught your eye, for all its indulgence, for a long and weary time, and I daresay you won't gainsay my confession. May the red glow of the Yuletide log diffuse itself at Underbank (with plenty of fenders and fireguards and raking out at night,) in a good old jovial manner. I think of you all on the Lincombes, &c., in these months, as a very high-feeding, champagne-quaffing, orchid-arranging society; and my gaze wanders a little wistfully toward you—away from my plain broth and barley-water. I in fact, some three weeks ago, fled from that Spartan diet up to town, hoping to be in the mood to remain there till Easter, and the experience is still going on, with this week here inserted as a picturesque parenthesis. I asked my young niece in the glow of last August not to fail to spend her Xmas with me, as I then expected to be, Promethean-like, on my rock; and I've returned to my rock not to leave her in the lurch. And I find a niece does temper solitude....

London, at all events, seems to me, after long expatriation, rather thrilling—all the more that I have the thrill, the quite anxious throb, of a new little habitation—which makes, alas, the third that I am actually master of! I've taken (with 34 De Vere Gardens still on my hands, but blessedly let for another year to come, and *then* to be wriggled out of with heaven's help) a permanent room at a club (Reform,) which seems to solve the problem of town on easy terms. They are let by the year only, and one waits one's turn long—(for years;) but when mine the other day came round I went it blind instead of letting it pass. One has to furnish and do all one's self—but the results, and conditions, generally, repay. My cell is spacious, southern, looking over Carlton Gardens: and tranquil, utterly, and singularly well-serviced; and I find I can work there—there being ample margin for a type-writer and its priest, or even priestess. It all hung by *that*—but I think I am not deceived; so I bear up. And the next time you come to perch at a neighbouring establishment, I shall sweep down on you from my eyrie. It's astonishing how remote, cumbrous and expensive it makes 34 De Vere Gardens seem. Worse luck that that millstone still dangles gracefully from my neck!...

I've now dined, and re-established my niece with the second volume of *Redgauntlet*—besides plying her, at dessert, with delicacies brought down, à son intention, from Fortnum & Mason; and thus with a good conscience I prepare to close this and to sally forth into the sea-fog to post it with my own hand—if it's to reach you at any congruous moment. I yesterday dismissed a servant at an hour's notice—the house of the Lamb scarce knew itself and felt like that of the Wolf—so that, with reduced resources, I make myself generally useful. Besides, at little, huddled, neighbourly Rye, even a white December sea-fog is a cosy and convenient thing.

So good night and all blessings on your tropic home. May your table groan with the memorials of friendship, and may Miss Effie's midnight masses not make her late for breakfast and *her* share of them—which is a little even in these poor words from yours, my dear Norris, always,

HENRY JAMES.

TO A. F. DE NAVARRO.

Lamb House, Rye.

December 29th, 1900.

Dear and splendid Tony!

They are all admirable and exquisite—for I seem to have received so much from you that "all" is the only indication comprehensive enough. I came down from ten days in town the other day to find *L'Aiglon*, and within three or four the beautiful little pocket-diary has added itself to that obligation. Dear and splendid Tony, let me not even (scarcely) *speak* of my obligations. That way lies prostration, the sense of deep unworthyness (wrongly spelled—to show how unworthi I *am*:) the memory and vision of a little library of Bond St. booklets that collectors (toward the end of 1901) will cut each others' throats for: and what do I know besides? I am more touched than I can say, in short, by your fidelity in every particular. *L'Aiglon*, now that we at last have the glittering text, has been a joy to me, of the finest kind, here by the Xmas fireside. I haven't seen the thing done—and I don't hugely want to: I so represent it to myself as I go. The talent, the effect, the art, the mastery, the brilliancy, are all prodigious. The man really has talent like an attack of smallpox—I mean it rages with as purple an intensity, and might almost (one vainly feels as one reads) be contagious. You have given me, by your admirable consideration, an exquisite pleasure. I wish we could talk of these things: but we are like the buckets in the well.... Make me a preliminary sign the first time you pass. For the present good-night. My Xmas letters are still mainly unwritten and they are many and much. I greet you and Mrs.

Tony very constantly: I wish you a big slice of the new century: and I am yours ever so gratefully,

HENRY JAMES.

TO THE VISCOUNTESS WOLSELEY.

Lamb House, Rye.

Dec. 29, 1900.

Dearest Lady Wolseley,

This is a very faint and meagre little word, addressed to you late of a terrifically windy winter's night by an old friend who doesn't happen[B] to be in very good physical case (only for the moment, thank goodness, probably!) and yet who doesn't want the New Year to edge an hour nearer before he has made you Both—made you all Three—a sign of affectionate remembrance amounting to tenderness pure and simple. I wish there were a benediction I could call down on your house and your associated life in sufficiently immediate and visible form: you would then see it flutter into your midst and perch upon your table even while you read these lines. I have thought of you constantly these past weeks, and have only not written to you from the fear of appearing to assume that your retirement has been to you woeful or in any degree heart-breaking. I couldn't congratulate you positively, on the event, and yet I hated to *condole*, in the case of people so gallant and distinguished. So I have been hovering about you in thought like an anxious mother armed, in the evening air, with a shawl or extra wrap, for a pair of belated but high-spirited children liable to feel a chill, but not quite venturing to approach the young people and clap the article on their shoulders. I have remained in short with my warm shawl on my hands, but if I were near you I should clap it straight on your shoulders at the first symptom of a shiver, and wrap it close round and tuck it thoroughly in. Forgive this feeble image of the confirmed devotion I hold at your service. To see you will be a joy and a relief—the next time I go up to town: I mean if it so befalls that you are then in residence at the Palace. I do go up on the 31st—Monday next—to stay till Easter: where my address is 105 *Pall Mall, S. W.*, and if you *should* be at Hampton Court the least sign from you would bring me begging for a cup of tea. I hope, meanwhile, with all my heart, that these weeks spent in looking, after so many years, Comparative Leisure in the face, have had somewhat the effect of mitigating the austerity of that countenance. There are opportunities always lurking in it—the opportunity, heaven-sent, in Lord Wolseley's case—as I venture to think of it—of sitting down again to the engaging Marlborough. But here I am talking as if you wouldn't know what to do! Whatever you do, or don't, please believe, both of you, in the great personal affection that prompts this and that calls toward you, to the threshold of the New Year, every pleasant possibility and all ease and honour and, so far as you will consent to it, rest.

Yours, dear Lady Wolseley, always and ever, and more than ever,

HENRY JAMES.

[B] This to attenuate his feebleness of hand!

TO WILLIAM JAMES.

The news had just arrived of the death of F. W. H. Myers at Rome, where William James was spending the winter.

Reform Club, Pall Mall, S. W.

Jan. 24, 1901.

My dear William,

A laggard in response you and Alice will indeed feel that I have become. I've had for three or four days your so interesting and relieving letter dictated to Alice at the hour of poor Myers's death, and though it greatly eased me off (as to my fears that the whole thing would have worn you out,) yet till this moment my hand has been stayed. I wrote you very briefly, moreover, as soon as the papers here gave the news. Blessed seems it to have been that everything round about Myers was so sane and comfortable; the reasonableness and serenity of his wife and children etc., not to speak of his own high philosophy, which it must have been fine to see in operation. But I hope the sequel hasn't been prolonged, and have been supposing that, by the necessary quick departure of his "party," you will have been left independent again and not too exhausted. We here, on our side, have been gathering close round the poor old dying and dead Queen, and are plunged in universal mourning tokens—which accounts for my black-edged paper. It has really been, the event, most moving, interesting and picturesque. I have felt *more* moved, much, than I should have expected (such is *community* of sentiment,) and one has realized all sorts of things about the brave old woman's beneficent duration and holding-together virtue. The thing has been journalistically overdone, of course—greatly; but the people have appeared to advantage—serious and sincere and decent—*really* caring. Meanwhile the drama of the accession, new reign, &c., has its lively spectacular interest—even with the P. of W. for hero. I dined last night in company with some Privy Councillors who had met him ceremonially, in the a.m., and they said (John Morley in particular said) that he made a very good impression. Speriamo!

I find London answering very well, but with so much more crowdedness on one's hours and minutes than in the country that I shall be glad indeed when the end comes. Meanwhile, however, work proceeds.... The war has *doubled* the income tax here; it is hideous.

Ever tenderly your

HENRY.

TO MISS MUIR MACKENZIE.

Miss Muir Mackenzie, during a recent visit to Rye, had been nominated "Hereditary Grand Governess" of the garden of Lamb House, and is addressed accordingly.

Lamb House, Rye.

June 15th, 1901.

Dear Grand Governess,

You are grand indeed, and no mistake, and we are bathed in gratitude for what you have done for us, and, in general, for all your comfort, support and illumination. We cling to you; we will walk but by your wisdom and live in your light; we cherish and inscribe on our precious records every word that drops from you, and we have begun by taking up your delightful tobacco-leaves with pious and reverent hands and consigning them to the lap of earth (in the big vague blank unimaginative border with the lupines, etc.) exactly in the manner you prescribe; where they have already done wonders toward peopling its desolation. It is really most kind and beneficent of you to have taken this charming trouble for us. We acted, further, instantaneously on your hint in respect to the poor formal fuchsias—sitting up in their hot stuffy drawing-room with never so much as a curtain to draw over their windows. We haled them forth on the spot, everyone, and we clapped them (in thoughtful clusters) straight into the same capacious refuge or omnium gatherum. Then, while the fury and the frenzy were upon us, we did the same by the senseless stores of geranium (my poor little 22/-a-week-gardener's idée fixe!)—we enriched the boundless receptacle with *them* as well—in consequence of which it looks now quite sociable and civilised. Your touch is magical, in short, and your influence infinite. The little basket went immediately to its address, and George Gammon (!!) my 22-shillinger, permitted himself much appreciation of your humour on the little tin soldiers. That regiment, I see, will be more sparingly recruited in future. The total effect of all this, and of your discreet and benevolent glance at my ineffective economy, is to make me feel it fifty times a pity, a shame, a crime, that, as John Gilpin said to his wife "you should dine at Edmonton, and I should dine at Ware!"—that you should bloom at Effingham and I should fade at Rye! Your real place is *here*—where I would instantly ask your leave to farm myself out to you. I want to *be* farmed; I am utterly unfit to farm myself; and I do it, all round, for (seeing, alas, what it is) not nearly little enough money. Therefore you ought to be over the wall and "march" with me, as you say in Scotland. However, even as it is, your mere "look round" makes for salvation. I am, I rejoice to say, clothed and in my right mind—compared with what I was when you left me; and so shall go on, I trust, for a year and a day. I have been alone—but next week bristles with possibilities—two men at the beginning, two women (postponed—the Americans) in the middle—and madness, possibly, at the end. I shall have to move over to Winchelsea! But while my reason abides I shall not cease to thank you for your truly generous and ministering visit and for everything that is yours. Which *I* am, very faithfully and gratefully,

HENRY JAMES.

TO W. D. HOWELLS.

Strether's outburst to little Bilham, in Book V. of *The Ambassadors*, during their colloquy in the Parisian garden, represents the germ from which the novel sprang, and which H. J. owed, as he here tells, to Mr. Howells. The development of the subject from this origin is described in the preface afterwards written for the book.

Lamb House, Rye.

August 10th, 1901.

My dear Howells,

Ever since receiving and reading your elegant volume of short tales—the arrival of which from you was affecting and delightful to me—I've meant to write to you, but the wish has struggled in vain with the daily distractions of a tolerably busy summer. I should blush, however, if the season were to melt away without my greeting and thanking you. I read your book with joy and found in it recalls from far far away—stray echoes and scents as from another, the American, the prehistoric existence. The thing that most took me was that entitled A Difficult Case, which I found beautiful and admirable, ever so true and ever so *done*. But I fear I more, almost, than anything else, lost myself in mere envy of your freedom to do, and, speaking vulgarly, to place, things of that particular and so agreeable dimension—I mean the dimension of most of the stories in the volume. It is sternly enjoined upon one here (where an agent-man does what he can for me) that everything—every hundred—above 6 or 7 thousand words is fatal to "placing"; so that I do them of that length, with great care, art and time (much reboiling,) and then, even then, can scarcely get them worked off—published even when they've been accepted.... So that (though I don't know why I inflict on you these sordid groans—except that I haven't any one else to inflict them on—and the mere affront—of being unused so inordinately long—is almost intolerable) I don't feel incited in that direction. Fortunately, however, I am otherwise immersed. I lately finished a tolerably long novel, and I've written a third of another—with still another begun and two or three more subjects awaiting me thereafter like carriages drawn up at the door and horses champing their bits. And àpropos of the first named of these, which is in the hands of the Harpers, I have it on my conscience to let you know that the idea of the fiction in question had its earliest origin in a circumstance mentioned to me—years ago—in respect to no less a person than yourself. At Torquay, once, our young friend Jon. Sturges came down to spend some days near me, and, lately from Paris, repeated to me five words you had said to him one day on his meeting you during a call at Whistler's. I thought the words charming—you have probably quite forgotten them; and the whole incident suggestive—so far as it was an incident; and, more than this, they presently caused me to see in them the faint vague germ, the mere point of the *start*, of a subject. I noted them, to that end, as I note everything; and years afterwards (that is three or four) the subject sprang at me, one day, out of my notebook. I don't know if it be good; at any rate it has been treated, now, for whatever it is; and my point is that it had long before—it had in the very act of striking me as a germ—got away from *you* or from anything like you! had become impersonal and independent. Nevertheless your initials figure in my little note; and if you hadn't said the five words to Jonathan he wouldn't have had them (most sympathetically and interestingly) to relate, and I shouldn't have had them to work in my imagination. The moral is that you are responsible for the whole business. But I've had it, since the book was finished, much at heart to tell you so. May you carry the burden bravely!—I hope you are on some thymy promontory and that the winds of heaven blow upon you all— perhaps in that simplified scene that you wrote to me from, with so gleaming a New England evocation, last year. The summer has been wondrous again in these islands—four or five months, from April 1st, of almost merciless fine weather—a rainlessness absolute and without precedent. It has made my hermitage, as a retreat, a blessing, and I have been able, thank goodness, to work without breaks—other than those of prospective readers' hearts.—It almost broke mine, the other day, by the way, to go down into the New Forest (where he has taken a house) to see Godkin, dear old stricken friend. He gave me, in a manner, news of you—told me he had seen you lately.... I am lone here just now with my sweet niece Peggy, but my brother and his wife are presently to be with me again for fifteen days before sailing (31st) for the U.S. He is immensely better in health, but he must take in sail hand over hand at home to remain so. Stia bene, caro amico, anche Lei (my Lei is my joke!) Tell Mrs. Howells and Mildred that I yearn toward them tenderly.

Yours always and ever,

HENRY JAMES.

TO EDMUND GOSSE.

Lamb House, Rye.

Sept. 16th [1901].

My dear Gosse,

I hurl this after you, there, for good luck, like the outworn shoe of ancient usage. Even a very, very old shoe will take you properly over Venice. I wrote a week ago to Mrs. Curtis about you, and you will doubtless hear from her, beckoningly, in respect to the ever-so-amiable Barbaro: an impression well worth your having. For the rest I commit you both, paternally, to Brown, to whose friendly memory I beg you to recall me. I wish I could assist at some of your raptures. *Go to see the Tintoretto Crucifixion at San Cossiano*—or never more be officer of mine. And, àpropos of master-pieces, read a thing called *Venice* in a thing called *Portraits of Places* by a thing called H. J., if you can get the book: I'm not sure if it's in Tauchnitz, but Mrs. Curtis may have the same. Brown certainly won't, though J. A. Symonds, in the only communication I ever got from him, told me he thought it the best image of V. he had ever seen made. This is the first time in my life, I believe, by the way, I ever indulged in any such—in *any* fatuous reference to a fruit of my pen. So there may be something in it. Drink deep, both of you, and come home remorselessly intoxicated, and reeking of the purple vine, to your poor old attached abstainer,

HENRY JAMES.

TO MISS JESSIE ALLEN.

The "hideous American episode" was the recent assassination of President McKinley, on which Mr. Roosevelt succeeded to the Presidency. The "heavenly mansion" was the Palazzo Barbaro (referred to in the preceding letter to Mr. Gosse), where H. J. had stayed in company with Miss Allen.

Lamb House, Rye.

September 19th, 1901.

Dear bountiful and beautiful lady!

It is equally impossible to respond to you adequately and not to respond to you somehow. You flash your many-coloured lantern, over my small grey surface, from every corner of these islands, and I sit blinking, gaping, clapping my hands, at the purple and orange tints to such a tune that I've scarce presence of mind left for an articulate "Thank you." How you keep it up, and how exactly you lead the life that, long years ago, when I was young, I used to believe a very, very few fantastically happy mortals on earth *could* lead, and could survive the bliss of leading—the waltz-like, rhythmic rotation from great country-house to great country-house, to the sound of perpetual music and the acclamation of the "house-parties" that gather to await you. You are the dream come true—you really do it, and I get the side-wind of the fairy-tale—which is more than I can really quite believe of myself—such a living—almost—*near* the rose! You make me feel near, at any rate, when you write me so kindly about the hideous American episode—almost the worst feature of which is that I don't either like or trust the new President, a dangerous and ominous Jingo—of whom the most hopeful thing to say is that he may be rationalized by this sudden real responsibility. *Speriamo*, as we used to say in the golden age, in the heavenly mansion, along with the ministering angel, long, long ago. And all thanks meanwhile for your sympathetic thought. It must indeed—the base *success* of the act—cause a sinking of the heart among the potentates in circulation. One wonders, for instance, just now, who is most nervous, the poor little Tsar for himself or M. Loubet for him. Let us thank our stars that we are not travelling stars, I not even a Loubet, nor you a Loubette, and that though we have many annoyances we are probably not marked for the dagger of the assassin.

20th, p.m. I had to break off last night, and I resume—perhaps a trifle precariously at this midnight hour of what is just no longer Friday, but about to be Saturday. I have seen, as it were, my two guests, and my tardy servants, to bed, and I put in again this illegible little talk with (poor) you! It has been a more convivial 24 hours than my general scheme of life often permits.... Such are the modest annals of Lamb House—or rather its daily and nightly chronicle. But don't let it depress you—for everything passes, and I bow my head to the whirlwind. But I hate the care of even a tiny and twopenny house and wish I could farm out the same. If some one would only undertake it—and the backgarden—at so much a year I would close with the offer and ask no questions. I may still have to try Whiteley. But I shall try a winter in town first. I blush for my meagreness of response to all your social lights and shadows, your rich record of adventures.... But it's now—as usual over my letters—tomorrow a.m. (I mean 1 a.m.) and I am, dear Miss Allen, very undecipherably but constantly yours,

HENRY JAMES.

TO MRS. W. K. CLIFFORD.

Lamb House, Rye.

Wednesday night.

Dearest Lucy C.

I have waited to welcome you, to thank you for your dear and brilliant Vienna letter, because you stayed my hand (therein) from writing—for want of an address; and because I've believed that not till now (if even now) would you be disengaged from the tangled skein of your adventures. And even at this hour (of loud-ticking midnight stillness,) I don't pretend to do more than greet you affectionately on the threshold of home; promise you a better equivalent (for your so interesting, so envy-squeezing, so vivid record of adventure) at some very near date; and, above all, renew my jubilation at your having made so good and brave a thing of it all—especially as *full* and unstinted a one as you desired. Never mind the money, I handsomely say— you will get it all back and much more—in the refreshment and renewal and general intellectual ventilation your six weeks will have been to you. I'm sure the effect will go far—I want details so much that I wish I were to see you soon—but, alas, I don't quite see when. I'm just emerging from a domestic cyclone that has, in one way and another, cost me so much time, that, pressed as I am with a woefully backward book, I can only for the present hug my writing-table with convulsive knees. The figure doesn't fit—but the postponement of all joy, alas, does. My two old man-and-wife servants (who had been with me sixteen years) were, a few days ago, shot into space (thank heaven at last!) by a whirlwind of but 48 hours duration; and though the absolute rupture came and went in that time, the horrid accompaniments and upheaved neighbourhoods have represented a woeful interruption. But it's over, and I have plunged again (and am living, blissfully, for the present, with a house-maid and a charwoman, and immensely enjoying my simplified state and my relief from what I see now was a long nightmare).

I read your play in the Nineteenth Century, as you invited me, but I can't *write* of it now beyond saying that I was greatly struck by the care and finish you had given it. If I must tell you categorically, however, I don't think it a scenic subject *at all*; I think it bears all the mark of a subject selected for a tale and done as a play as an after-thought. I don't see, that is, what the scenic form does, or *can* do, for it, that the narrative couldn't do better—or what it, in turn, does for the scenic form. The inwardness is a kind of inwardness that doesn't become an outwardness—effectively—theatrically; and the part played in the whole by the painting of the portrait seems to me the kind of thing for which the play is a non-conductor. And here I am *douching* you on your doorstep with cold water. We must *talk*, we must colloquise and compare and *renew* the first moment we can, and I am all the while and ever your affectionate old friend,

HENRY JAMES.

TO MISS MUIR MACKENZIE.

Lamb House, Rye.

Wednesday night. [Oct. 17, 1901].

Dear Miss Muir Mackenzie,

One almost infallibly begins—at least the perpetually criminal *I* do—with the assurance that one has, from long since, been on the point—! And it remains eternally true; which makes no difference, however, in your being bored to hear it. Besides, if I *had* been writing a month ago I shouldn't, perhaps, be writing now; and that I *am* writing now is a present joy to me—which I would barter for none other, no mere luxury of conscience. I haven't, for weeks, strolled through my now blighted and stricken *jardinet* without reverting gratefully in thought to you as its titular directress; without wishing, at once, that it were more worthy of you, and recognising, recalling your hand and mind, in most of its least humiliating features. Your kind visit, so scantly honoured, so meagerly recorded (I mean by commemorative tablet, or other permanent demonstration,) lives again in some of the faded phenomena of the scene—and the blush revives which the sense of how poor a host I was caused even then to visit my cheek. I want you in particular to know what a joy and pride your great proud and pink tobacco-present has proved. It has overlorded the confused and miscellaneous border in which your masterly eye recognised its imperative—not to say imperial—place, and it has reduced by its mere personal success all the incoherence around it to comparative insignificance. What a bliss, what a daily excitement, all summer, to see it grow by leaps and bounds and to feel it happy and hearty—as much as it could be in its strange exile and inferior company. It has all prospered—though some a little smothered by more vulgar neighbours; and the tallest of the brotherhood are still as handsome as ever, with a particular shade of watered wine-colour in the flower that I much delight in. And yet—niny that I am!—I don't know what to do with them for next year. My gardener opines that we leave them, as your perennial monument, just as they are. But I have vague glimmerings of conviction that we cut them down to a mere small protrusion above ground—and we probably both are fully wrong. Or do we extract precious seed and plant afresh? Forgive my feeble (I repeat) flounderings. I feel as the dunce of an infant school trying to babble Greek to Professor Jebb (or suchlike.) I am none the less hoping that the garden will be less dreadful and casual next year. We've ordered 105 roses—also divers lilies—and made other vague dashes. Oh, you should be in controlling permanence! Actually we are painfully preparing to become bulbous and particoloured. One *must* occupy the gardener. The grapes have been bad (bless their preposterous little pretensions!) but the figs unprecedently numerous. And so on, and so on. And it has been for me a rather feverish and *accidenté* summer; I mean through the constant presence of family till a month ago, and through a prolonged domestic upheaval ever since. I sit amid the ruins of a once happy household, clutching a charwoman with one hand, and a knife-boy—from Lilliput—with the other. A man and his wife, who had lived with me for long, long years, and were (in spite of growing infirmities and the darker and darker shadow of approaching doom) the mainstay of my existence, were sacrificed to the just gods three or four weeks ago, and I've picnicked (for very relief) ever since—making futile attempts at reconstruction for which I have had no time, and yet which have consumed so much of it that none has been left, as I began by hinting, for correspondence. I've been up to London over it, and haunted Hastings, and wired to friends, and almost appealed to the Grand Governess—only deterred by the fear of hearing from her that it isn't her province. Yet I did wonder if I couldn't lawfully work it in under kitchen-garden. No matter; my fate closes round me again, and the first thing I think of now when I wake up in the morning is that a "cook-housekeeper" in a

Gorringe (?) costume (?) is to arrive next week. I tremble at her. If the worst comes to the worst I *shall* make you responsible. I walked over to Winchelsea this afternoon and returned, in darkness and wet, by the far-off station and the merciful train—always re-weaving the legend of your wet exile there. It blows, it rains, it rages to-night—for the first time here for six months. I hope you haven't had again to eat overmuch the bread of banishment. I haven't asked you for your news—have only jabbered my own; but I believe you not unaware that this is but a subtler art for extracting from you the whole of your herbaceous (and other) history. May it have been mild and merciful. Good-night—or, as usual, good-morning—I am going to bed, but it has been for some time to-morrow. Yours, dear Miss Muir Mackenzie, very gratefully and faithfully,

HENRY JAMES.

TO EDMUND GOSSE.

The reference in the following is to W. E. Henley's provocative article in the *Pall Mall Magazine* on Mr. Graham Balfour's recently published Life of Robert Louis Stevenson.

Lamb House, Rye.

November 20th, 1901.

My dear Gosse,

I have been very sorry to hear from you of renewed upsets on quitting these walls—the same fate having, I remember, overtaken you most of the other times you've been here. I trust it isn't the infection of the walls themselves, nor of the *re*fection (so scant last time) enjoyed within them. Is it some baleful effluence of your host? He will try and exercise next time some potent counter-charm—and meanwhile he rejoices that your devil is cast out.

All thanks for your so vivid news of the overflow of Henley's gall. Ça ne pouvait manquer—ça *devait* venir. I have sent for the article and will write you when I've read it. I gather from you that it's really rather a striking and lurid—and so far interesting case—of long discomfortable jealousy and ranklement turned at last to posthumous (as it were!) malignity, and making the man do, coram publico, his ugly act, risking the dishonour for the assuagement. That *is*, on the part of a favourite of the press etc., a remarkable "psychologic" incident—or perhaps I'm talking in the air, from not having read the thing. I dare say, moreover, at all events, that H. *did* very seriously—I mean sincerely—deplore all the graces that had crept into Louis's writing—all the more that they had helped it so to be loved: he honestly thinks that L. should have written like—well, like who but Henley's self? But the whole business illustrates how life takes upon itself to give us more true and consistent examples of human unpleasantness than expectation could suggest—makes a given man, I mean, live up to his ugliness. This one's whole attitude in respect to these recent amiable commemorations of Louis—the having (I, "self-conscious and alone") nothing to do with them, contained singularly the promise of some positive aggression. I have, however, this a.m., a letter from Graham Balfour (in answer to one I had written him on reading his book,) in which, speaking of Henley's paper, he says it's less bad than he expected. He apparently feared more. It's since you were here, by the way, that I've read his record, in which, as to its second volume, I found a good deal of fresh interest and charm. It seems to me, the whole thing, very neatly and tactfully done for an amateur, a non-expert. *But*, I see now that a really curious thing has happened, a "case" occurred much more interesting than the *cas* Henley. Insistent publicity, so to speak, has done its work (I only knew it was *doing* it, but G. B.'s book's a settler,) and Louis, *qua* artist, is now, definitely, the victim thereof. That is, he has *superseded*, personally, his books, and this last re-placement of himself so *en scène* (so largely by his own aid, too) has *killed* the literary baggage. Out of no mystery now do they issue, the creations in question—and they couldn't afford to lose it. Louis himself never understood that; he too publicly caressed and accounted for them—but I needn't insist on what I mean. As I *see* it, at all events, it's a strange little evolution and all taking place here, quite compactly, under one's nose.

I don't come up to town, alas, for more than a few necessary hours, till I've finished my book, and that will be when God pleases. I pray for early in January. But then I shall stay as long as ever I can. All thanks for your news of Norris, to whom I shall write. I envy your Venetian newses—but I myself have written for some. I rain good wishes on your house and am yours always,

HENRY JAMES.

TO H. G. WELLS.

Lamb House, Rye.

January 20th, 1902.

My dear Wells,

Don't, I beseech you, measure the interest I've taken in your brilliant book (that is in the prior of the recent pair of them,) and don't measure any other decency or humanity of mine (in relation to anything that is yours,) by my late abominable and aggravated silence. You most handsomely sent me *Anticipations* when the volume appeared, and I was not able immediately to read it; I was bothered and preoccupied with many things, wished for a free mind and an attuned ear for it, so let it wait till the right hour, knowing that neither you nor I would lose by the process. The right hour came, and I gave myself up—utterly, admirably up—to the charm; but the charm, on its side, left me so spent, as it were, with saturation, that I had scarce pulled myself round before the complications of Xmas set in, and the New Year's flood—in respect to correspondence—was upon me; which I've been till now buffeting and breasting. And then I was ashamed—and I'm ashamed still. That is the penalty of vice—one's shame disqualifies one for the company of virtue. Yet, all this latter time, I've taken the greatest pleasure in my still throbbing and responding sense of the book.

I found it then, I assure you, extraordinarily and unceasingly interesting. It's not that I haven't—hadn't—reserves and reactions, but that the great source of interest never failed: which great source was simply H. G. W.

himself. You, really, come beautifully out of your adventure, come out of it immensely augmented and extended, like a belligerent who has annexed half-a-kingdom, with drums and trumpets and banners all sounding and flying. And this is because the thing, in our deadly day, is such a charming exhibition of complete freedom of mind. That's what I enjoyed in it—your intellectual disencumberedness; very interesting to behold as the direct fruit of training and observation. A gallant show altogether—and a gallant temper and a gallant tone. For the rest, you will be tired of hearing that, for vatication, you, to excess, simplify. Besides, the phrophet (see how I recklessly spell him, to do him the greater honour!) *must*—I can't imagine a subtilizing prophet. At any rate I don't make you a reproach of simplifying, for if you hadn't I shouldn't have been able to understand you. But on the other hand I think your reader asks himself too much "Where is *life* in all this, life as I feel it and know it?" Subject of your speculations as it is, it is nevertheless too much left out. That comes partly from your fortunate youth—it's a more limited mystery for you than for the Methuselah who now addresses you. There's less of it with you to provide for, and it's less a perturber of your reckoning. There are for instance more kinds of people, I think, in the world—more irreducible kinds—than your categories meet. However, your categories do you, none the less, great honour, the greatest, worked out as they are; and I quite agree that, as before hinted, if one wants more life, there is Mr. Lewisham himself, of Spade House, exhaling it from every pore and in the centre of the picture. That is the great thing: he *makes*, Mr. Lewisham does, your heroic red-covered romance. It had to have a hero—and it has an irresistible one. Such is my criticism. I can't go further. I can't take you up in detail. I am under the charm. My world *is*, somehow, other; but I can't produce it. Besides, I don't want to. You can, and do, produce yours—so you've a right to talk. Finally, moreover, your book is full of truth and wit and sanity—that's where I mean you come out so well. I go to London next week for three months; but on my return, in May, I should like well to see you. What a season you must have had, with philosophy, poetry and the banker! I had a saddish letter from Gissing—but rumours of better things for him (I mean reviving powers) have come to me, I don't quite know how, since. Conrad haunts Winchelsea, and Winchelsea (in discretion) haunts Rye. So foot it up, and accept, at near one o'clock in the morning, the cordial good-night and general benediction of yours, my dear Wells, more than ever,

HENRY JAMES.

TO PERCY LUBBOCK.

Lamb House, Rye.

March 9th, 1902.

My dear Percy Lubbock,

I've been very uncivilly silent, but I've also been still more dismally hindered—I mean ever since receiving your good note of Feb. 22d. It found me wearily, drearily ill, in bed; such had been my state ever since Jan. 29th, and it ceased to be my state only ten days ago—since when I have sat feebly staring at a mountain of unanswered letters. I did go to London, Jan. 27th, but was immediately stricken, and scrambled back here to be more commodiously prostrate. I've had to stay and recuperate. But I am infinitely better—only universally behind. Still, it isn't too late, I hope, to tell you it would have given me extreme pleasure to see you in town had everything been different. Also that I congratulate you with all my heart on the great event of your young, your first, your never to be surpassed or effaced, prime Italiänische Reise. It's a great event (*the* revelation) at any time of life, but it's altogether immeasurable at *your* lucky one. Yet there are things to be said too. As that there would be no use whatever in my having "told you what to do." There wouldn't be the remotest chance of your doing it. The place, the time, the aspect, the colour of the light and the inclination of Percy Lubbock, will already be making for you their own law, or, better still, causing you to live generally lawless and promiscuous. *Be* promiscuous and incoherent and intelligent, absorbent, happy: it's your great chance. Be further glad of every Italian vocable you take to your heart, and help me to hope that our meeting over it all is only moderately put off—when you'll have ever so interesting things to tell to yours most truly,

HENRY JAMES.

TO GAILLARD T. LAPSLEY.

Lamb House, Rye.

June 22nd, 1902.

My dear, dear Boy!

The penalty of shameful turpitude is that even reparation and contrition are made almost impossible by the dimensions of the abyss that separates the criminal from virtue. Or, more simply, the amount of explanation (of my baseness) that I have felt myself saddled with toward you, has long operated as a further and a fatal deterrent in respect to writing to you at all. The burden of my shame has in short piled up my silence, and to break that hideous spell I must now cast explanations to the winds—ere they crush me altogether. I've had a rather blighted and broken winter—a good deal of somewhat ominous unwellness, now happily (D.V.) over-past. Under the effect of it *all* my correspondence has gone to pieces, and though I've managed to write two books I've done so mainly by an economy of *moyens* that has forbidden my answering even a note or two. I've thought of you, dreamed of you, followed you, admired you, in fine tenderly loved you: done everything accordingly but treat you decently. But I'm all right in the long, the very long run, and your admirably interesting and charming letter of ever so many months ago has never ceased to be a joy and pride to me. Those emotions have just been immeasureably quickened by something told me by my brave little cousin Bay Emmet (the paintress)—viz. her having lately met you in New York and heard on your lips words (à mon adresse) not of resentment or scorn, but of divine magnanimity and gentleness. You appear to have spoken to her "as if you still liked me," and I like you so much for that that the vibration has started these stammering accents. I really write you these words not from my peaceful hermitage by the southern sea, but from the depths of the meretricious metropolis, which I've never known so detestable as at this most tawdry of crises, and from which I hope to escape in a day or two, utterly dodging the insane crush of the Coronation. The place is vilely disfigured by league-long hoardings (for spectators at £10 0. 0. a head,) and cheap and awful decorations, and the dear old Abbey in particular smothered into the likeness of the Earl's Court Exhibition—not to be distinguished from the Westminster Aquarium, in fact, opposite. And then the crowds, the gregarious, gaping millions, are appalling, and I fly, in fine, back to the Southern Sea—on the shore of which I've spent almost all my time for almost a year past. I've lately been dabbling a little, for compensation, in town; but I find small doses of London now go further, for my organisation, than they used.

B. Emmet tells me that you still sit aloft in California and I permit myself to rejoice in it, in spite of some of the lurid lights projected by your so vivid letter over the composition of that *milieu*. You tell me things of awful suggestion—and in respect to which I would give anything for more talk with you and more chance for question and answer.

June 26th. The foregoing, my dear Boy, though dated here, was written in London—which means that in the confusion and distraction, the present chaotic crash of things there, it was also interrupted. I had been there for a snatch of but three or four days, and I rushed back here, in horror and dismay (24 hours since), just *before* the poor King's collapse set the seal on the general gregarious madness. I had "chucked" the Coronation, thank heaven, before the Coronation chucked *me*, and this little russet and green corner, as so often before, has been breathing balm and peace to me after the huge bear-garden. The latter beggars description at the present moment—and must now do so doubly while reeling under the smash of everything. I feel like a man who has jumped, safe, from an express-train before a collision—and to make really sure of my *not* having broken my neck I take up again this distempered scrawl to you. But I won't talk of all this dreary pandemonium here—dreary *whatever* the issue of the poor King's illness; inasmuch as, either way, it can only mean more gregarious madness, more league-long hoarding, more blocks of traffic and deluges of dust and tons of newspaper verbiage. Amen!

What I didn't begin to say to you the other day was how interesting and awful I found your picture of your seat of learning. I rejoice with all my heart that it has attached you, for just "the likes of you" are what must make a difference (by influence, by example, by civilization, by revelation) in the strange mixture—or absence of mixture—of its elements. I gather from you that its air is *all* female, so to speak, and that in this buoyant medium you triumphantly float. It must be very wonderful and fearful and indescribable, all of it, lifelike indeed though your sketch appears to me. I wish immensely I could see you, so that we could get nearer, together, to everything. You come out most summers—is there no chance of your doing so this year? I seem to infer the sad contrary, from my little cousin's not having told me that you mentioned anything of the sort to her. I have the sense of having seen you odiously little last year—a blighted and distracted season. As I read over at present your generous letter I feel a special horror and dismay at having failed so long and so abominably to give you the promised word of introduction to Fanny Stevenson. I enclose one herewith—but I must tell you that I feel myself to be launching it rather into the dark. That is, I have a fear that she is rather changed—or rather exaggerated—with time, illness etc.—and that you may find her somewhat aged, queer, eccentric etc. And I'm not sure I'm possessed of her address. Only remember this—that *she* (with all deference to her) was never the person to have seen, it was R. L. S. himself. But good-night. I haven't half responded to you, nor met you—in your charming details; yet I *am*, none the less, my dear Lapsley, very affectionately yours,

HENRY JAMES.

TO MRS. CADWALADER JONES.

Mrs. Jones, it will be understood, had sent him two of the books of her sister-in-law, Mrs. Wharton.

Lamb House, Rye.

August 20th, 1902.

Dictated.

Dear and bountiful Lady,

My failure, during these few days, to thank you for everything has not come from a want of appreciation of *anything*—or from a want of gratitude, or lively remembrance, or fond hope; or, in short, from anything but a quite calculating and canny view that I shall perhaps come in, during your present episode, with a slightly greater effect of direct support and encouragement than if I had come during the fever of your late short interval in London. It seems to be "borne in" to me that you may be feeling—là où vous êtes—a little lone and lorn, a little alien and exotic; so that the voice of the compatriot, counsellor and moderator, may fall upon your ears with an approach to sweetness. I am sure, all the same, that you are in a situation of great and refreshing novelty and of general picturesque interest. At your leisure you will give me news of it, and I wish you meanwhile, as the best advice, to drain it to the dregs and leave no element of it untasted.

My situation has, en attendant, been made picturesque by the successive arrivals of your different mementoes, each one of which has done its little part to assuage my solitude and relieve my gloom. Putting them in their order, Mrs. Wharton comes in an easy first; the unspeakable Postum follows handsomely, and Protoplasm—by which I mean Plasmon—pants far behind. How shall I thank you properly for these prompt and valued missives? Postum *does* taste like a ferociously mild coffee—a coffee reduced to second childhood, the prattle of senility. I hasten to add, however, that it accords thereby but the better with my enfeebled powers of assimilation, and that I am taking it regular and blessing your name for it. It interposes a little ease after the long and unattenuated grimness of cocoa. Since Jackson was able to provide it with so little delay, I feel I may count on him for blessed renewals. But I shall never count on any one again for Plasmon, which is gruesome and medicinal, or at all events an "acquired taste," which the rest of my life will not be long enough to acquire.

Mrs. Wharton is another affair, and I take to her very kindly as regards her diabolical little cleverness, the quantity of intention and intelligence in her style, and her sharp eye for an interesting *kind* of subject. I had read neither of these two volumes, and though the "Valley" is, for significance of ability, several pegs above either, I have extracted food for criticism from both. As criticism, in the nobler sense of the word, is for me enjoyment, I've in other words much liked them. Only they've made me again, as I hinted to you other things had, want to get hold of the little lady and pump the pure essence of my wisdom and experience into her. She *must* be tethered in native pastures, even if it reduces her to a back-yard in New York. If a work of imagination, of fiction, interests me at all (and very few, alas, do!) I always want to write it over in my own way, handle the subject from my own sense of it. *That* I always find a pleasure in, and I found it extremely in the "Vanished Hand"—over which I should have liked, at several points, to contend with her. But I can't speak more highly for any book, or at least for my interest in any. I take liberties with the greatest.

But you will say that in ticking out this amount of Remingtonese at you I am taking a great liberty with *you*; or rather, of course, I know you won't, since you gave me kind leave—for which I shamelessly bless you.... Good-bye with innumerable good wishes. Please tell Miss Beatrix that these are addressed equally to her, as in fact my whole letter is, and that my liveliest interest attends her on her path.

Yours and hers always affectionately,

HENRY JAMES.

TO W. D. HOWELLS.

Lamb House, Rye.

Sept. 12th, 1902.

Dictated.

My dear Howells,

An inscrutable and untoward fate condemns me to strange delinquencies—though it is no doubt the weakness of my nature as well as the strength of the said treacherous principle that the "undone vast," in my existence, lords it chronically and shamelessly over the "petty done." It strikes me indeed both *as* vast, and yet in a monstrous way as petty too, that I should have joyed so in "*The Kentons*," which you sent me, ever so kindly, more weeks ago than it would be decent in me to count—should have eaten and drunk and dreamed and thought of them as I did, should have sunk into them, in short, so that they closed over my head like living waters and kept me down, down in subaqueous prostration, and all the while should have remained, so far as *you* are concerned, brutishly and ungratefully dumb. I haven't been otherwise dumb, I assure you—that is so far as they themselves are concerned: there was a time when I talked of nothing and nobody else, and I have scarcely even now come to the end of it. I think in fact it is *because* I have been so busy vaunting and proclaiming them, up and down the more or less populated avenues of my life, that I have had no time left for anything else. The avenue on which you live, worse luck, is perversely out of my beat. Why, however, do I talk thus? I know too well how *you* know too well that letters, in the writing life, are the last things that get themselves written. You see the way that this one tries to manage it—which at least is better than no way. All the while, at any rate, the impression of the book remains, and I have infinitely pleased myself, even in my shame, with thinking of the pleasure that must have come to yourself from so acclaimed and attested a demonstration of the freshness, within you still, of the spirit of evocation. Delightful, in one's golden afternoon, and after many days and many parturitions, to put forth thus a young, strong, living flower. You have done nothing more true and complete, more thoroughly homogeneous and hanging-together, without the faintest ghost of a false note or a weak touch—all as sharply ciphered-up and tapped-out as the "proof" of a prize scholar's sum on a slate. It is in short miraculously felt and beautifully done, and the aged—by which I mean the richly-matured—sposi *as* done as if sposi were a new and fresh idea to you. Of all your sposi they are, I think, the most penetrated and most penetrating. I took in short true comfort in the whole manifestation, the only bitterness in the cup being that it made me feel old. *I* shall never again so renew myself. But I want to hear from you that it has really—the sense and the cheer of having done it—set you spinning again with a quickened hum. When you mentioned to me, I think in your last letter, that you had done the Kentons, you mentioned at the same time the quasi-completion of something else. It is this thing I now want—won't it soon be coming due?—and if you will magnanimously send it to me I promise you to have, for it, better manners. Meanwhile, let me add, I have directed the Scribners to send you a thing of my own, too long-winded and minute a thing, but well-meaning, just put forth under the name of *The Wings of the Dove.*

I hope the summer's end finds you still out of the streets, and that it has all been a comfortable chapter. I hear of it from my brother as the Great Cool Time, which makes for me a pleasant image, since I generally seem to sear my eyeballs, from June to September, when I steal a glance, across the sea, at the bright American picture. Here, of course, we have been as grey and cold, as "braced" and rheumatic and uncomfortable as you please. But that has little charm of novelty—though (not to blaspheme) we *have*, since I've been living here, occasionally perspired. I live here, as you see, still, and am by this time, like the dyer's hand, subdued to what I work in, or at least try to economise in. It is pleasant enough, for five or six months of the year, for me to wish immensely that some crowning stroke of fortune may still take the form of driving you over to see me before I fall to pieces. Apropos of which I am forgetting what has been half my reason—no, not half—for writing to you. Many weeks ago there began to be blown about the world— from what fountain of lies proceeding I know not—a rumour that you were staying with me here, a rumour flaunting its little hour as large as life in some of the London papers. It brought me many notes of inquiry, invitations to you, and other tributes to your glory—damn it! (I don't mean damn your glory, but damn the wanton and worrying rumour). Among other things it brought me a fattish letter addressed to you and which I have been so beastly procrastinating as not to forward you till now, when I post it with this. Its aspect somehow denotes insignificance and impertinence, and I haven't wanted to do it, as a part of the so grossly newspaperistic impudence, too much honour; besides, verily, the intention day after day of writing you at the same time. Well, there it all is. You will think my letter as long as my book. So I add only my benediction, as ever, on your house, beginning with Mrs. Howells, going straight through, and ramifying as far as you permit me.

Yours, my dear Howells, always and ever,

HENRY JAMES.

TO H. G. WELLS.

Lamb House, Rye.

September 23rd, 1902.

My dear Wells,

All's well that ends well and everything is to hand. I thank you heartily for the same, and I have read the *Two Men*, dangling breathlessly at the tail of their tub while in the air and plying them with indiscreet questions while out of it. It is, the whole thing, stupendous, but do you know what the main effect of it was on my cheeky consciousness? To make me sigh, on some such occasion, to *collaborate* with you, to intervene in the interest of—well, I scarce know what to call it: I must wait to find the right name when we meet. You can so easily avenge yourself by collaborating with *me*! Our mixture would, I think, be effective. I hope you are thinking of doing Mars—in some detail. Let me in *there*, at the right moment—or in other words at an early stage. I really shall, opportunity serving, venture to try to say two or three things to you about the Two Men—or rather not so much about them as about the cave of conceptions whence they issue. All I can say now however is that the volume *goes* like a bounding ball, that it is 12.30 a.m., and that I am goodnightfully yours,

HENRY JAMES.

TO MRS. CADWALADER JONES.

Dictated.

Lamb House, Rye.

October 23d, 1902.

Dear Mrs. Cadwalader,

Both your liberal letters have reached me, and have given me, as the missives of retreating friends never fail to do, an almost sinister sense of the rate at which the rest of the world goes, moves, rushes, voyages, railroads, passing from me through a hundred emotions and adventures, and pulling up in strange habitats, while I sit in this grassy corner artlessly thinking that the days are few and the opportunities small (quite big enough for the likes of *me* though the latter be even here.) All of which means of course simply that you take away my breath. But that was on the cards and it's not worth mentioning. Your best news for me is of your being, for complete convalescence, in the superlative hands you describe—to which I hope you are already doing infinite credit. I kind of make you out, "down there," I mean in the pretty, very pretty, as it used to be, New York Autumn, and in the Washington Squareish region trodden by the steps of my childhood, and I wonder if you ever kick the October leaves as you walk in Fifth Avenue, as I can to this hour feel myself, hear myself, positively *smell* myself doing. But perhaps there are no leaves and no trees now in Fifth Avenue—nothing but patriotic arches, Astor hotels and Vanderbilt palaces. (My secretary was on the point of writing the great name "aster"—which I think the most delightful irony of fate! they are so flowerlike a race!) The October leaves are at any rate gathering about me here—and that I have watched them fall, and lighted my fire and trimmed my lamp, is about the only thing that has happened to me—though I *should* count in a visit from a delightful nephew, who has just been with me for a fortnight, and left me for Geneva, where he spends the winter.

I assisted dimly, through your discreet page, at your visit to Mrs. Wharton, whose Lenox house must be a love, and I wish I could have been less remotely concerned. In the way of those I know I hope you have by this time, on your own side, gathered in John La Farge, and are not allowing him to feel anything but that he is well and happy—except, also, that I very affectionately remember him....

But I am not thanking you, all this time, for the interesting remarks about the book I had last placed in your hands (The Wings of the Dove), which you so heroically flung upon paper even on the heaving deep—a feat to *me* very prodigious. I won't say your criticism was eminent for the time and place—I'll say, frankly, that it was eminent in itself, and all full of suggestion. The fact is, however, that one is so aware one's self, even to satiety, of the rights and wrongs of these matters—especially of the wrongs—that freshness of mind almost fails for discriminations, however benevolent, of others. Such is the price of having written many books and lived many years. The thing in question is, by a complicated accident which it would take too long to describe to you, too inordinately drawn out, and too inordinately rubbed in. The centre, moreover, isn't in the middle, or the middle, rather, isn't in the centre, but ever so much too near the end, so that what was to come after it is truncated. The book, in fine, has too big a head for its body. I am trying, all the while, to write one with the opposite disproportion—the body too big for its head. So I shall perhaps do if I live to 150. Don't therefore undermine me by general remarks. And dictating, please, has moreover nothing to do with it. The value of that process for me is in its help to do over and over, for which it is extremely adapted, and which is the only way I can do at all. It soon enough, accordingly, becomes, *intellectually*, absolutely identical with the act of writing—or has become so, after five years now, with me; so that the difference is only material and illusory—only the difference, that is, that I walk up and down: which is so much to the good.—But I must stop walking now. I stand quite still to send my hearty benediction to Miss Beatrix and I am yours and hers very constantly,

HENRY JAMES.

TO H. G. WELLS.

The only two "effusions," of the kind described in this letter, that have survived are the preliminary schemes for the unfinished novels, *The Ivory Tower* and *The Sense of the Past*, published with them in 1917.

Lamb House, Rye.

November 15th, 1902.

My dear Wells,

It is too horribly long that I have neglected an interesting (for I can't say an interested) inquiry of yours—in your last note; and neglected it precisely *because* the acknowledgment involved had to be an explanation. I have somehow, for the last month, not felt capable of explanations, it being my infirmity that when "finishing a book" (and that seems my chronic condition) my poor enfeebled cerebration becomes incapable of the least extra effort, however slight and simple. My correspondence then shrinks and shrinks—only the least explicit of my letters get themselves approximately written. And somehow it has seemed highly explicit to tell you that (in reply to your suggestive last) those wondrous and copious preliminary statements (of my fictions that are to be) don't really exist in any form in which they can be imparted. I think I know to whom you allude as having seen their semblance—and indeed their very substance; but in two exceptional (as it were) cases. In these cases what was seen was the statement drawn up on the basis of the serialization of the work—drawn up in one case with extreme detail and at extreme length (in 20,000 words!) Pinker saw that: it referred to a long novel, afterwards (this more than a year) written and finished, but not yet, to my great inconvenience, published; but it went more than two years ago to America, to the Harpers, and there remained and has probably been destroyed. Were it here I would with pleasure transmit it to you; for, though I say it who should not, it *was*, the statement, full and vivid, I think, as a statement could be, of a subject as worked out. Then Conrad saw a shorter one of the *Wings of the D.*—also well enough in its way, but only half as long and proportionately less developed. *That* had been prepared so that the book might be serialized in another American periodical, but this wholly failed (what secrets and shames I reveal to you!) and the thing (the book) was then written, the subject treated, on a more free and independent scale. But *that* synopsis too has been destroyed; it was returned from the U.S., but I had then no occasion to preserve it. And evidently no fiction of mine can or *will* now be serialized; certainly I shall not again draw up detailed and explicit plans for unconvinced and ungracious editors; so that I fear I shall have nothing of that sort to show. A plan for *myself*, as copious and developed as possible, I always do draw up—that is the two documents I speak of were based upon, and extracted from, such a preliminary *private* outpouring. But this latter voluminous effusion is, ever, so extremely familiar, confidential and intimate—in the form of an interminable garrulous letter addressed to my own fond fancy—that, though I always for easy reference, have it carefully typed, it isn't a thing I would willingly expose to any eye but my own. And even *then*, sometimes, I shrink! So there it is. I am greatly touched by your respectful curiosity, but I haven't, you see, anything coherent to produce. Let me promise however that if I ever do, within any calculable time, address a manifesto to the dim editorial mind, you shall certainly have the benefit of a copy. Candour compels me to add that that consummation has now become unlikely. It is too wantonly expensive a treat to them. In the first place they will none of me, and in the second the relief, and greater intellectual dignity, so to speak, of working on one's own scale, one's own line of continuity and in one's own absolutely independent *tone*, is too precious to me to be again forfeited. Pardon my too many words. I only add that I hope the domestic heaven bends blue above you.

Yours, my dear Wells, always,

HENRY JAMES.

TO MRS. FRANK MATHEWS.

Lamb House, Rye.

November 18th, 1902.

My dear Mary,

You have made me a most beautiful and interesting present, and I thank you heartily for the lavish liberality and trouble of the same. It arrived this a.m. swathed like a mummy of the Pharaohs, and is a monument to the care and skill of every one concerned. The photographer has *retouched* the impression rather too freely, especially the eyes (if one could but keep their hands off!) but the image has a pleasing ghostliness, as out of the far past, and affects me pathetically as if it were of the dead—of one who died young and innocent. Well, so he did, and I can speak of him or admire him, poor charming slightly mawkish youth, quite as I would another. I remember (it now all comes back to me) when (and where) I was so taken: at the age of *20*, though I look younger, and at a time when I had had an accident (an injury to my back,) and was rather sick and sorry. I look rather as if I wanted propping up. But you have propped me up, now, handsomely for all time, and I feel that I shall go down so to the remotest posterity. There is a great Titian, you know, at the Louvre—*l'homme au gant*; but I, in my gloved gentleness, shall run him close. All thanks again, then: you have renewed my youth for me and diverted my antiquity and I really, as they say, fancy myself, and am yours, my dear Mary, very constantly,

HENRY JAMES.

TO W. D. HOWELLS.

Lamb House, Rye.

December 11th, 1902.

My dear Howells,

Nothing more delightful, or that has touched me more closely, even to the spring of tears, has befallen me for years, literally, than to receive your beautiful letter of Nov. 30th, so largely and liberally anent *The W. of the D.* Every word of it goes to my heart and to "thank" you for it seems a mere grimace. The same post brought me a letter from dear John Hay, so that my measure has been full. I haven't known anything about the American "notices," heaven save the mark! any more than about those here (which I am told, however, have been remarkably genial;) so that I have *not* had the sense of confrontation with a public more than usually childish—I mean had it in any special way. I confess, however, that that is my chronic sense—the more than usual childishness of publics: and it is (has been,) in my mind, long since discounted, and my work definitely insists upon being independent of such phantasms and on unfolding itself wholly from its own "innards." Of course, in our conditions, doing anything decent is pure disinterested, unsupported, unrewarded heroism; but that's in the day's work. The *faculty of attention* has utterly vanished from the general anglo-saxon mind, extinguished at its source by the big blatant *Bayadère* of Journalism, of the newspaper and the *picture* (above all) magazine; who keeps screaming "Look at *me*, *I* am the thing, and I only, the thing that will keep you in relation with me *all the time* without your having to attend *one minute* of the time." If you are moved to write anything anywhere about the *W. of the D.* do say something of that— it so awfully wants saying. But we live in a lovely age for literature or for any art but the mere visual. Illustrations, loud simplifications and *grossissements*, the big building (good for John,) the "mounted" play, the prose that is careful to be in the tone of, and with the distinction of a newspaper or bill-poster advertisement—these, and these only, meseems, "stand a chance." But why do I talk of such chances? I am melted at your reading *en famille The Sacred Fount*, which you will, I fear, have found chaff in the mouth and which is one of several things of mine, in these last years, that have paid the penalty of having been conceived only as the "short story" that (alone, apparently) I could hope to work off somewhere (which I mainly failed of,) and then *grew* by a rank force of its own into something of which the idea had, modestly, never been to be a book. That is essentially the case with the *S. F.*, planned, like The Spoils of Poynton, What Maisie Knew, The Turn of the Screw, and various others, as a story of the "8 to 10 thousand words"!! and then having accepted its bookish necessity or destiny in consequence of becoming already, at the start, 20,000, accepted it ruefully and blushingly, moreover, since, *given the tenuity of the idea*, the larger quantity of treatment hadn't been aimed at. I remember how I would have "chucked" *The Sacred Fount* at the 15th thousand word, if in the first place I could have afforded to "waste" 15,000, and if in the second I were not always ridden by a superstitious terror of not finishing, for finishing's and for the precedent's sake, what I have begun. I am a fair coward about *dropping*, and the book in question, I fear, is, more than anything else, a monument to that superstition. When, if it meets my eye, I say to myself, "You know you might not have finished it," I make the remark not in natural reproach, but, I confess, in craven relief.

But why am I thus grossly expatiative on the airy carpet of the bridal altar? I spread it beneath Pilla's feet with affectionate jubilation and gratification and stretch it out further, in the same spirit, beneath yours and her mother's. I wish her and you, and the florally-minded young man (he *must* be a good 'un,) all joy in the connection. If he stops short of gathering samphire it's a beautiful trade, and I trust he will soon come back to claim the redemption of the maiden's vows. Please say to her from me that I bless her—*hard*.

Your visit to Cambridge makes me yearn a little, and your watching over it with C. N. and your sitting in it with Grace. Did the ghost of other walks (I'm told Fresh Pond is no longer a Pond, or no longer Fresh, only stale, or something) ever brush you with the hem of its soft shroud? Haven't you lately published some volume of Literary Essays or Portraits (*since* the Heroines of Fiction) and won't you, munificently, send me either that *or* the Heroines— neither of which have sprung up in my here so rustic path? I will send you in partial payment another book of mine to be published on February 27th.

Good-night, with renewed benedictions on your house and your spirit.

Yours always and ever,

HENRY JAMES.

TO MADAME PAUL BOURGET.

Lamb House, Rye.

January 5th, 1903.

Dear Madame Paul,

Very welcome, very delightful, to me your kind New Year's message, and meeting a solicitude (for news of you both) which was as a shadow across my (not very glowing indeed) Christmas hearth. Your note finds me still incorrigibly rustic; I have been spending here the most solitary Christmas-tide of my life (absolutely solitary) and I have not, for long months, been further from home than for an occasional day or two in London. I go there on the 10th to remain till May; but I am sorry to say I see little hope of my being able to peregrinate to far Provence—all benignant though your invitation be. We must meet—*some* time!—again in the loved *Italy*; but I blush, almost, to say it, when I have to say at the same time that my present prospect of that bliss is of the smallest. I long unspeakably to go back there—before I descend into the dark deep tomb—for a *long* visit (of upwards of a year); yet it proves more difficult for me than it ought, or than it looks, and, in short, I oughtn't to speak of it again save to announce it as definite. Unfortunately I also want to return for a succession of months to the land of my birth—also in anticipation of the tomb; and the one doesn't help the other. Europe has ceased to be romantic to me, and my own country, in the evening of my days, has become so; but this senile passion too is perhaps condemned to remain platonic.—Bourget's benevolence continues to shine on me, his generosity to descend, in the form of heavenly-blue volumes, the grave smile of my dull library shelves, for which I blush that I make so meagre returns. I shall send you a volume in February, but it will have no such *grande allure*; though the best thing in it will be a little story of which you gave me long ago, at Torquay, the motive, and which I will mark. I congratulate you on not being absentees from your high-walled—or much-walled—Eden, and I hope it means a happy distillation for Bourget and much health and peace for both of you. May you have a mild and merciful year! Deserve it by continuing to have patience tous les deux with your very faithful (and very inky) old friend,

HENRY JAMES.

TO MRS. WALDO STORY.

The book to which the following refers is of course *William Wetmore Story and his Friends*, published in 1903.

Dictated.

Lamb House, Rye.

Jan. 6th, 1903.

Dear Mrs. Waldo,

Let my first word be to ask you to pardon this vulgar machinery and this portentous legibility: the fruit of dictation, in the first place (now made absolutely necessary to me;) and the fruit, in the second place, of the fact that, pegging away as I am at present, in your interest and Waldo's (and with the end of our business now, I am happy to say, well in sight), I so live, as it were, from day to day and from hour to hour, by the aid of this mechanism, that it is an effort to me to break with it even for my correspondence. I had promised myself to write you so that you should receive my letter on the very Capo d'Anno; and if I had *then* overcome my scruple as to launching at you a dictated thing, you would some time ere this have been in possession of my news. I have delayed till now because I was every day hoping to catch the right moment to address you a page or two of my own proper hieroglyphics. But one's Christmas-tide burden (of writing) here is heavy; I didn't snatch the moment; and *this* is a brave precaution lest it should again elude me; which, in the interest of lucidity, please again forgive.

So much as that about a minor matter. The more important one is that, as you will both be glad to know, I have (in spite of a most damnable interruption of several weeks, this autumn, a detested compulsion to attend, for the time, to something else) got on so straight with the Book that three quarters of it are practically written, and four or five weeks more will see me, I calculate, at the end of the matter.... All the material I received from you has been of course highly useful—indispensable; yet, none the less, all of it put together was not material for a Biography pure and simple. The subject itself didn't lend itself to *that*, in the strict sense of the word: and I had to make out, for myself, what my material *did* lend itself to. I *have*, I think, made out successfully and happily; if I haven't, at any rate, it has not been for want of a great expenditure of zeal, pains, taste (though I say it who shouldn't!) and

355

talent! But the Book will, without doubt, be an agreeable and, in a literary sense, really artistic and honourable one. I shall not have made you all so patiently, amiably, admirably wait so long for nothing.... I have looked at the picture, as it were, given me by all your material, *as* a picture—the image or evocation, charming, heterogeneous, and a little ghostly, of a great cluster of people, a society practically extinct, with Mr. and Mrs. Story, naturally, all along, the centre, the pretext, so to speak, and the *point d'appui*. This course was the only one open to me—it was imposed with absolute logic. The Book was not makeable at all unless I used the letters of other people, and the letters of other people were useable with effect only so far as I could more or less evoke and present the other people....

But I am writing you at hideous length—and crowding out all space for matters more personal to ourselves. When once the Book is out I shall want, I shall need, exceedingly, to see you all; and I don't think that, unless some morbid madness settles on me, I shall fear to. But that is arrangeable and shall be arranged.... My blessing on all of you.

Yours, dear Mrs. Waldo, most faithfully,

HENRY JAMES.

TO W. D. HOWELLS.

The Ambassadors began at length to appear in the *North American Review*, January 1903, where it ran throughout the year.

Dictated.

Lamb House, Rye.

Jan. 8th, 1903.

My dear Howells,

Let me beg you first of all not to be disconcerted by this chill legibility. I want to write to you *to-day*, immediately, your delightful letter of Dec. 29th having arrived this morning, and I can only manage it by dictation as I am, in consequence of some obscure indiscretion of diet yesterday, temporarily sick, sorry, and seedy; so that I can only loll, rather listless (but already better of my poison), in an armchair. My feelings don't permit me to wait to tell you that the communication I have just had from you surpasses for pure unadulterated charm any communication I have *ever* received. I am really quite overcome and weakened by your recital of the generous way in which you threw yourself into the scale of the arrangement, touching my so long unserialized serial, which is manifestly so excellent a thing for me. I had begun to despair of anything, when, abruptly, this brightens the view. For I *like*, extremely, the place the N.A.R. makes for my novel; it meets quite my ideal in respect to that isolation and relief one has always fondly conceived as the proper *due* of one's productions, and yet never, amid the promiscuous petticoats and other low company of the usual magazine table-of-contents, seen them in the remotest degree attended with. One had dreamed, in private fatuity, that one would really be the better for "standing out" a little; but one had, to one's own sense, never really "stood" at all, but simply lain very flat, for the petticoats and all the foolish feet aforesaid to trample over with the best conscience in the world. Charming to me also is the idea of your own beneficent paper in the same quarter—the complete detachment of which, however, from the current fiction itself I equally apprehend and applaud: just as I see how the (not-to-be-qualified) editorial mind would indulge one of its most characteristic impulses by suggesting a connection. Never mind suggestions—and how you echo one of the most sacred laws of my own effort toward wisdom in not caring to know the source of *that* one! I care to know nothing but that your relation to my stuff, as it stands, gives me clear joy. Within a couple of days, moreover, your three glorious volumes of illustrated prose have arrived to enrich my existence, adorn my house and inflame my expectations. With many things pressing upon me at this moment as preliminary to winding-up here and betaking myself, till early in the summer, to London, my more penetrative attention has not yet been free for them; but I am gathering for the swoop. Please meanwhile be tenderly thanked for the massive and magnificent character of the gift. What a glorious quantity of work it brings home to me that you do! I feel like a hurdy-gurdy man listening outside a cathedral to the volume of sound poured forth there by the enthroned organist.... But good-night, my dear Howells, with every feebly-breathed, but forcibly-felt good wish of yours always and ever,

HENRY JAMES.

TO WILLIAM JAMES.

The special business that H. J. hints at in connexion with his projected visit to America was to be the arrangement for a collected edition of his works, a scheme that was now beginning to take shape. With regard to another allusion in this letter, it may be said that the threatened destruction of the old cottages, a few yards from Lamb House, was averted.

Dictated.

Lamb House, Rye.

May 24th, 1903.

Dearest William,

How much I feel in arrears with you let this gross machinery testify—which I shamelessly use to help to haul myself into line. However, you have most beneficently, from of old, given me free licence for it. Other benefits, unacknowledged as yet, have I continued to receive from you: I think I've been silent even since *before* your so cheering (about yourself) letter from Ashville, followed, a few days before I left town (which I did five days ago), by your still more interesting and important one (of May 3d) in answer to mine dealing (so tentatively!) with the question of my making plans, so far as complicatedly and remotely possible, for going over to you for 6 or 8 months. There is—and there *was* when I wrote—no conceivability of my doing this for a year at least to come—before August 1904, at nearest; but it kind of eases my mind to thresh the idea out sufficiently to have a direction to *tend* to meanwhile, and an aim to work at. It is in fact a practical necessity for me, *dès maintenant*, to know whether or no I absolutely want to go if, and when, I *can*: such a difference in many ways (more than I need undertake to explain) do the prospect of going and the prospect of *not* going make. Luckily, for myself, I do already (as I feel) quite adequately remain convinced that I *shall* want to whenever I can: that is [if] I don't put it off for much *more* than a year—after which period I certainly shall *lose* the impulse to return to my birth-place under the mere blight of incipient senile decay. If I go at all I must go before I'm too old, and, above all, before I mind being older. You are very dissuasive—even more than I expected; but I think it comes from your understanding even less than I expected the motives, considerations, advisabilities etc., that have gradually, cumulatively, and under much study of the question, much carefully invoked *light* on it, been acting upon me. I won't undertake just now to tell you what all these reasons are, and how they show to me—for there is still plenty of time to do that. Only I *may* even at present say that I don't despair of bringing you round in the interval (if what is beyond the interval *can* realise itself) to a better perception of my situation. It is, roughly—and you will perhaps think too cryptically—speaking, a situation for which 6 or 8 months in my native land shine before me as a very possible and profitable remedy: and I don't speak *not* by book. Simply and supinely to shrink—on mere grounds of general fear and encouraged shockability—has to me all the air of giving up, chucking away without a struggle, the one chance that remains to me in life of anything that can be called a *movement*: my one little ewe-lamb of possible exotic experience, such experience as may convert itself, through the senses, through observation, imagination and reflection now at their maturity, into vivid and solid *material*, into a general renovation of one's too monotonised grab-bag. You speak of the whole matter rather, it seems to me, "à votre aise"; you make, comparatively, and have always made, so many movements; you have travelled and gone to and fro—always comparatively!—so often and so much. I have practically never travelled at all—having never been economically able to; I've only gone, for short periods, a few times—so much fewer than I've wanted—to Italy: never anywhere else that I've seen every one about me here (who is, or was, anyone) perpetually making for. These visions I've had, one by one, all to give up—Spain, Greece, Sicily, any glimpse of the East, or in fact of anything; even to the extent of rummaging about in France; even to the extent of trudging about, a little, in Switzerland. Counting out my few dips into Italy, there has been no time at which *any* "abroad" was financially convenient or possible.

And now, more and more, all such adventures present themselves in the light of mere agreeable *luxuries*, expensive and supererogatory, inasmuch as not resolving themselves into new material or assimilating with my little acquired stock, my accumulated capital of (for convenience) "international" items and properties. There's nothing to be done by me, any more, in the way of writing, *de chic*, little worthless, superficial, *poncif* articles about Spain, Greece, or Egypt. They are the sort of thing that doesn't work in at all to what now most interests me: which is human Anglo-Saxonism, with the American extension, or opportunity for it, so far as it may be given me still to work the same. If I *shouldn't*, in other words, bring off going to the U.S., it would simply mean giving up, for the remainder of my days, all chance of such experience as is represented by interesting "travel"—and which in this special case of my own would be much more than so represented (granting the travel to be American.) I should settle down to a mere mean oscillation from here to London and from London here—with nothing (to speak of) left, more, to happen to me in life in the way of (the poetry of) motion. That spreads before me as for mind, imagination, special, "professional" labour, a thin, starved, lonely, defeated, beaten, prospect: in comparison with which your own circumgyrations have been as the adventures of Marco Polo or H.M. Stanley. I *should* like to think of going once or twice more again, for a sufficient number of months, to Italy, where I know my ground sufficiently to be able to plan for such quiet work there as might be needfully involved. But the day is past when I can "write" stories about Italy with a mind otherwise pre-occupied. My native land, which time, absence and change have, in a funny sort of way, made almost as romantic to me as "Europe," in dreams or in my earlier time here, used to be—the actual bristling (as fearfully bristling as you like) U.S.A. have the merit and the precious property that they meet and fit into my ("creative") preoccupations; and that the period there which should represent the poetry of motion, the one big taste of travel not supremely missed, would carry with it also possibilities of the prose of *production* (that is of the production of prose) such as no other mere bought, paid for, sceptically and half-heartedly worried-through adventure, by land or sea, would be able to give me. My primary idea in the matter is absolutely economic—and on a basis that I can't make clear to you now, though I probably shall be able to later on if you demand it: that is if you also are accessible to the impression of my having *any* "professional standing" là-bas big enough to be improved on. I am not thinking (I'm sure) vaguely or blindly (but recognising direct intimations) when I take for granted some such Chance as my personal presence there *would* conduce to improve: I don't mean by its beauty or brilliancy, but simply by the benefit of my managing for once in my life not to fail to be on the spot. Your allusion to an American [agent] as all sufficient for any purpose I could entertain doesn't, for me, begin to cover the ground— which is antecedent to that altogether. It isn't in the least a question of my trying to make old copy-rights pay better or look into arrangements actually existing; it's a question—well, of too much more than I can go into the detail of now (or, much rather, into the general and comprehensive truth of); or even than I can ever do, so long as I only have from you Doubt. What you say of the Eggs (!!!), of the Vocalisation, of the Shocks in general, and of everything else, is utterly beside the mark—it being absolutely *for* all that class of phenomena, and every other class, that I nurse my infatuation. I want to see them, I want to see everything. I want to see the Country (scarcely a bit New York and Boston, but intensely the Middle and Far West and California and the South)—in *cadres* as complete, and immeasurably more mature than those of the celebrated Taine when he went, early in the sixties, to Italy for six weeks, in order to write his big book. Moreover, besides the general "professional" I have thus a conception of, have really in definite view, there hangs before me a very special other probability—which, however, I must ask you to take on trust, if you can, as it would be a mistake for me to bruit it at all abroad as yet. To make anything of this last-mentioned business I must be on the spot—I mean not only to carry the business out, of course, but to arrange in advance its indispensable basis. It would be the last of follies for me to attempt to do that from here—I should simply spoil my chance. So you see what it all comes to, roughly stated—that the 6 or 8 months in question are all I have to look to unless I give up the prospect of ever stirring again. They are the only "stir" I shall ever be able to afford, because, though they will cost something, cost even a good bit, they will bring in a great deal more, in proportion, than they will cost. Anything else (other than a mere repeated and too aridly Anglo-American winter in Florence, perhaps, say) would

361

almost only cost. But enough of all this—I am saying, *have* said, much more than I meant to say at the present date. Let it, at any rate, simmer in your mind, if your mind has any room for it, and take *time*, above all, if there is any danger of your still replying adversely. Let me add this word more, however, that I mention August 1904 very advisedly. If I want (and it's half the battle) to go to the West and South, and even, dreamably, to Mexico, I [could not] do these things during that part of the summer during which (besides feeling, I fear, very ill from the heat) I should simply have to sit still. On the other hand I should like immensely not to fail of coming in for the *whole* American autumn, and like hugely, in especial, to arrive in time for the last three or four weeks of your stay in Chocorua—which I suppose I should do if I quitted this by *about* mid-August. Then I should have the music of *toute la lyre*, coming away after, say, three or four Spring weeks at Washington, the next April or May. But I *must* stop. These castles in Spain all hang by the thread of my finding myself in fact economically able, 14 months hence, to *face* the music. If I am not, the whole thing must drop. All I can do meanwhile is to try and arrange that I *shall* be. I am scared, rather—well in advance—by the vision of American expenses. But the "special" possibility that shines before me has the virtue of covering (potentially) all that. One thing is very certain—I shall not be able to hoard by "staying" with people. This will be impossible to me (though I *will*, assuredly, by a rich and rare exception, dedicate to you and Alice as many days as you will take me in for, whether in country or town.) Basta!

I talk of your having room in mind, but you must be having at the present moment little enough for anything save your Emerson speech, which you are perhaps now, for all I know, in the very act of delivering. This morning's Times has, in its American despatch, an account of the beginning, either imminent or actual, of the Commemoration—and I suppose your speech is to be uttered at Concord. Would to God I could sit there entranced by your accents—side by side, I suppose, with the genial Bob! May you be floated grandly over your cataract—by which I don't mean have any manner of fall, but only be a Niagara of eloquence, all continuously, whether above or below the rapids. You will send me, I devoutly hope, some report of the whole thing. It affects me much even at this distance and in this so grossly alien air—

this overt dedication of dear old Emerson to his immortality. I hope all the attendant circumstances will be graceful and beautiful. I came back hither as I believe I have mentioned, some six days ago, after some 18 weeks in London, which went, this time, very well, and were very easy, on my present extremely convenient basis, to manage. The Spring here, till within a week, has been backward and blighted; but Summer has arrived at last with a beautiful jump, and Rye is quite adorable in its outbreak of greenery and blossom. I never saw it more lovely than yesterday, a supreme summer (early summer) Sunday. The dear little charm of the place at such times consoles me for the sordid vandalisms that are rapidly disfiguring and that I fear will soon quite destroy it. Another scare for me just now is the threatened destruction of the two little charmingly-antique silver-grey cottages on the right of the little vista that stretches from my door to the church—the two that you may remember just beyond my garden wall, and in one of which my gardener has lately been living. They will be replaced, if destroyed, by a pair of hideous cheap modern workingman's cottages—a horrid inhuman stab at the very heart of old Rye. There is a chance it may be still averted—but only just a bare chance. One would buy them, in a moment, to save them and to save one's little prospect; but one is, naturally, quite helpless for that, and the price asked is impudently outrageous, quite of the blackmailing order. On the other hand, let me add, I'm gradually consoling myself now for having been blackmailed in respect to purchase of the neighbouring garden I wrote you of. Now that I have got it and feel the value of the protection, my greater peace seems almost worth the imposition. This, however, is all my news—except that I have just acquired by purchase a very beautiful and valuable little Dachshund pup of the "red" species, who has been promising to be the joy of my life up to a few hours since—when he began to develop a mysterious and increasing tumification of one side of his face, about which I must immediately have advice. The things my dogs have, and the worries I have in consequence! I already see this one settled beneath monumental alabaster in the little cemetery in the angle of my garden, where he will make the fifth. I have heard, most happily, from Billy at Marburg. He seems to fall everywhere blessedly on his feet. But you will know as much, and more, about him than I. I am already notching off the days till I hope to have him here in August. I count on his then staying through September. But good-bye, with every fond *vœu*. I delight in the news of Aleck's free wild life—and also of Peggy's (which the accounts of her festivities, feathers and frills, in a manner reproduce for me.) Tender love to Alice. I embrace you all and am always yours,

HENRY JAMES.

TO MISS VIOLET HUNT.

Dictated.

Lamb House, Rye.

Aug. 26th, 1903.

Dear Violet Hunt,

I am very backward with you, being in receipt of more than one unanswered communication. Please set this down to many things; not least my having, ever since you were here, been carrying on uninterruptedly a small but crowded hotel.... I have still, all the same, to thank you for the photographs of the admirable little niece, one of which, the one with the hat, I retain, sending the other back to you if not by this very post, then, at least, by the very next. Both are very pleasing, but no photograph does much more than rather civilly extinguish the life and bloom (so exquisite a thing) in a happy child's face. Also came the Shakespeare-book back with your accompanying letter—for which also thanks, but to which I can't now pretend to reply. You rebound lightly, I judge, from any pressure exerted on you by the author—but *I* don't rebound: I am "a sort of" haunted by the conviction that the divine William is the biggest and most successful fraud ever practised on a patient world. The more I turn him round and round the more he so affects me. But that is all—I am not pretending to treat the question or to carry it any further. It bristles with difficulties, and I can only express my general sense by saying that I find it *almost* as impossible to conceive that Bacon wrote the plays as to conceive that the man from Stratford, as we know the man from Stratford, did.

For the rest, I have been trying to sit tight and get on with work that has been much retarded, these two months, and much interrupted and blighted.... I hope you will be able to give me, when we next meet, as good an account of *your* adventures and emotions. I have taken again the liberty of this machinery with you, for having broken in your great amiability I don't want to waste my advantage. Wherever you are *buon divertimento*! I really hope for you that you are in town, which has resources and defences against this execrable August that the bare bosom of Nature, as we mainly know it here, sadly lacks.

Believe me yours always,

HENRY JAMES.

TO W. E. NORRIS.

Lamb House, Rye.

September 17th, 1903.

My dear Norris,

Your letter from the unpronounceable Japanese steamer is magnificent—so magnificent, so appreciated and so *felt*, that it really almost has an effect contrary to the case it incidentally urges—the effect of undermining my due disposition to write to you! Your adventures by land and sea, your commerce with the great globe, your grand imperial and cosmic life, hover before me on your admirable page to make me ask what you can possibly want of the small beer of any chronicle of mine. My "beer," always, to my sense, of the smallest, sinks to positively ignoble dregs in the presence of your splendid record—of which I think also I am even moved to a certain humiliated jealousy. "All this and heaven too?"—all this and letters from Lamb House, Rye, into the bargain? That slightly sore sense has in fact been at the bottom of my failure to write to you altogether—that and a wholly blank mind as to where to address, catch or otherwise waylay you. Frankly, *really*, I seemed to imagine you out of tune (very naturally and inevitably) with *our* dull lives and only saying to yourself that you would have quite enough of them on getting back to them and finding them creep along as tamely as ever. Let me hasten to add that I now rejoice to learn that you have actually missed the sound of my voice, the scratch of my poor pen, and I "sit down" as promptly, almost, as you enjoin, to prepare a message which shall overtake you, or meet you somewhere. May it not have failed of this before we (you sternly, I guiltily) are confronted! Your appeal, scented with all the spices of the East and the airs of the Antipodes, arrived in fact four or five days ago, and would have had my more instant attention if the world, in these days, the small world of my tiny point on the globe, were not inconveniently and oppressively with me, making great holes in my all too precious, my all too hoarded and shrunken treasure of Time. We have had an execrable, an infamous summer of rain—endless rain and wild wintry tempest (the very worst of my long lifetime;) but it has not in the least stayed the circulation of my country-people (in particular,) and I have been running a small crammed and wholly unlucrative hotel for their benefit, without interruption, ever since I returned here from London the middle of May. As I have to run it, socially and personally speaking, all unaided and alone, I am always in the breach, and my fond dream of this place as a little sheltered hermitage is exposed to rude shocks. I am just now, in short, receiving a fresh shock every day, and the end is so far from being in sight that the rest of this month and the replete form of October loom before me as truly formidable. This once comparatively quiet corner has, it is impossible to doubt, quite changed its convenient little character since I first knew and adopted it, and has become, for the portion of the year for which I most so prized it, a vulgarly bustling rendezvous of indiscreet and inferior people. (I don't so qualify my own visitors, poor dears—but the total effect of these harried and haunted months, whereof the former golden air has been turned to tinkling brass. It all makes me glad I am old, and thereby soon to take leave of a world in which one is driven, unoffending, from pillar to post.) You see I don't pretend to take up *your* wondrous tale or to treat you to responsive echoes and ejaculations. It will be delightful to do so when we meet again and I can ask you face to face the thousand questions that your story calls to my lips. Let me even now and thus, however, congratulate you with all my heart on such a fine bellyful of raw (and other) material as your so varied and populated experience must have provided you withal. You have had to ingurgitate a bigger dose of salt water than I should personally care for, and I don't directly wish that *any* of your opportunities should have been mine—so wholly, with the lack of means to move, has the appetite for movement abandoned my aged carcass. But I applaud and enjoy the sight of these high energies in those who are capable and worthy of them, and distinctly like to think that there are quasi-contemporaries of longer wind (and purse,) and of stouter heart than mine—though I *am* planning at last to go to the U.S. (for the first time for 21 years) next summer, and remain there some 6 or 8 months. (But there is time to talk of this.).. Your letter is full of interesting things that I can, however, send back to you no echo of—since if I do I shall still be writing it when you get back, and you will come and look at it over my shoulder. Interesting above all your hints of your convictions or impressions or whatever, about the great colonial question and the great Joseph's probable misadventure—as to which I find it utterly impossible to have a competent opinion. I have nothing but an obscure and superstitious sense that this country's "fiscal" attitude and faith has for the last half century been *superior* and distinguished, and that the change proposed to her reeks, probably, with political and economical vulgarity. But that way, just now, madness lies—you will find plenty of it when you get back. As to the probable date of that event you give me no hint, but I look forward to your return with an eager appetite for your high exotic flavour, which please do everything further possible, meanwhile, to intensify: unless indeed the final effort of everything shall have been (as I shrewdly suspect) to make you more brutally British. You will even then, anyway, be an exceedingly welcome reappearance to yours always and ever,

HENRY JAMES.

TO HOWARD STURGIS.

The proof-sheets in question were those of Mr. Sturgis's forthcoming novel, *Belchamber*.

Lamb House, Rye.

November 8th, 1903.

My dear Howard,

I send you back the blooming proofs with my thanks and with no marks or comments at all. In the first place there are none, of the marginal kind, to make, and in the second place it is too late to make them if there were. The thing goes on very solidly and smoothly, interesting and amusing as it moves, very well written, well felt, well composed, well written perhaps in particular. I am a bad person, really, to expose "fictitious work" to—I, as a battered producer and "technician" myself, have long since inevitably ceased to read with *naïveté*; I can only read critically, constructively, reconstructively, writing the thing over (if I can swallow it at all) *my* way, and looking at it, so to speak, from within. But even thus I "pass" your book very—tenderly! There is only one thing that, as a matter of detail, I am moved to say—which is that I feel you have a great deal increased your difficulty by screwing up the "social position" of all your people so very high. When a man is an English Marquis, even a lame one, there are whole masses of Marquisate things and items, a multitude of inherent detail in his existence, which it isn't open to the painter *de gaieté de cœur* not to make some picture of. And yet if I mention this because it is *the* place where people will challenge you, and to suggest to you therefore to expect it—if I do so I am probably after all quite wrong. No one notices or understands *any*thing, and no one will make a single intelligent or intelligible observation about your work. They will make plenty of others. What I applaud is your sticking to the real line and centre of your theme—the consciousness and view of Sainty himself, and your dealing with things, with the whole fantasmagoria, as presented to him only, not otherwise going behind them.

And also I applaud, dearest Howard, your expression of attachment to him who holds this pen (and passes it at this moment over very dirty paper:) for he is extremely accessible to such demonstrations and touched by them—more than ever in his lonely (more than) maturity. Keep it up as hard as possible; continue to pass your hand into my arm and believe that I always like greatly to feel it. We are two who can communicate freely.

I send you back also Temple Bar, in which I have found your paper a moving and charming thing, waking up the pathetic ghost only too effectually. The ancient years and images that I too more or less remember swarm up and vaguely moan round about one like Banshees or other mystic and melancholy presences. It's *all* a little mystic and melancholy to me here when I am quite alone, as I more particularly am after "grand" company has come and gone. You are essentially grand company, and felt as such—and the subsidence is proportionally flat. But I took a long walk with Max this grey still Sabbath afternoon—have indeed taken one each day, and am possessed of means, thank goodness, to make the desert (of being quite to myself) blossom like the rose.

Good-night—it's 12.30, the clock ticks loud and Max snoozes audibly in the armchair I lately vacated.... Yours, my dear Howard always and ever,

HENRY JAMES.

TO HENRY ADAMS.

Henry Adams, the well-known American historian, was a friend of long standing. The following refers to H. J.'s recently published *W. W. Story and his Friends*.

Lamb House, Rye.

November 19, 1903.

My dear Adams,

I am so happy at hearing from you *at all* that the sense of the particular occasion of my doing so is almost submerged and smothered. You did bravely well to write—make a note of the act, for your future career, as belonging to a class of impulses to be precipitately obeyed, and, if possible, even tenderly nursed. Yet it has been interesting, exceedingly, in the narrower sense, as well as delightful in the larger, to have your letter, with its ingenious expression of the effects on you of poor *W. W. S.*—with whom, and the whole business of whom, there is (yes, I can see!) a kind of *inevitableness* in my having made you squirm—or whatever is the proper name for the sensation engendered in you! Very curious, and even rather terrible, this so far-reaching action of a little biographical vividness—which did indeed, in a manner, begin with me, myself, even as I put the stuff together—though putting me to conclusions less grim, as I may call them, than in your case. The truth is that *any* retraced story of bourgeois lives (lives other than great lives of "action"—*et encore!*) throws a chill upon the scene, the time, the subject, the small mapped-out facts, and if you find "great men thin" it isn't really so much their fault (and least of all yours) as that the art of the biographer—devilish art!—is somehow practically *thinning*. It simplifies even while seeking to enrich—and even the Immortal are so helpless and passive in death. The proof is that I wanted to invest dull old Boston with a mellow, a golden glow—and that for those who know, like yourself, I only make it bleak—and weak! Luckily those who know are indeed but three or four—and they won't, I hope, too promiscuously tell....

Yours, my dear Adams, always and ever,

HENRY JAMES.

TO SIR GEORGE O. TREVELYAN.

The second part of Sir George Trevelyan's *American Revolution* had just appeared at this time.

Lamb House, Rye.

Nov. 25th, 1903.

Dear Sir George,

I should be a poor creature if I had read your two last volumes without feeling the liveliest desire to write to you. That is the desire you must have kindled indeed in more quarters than you will care to reckon with; but even this reflection doesn't stay my pen, save to make me parenthise that I should be absolutely distressed to receive from you any acknowledgment of these few lines.

This new instalment of your admirable book has held me so tight, from chapter to chapter, that it is as if I were hanging back from mere force of appreciation, and yet I found myself, as I read, vibrating responsively, in so many different ways, that my emotions carried me at the same time all over the place. You of course know far better than I how you have dealt with your material; but I doubt whether you know what a work of civilization you are perpetrating internationally by the very fact of your producing so exquisite a work of art. The American, the Englishman, the artist, and the critic in me—to say nothing of the friend!—all drink you down in a deep draught, each in turn feeling that he is more deeply concerned. But it is of course, as with the other volume, the book's being so richly and authoritatively English, so validly true, and yet so projected as it were into the American consciousness, that will help to build the bridge across the Atlantic; and I think it is the mystery of this large fusion, carried out in so many ways, that makes the thing so distinguished a work of art; yet who shall say, so familiarly—when a thing is such a work of art—I mean who shall say how it has, by a thousand roads, got itself made so?

It is this literary temperament of your work, this beautiful quality of composition, and feeling of the presentation, grasping reality all the while, and controlling and playing with the detail, it is this in our chattering and slobbering day that gives me the sense of the ampler tread and deeper voice of the man—in fact of his speaking in his own voice at all, or moving with his own step. You will make my own country people touch as with reverence the hem of his garment; but I think that I most envy you your having such a method at all—your being able to see so many facts and yet to see them each, imaged and related and lighted, as a painter sees the objects, together, that are before his canvas. They become, I mean, so amusingly concrete and individual for you; but that is just the inscrutable luxury of your book; and you bring home further, to me, at least, who had never so fully felt it, what a difficult and precarious, and even might-not-have been, Revolution it was, altogether, as a Revolution. Wasn't it as nearly as possible not being that, whatever else it might have been? The Tail might in time have taken to wagging the dog if the Tail could only, as seemed so easy, have been left on! But I didn't mean to embark on these reflections. I only wanted really to make you feel a little responsible for my being, through living with you this succession of placid country evenings, far from the London ravage, extravagantly agitated. But take your responsibility philosophically; recall me to the kind consideration of Lady Trevelyan, and believe me very constantly yours,

HENRY JAMES.

THE LESSON OF THE
MASTER

I

HE had been told the ladies were at church, but this was corrected by what he saw from the top of the steps—they descended from a great height in two arms, with a circular sweep of the most charming effect—at the threshold of the door which, from the long bright gallery, overlooked the immense lawn. Three gentlemen, on the grass, at a distance, sat under the great trees, while the fourth figure showed a crimson dress that told as a "bit of colour" amid the fresh rich green. The servant had so far accompanied Paul Overt as to introduce him to this view, after asking him if he wished first to go to his room. The young man declined that privilege, conscious of no disrepair from so short and easy a journey and always liking to take at once a general perceptive possession of a new scene. He stood there a little with his eyes on the group and on the admirable picture, the wide grounds of an old country-house near London—that only made it better—on a splendid Sunday in June. "But that lady, who's *she*?" he said to the servant before the man left him.

"I think she's Mrs. St. George, sir."

"Mrs. St. George, the wife of the distinguished—" Then Paul Overt checked himself, doubting if a footman would know.

"Yes, sir—probably, sir," said his guide, who appeared to wish to intimate that a person staying at Summersoft would naturally be, if only by alliance, distinguished. His tone, however, made poor Overt himself feel for the moment scantly so.

"And the gentlemen?" Overt went on.

"Well, sir, one of them's General Fancourt."

"Ah yes, I know; thank you." General Fancourt was distinguished, there was no doubt of that, for something he had done, or perhaps even hadn't done—the young man couldn't remember which—some years before in India. The servant went away, leaving the glass doors open into the gallery, and Paul Overt remained at the head of the wide double staircase, saying to himself that the place was sweet and promised a pleasant visit, while he leaned on the balustrade of fine old ironwork which, like all the other details, was of the same period as the house. It all went together and spoke in one voice—a rich English voice of the early part of the eighteenth century. It might have been church-time on a summer's day in the reign of Queen Anne; the stillness was too perfect to be modern, the nearness counted so as distance, and there was something so fresh and sound in the originality of the large smooth house, the expanse of beautiful brickwork that showed for pink rather than red and that had been kept clear of messy creepers by the law under which a woman with a rare complexion disdains a veil. When Paul Overt became aware that the people under the trees had noticed him he turned back through the open doors into the great gallery which was the pride of the place. It marched across from end to end and seemed—with its bright colours, its high panelled windows, its faded flowered chintzes, its quickly-recognised portraits and pictures, the blue-and-white china of its cabinets and the attenuated festoons and rosettes of its ceiling—a cheerful upholstered avenue into the other century.

Our friend was slightly nervous; that went with his character as a student of fine prose, went with the artist's general disposition to vibrate; and there was a particular thrill in the idea that Henry St. George might be a member of the party. For the young aspirant he had remained a high literary figure, in spite of the lower range of production to which he had fallen after his first three great successes, the comparative absence of quality in his later work. There had been moments when Paul Overt almost shed tears for this; but now that he was near him—he had never met him—he was conscious only of the fine original source and of his own immense debt. After he had taken a turn or two up and down the gallery he came out again and descended the steps. He was but slenderly supplied with a certain social boldness—it was really a weakness in him—so that, conscious of a want of acquaintance with the four persons in the distance, he gave way to motions recommended by their not committing him to a positive approach. There was a fine English awkwardness in this—he felt that too as he sauntered vaguely and obliquely across the lawn, taking an independent line. Fortunately there was an equally fine English directness in the way one of the gentlemen presently rose and made as if to "stalk" him, though with an air of conciliation and reassurance. To this demonstration Paul Overt instantly responded, even if the gentleman were not his host. He was tall, straight and elderly and had, like the great house itself, a pink smiling face, and into the bargain a white moustache. Our young man met him halfway while he laughed and said: "Er—Lady Watermouth told us you were coming; she asked me just to look after you." Paul Overt thanked him, liking him on the spot, and turned round with him to walk toward the others. "They've all gone to church—all except us," the stranger continued as they went; "we're just sitting here—it's so jolly." Overt pronounced it jolly indeed: it was such a lovely place. He mentioned that he was having the charming impression for the first time.

"Ah you've not been here before?" said his companion. "It's a nice little place—not much to *do*, you know". Overt wondered what he wanted to "do"—he felt that he himself was doing so much. By the time they came to where the others sat he had recognised his initiator for a military man and—such was the turn of Overt's imagination—had found him thus still more sympathetic. He would naturally have a need for action, for deeds at variance with the pacific pastoral scene. He was evidently so good-natured, however, that he accepted the inglorious hour for what it was worth. Paul Overt shared it with him and with his companions for the next twenty minutes; the latter looked at him and he looked at them without knowing much who they were, while the talk went on without much telling him even what it meant. It seemed indeed to mean nothing in particular; it wandered, with casual pointless pauses and short terrestrial flights, amid names of persons and places—names which, for our friend, had no great power of evocation. It was all sociable and slow, as was right and natural of a warm Sunday morning.

His first attention was given to the question, privately considered, of whether one of the two younger men would be Henry St. George. He knew many of his distinguished contemporaries by their photographs, but had never, as happened, seen a portrait of the great misguided novelist. One of the gentlemen was unimaginable—he was too young; and the other scarcely looked clever enough, with such mild undiscriminating eyes. If those eyes were St. George's the problem, presented by the ill-matched parts of his genius would be still more difficult of solution. Besides, the deportment of their proprietor was not, as regards the lady in the red dress, such as could be natural, toward the wife of his bosom, even to a writer accused by several critics of sacrificing too much to manner. Lastly Paul Overt had a vague sense that if the gentleman with the expressionless eyes bore the name that had set his heart beating faster (he also had contradictory conventional whiskers— the young admirer of the celebrity had never in a mental vision seen *his* face in so vulgar a frame) he would have given him a sign of recognition or of friendliness, would have heard of him a little, would know something about "Ginistrella," would have an impression of how that fresh fiction had caught the eye of real criticism. Paul Overt had a dread of being grossly proud, but even morbid modesty might view the authorship of "Ginistrella" as constituting a degree of identity. His soldierly friend became clear enough: he was "Fancourt," but was also "the General"; and he mentioned to the new visitor in the course of a few moments that he had but lately returned from twenty years service abroad.

"And now you remain in England?" the young man asked.

"Oh yes; I've bought a small house in London."

"And I hope you like it," said Overt, looking at Mrs. St. George.

"Well, a little house in Manchester Square—there's a limit to the enthusiasm *that* inspires."

"Oh I meant being at home again—being back in Piccadilly."

"My daughter likes Piccadilly—that's the main thing. She's very fond of art and music and literature and all that kind of thing. She missed it in India and she finds it in London, or she hopes she'll find it. Mr. St. George has promised to help her—he has been awfully kind to her. She has gone to church—she's fond of that too—but they'll all be back in a quarter of an hour. You must let me introduce you to her—she'll be so glad to know you. I dare say she has read every blest word you've written."

"I shall be delighted—I haven't written so very many," Overt pleaded, feeling, and without resentment, that the General at least was vagueness itself about that. But he wondered a little why, expressing this friendly disposition, it didn't occur to the doubtless eminent soldier to pronounce the word that would put him in relation with Mrs. St. George. If it was a question of introductions Miss Fancourt—apparently as yet unmarried—was far away, while the wife of his illustrious confrère was almost between them. This lady struck Paul Overt as altogether pretty, with a surprising juvenility and a high smartness of aspect, something that—he could scarcely have said why— served for mystification. St. George certainly had every right to a charming wife, but he himself would never have imagined the important little woman in the aggressively Parisian dress the partner for life, the alter ego, of a man of letters. That partner in general, he knew, that second self, was far from presenting herself in a single type: observation had taught him that she was not inveterately, not necessarily plain. But he had never before seen her look so much as if her prosperity had deeper foundations than an ink-spotted study-table littered with proof-sheets. Mrs. St. George might have been the wife of a gentleman who "kept" books rather than wrote them, who carried on great affairs in the City and made better bargains than those that poets mostly make with publishers. With this she hinted at a success more personal—a success peculiarly stamping the age in which society, the world of conversation, is a great drawing-room with the City for its antechamber. Overt numbered her years at first as some thirty, and then ended by believing that she might approach her fiftieth. But she somehow in this case juggled away the excess and the difference—you only saw them in a rare glimpse, like the rabbit in the conjurer's sleeve. She was extraordinarily white, and her every element and item was pretty; her eyes, her ears, her hair, her voice, her hands, her feet—to which her relaxed attitude in her wicker chair gave a great publicity—and the numerous ribbons and trinkets with which she was bedecked. She looked as if she had put on her best clothes to go to church and then had decided they were too good for that and had stayed at home. She told a story of some length about the shabby way Lady Jane had treated the Duchess, as well as an anecdote in relation to a purchase she had made in Paris—on her way back from Cannes; made for Lady Egbert, who had never refunded the money. Paul Overt suspected her of a tendency to figure great people as larger than life, until he noticed the manner in which she handled Lady Egbert, which was so sharply mutinous that it reassured him. He felt he should have understood her better if he might have met her eye; but she scarcely so much as glanced at him. "Ah here they come—all the good ones!" she said at last; and Paul Overt admired at his distance the return of the church-goers—several persons, in couples and threes, advancing in a flicker of sun and shade at the end of a large green vista formed by the level grass and the overarching boughs.

"If you mean to imply that *we're* bad, I protest," said one of the gentlemen—"after making one's self agreeable all the morning!"

"Ah if they've found you agreeable—!" Mrs. St. George gaily cried. "But if we're good the others are better."

"They must be angels then," said the amused General.

"Your husband was an angel, the way he went off at your bidding," the gentleman who had first spoken declared to Mrs. St. George.

"At my bidding?"

"Didn't you make him go to church?"

"I never made him do anything in my life but once—when I made him burn up a bad book. That's all!" At her "That's all!" our young friend broke into an irrepressible laugh; it lasted only a second, but it drew her eyes to him. His own met them, though not long enough to help him to understand her; unless it were a step towards this that he saw on the instant how the burnt book—the way she alluded to it!—would have been one of her husband's finest things.

"A bad book?" her interlocutor repeated.

"I didn't like it. He went to church because your daughter went," she continued to General Fancourt. "I think it my duty to call your attention to his extraordinary demonstrations to your daughter."

"Well, if you don't mind them I don't," the General laughed.

"Il s'attache à ses pas. But I don't wonder—she's so charming."

"I hope she won't make him burn any books!" Paul Overt ventured to exclaim.

"If she'd make him write a few it would be more to the purpose," said Mrs. St. George. "He has been of a laziness of late—!"

Our young man stared—he was so struck with the lady's phraseology. Her "Write a few" seemed to him almost as good as her "That's all." Didn't she, as the wife of a rare artist, know what it was to produce one perfect work of art? How in the world did she think they were turned on? His private conviction was that, admirably as Henry St. George wrote, he had written for the last ten years, and especially for the last five, only too much, and there was an instant during which he felt inwardly solicited to make this public. But before he had spoken a diversion was effected by the return of the absentees. They strolled up dispersedly—there were eight or ten of them—and the circle under the trees rearranged itself as they took their place in it. They made it much larger, so that Paul Overt could feel—he was always feeling that sort of thing, as he said to himself—that if the company had already been interesting to watch the interest would now become intense. He shook hands with his hostess, who welcomed him without many words, in the manner of a woman able to trust him to understand and conscious that so pleasant an occasion would in every way speak for itself. She offered him no particular facility for sitting by her, and when they had all subsided again he found himself still next General Fancourt, with an unknown lady on his other flank.

"That's my daughter—that one opposite," the General said to him without lose of time. Overt saw a tall girl, with magnificent red hair, in a dress of a pretty grey-green tint and of a limp silken texture, a garment that clearly shirked every modern effect. It had therefore somehow the stamp of the latest thing, so that our beholder quickly took her for nothing if not contemporaneous.

"She's very handsome—very handsome," he repeated while he considered her. There was something noble in her head, and she appeared fresh and strong.

Her good father surveyed her with complacency, remarking soon: "She looks too hot—that's her walk. But she'll be all right presently. Then I'll make her come over and speak to you."

"I should be sorry to give you that trouble. If you were to take me over *there*—!" the young man murmured.

"My dear sir, do you suppose I put myself out that way? I don't mean for you, but for Marian," the General added.

"*I* would put myself out for her soon enough," Overt replied; after which he went on: "Will you be so good as to tell me which of those gentlemen is Henry St. George?"

"The fellow talking to my girl. By Jove, he *is* making up to her—they're going off for another walk."

"Ah is that he—really?" Our friend felt a certain surprise, for the personage before him seemed to trouble a vision which had been vague only while not confronted with the reality. As soon as the reality dawned the mental image, retiring with a sigh, became substantial enough to suffer a slight wrong. Overt, who had spent a considerable part of his short life in foreign lands, made now, but not for the first time, the reflexion that whereas in those countries he had almost always recognised the artist and the man of letters by his personal "type," the mould of his face, the character of his head, the expression of his figure and even the indications of his dress, so in England this identification was as little as possible a matter of course, thanks to the greater conformity, the habit of sinking the profession instead of advertising it, the general diffusion of the air of the gentleman—the gentleman committed to no particular set of ideas. More than once, on returning to his own country, he had said to himself about people met in society: "One sees them in this place and that, and one even talks with them; but to find out what they *do* one would really have to be a detective." In respect to several individuals whose work he was the opposite of "drawn to"—perhaps he was wrong—he found himself adding "No wonder they conceal it—when it's so bad!" He noted that oftener than in France and in Germany his artist looked like a gentleman—that is like an English one—while, certainly outside a few exceptions, his gentlemen didn't look like an artist. St. George was not one of the exceptions; that circumstance he definitely apprehended before the great man had turned his back to walk off with Miss Fancourt. He certainly looked better behind than any foreign man of letters—showed for beautifully correct in his tall black hat and his superior frock coat. Somehow, all the same, these very garments—he wouldn't have minded them so much on a weekday— were disconcerting to Paul Overt, who forgot for the moment that the head of the profession was not a bit better dressed than himself. He had caught a glimpse of a regular face, a fresh colour, a brown moustache and a pair of eyes surely never visited by a fine frenzy, and he promised himself to study these denotements on the first occasion. His superficial sense was that their owner might have passed for a lucky stockbroker—a gentleman driving eastward every morning from a sanitary suburb in a smart dog-cart. That carried out the impression already derived from his wife. Paul's glance, after a moment, travelled back to this lady, and he saw how her own had followed her husband as he moved off with Miss Fancourt. Overt permitted himself to wonder a little if she were jealous when another woman took him away. Then he made out that Mrs. St. George wasn't glaring at the indifferent maiden. Her eyes rested but on her husband, and with unmistakeable serenity. That was the way she wanted him to be—she liked his conventional uniform. Overt longed to hear more about the book she had induced him to destroy.

II

As they all came out from luncheon General Fancourt took hold of him with an "I say, I want you to know my girl!" as if the idea had just occurred to him and he hadn't spoken of it before. With the other hand he possessed himself all paternally of the young lady. "You know all about him. I've seen you with his books. She reads everything—everything!" he went on to Paul. The girl smiled at him and then laughed at her father. The General turned away and his daughter spoke—"Isn't papa delightful?"

"He is indeed, Miss Fancourt."

"As if I read you because I read 'everything'!"

"Oh I don't mean for saying that," said Paul Overt. "I liked him from the moment he began to be kind to me. Then he promised me this privilege."

"It isn't for you he means it—it's for me. If you flatter yourself that he thinks of anything in life but me you'll find you're mistaken. He introduces every one. He thinks me insatiable."

"You speak just like him," laughed our youth.

"Ah but sometimes I want to"—and the girl coloured. "I don't read everything—I read very little. But I *have* read you."

"Suppose we go into the gallery," said Paul Overt. She pleased him greatly, not so much because of this last remark—though that of course was not too disconcerting—as because, seated opposite to him at luncheon, she had given him for half an hour the impression of her beautiful face. Something else had come with it—a sense of generosity, of an enthusiasm which, unlike many enthusiasms, was not all manner. That was not spoiled for him by his seeing that the repast had placed her again in familiar contact with Henry St. George. Sitting next her this celebrity was also opposite our young man, who had been able to note that he multiplied the attentions lately brought by his wife to the General's notice. Paul Overt had gathered as well that this lady was not in the least discomposed by these fond excesses and that she gave every sign of an unclouded spirit. She had Lord Masham on one side of her and on the other the accomplished Mr. Mulliner, editor of the new high-class lively evening paper which was expected to meet a want felt in circles increasingly conscious that Conservatism must be made amusing, and unconvinced when assured by those of another political colour that it was already amusing enough. At the end of an hour spent in her company Paul Overt thought her still prettier than at the first radiation, and if her profane allusions to her husband's work had not still rung in his ears he should have liked her—so far as it could be a question of that in connexion with a woman to whom he had not yet spoken and to whom probably he should never speak if it were left to her. Pretty women were a clear need to this genius, and for the hour it was Miss Fancourt who supplied the want. If Overt had promised himself a closer view the occasion was now of the best, and it brought consequences felt by the young man as important. He saw more in St. George's face, which he liked the better for its not having told its whole story in the first three minutes. That story came out as one read, in short instalments—it was excusable that one's analogies should be somewhat professional—and the text was a style considerably involved, a language not easy to translate at sight. There were shades of meaning in it and a vague perspective of history which receded as you advanced. Two facts Paul had particularly heeded. The first of these was that he liked the measured mask much better at inscrutable rest than in social agitation; its almost convulsive smile above all displeased him (as much as any impression from that source could), whereas the quiet face had a charm that grew in proportion as stillness settled again. The change to the expression of gaiety excited, he made out, very much the private protest of a person sitting gratefully in the twilight when the lamp is brought in too soon. His second reflexion was that, though generally averse to the flagrant use of ingratiating arts by a man of age "making up" to a pretty girl, he was not in this case too painfully affected: which seemed to prove either that St. George had a light hand or the air of being younger than he was, or else that Miss Fancourt's own manner somehow made everything right.

Overt walked with her into the gallery, and they strolled to the end of it, looking at the pictures, the cabinets, the charming vista, which harmonised with the prospect of the summer afternoon, resembling it by a long brightness, with great divans and old chairs that figured hours of rest. Such a place as that had the added merit of giving those who came into it plenty to talk about. Miss Fancourt sat down with her new acquaintance on a flowered sofa, the cushions of which, very numerous, were tight ancient cubes of many sizes, and presently said: "I'm so glad to have a chance to thank you."

"To thank me—?" He had to wonder.

"I liked your book so much. I think it splendid."

She sat there smiling at him, and he never asked himself which book she meant; for after all he had written three or four. That seemed a vulgar detail, and he wasn't even gratified by the idea of the pleasure she told him—her handsome bright face told him—he had given her. The feeling she appealed to, or at any rate the feeling she excited, was something larger, something that had little to do with any quickened pulsation of his own vanity. It was responsive admiration of the life she embodied, the young purity and richness of which appeared to imply that real success was to resemble *that*, to live, to bloom, to present the perfection of a fine type, not to have hammered out headachy fancies with a bent back at an ink-stained table. While her grey eyes rested on him—there was a wideish space between these, and the division of her rich-coloured hair, so thick that it ventured to be smooth, made a free arch above them—he was almost ashamed of that exercise of the pen which it was her present inclination to commend. He was conscious he should have liked better to please her in some other way. The lines of her face were those of a woman grown, but the child lingered on in her complexion and in the sweetness of her mouth. Above all she was natural—that was indubitable now; more natural than he had supposed at first, perhaps on account of her æsthetic toggery, which was conventionally unconventional, suggesting what he might have called a tortuous spontaneity. He had feared that sort of thing in other cases, and his fears had been justified; for, though he was an artist to the essence, the modern reactionary nymph, with the brambles of the woodland caught in her folds and a look as if the satyrs had toyed with her hair, made him shrink not as a man of starch and patent leather, but as a man potentially himself a poet or even a faun. The girl was really more candid than her costume, and the best proof of it was her supposing her liberal character suited by any uniform. This was a fallacy, since if she was draped as a pessimist he was sure she liked the taste of life. He thanked her for her appreciation—aware at the same time that he didn't appear to thank her enough and that she might think him ungracious. He was afraid she would ask him to explain something he had written, and he always winced at that—perhaps too timidly—for to his own ear the explanation of a work of art sounded fatuous. But he liked her so much as to feel a confidence that in the long run he should be able to show her he wasn't rudely evasive. Moreover she surely wasn't quick to take offence, wasn't irritable; she could be trusted to wait. So when he said to her, "Ah don't talk of anything I've done, don't talk of it *here*; there's another man in the house who's the actuality!"— when he uttered this short sincere protest it was with the sense that she would see in the words neither mock humility nor the impatience of a successful man bored with praise.

"You mean Mr. St. George—isn't he delightful?"

Paul Overt met her eyes, which had a cool morning-light that would have half-broken his heart if he hadn't been so young. "Alas I don't know him. I only admire him at a distance."

"Oh you must know him—he wants so to talk to you," returned Miss Fancourt, who evidently had the habit of saying the things that, by her quick calculation, would give people pleasure. Paul saw how she would always calculate on everything's being simple between others.

"I shouldn't have supposed he knew anything about me," he professed.

"He does then—everything. And if he didn't I should be able to tell him."

"To tell him everything?" our friend smiled.

"You talk just like the people in your book!" she answered.

"Then they must all talk alike."

She thought a moment, not a bit disconcerted. "Well, it must be so difficult. Mr. St. George tells me it *is*—terribly. I've tried too—and I find it so. I've tried to write a novel."

"Mr. St. George oughtn't to discourage you," Paul went so far as to say.

"You do much more—when you wear that expression."

"Well, after all, why try to be an artist?" the young man pursued. "It's so poor—so poor!"

"I don't know what you mean," said Miss Fancourt, who looked grave.

"I mean as compared with being a person of action—as living your works."

"But what's art but an intense life—if it be real?" she asked. "I think it's the only one—everything else is so clumsy!" Her companion laughed, and she brought out with her charming serenity what next struck her. "It's so interesting to meet so many celebrated people."

"So I should think—but surely it isn't new to you."

"Why I've never seen any one—any one: living always in Asia."

The way she talked of Asia somehow enchanted him. "But doesn't that continent swarm with great figures? Haven't you administered provinces in India and had captive rajahs and tributary princes chained to your car?"

It was as if she didn't care even *should* he amuse himself at her cost. "I was with my father, after I left school to go out there. It was delightful being with him—we're alone together in the world, he and I—but there was none of the society I like best. One never heard of a picture—never of a book, except bad ones."

"Never of a picture? Why, wasn't all life a picture?"

She looked over the delightful place where they sat. "Nothing to compare to this. I adore England!" she cried.

It fairly stirred in him the sacred chord. "Ah of course I don't deny that we must do something with her, poor old dear, yet."

"She hasn't been touched, really," said the girl.

"Did Mr. St. George say that?"

There was a small and, as he felt, harmless spark of irony in his question; which, however, she answered very simply, not noticing the insinuation. "Yes, he says England hasn't been touched—not considering all there is," she went on eagerly. "He's so interesting about our country. To listen to him makes one want so to do something."

"It would make *me* want to," said Paul Overt, feeling strongly, on the instant, the suggestion of what she said and that of the emotion with which she said it, and well aware of what an incentive, on St. George's lips, such a speech might be.

"Oh you—as if you hadn't! I should like so to hear you talk together," she added ardently.

"That's very genial of you; but he'd have it all his own way. I'm prostrate before him."

She had an air of earnestness. "Do you think then he's so perfect?"

"Far from it. Some of his later books seem to me of a queerness—!"

"Yes, yes—he knows that."

Paul Overt stared. "That they seem to me of a queerness—!"

"Well yes, or at any rate that they're not what they should be. He told me he didn't esteem them. He has told me such wonderful things—he's so interesting."

There was a certain shock for Paul Overt in the knowledge that the fine genius they were talking of had been reduced to so explicit a confession and had made it, in his misery, to the first comer; for though Miss Fancourt was charming what was she after all but an immature girl encountered at a country-house? Yet precisely this was part of the sentiment he himself had just expressed: he would make way completely for the poor peccable great man not because he didn't read him clear, but altogether because he did. His consideration was half composed of tenderness for superficialities which he was sure their perpetrator judged privately, judged more ferociously than any one, and which represented some tragic intellectual secret. He would have his reasons for his psychology à fleur de peau, and these reasons could only be cruel ones, such as would make him dearer to those who already were fond of him. "You excite my envy. I have my reserves, I discriminate—but I love him," Paul said in a moment. "And seeing him for the first time this way is a great event for me."

"How momentous—how magnificent!" cried the girl. "How delicious to bring you together!"

"Your doing it—that makes it perfect," our friend returned.

"He's as eager as you," she went on. "But it's so odd you shouldn't have met."

"It's not really so odd as it strikes you. I've been out of England so much—made repeated absences all these last years."

She took this in with interest. "And yet you write of it as well as if you were always here."

"It's just the being away perhaps. At any rate the best bits, I suspect, are those that were done in dreary places abroad."

"And why were they dreary?"

"Because they were health-resorts—where my poor mother was dying."

"Your poor mother?"—she was all sweet wonder.

"We went from place to place to help her to get better. But she never did. To the deadly Riviera (I hate it!) to the high Alps, to Algiers, and far away—a hideous journey—to Colorado."

"And she isn't better?" Miss Fancourt went on.

"She died a year ago."

"Really?—like mine! Only that's years since. Some day you must tell me about your mother," she added.

He could at first, on this, only gaze at her. "What right things you say! If you say them to St. George I don't wonder he's in bondage."

It pulled her up for a moment. "I don't know what you mean. He doesn't make speeches and professions at all—he isn't ridiculous."

"I'm afraid you consider then that I am."

"No, I don't"—she spoke it rather shortly. And then she added: "He understands—understands everything."

The young man was on the point of saying jocosely: "And I don't—is that it?" But these words, in time, changed themselves to others slightly less trivial: "Do you suppose he understands his wife?"

Miss Fancourt made no direct answer, but after a moment's hesitation put it: "Isn't she charming?"

"Not in the least!"

"Here he comes. Now you must know him," she went on. A small group of visitors had gathered at the other end of the gallery and had been there overtaken by Henry St. George, who strolled in from a neighbouring room. He stood near them a moment, not falling into the talk but taking up an old miniature from a table and vaguely regarding it. At the end of a minute he became aware of Miss Fancourt and her companion in the distance; whereupon, laying down his miniature, he approached them with the same procrastinating air, his hands in his pockets and his eyes turned, right and left, to the pictures. The gallery was so long that this transit took some little time, especially as there was a moment when he stopped to admire the fine Gainsborough. "He says Mrs. St. George has been the making of him," the girl continued in a voice slightly lowered.

"Ah he's often obscure!" Paul laughed.

"Obscure?" she repeated as if she heard it for the first time. Her eyes rested on her other friend, and it wasn't lost upon Paul that they appeared to send out great shafts of softness. "He's going to speak to us!" she fondly breathed. There was a sort of rapture in her voice, and our friend was startled.

"Bless my soul, does she care for him like *that*?—is she in love with him?" he mentally enquired. "Didn't I tell you he was eager?" she had meanwhile asked of him.

"It's eagerness dissimulated," the young man returned as the subject of their observation lingered before his Gainsborough. "He edges toward us shyly. Does he mean that she saved him by burning that book?"

"That book? what book did she burn?" The girl quickly turned her face to him.

"Hasn't he told you then?"

"Not a word."

"Then he doesn't tell you everything!" Paul had guessed that she pretty much supposed he did. The great man had now resumed his course and come nearer; in spite of which his more qualified admirer risked a profane observation: "St. George and the Dragon is what the anecdote suggests!"

His companion, however, didn't hear it; she smiled at the dragon's adversary. "He *is* eager—he is!" she insisted.

"Eager for you—yes."

But meanwhile she had called out: "I'm sure you want to know Mr. Overt. You'll be great friends, and it will always be delightful to me to remember I was here when you first met and that I had something to do with it."

There was a freshness of intention in the words that carried them off; nevertheless our young man was sorry for Henry St. George, as he was sorry at any time for any person publicly invited to be responsive and delightful. He would have been so touched to believe that a man he deeply admired should care a straw for him that he wouldn't play with such a presumption if it were possibly vain. In a single glance of the eye of the pardonable Master he read—having the sort of divination that belonged to his talent—that this personage had ever a store of friendly patience, which was part of his rich outfit, but was versed in no printed page of a rising scribbler. There was even a relief, a simplification, in that: liking him so much already for what he had done, how could one have liked him any more for a perception which must at the best have been vague? Paul Overt got up, trying to show his compassion, but at the same instant he found himself encompassed by St. George's happy personal art—a manner of which it was the essence to conjure away false positions. It all took place in a moment. Paul was conscious that he knew him now, conscious of his handshake and of the very quality of his hand; of his face, seen nearer and consequently seen better, of a general fraternising assurance, and in particular of the circumstance that St. George didn't dislike him (as yet at least) for being imposed by a charming but too gushing girl, attractive enough without such danglers. No irritation at any rate was reflected in the voice with which he questioned Miss Fancourt as to some project of a walk—a general walk of the company round the park. He had soon said something to Paul about a talk—"We must have a tremendous lot of talk; there are so many things, aren't there?"—but our friend could see this idea wouldn't in the present case take very immediate effect. All the same he was extremely happy, even after the matter of the walk had been settled— the three presently passed back to the other part of the gallery, where it was discussed with several members of the party; even when, after they had all gone out together, he found himself for half an hour conjoined with Mrs. St. George. Her husband had taken the advance with Miss Fancourt, and this pair were quite out of sight. It was the prettiest of rambles for a summer afternoon—a grassy circuit, of immense extent, skirting the limit of the park within. The park was completely surrounded by its old mottled but perfect red wall, which, all the way on their left, constituted in itself an object of interest. Mrs. St. George mentioned to him the surprising number of acres thus enclosed, together with numerous other facts relating to the property and the family, and the family's other properties: she couldn't too strongly urge on him the importance of seeing their other houses. She ran over the names of these and rang the changes on them with the facility of practice, making them appear an almost endless list. She had received Paul Overt very amiably on his breaking ground with her by the mention of his joy in having just made her husband's acquaintance, and struck him as so alert and so accommodating a little woman that he was rather ashamed of his *mot* about her to Miss Fancourt; though he reflected that a hundred other people, on a hundred occasions, would have been sure to make it. He got on with Ms. St. George, in short, better than he expected; but this didn't prevent her suddenly becoming aware that she was faint with fatigue and must take her way back to the house by the shortest cut. She professed that she hadn't the strength of a kitten and was a miserable wreck; a character he had been too preoccupied to discern in her while he wondered in what sense she could be held to have been the making of her husband. He had arrived at a glimmering of the answer when she announced that she must leave him, though this perception was of course provisional. While he was in the very act of placing himself at her disposal for the return the situation underwent a change; Lord Masham had suddenly turned up, coming back to them, overtaking them, emerging from the shrubbery—Overt could scarcely have said how he appeared—and Mrs. St. George had protested that she wanted to be left alone and not to break up the party. A moment later she was walking off with Lord Masham. Our friend fell back and joined Lady Watermouth, to whom he presently mentioned that Mrs. St. George had been obliged to renounce the attempt to go further.

"She oughtn't to have come out at all," her ladyship rather grumpily remarked.

"Is she so very much of an invalid?"

"Very bad indeed." And his hostess added with still greater austerity: "She oughtn't really to come to one!" He wondered what was implied by this, and presently gathered that it was not a reflexion on the lady's conduct or her moral nature: it only represented that her strength was not equal to her aspirations.

III

THE smoking-room at Summersoft was on the scale of the rest of the place; high light commodious and decorated with such refined old carvings and mouldings that it seemed rather a bower for ladies who should sit at work at fading crewels than a parliament of gentlemen smoking strong cigars. The gentlemen mustered there in considerable force on the Sunday evening, collecting mainly at one end, in front of one of the cool fair fireplaces of white marble, the entablature of which was adorned with a delicate little Italian "subject." There was another in the wall that faced it, and, thanks to the mild summer night, a fire in neither; but a nucleus for aggregation was furnished on one side by a table in the chimney-corner laden with bottles, decanters and tall tumblers. Paul Overt was a faithless smoker; he would puff a cigarette for reasons with which tobacco had nothing to do. This was particularly the case on the occasion of which I speak; his motive was the vision of a little direct talk with Henry St. George. The "tremendous" communion of which the great man had held out hopes to him earlier in the day had not yet come off, and this saddened him considerably, for the party was to go its several ways immediately after breakfast on the morrow. He had, however, the disappointment of finding that apparently the author of "Shadowmere" was not disposed to prolong his vigil. He wasn't among the gentlemen assembled when Paul entered, nor was he one of those who turned up, in bright habiliments, during the next ten minutes. The young man waited a little, wondering if he had only gone to put on something extraordinary; this would account for his delay as well as contribute further to Overt's impression of his tendency to do the approved superficial thing. But he didn't arrive—he must have been putting on something more extraordinary than was probable. Our hero gave him up, feeling a little injured, a little wounded, at this loss of twenty coveted words. He wasn't angry, but he puffed his cigarette sighingly, with the sense of something rare possibly missed. He wandered away with his regret and moved slowly round the room, looking at the old prints on the walls. In this attitude he presently felt a hand on his shoulder and a friendly voice in his ear "This is good. I hoped I should find you. I came down on purpose." St. George was there without a change of dress and with a fine face—his graver one—to which our young man all in a flutter responded. He explained that it was only for the Master—the idea of a little talk—that he had sat up, and that, not finding him, he had been on the point of going to bed.

"Well, you know, I don't smoke—my wife doesn't let me," said St. George, looking for a place to sit down. "It's very good for me—very good for me. Let us take that sofa."

"Do you mean smoking's good for you?"

"No no—her not letting me. It's a great thing to have a wife who's so sure of all the things one can do without. One might never find them out one's self. She doesn't allow me to touch a cigarette." They took possession of a sofa at a distance from the group of smokers, and St. George went on: "Have you got one yourself?"

"Do you mean a cigarette?"

"Dear no—a wife."

"No; and yet I'd give up my cigarette for one."

"You'd give up a good deal more than that," St. George returned. "However, you'd get a great deal in return. There's a something to be said for wives," he added, folding his arms and crossing his outstretched legs. He declined tobacco altogether and sat there without returning fire. His companion stopped smoking, touched by his courtesy; and after all they were out of the fumes, their sofa was in a far-away corner. It would have been a mistake, St. George went on, a great mistake for them to have separated without a little chat; "for I know all about you," he said, "I know you're very remarkable. You've written a very distinguished book."

"And how do you know it?" Paul asked.

"Why, my dear fellow, it's in the air, it's in the papers, it's everywhere." St. George spoke with the immediate familiarity of a confrère—a tone that seemed to his neighbour the very rustle of the laurel. "You're on all men's lips and, what's better, on all women's. And I've just been reading your book."

"Just? You hadn't read it this afternoon," said Overt.

"How do you know that?"

"I think you should know how I know it," the young man laughed.

"I suppose Miss Fancourt told you."

"No indeed—she led me rather to suppose you had."

"Yes—that's much more what she'd do. Doesn't she shed a rosy glow over life? But you didn't believe her?" asked St. George.

"No, not when you came to us there."

"Did I pretend? did I pretend badly?" But without waiting for an answer to this St. George went on: "You ought always to believe such a girl as that—always, always. Some women are meant to be taken with allowances and reserves; but you must take *her* just as she is."

"I like her very much," said Paul Overt.

Something in his tone appeared to excite on his companion's part a momentary sense of the absurd; perhaps it was the air of deliberation attending this judgement. St. George broke into a laugh to reply. "It's the best thing you can do with her. She's a rare young lady! In point of fact, however, I confess I hadn't read you this afternoon."

"Then you see how right I was in this particular case not to believe Miss Fancourt."

"How right? how can I agree to that when I lost credit by it?"

"Do you wish to pass exactly for what she represents you? Certainly you needn't be afraid," Paul said.

"Ah, my dear young man, don't talk about passing—for the likes of me! I'm passing away—nothing else than that. She has a better use for her young imagination (isn't it fine?) than in 'representing' in any way such a weary wasted used-up animal!" The Master spoke with a sudden sadness that produced a protest on Paul's part; but before the protest could be uttered he went on, reverting to the latter's striking novel: "I had no idea you were so good—one hears of so many things. But you're surprisingly good."

"I'm going to be surprisingly better," Overt made bold to reply.

"I see that, and it's what fetches me. I don't see so much else—as one looks about—that's going to be surprisingly better. They're going to be consistently worse—most of the things. It's so much easier to be worse—heaven knows I've found it so. I'm not in a great glow, you know, about what's breaking out all over the place. But you *must* be better—you really must keep it up. I haven't of course. It's very difficult—that's the devil of the whole thing, keeping it up. But I see you'll be able to. It will be a great disgrace if you don't."

"It's very interesting to hear you speak of yourself; but I don't know what you mean by your allusions to your having fallen off," Paul Overt observed with pardonable hypocrisy. He liked his companion so much now that the fact of any decline of talent or of care had ceased for the moment to be vivid to him.

"Don't say that—don't say that," St. George returned gravely, his head resting on the top of the sofa-back and his eyes on the ceiling. "You know perfectly what I mean. I haven't read twenty pages of your book without seeing that you can't help it."

"You make me very miserable," Paul ecstatically breathed.

"I'm glad of that, for it may serve as a kind of warning. Shocking enough it must be, especially to a young fresh mind, full of faith—the spectacle of a man meant for better things sunk at my age in such dishonour." St. George, in the same contemplative attitude, spoke softly but deliberately, and without perceptible emotion. His tone indeed suggested an impersonal lucidity that was practically cruel—cruel to himself—and made his young friend lay an argumentative hand on his arm. But he went on while his eyes seemed to follow the graces of the eighteenth-century ceiling: "Look at me well, take my lesson to heart—for it *is* a lesson. Let that good come of it at least that you shudder with your pitiful impression, and that this may help to keep you straight in the future. Don't become in your old age what I have in mine— the depressing, the deplorable illustration of the worship of false gods!"

"What do you mean by your old age?" the young man asked.

"It has made me old. But I like your youth."

Paul answered nothing—they sat for a minute in silence. They heard the others going on about the governmental majority. Then "What do you mean by false gods?" he enquired.

His companion had no difficulty whatever in saying, "The idols of the market; money and luxury and 'the world;' placing one's children and dressing one's wife; everything that drives one to the short and easy way. Ah the vile things they make one do!"

"But surely one's right to want to place one's children."

"One has no business to have any children," St. George placidly declared. "I mean of course if one wants to do anything good."

"But aren't they an inspiration—an incentive?"

"An incentive to damnation, artistically speaking."

"You touch on very deep things—things I should like to discuss with you," Paul said. "I should like you to tell me volumes about yourself. This is a great feast for *me*!"

"Of course it is, cruel youth. But to show you I'm still not incapable, degraded as I am, of an act of faith, I'll tie my vanity to the stake for you and burn it to ashes. You must come and see me—you must come and see us," the Master quickly substituted. "Mrs. St. George is charming; I don't know whether you've had any opportunity to talk with her. She'll be delighted to see you; she likes great celebrities, whether incipient or predominant. You must come and dine—my wife will write to you. Where are you to be found?"

"This is my little address"—and Overt drew out his pocketbook and extracted a visiting-card. On second thoughts, however, he kept it back, remarking that he wouldn't trouble his friend to take charge of it but would come and see him straightway in London and leave it at his door if he should fail to obtain entrance.

"Ah you'll probably fail; my wife's always out—or when she isn't out is knocked up from having been out. You must come and dine—though that won't do much good either, for my wife insists on big dinners." St. George turned it over further, but then went on: "You must come down and see us in the country, that's the best way; we've plenty of room, and it isn't bad."

"You've a house in the country?" Paul asked enviously.

"Ah not like this! But we have a sort of place we go to—an hour from Euston. That's one of the reasons."

"One of the reasons?"

"Why my books are so bad."

"You must tell me all the others!" Paul longingly laughed.

His friend made no direct rejoinder to this, but spoke again abruptly. "Why have I never seen you before?"

The tone of the question was singularly flattering to our hero, who felt it to imply the great man's now perceiving he had for years missed something. "Partly, I suppose, because there has been no particular reason why you should see me. I haven't lived in the world—in your world. I've spent many years out of England, in different places abroad."

"Well, please don't do it any more. You must do England—there's such a lot of it."

"Do you mean I must write about it?" and Paul struck the note of the listening candour of a child.

"Of course you must. And tremendously well, do you mind? That takes off a little of my esteem for this thing of yours—that it goes on abroad. Hang 'abroad!' Stay at home and do things here—do subjects we can measure."

"I'll do whatever you tell me," Overt said, deeply attentive. "But pardon me if I say I don't understand how you've been reading my book," he added. "I've had you before me all the afternoon, first in that long walk, then at tea on the lawn, till we went to dress for dinner, and all the evening at dinner and in this place."

St. George turned his face about with a smile. "I gave it but a quarter of an hour."

"A quarter of an hour's immense, but I don't understand where you put it in. In the drawing-room after dinner you weren't reading—you were talking to Miss Fancourt."

"It comes to the same thing, because we talked about 'Ginistrella.' She described it to me—she lent me her copy."

"Lent it to you?"

"She travels with it."

"It's incredible," Paul blushed.

"It's glorious for you, but it also turned out very well for me. When the ladies went off to bed she kindly offered to send the book down to me. Her maid brought it to me in the hall and I went to my room with it. I hadn't thought of coming here, I do that so little. But I don't sleep early, I always have to read an hour or two. I sat down to your novel on the spot, without undressing, without taking off anything but my coat. I think that's a sign my curiosity had been strongly roused about it. I read a quarter of an hour, as I tell you, and even in a quarter of an hour I was greatly struck."

"Ah the beginning isn't very good—it's the whole thing!" said Overt, who had listened to this recital with extreme interest. "And you laid down the book and came after me?" he asked.

"That's the way it moved me. I said to myself 'I see it's off his own bat, and he's there, by the way, and the day's over and I haven't said twenty words to him.' It occurred to me that you'd probably be in the smoking-room and that it wouldn't be too late to repair my omission. I wanted to do something civil to you, so I put on my coat and came down. I shall read your book again when I go up."

Our friend faced round in his place—he was touched as he had scarce ever been by the picture of such a demonstration in his favour. "You're really the kindest of men. Cela s'est passé comme ça?—and I've been sitting here with you all this time and never apprehended it and never thanked you!"

"Thank Miss Fancourt—it was she who wound me up. She has made me feel as if I had read your novel."

"She's an angel from heaven!" Paul declared.

"She is indeed. I've never seen any one like her. Her interest in literature's touching—something quite peculiar to herself; she takes it all so seriously. She feels the arts and she wants to feel them more. To those who practise them it's almost humiliating—her curiosity, her sympathy, her good faith. How can anything be as fine as she supposes it?"

"She's a rare organisation," the younger man sighed.

"The richest I've ever seen—an artistic intelligence really of the first order. And lodged in such a form!" St. George exclaimed.

"One would like to represent such a girl as that," Paul continued.

"Ah there it is—there's nothing like life!" said his companion. "When you're finished, squeezed dry and used up and you think the sack's empty, you're still appealed to, you still get touches and thrills, the idea springs up— out of the lap of the actual—and shows you there's always something to be done. But I shan't do it—she's not for me!"

"How do you mean, not for you?"

"Oh it's all over—she's for you, if you like."

"Ah much less!" said Paul. "She's not for a dingy little man of letters; she's for the world, the bright rich world of bribes and rewards. And the world will take hold of her—it will carry her away."

"It will try—but it's just a case in which there may be a fight. It would be worth fighting, for a man who had it in him, with youth and talent on his side."

These words rang not a little in Paul Overt's consciousness—they held him briefly silent. "It's a wonder she has remained as she is; giving herself away so—with so much to give away."

"Remaining, you mean, so ingenuous—so natural? Oh she doesn't care a straw—she gives away because she overflows. She has her own feelings, her own standards; she doesn't keep remembering that she must be proud. And then she hasn't been here long enough to be spoiled; she has picked up a fashion or two, but only the amusing ones. She's a provincial—a provincial of genius," St. George went on; "her very blunders are charming, her mistakes are interesting. She has come back from Asia with all sorts of excited curiosities and unappeased appetites. She's first-rate herself and she expends herself on the second-rate. She's life herself and she takes a rare interest in imitations. She mixes all things up, but there are none in regard to which she hasn't perceptions. She sees things in a perspective—as if from the top of the Himalayas—and she enlarges everything she touches. Above all she exaggerates—to herself, I mean. She exaggerates you and me!"

There was nothing in that description to allay the agitation caused in our younger friend by such a sketch of a fine subject. It seemed to him to show the art of St. George's admired hand, and he lost himself in gazing at the vision—this hovered there before him—of a woman's figure which should be part of the glory of a novel. But at the end of a moment the thing had turned into smoke, and out of the smoke—the last puff of a big cigar—proceeded the voice of General Fancourt, who had left the others and come and planted himself before the gentlemen on the sofa. "I suppose that when you fellows get talking you sit up half the night."

"Half the night?—jamais de la vie! I follow a hygiene"—and St. George rose to his feet.

"I see—you're hothouse plants," laughed the General. "That's the way you produce your flowers."

"I produce mine between ten and one every morning—I bloom with a regularity!" St. George went on.

"And with a splendour!" added the polite General, while Paul noted how little the author of "Shadowmere" minded, as he phrased it to himself, when addressed as a celebrated story-teller. The young man had an idea *he* should never get used to that; it would always make him uncomfortable—from the suspicion that people would think they had to—and he would want to prevent it. Evidently his great colleague had toughened and hardened—had made himself a surface. The group of men had finished their cigars and taken up their bedroom candlesticks; but before they all passed out Lord Watermouth invited the pair of guests who had been so absorbed together to "have" something. It happened that they both declined; upon which General Fancourt said: "Is that the hygiene? You don't water the flowers?"

"Oh I should drown them!" St. George replied; but, leaving the room still at his young friend's side, he added whimsically, for the latter's benefit, in a lower tone: "My wife doesn't let me."

"Well I'm glad I'm not one of you fellows!" the General richly concluded.

The nearness of Summersoft to London had this consequence, chilling to a person who had had a vision of sociability in a railway-carriage, that most of the company, after breakfast, drove back to town, entering their own vehicles, which had come out to fetch them, while their servants returned by train with their luggage. Three or four young men, among whom was Paul Overt, also availed themselves of the common convenience; but they stood in the portico of the house and saw the others roll away. Miss Fancourt got into a victoria with her father after she had shaken hands with our hero and said, smiling in the frankest way in the world, "I *must* see you more. Mrs. St. George is so nice: she has promised to ask us both to dinner together." This lady and her husband took their places in a perfectly-appointed brougham—she required a closed carriage—and as our young man waved his hat to them in response to their nods and flourishes he reflected that, taken together, they were an honourable image of success, of the material rewards and the social credit of literature. Such things were not the full measure, but he nevertheless felt a little proud for literature.

IV

Before a week had elapsed he met Miss Fancourt in Bond Street, at a private view of the works of a young artist in "black-and-white" who had been so good as to invite him to the stuffy scene. The drawings were admirable, but the crowd in the one little room was so dense that he felt himself up to his neck in a sack of wool. A fringe of people at the outer edge endeavoured by curving forward their backs and presenting, below them, a still more convex surface of resistance to the pressure of the mass, to preserve an interval between their noses and the glazed mounts of the pictures; while the central body, in the comparative gloom projected by a wide horizontal screen hung under the skylight and allowing only a margin for the day, remained upright dense and vague, lost in the contemplation of its own ingredients. This contemplation sat especially in the sad eyes of certain female heads, surmounted with hats of strange convolution and plumage, which rose on long necks above the others. One of the heads Paul perceived, was much the so most beautiful of the collection, and his next discovery was that it belonged to Miss Fancourt. Its beauty was enhanced by the glad smile she sent him across surrounding obstructions, a smile that drew him to her as fast as he could make his way. He had seen for himself at Summersoft that the last thing her nature contained was an affectation of indifference; yet even with this circumspection he took a fresh satisfaction in her not having pretended to await his arrival with composure. She smiled as radiantly as if she wished to make him hurry, and as soon as he came within earshot she broke out in her voice of joy: "He's here—he's here—he's coming back in a moment!"

"Ah your father?" Paul returned as she offered him her hand.

"Oh dear no, this isn't in my poor father's line. I mean Mr. St. George. He has just left me to speak to some one—he's coming back. It's he who brought me—wasn't it charming?"

"Ah that gives him a pull over me—I couldn't have 'brought' you, could I?"

"If you had been so kind as to propose it—why not you as well as he?" the girl returned with a face that, expressing no cheap coquetry, simply affirmed a happy fact.

"Why he's a père de famille. They've privileges," Paul explained. And then quickly: "Will you go to see places with *me*?" he asked.

"Anything you like!" she smiled. "I know what you mean, that girls have to have a lot of people—" Then she broke off: "I don't know; I'm free. I've always been like that—I can go about with any one. I'm so glad to meet you," she added with a sweet distinctness that made those near her turn round.

"Let me at least repay that speech by taking you out of this squash," her friend said. "Surely people aren't happy here!"

"No, they're awfully mornes, aren't they? But I'm very happy indeed and I promised Mr. St. George to remain in this spot till he comes back. He's going to take me away. They send him invitations for things of this sort—more than he wants. It was so kind of him to think of me."

"They also send me invitations of this kind—more than *I* want. And if thinking of *you* will do it—!" Paul went on.

"Oh I delight in them—everything that's life—everything that's London!"

"They don't have private views in Asia, I suppose," he laughed. "But what a pity that for this year, even in this gorged city, they're pretty well over."

"Well, next year will do, for I hope you believe we're going to be friends always. Here he comes!" Miss Fancourt continued before Paul had time to respond.

He made out St. George in the gaps of the crowd, and this perhaps led to his hurrying a little to say: "I hope that doesn't mean I'm to wait till next year to see you."

"No, no—aren't we to meet at dinner on the twenty-fifth?" she panted with an eagerness as happy as his own.

"That's almost next year. Is there no means of seeing you before?"

She stared with all her brightness. "Do you mean you'd *come?*"

"Like a shot, if you'll be so good as to ask me!"

"On Sunday then—this next Sunday?"

"What have I done that you should doubt it?" the young man asked with delight.

Miss Fancourt turned instantly to St. George, who had now joined them, and announced triumphantly: "He's coming on Sunday—this next Sunday!"

"Ah my day—my day too!" said the famous novelist, laughing, to their companion.

"Yes, but not yours only. You shall meet in Manchester Square; you shall talk—you shall be wonderful!"

"We don't meet often enough," St. George allowed, shaking hands with his disciple. "Too many things—ah too many things! But we must make it up in the country in September. You won't forget you've promised me that?"

"Why he's coming on the twenty-fifth—you'll see him then," said the girl.

"On the twenty-fifth?" St. George asked vaguely.

"We dine with you; I hope you haven't forgotten. He's dining out that day," she added gaily to Paul.

"Oh bless me, yes—that's charming! And you're coming? My wife didn't tell me," St. George said to him. "Too many things—too many things!" he repeated.

"Too many people—too many people!" Paul exclaimed, giving ground before the penetration of an elbow.

"You oughtn't to say that. They all read you."

"Me? I should like to see them! Only two or three at most," the young man returned.

"Did you ever hear anything like that? He knows, haughtily, how good he is!" St. George declared, laughing to Miss Fancourt. "They read *me*, but that doesn't make me like them any better. Come away from them, come away!" And he led the way out of the exhibition.

"He's going to take me to the Park," Miss Fancourt observed to Overt with elation as they passed along the corridor that led to the street.

"Ah does he go there?" Paul asked, taking the fact for a somewhat unexpected illustration of St. George's moeurs.

"It's a beautiful day—there'll be a great crowd. We're going to look at the people, to look at types," the girl went on. "We shall sit under the trees; we shall walk by the Row."

"I go once a year—on business," said St. George, who had overheard Paul's question.

"Or with a country cousin, didn't you tell me? I'm the country cousin!" she continued over her shoulder to Paul as their friend drew her toward a hansom to which he had signalled. The young man watched them get in; he returned, as he stood there, the friendly wave of the hand with which, ensconced in the vehicle beside her, St. George took leave of him. He even lingered to see the vehicle start away and lose itself in the confusion of Bond Street. He followed it with his eyes; it put to him embarrassing things. "She's not for *me*!" the great novelist had said emphatically at Summersoft; but his manner of conducting himself toward her appeared not quite in harmony with such a conviction. How could he have behaved differently if she *had* been for him? An indefinite envy rose in Paul Overt's heart as he took his way on foot alone; a feeling addressed alike strangely enough, to each of the occupants of the hansom. How much he should like to rattle about London with such a girl! How much he should like to go and look at "types" with St. George!

The next Sunday at four o'clock he called in Manchester Square, where his secret wish was gratified by his finding Miss Fancourt alone. She was in a large bright friendly occupied room, which was painted red all over, draped with the quaint cheap florid stuffs that are represented as coming from southern and eastern countries, where they are fabled to serve as the counterpanes of the peasantry, and bedecked with pottery of vivid hues, ranged on casual shelves, and with many water-colour drawings from the hand (as the visitor learned) of the young lady herself, commemorating with a brave breadth the sunsets, the mountains, the temples and palaces of India. He sat an hour—more than an hour, two hours—and all the while no one came in. His hostess was so good as to remark, with her liberal humanity, that it was delightful they weren't interrupted; it was so rare in London, especially at that season, that people got a good talk. But luckily now, of a fine Sunday, half the world went out of town, and that made it better for those who didn't go, when these others were in sympathy. It was the defect of London—one of two or three, the very short list of those she recognised in the teeming world-city she adored—that there were too few good chances for talk; you never had time to carry anything far.

"Too many things—too many things!" Paul said, quoting St. George's exclamation of a few days before.

"Ah yes, for him there are too many—his life's too complicated."

"Have you seen it *near*? That's what I should like to do; it might explain some mysteries," her visitor went on. She asked him what mysteries he meant, and he said: "Oh peculiarities of his work, inequalities, superficialities. For one who looks at it from the artistic point of view it contains a bottomless ambiguity."

She became at this, on the spot, all intensity. "Ah do describe that more—it's so interesting. There are no such suggestive questions. I'm so fond of them. He thinks he's a failure—fancy!" she beautifully wailed.

"That depends on what his ideal may have been. With his gifts it ought to have been high. But till one knows what he really proposed to himself—? Do *you* know by chance?" the young man broke off.

"Oh he doesn't talk to me about himself. I can't make him. It's too provoking."

Paul was on the point of asking what then he did talk about, but discretion checked it and he said instead: "Do you think he's unhappy at home?"

She seemed to wonder. "At home?"

"I mean in his relations with his wife. He has a mystifying little way of alluding to her."

"Not to me," said Marian Fancourt with her clear eyes. "That wouldn't be right, would it?" she asked gravely.

"Not particularly; so I'm glad he doesn't mention her to you. To praise her might bore you, and he has no business to do anything else. Yet he knows you better than me."

"Ah but he respects *you*!" the girl cried as with envy.

Her visitor stared a moment, then broke into a laugh. "Doesn't he respect you?"

"Of course, but not in the same way. He respects what you've done—he told me so, the other day."

Paul drank it in, but retained his faculties. "When you went to look at types?"

"Yes—we found so many: he has such an observation of them! He talked a great deal about your book. He says it's really important."

"Important! Ah the grand creature!"—and the author of the work in question groaned for joy.

"He was wonderfully amusing, he was inexpressibly droll, while we walked about. He sees everything; he has so many comparisons and images, and they're always exactly right. C'est d'un trouvé, as they say."

"Yes, with his gifts, such things as he ought to have done!" Paul sighed.

"And don't you think he *has* done them?"

Ah it was just the point. "A part of them, and of course even that part's immense. But he might have been one of the greatest. However, let us not make this an hour of qualifications. Even as they stand," our friend earnestly concluded, "his writings are a mine of gold."

To this proposition she ardently responded, and for half an hour the pair talked over the Master's principal productions. She knew them well—she knew them even better than her visitor, who was struck with her critical intelligence and with something large and bold in the movement in her mind. She said things that startled him and that evidently had come to her directly; they weren't picked-up phrases—she placed them too well. St. George had been right about her being first-rate, about her not being afraid to gush, not remembering that she must be proud. Suddenly something came back to her, and she said: "I recollect that he did speak of Mrs. St. George to me once. He said, apropos of something or other, that she didn't care for perfection."

"That's a great crime in an artist's wife," Paul returned.

"Yes, poor thing!" and the girl sighed with a suggestion of many reflexions, some of them mitigating. But she presently added: "Ah perfection, perfection—how one ought to go in for it! I wish *I* could."

"Every one can in his way," her companion opined.

"In *his* way, yes—but not in hers. Women are so hampered—so condemned! Yet it's a kind of dishonour if you don't, when you want to *do* something, isn't it?" Miss Fancourt pursued, dropping one train in her quickness to take up another, an accident that was common with her. So these two young persons sat discussing high themes in their eclectic drawing-room, in their London "season"—discussing, with extreme seriousness, the high theme of perfection. It must be said in extenuation of this eccentricity that they were interested in the business. Their tone had truth and their emotion beauty; they weren't posturing for each other or for some one else.

The subject was so wide that they found themselves reducing it; the perfection to which for the moment they agreed to confine their speculations was that of the valid, the exemplary work of art. Our young woman's imagination, it appeared, had wandered far in that direction, and her guest had the rare delight of feeling in their conversation a full interchange. This episode will have lived for years in his memory and even in his wonder; it had the quality that fortune distils in a single drop at a time—the quality that lubricates many ensuing frictions. He still, whenever he likes, has a vision of the room, the bright red sociable talkative room with the curtains that, by a stroke of successful audacity, had the note of vivid blue. He remembers where certain things stood, the particular book open on the table and the almost intense odour of the flowers placed, at the left, somewhere behind him. These facts were the fringe, as it were, of a fine special agitation which had its birth in those two hours and of which perhaps the main sign was in its leading him inwardly and repeatedly to breathe "I had no idea there was any one like this—I had no idea there was any one like this!" Her freedom amazed him and charmed him—it seemed so to simplify the practical question. She was on the footing of an independent personage—a motherless girl who had passed out of her teens and had a position and responsibilities, who wasn't held down to the limitations of a little miss. She came and went with no dragged duenna, she received people alone, and, though she was totally without hardness, the question of protection or patronage had no relevancy in regard to her. She gave such an impression of the clear and the noble combined with the easy and the natural that in spite of her eminent modern situation she suggested no sort of sister-hood with the "fast" girl. Modern she was indeed, and made Paul Overt, who loved old colour, the golden glaze of time, think with some alarm of the muddled palette of the future. He couldn't get used to her interest in the arts he cared for; it seemed too good to be real—it was so unlikely an adventure to tumble into such a well of sympathy. One might stray into the desert easily—that was on the cards and that was the law of life; but it was too rare an accident to stumble on a crystal well. Yet if her aspirations seemed at one moment too extravagant to be real they struck him at the next as too intelligent to be false. They were both high and lame, and, whims for whims, he preferred them to any he had met in a like relation. It was probable enough she would leave them behind— exchange them for politics or "smartness" or mere prolific maternity, as was the custom of scribbling daubing educated flattered girls in an age of luxury and a society of leisure. He noted that the water-colours on the walls of the room she sat in had mainly the quality of being naïves, and reflected that naïveté in art is like a zero in a number: its importance depends on the figure it is united with. Meanwhile, however, he had fallen in love with her. Before he went away, at any rate, he said to her: "I thought St. George was coming to see you to-day, but he doesn't turn up."

For a moment he supposed she was going to cry "Comment donc? Did you come here only to meet him?" But the next he became aware of how little such a speech would have fallen in with any note of flirtation he had as yet perceived in her. She only replied: "Ah yes, but I don't think he'll come. He recommended me not to expect him." Then she gaily but all gently added: "He said it wasn't fair to you. But I think I could manage two."

"So could I," Paul Overt returned, stretching the point a little to meet her. In reality his appreciation of the occasion was so completely an appreciation of the woman before him that another figure in the scene, even so esteemed a one as St. George, might for the hour have appealed to him vainly. He left the house wondering what the great man had meant by its not being fair to him; and, still more than that, whether he had actually stayed away from the force of that idea. As he took his course through the Sunday solitude of Manchester Square, swinging his stick and with a good deal of emotion fermenting in his soul, it appeared to him he was living in a world strangely magnanimous. Miss Fancourt had told him it was possible she should be away, and that her father should be, on the following Sunday, but that she had the hope of a visit from him in the other event. She promised to let him know should their absence fail, and then he might act accordingly. After he had passed into one of the streets that open from the Square he stopped, without definite intentions, looking sceptically for a cab. In a moment he saw a hansom roll through the place from the other side and come a part of the way toward him. He was on the point of hailing the driver when he noticed a "fare" within; then he waited, seeing the man prepare to deposit his passenger by pulling up at one of the houses. The house was apparently the one he himself had just quitted; at least he drew that inference as he recognised Henry St. George in the person who stepped out of the hansom. Paul turned off as quickly as if he had been caught in the act of spying. He gave up his cab—he preferred to walk; he would go nowhere else. He was glad St. George hadn't renounced his visit altogether—that would have been too absurd. Yes, the world was magnanimous, and even he himself felt so as, on looking at his watch, he noted but six o'clock, so that he could mentally congratulate his successor on having an hour still to sit in Miss Fancourt's drawing-room. He himself might use that hour for another visit, but by the time he reached the Marble Arch the idea of such a course had become incongruous to him. He passed beneath that architectural effort and walked into the Park till he got upon the spreading grass. Here he continued to walk; he took his way across the elastic turf and came out by the Serpentine. He watched with a friendly eye the diversions of the London people, he bent a glance almost encouraging on the young ladies paddling their sweethearts about the lake and the guardsmen tickling tenderly with their bearskins the artificial flowers in the Sunday hats of their partners. He prolonged his meditative walk; he went into Kensington Gardens, he sat upon the penny chairs, he looked at the little sail-boats launched upon the round pond and was glad he had no engagement to dine. He repaired for this purpose, very late, to his club, where he found himself unable to order a repast and told the waiter to bring whatever there was. He didn't even observe what he was served with, and he spent the evening in the library of the establishment, pretending to read an article in an American magazine. He failed to discover what it was about; it appeared in a dim way to be about Marian Fancourt.

Quite late in the week she wrote to him that she was not to go into the country—it had only just been settled. Her father, she added, would never settle anything, but put it all on her. She felt her responsibility—she had to—and since she was forced this was the way she had decided. She mentioned no reasons, which gave our friend all the clearer field for bold conjecture about them. In Manchester Square on this second Sunday he esteemed his fortune less good, for she had three or four other visitors. But there were three or four compensations; perhaps the greatest of which was that, learning how her father had after all, at the last hour, gone out of town alone, the bold conjecture I just now spoke of found itself becoming a shade more bold. And then her presence was her presence, and the personal red room was there and was full of it, whatever phantoms passed and vanished, emitting incomprehensible sounds. Lastly, he had the resource of staying till every one had come and gone and of believing this grateful to her, though she gave no particular sign. When they were alone together he came to his point. "But St. George did come—last Sunday. I saw him as I looked back."

"Yes; but it was the last time."

"The last time?"

"He said he would never come again."

Paul Overt stared. "Does he mean he wishes to cease to see you?"

"I don't know what he means," the girl bravely smiled. "He won't at any rate see me here."

"And pray why not?"

"I haven't the least idea," said Marian Fancourt, whose visitor found her more perversely sublime than ever yet as she professed this clear helplessness.

V

"Oh I say, I want you to stop a little," Henry St. George said to him at eleven o'clock the night he dined with the head of the profession. The company—none of it indeed *of* the profession—had been numerous and was taking its leave; our young man, after bidding good-night to his hostess, had put out his hand in farewell to the master of the house. Besides drawing from the latter the protest I have cited this movement provoked a further priceless word about their chance now to have a talk, their going into his room, his having still everything to say. Paul Overt was all delight at this kindness; nevertheless he mentioned in weak jocose qualification the bare fact that he had promised to go to another place which was at a considerable distance.

"Well then you'll break your promise, that's all. You quite awful humbug!" St. George added in a tone that confirmed our young man's ease.

"Certainly I'll break it—but it was a real promise."

"Do you mean to Miss Fancourt? You're following her?" his friend asked.

He answered by a question. "Oh is *she* going?"

"Base impostor!" his ironic host went on. "I've treated you handsomely on the article of that young lady: I won't make another concession. Wait three minutes—I'll be with you." He gave himself to his departing guests, accompanied the long-trained ladies to the door. It was a hot night, the windows were open, the sound of the quick carriages and of the linkmen's call came into the house. The affair had rather glittered; a sense of festal things was in the heavy air: not only the influence of that particular entertainment, but the suggestion of the wide hurry of pleasure which in London on summer nights fills so many of the happier quarters of the complicated town. Gradually Mrs. St. George's drawing-room emptied itself; Paul was left alone with his hostess, to whom he explained the motive of his waiting. "Ah yes, some intellectual, some *professional*, talk," she leered; "at this season doesn't one miss it? Poor dear Henry, I'm so glad!" The young man looked out of the window a moment, at the called hansoms that lurched up, at the smooth broughams that rolled away. When he turned round Mrs. St. George had disappeared; her husband's voice rose to him from below—he was laughing and talking, in the portico, with some lady who awaited her carriage. Paul had solitary possession, for some minutes, of the warm deserted rooms where the covered tinted lamplight was soft, the seats had been pushed about and the odour of flowers lingered. They were large, they were pretty, they contained objects of value; everything in the picture told of a "good house." At the end of five minutes a servant came in with a request from the Master that he would join him downstairs; upon which, descending, he followed his conductor through a long passage to an apartment thrown out, in the rear of the habitation, for the special requirements, as he guessed, of a busy man of letters.

St. George was in his shirt-sleeves in the middle of a large high room—a room without windows, but with a wide skylight at the top, that of a place of exhibition. It was furnished as a library, and the serried bookshelves rose to the ceiling, a surface of incomparable tone produced by dimly-gilt "backs" interrupted here and there by the suspension of old prints and drawings. At the end furthest from the door of admission was a tall desk, of great extent, at which the person using it could write only in the erect posture of a clerk in a counting-house; and stretched from the entrance to this structure was a wide plain band of crimson cloth, as straight as a garden-path and almost as long, where, in his mind's eye, Paul at once beheld the Master pace to and fro during vexed hours—hours, that is, of admirable composition. The servant gave him a coat, an old jacket with a hang of experience, from a cupboard in the wall, retiring afterwards with the garment he had taken off. Paul Overt welcomed the coat; it was a coat for talk, it promised confidences— having visibly received so many—and had tragic literary elbows. "Ah we're practical—we're practical!" St. George said as he saw his visitor look the place over. "Isn't it a good big cage for going round and round? My wife invented it and she locks me up here every morning."

Our young man breathed—by way of tribute—with a certain oppression. "You don't miss a window—a place to look out?"

"I did at first awfully; but her calculation was just. It saves time, it has saved me many months in these ten years. Here I stand, under the eye of day—in London of course, very often, it's rather a bleared old eye—walled in to my trade. I can't get away—so the room's a fine lesson in concentration. I've learnt the lesson, I think; look at that big bundle of proof and acknowledge it." He pointed to a fat roll of papers, on one of the tables, which had not been undone.

"Are you bringing out another—?" Paul asked in a tone the fond deficiencies of which he didn't recognise till his companion burst out laughing, and indeed scarce even then.

"You humbug, you humbug!"—St. George appeared to enjoy caressing him, as it were, with that opprobrium. "Don't I know what you think of them?" he asked, standing there with his hands in his pockets and with a new kind of smile. It was as if he were going to let his young votary see him all now.

"Upon my word in that case you know more than I do!" the latter ventured to respond, revealing a part of the torment of being able neither clearly to esteem nor distinctly to renounce him.

"My dear fellow," said the more and more interesting Master, "don't imagine I talk about my books specifically; they're not a decent subject—il ne manquerait plus que ça! I'm not so bad as you may apprehend! About myself, yes, a little, if you like; though it wasn't for that I brought you down here. I want to ask you something—very much indeed; I value this chance. Therefore sit down. We're practical, but there *is* a sofa, you see—for she does humour my poor bones so far. Like all really great administrators and disciplinarians she knows when wisely to relax." Paul sank into the corner of a deep leathern couch, but his friend remained standing and explanatory. "If you don't mind, in this room, this is my habit. From the door to the desk and from the desk to the door. That shakes up my imagination gently; and don't you see what a good thing it is that there's no window for her to fly out of? The eternal standing as I write (I stop at that bureau and put it down, when anything comes, and so we go on) was rather wearisome at first, but

420

we adopted it with an eye to the long run; you're in better order—if your legs don't break down!—and you can keep it up for more years. Oh we're practical—we're practical!" St. George repeated, going to the table and taking up all mechanically the bundle of proofs. But, pulling off the wrapper, he had a change of attention that appealed afresh to our hero. He lost himself a moment, examining the sheets of his new book, while the younger man's eyes wandered over the room again.

"Lord, what good things I should do if I had such a charming place as this to do them in!" Paul reflected. The outer world, the world of accident and ugliness, was so successfully excluded, and within the rich protecting square, beneath the patronising sky, the dream-figures, the summoned company, could hold their particular revel. It was a fond prevision of Overt's rather than an observation on actual data, for which occasions had been too few, that the Master thus more closely viewed would have the quality, the charming gift, of flashing out, all surprisingly, in personal intercourse and at moments of suspended or perhaps even of diminished expectation. A happy relation with him would be a thing proceeding by jumps, not by traceable stages.

"Do you read them—really?" he asked, laying down the proofs on Paul's enquiring of him how soon the work would be published. And when the young man answered "Oh yes, always," he was moved to mirth again by something he caught in his manner of saying that. "You go to see your grandmother on her birthday—and very proper it is, especially as she won't last for ever. She has lost every faculty and every sense; she neither sees, nor hears, nor speaks; but all customary pieties and kindly habits are respectable. Only you're strong if you *do* read 'em! *I* couldn't, my dear fellow. You are strong, I know; and that's just a part of what I wanted to say to you. You're very strong indeed. I've been going into your other things—they've interested me immensely. Some one ought to have told me about them before—some one I could believe. But whom can one believe? You're wonderfully on the right road—it's awfully decent work. Now do you mean to keep it up?— that's what I want to ask you."

421

"Do I mean to do others?" Paul asked, looking up from his sofa at his erect inquisitor and feeling partly like a happy little boy when the schoolmaster is gay, and partly like some pilgrim of old who might have consulted a world-famous oracle. St. George's own performance had been infirm, but as an adviser he would be infallible.

"Others—others? Ah the number won't matter; one other would do, if it were really a further step—a throb of the same effort. What I mean is have you it in your heart to go in for some sort of decent perfection?"

"Ah decency, ah perfection—!" the young man sincerely sighed. "I talked of them the other Sunday with Miss Fancourt."

It produced on the Master's part a laugh of odd acrimony. "Yes, they'll 'talk' of them as much as you like! But they'll do little to help one to them. There's no obligation of course; only you strike me as capable," he went on. "You must have thought it all over. I can't believe you're without a plan. That's the sensation you give me, and it's so rare that it really stirs one up—it makes you remarkable. If you haven't a plan, if you *don't* mean to keep it up, surely you're within your rights; it's nobody's business, no one can force you, and not more than two or three people will notice you don't go straight. The others—*all* the rest, every blest soul in England, will think you do—will think you are keeping it up: upon my honour they will! I shall be one of the two or three who know better. Now the question is whether you can do it for two or three. Is that the stuff you're made of?"

It locked his guest a minute as in closed throbbing arms. "I could do it for one, if you were the one."

"Don't say that; I don't deserve it; it scorches me," he protested with eyes suddenly grave and glowing. "The 'one' is of course one's self, one's conscience, one's idea, the singleness of one's aim. I think of that pure spirit as a man thinks of a woman he has in some detested hour of his youth loved and forsaken. She haunts him with reproachful eyes, she lives for ever before him. As an artist, you know, I've married for money." Paul stared and even blushed a little, confounded by this avowal; whereupon his host, observing the expression of his face, dropped a quick laugh and pursued:

"You don't follow my figure. I'm not speaking of my dear wife, who had a small fortune—which, however, was not my bribe. I fell in love with her, as many other people have done. I refer to the mercenary muse whom I led to the altar of literature. Don't, my boy, put your nose into *that* yoke. The awful jade will lead you a life!"

Our hero watched him, wondering and deeply touched. "Haven't you been happy!"

"Happy? It's a kind of hell."

"There are things I should like to ask you," Paul said after a pause.

"Ask me anything in all the world. I'd turn myself inside out to save you."

"To 'save' me?" he quavered.

"To make you stick to it—to make you see it through. As I said to you the other night at Summersoft, let my example be vivid to you."

"Why your books are not so bad as that," said Paul, fairly laughing and feeling that if ever a fellow had breathed the air of art—!

"So bad as what?"

"Your talent's so great that it's in everything you do, in what's less good as well as in what's best. You've some forty volumes to show for it—forty volumes of wonderful life, of rare observation, of magnificent ability."

"I'm very clever, of course I know that"—but it was a thing, in fine, this author made nothing of. "Lord, what rot they'd all be if I hadn't been I'm a successful charlatan," he went on—"I've been able to pass off my system. But do you know what it is? It's cartonpierre."

"Carton-pierre?" Paul was struck, and gaped.

"Lincrusta-Walton!"

"Ah don't say such things—you make me bleed!" the younger man protested. "I see you in a beautiful fortunate home, living in comfort and honour."

423

"Do you call it honour?"—his host took him up with an intonation that often comes back to him. "That's what I want *you* to go in for. I mean the real thing. This is brummagem."

"Brummagem?" Paul ejaculated while his eyes wandered, by a movement natural at the moment, over the luxurious room.

"Ah they make it so well to-day—it's wonderfully deceptive!"

Our friend thrilled with the interest and perhaps even more with the pity of it. Yet he wasn't afraid to seem to patronise when he could still so far envy. "Is it deceptive that I find you living with every appearance of domestic felicity—blest with a devoted, accomplished wife, with children whose acquaintance I haven't yet had the pleasure of making, but who *must* be delightful young people, from what I know of their parents?"

St. George smiled as for the candour of his question. "It's all excellent, my dear fellow—heaven forbid I should deny it. I've made a great deal of money; my wife has known how to take care of it, to use it without wasting it, to put a good bit of it by, to make it fructify. I've got a loaf on the shelf; I've got everything in fact but the great thing."

"The great thing?" Paul kept echoing.

"The sense of having done the best—the sense which is the real life of the artist and the absence of which is his death, of having drawn from his intellectual instrument the finest music that nature had hidden in it, of having played it as it should be played. He either does that or he doesn't—and if he doesn't he isn't worth speaking of. Therefore, precisely, those who really know *don't* speak of him. He may still hear a great chatter, but what he hears most is the incorruptible silence of Fame. I've squared her, you may say, for my little hour—but what's my little hour? Don't imagine for a moment," the Master pursued, "that I'm such a cad as to have brought you down here to abuse or to complain of my wife to you. She's a woman of distinguished qualities, to whom my obligations are immense; so that, if you please, we'll say nothing about her. My boys—my children are all boys—are straight and strong, thank God, and have no poverty of growth about them, no penury of needs. I receive periodically the most satisfactory attestation from Harrow, from Oxford, from Sandhurst—oh we've done the best for them!—of their eminence as living thriving consuming organisms."

"It must be delightful to feel that the son of one's loins is at Sandhurst," Paul remarked enthusiastically.

"It is—it's charming. Oh I'm a patriot!"

The young man then could but have the greater tribute of questions to pay. "Then what did you mean—the other night at Summersoft—by saying that children are a curse?"

"My dear youth, on what basis are we talking?" and St. George dropped upon the sofa at a short distance from him. Sitting a little sideways he leaned back against the opposite arm with his hands raised and interlocked behind his head. "On the supposition that a certain perfection's possible and even desirable—isn't it so? Well, all I say is that one's children interfere with perfection. One's wife interferes. Marriage interferes."

"You think then the artist shouldn't marry?"

"He does so at his peril—he does so at his cost."

"Not even when his wife's in sympathy with his work?"

"She never is—she can't be! Women haven't a conception of such things."

"Surely they on occasion work themselves," Paul objected.

"Yes, very badly indeed. Oh of course, often, they think they understand, they think they sympathise. Then it is they're most dangerous. Their idea is that you shall do a great lot and get a great lot of money. Their great nobleness and virtue, their exemplary conscientiousness as British females, is in keeping you up to that. My wife makes all my bargains with my publishers for me, and has done so for twenty years. She does it consummately well— that's why I'm really pretty well off. Aren't you the father of their innocent babes, and will you withhold from them their natural sustenance? You asked

425

me the other night if they're not an immense incentive. Of course they are—there's no doubt of that!"

Paul turned it over: it took, from eyes he had never felt open so wide, so much looking at. "For myself I've an idea I need incentives."

"Ah well then, n'en parlons plus!" his companion handsomely smiled.

"*You* are an incentive, I maintain," the young man went on. "You don't affect me in the way you'd apparently like to. Your great success is what I see—the pomp of Ennismore Gardens!"

"Success?"—St. George's eyes had a cold fine light. "Do you call it success to be spoken of as you'd speak of me if you were sitting here with another artist—a young man intelligent and sincere like yourself? Do you call it success to make you blush—as you would blush!—if some foreign critic (some fellow, of course I mean, who should know what he was talking about and should have shown you he did, as foreign critics like to show it) were to say to you: 'He's the one, in this country, whom they consider the most perfect, isn't he?' Is it success to be the occasion of a young Englishman's having to stammer as you would have to stammer at such a moment for old England? No, no; success is to have made people wriggle to another tune. Do try it!"

Paul continued all gravely to glow. "Try what?"

"Try to do some really good work."

"Oh I want to, heaven knows!"

"Well, you can't do it without sacrifices—don't believe that for a moment," the Master said. "I've made none. I've had everything. In other words I've missed everything."

"You've had the full rich masculine human general life, with all the responsibilities and duties and burdens and sorrows and joys—all the domestic and social initiations and complications. They must be immensely suggestive, immensely amusing," Paul anxiously submitted.

426

"Amusing?"

"For a strong man—yes."

"They've given me subjects without number, if that's what you mean; but they've taken away at the same time the power to use them. I've touched a thousand things, but which one of them have I turned into gold? The artist has to do only with that—he knows nothing of any baser metal. I've led the life of the world, with my wife and my progeny; the clumsy conventional expensive materialised vulgarised brutalised life of London. We've got everything handsome, even a carriage—we're perfect Philistines and prosperous hospitable eminent people. But, my dear fellow, don't try to stultify yourself and pretend you don't know what we *haven't* got. It's bigger than all the rest. Between artists—come!" the Master wound up. "You know as well as you sit there that you'd put a pistol-ball into your brain if you had written my books!"

It struck his listener that the tremendous talk promised by him at Summersoft had indeed come off, and with a promptitude, a fulness, with which the latter's young imagination had scarcely reckoned. His impression fairly shook him and he throbbed with the excitement of such deep soundings and such strange confidences. He throbbed indeed with the conflict of his feelings—bewilderment and recognition and alarm, enjoyment and protest and assent, all commingled with tenderness (and a kind of shame in the participation) for the sores and bruises exhibited by so fine a creature, and with a sense of the tragic secret nursed under his trappings. The idea of *his*, Paul Overt's, becoming the occasion of such an act of humility made him flush and pant, at the same time that his consciousness was in certain directions too much alive not to swallow—and not intensely to taste—every offered spoonful of the revelation. It had been his odd fortune to blow upon the deep waters, to make them surge and break in waves of strange eloquence. But how couldn't he give out a passionate contradiction of his host's last extravagance, how couldn't he enumerate to him the parts of his work he loved, the splendid things he had found in it, beyond the compass of any other writer of the day? St. George listened a while, courteously; then he said, laying his hand on his visitor's: "That's all very well; and if your idea's to do nothing better there's no reason you shouldn't have as many good things as I—as many human and material appendages, as many sons or daughters, a wife with as many gowns, a house with as many servants, a stable with as many horses, a heart with as many aches." The Master got up when he had spoken thus—he stood a moment—near the sofa looking down on his agitated pupil. "Are you possessed of any property?" it occurred to him to ask.

"None to speak of."

"Oh well then there's no reason why you shouldn't make a goodish income—if you set about it the right way. Study *me* for that—study me well. You may really have horses."

Paul sat there some minutes without speaking. He looked straight before him—he turned over many things. His friend had wandered away, taking up a parcel of letters from the table where the roll of proofs had lain. "What was the book Mrs. St. George made you burn—the one she didn't like?" our young man brought out.

"The book she made me burn—how did you know that?" The Master looked up from his letters quite without the facial convulsion the pupil had feared.

"I heard her speak of it at Summersoft."

"Ah yes—she's proud of it. I don't know—it was rather good."

"What was it about?"

"Let me see." And he seemed to make an effort to remember. "Oh yes— it was about myself." Paul gave an irrepressible groan for the disappearance of such a production, and the elder man went on: "Oh but *you* should write it—*you* should do me." And he pulled up—from the restless motion that had come upon him; his fine smile a generous glare. "There's a subject, my boy: no end of stuff in it!"

Again Paul was silent, but it was all tormenting. "Are there no women who really understand—who can take part in a sacrifice?"

"How can they take part? They themselves are the sacrifice. They're the idol and the altar and the flame."

"Isn't there even *one* who sees further?" Paul continued.

For a moment St. George made no answer; after which, having torn up his letters, he came back to the point all ironic. "Of course I know the one you mean. But not even Miss Fancourt."

"I thought you admired her so much."

"It's impossible to admire her more. Are you in love with her?" St. George asked.

"Yes," Paul Overt presently said.

"Well then give it up."

Paul stared. "Give up my 'love'?"

"Bless me, no. Your idea." And then as our hero but still gazed: "The one you talked with her about. The idea of a decent perfection."

"She'd help it—she'd help it!" the young man cried.

"For about a year—the first year, yes. After that she'd be as a millstone round its neck."

Paul frankly wondered. "Why she has a passion for the real thing, for good work—for everything you and I care for most."

"'You and I' is charming, my dear fellow!" his friend laughed. "She has it indeed, but she'd have a still greater passion for her children—and very proper too. She'd insist on everything's being made comfortable, advantageous, propitious for them. That isn't the artist's business."

"The artist—the artist! Isn't he a man all the same?"

St. George had a grand grimace. "I mostly think not. You know as well as I what he has to do: the concentration, the finish, the independence he must strive for from the moment he begins to wish his work really decent. Ah my young friend, his relation to women, and especially to the one he's most intimately concerned with, is at the mercy of the damning fact that whereas he can in the nature of things have but one standard, they have about fifty. That's what makes them so superior," St. George amusingly added. "Fancy an artist with a change of standards as you'd have a change of shirts or of dinner-plates. To *do* it—to do it and make it divine—is the only thing he has to think about. 'Is it done or not?' is his only question. Not 'Is it done as well as a proper solicitude for my dear little family will allow?' He has nothing to do with the relative—he has only to do with the absolute; and a dear little family may represent a dozen relatives."

"Then you don't allow him the common passions and affections of men?" Paul asked.

"Hasn't he a passion, an affection, which includes all the rest? Besides, let him have all the passions he likes—if he only keeps his independence. He must be able to be poor."

Paul slowly got up. "Why then did you advise me to make up to her?"

St. George laid his hand on his shoulder. "Because she'd make a splendid wife! And I hadn't read you then."

The young man had a strained smile. "I wish you had left me alone!"

"I didn't know that that wasn't good enough for you," his host returned.

"What a false position, what a condemnation of the artist, that he's a mere disfranchised monk and can produce his effect only by giving up personal happiness. What an arraignment of art!" Paul went on with a trembling voice.

"Ah you don't imagine by chance that I'm defending art? 'Arraignment'—I should think so! Happy the societies in which it hasn't made its appearance, for from the moment it comes they have a consuming ache, they have an incurable corruption, in their breast. Most assuredly is the artist in a false position! But I thought we were taking him for granted. Pardon me," St. George continued: "'Ginistrella' made me!"

Paul stood looking at the floor—one o'clock struck, in the stillness, from a neighbouring church-tower. "Do you think she'd ever look at me?" he put to his friend at last.

"Miss Fancourt—as a suitor? Why shouldn't I think it? That's why I've tried to favour you—I've had a little chance or two of bettering your opportunity."

"Forgive my asking you, but do you mean by keeping away yourself?" Paul said with a blush.

"I'm an old idiot—my place isn't there," St. George stated gravely.

"I'm nothing yet, I've no fortune; and there must be so many others," his companion pursued.

The Master took this considerably in, but made little of it. "You're a gentleman and a man of genius. I think you might do something."

"But if I must give that up—the genius?"

"Lots of people, you know, think I've kept mine," St. George wonderfully grinned.

"You've a genius for mystification!" Paul declared; but grasping his hand gratefully in attenuation of this judgement.

"Poor dear boy, I do worry you! But try, try, all the same. I think your chances are good and you'll win a great prize."

Paul held fast the other's hand a minute; he looked into the strange deep face. "No, I *am* an artist—I can't help it!"

"Ah show it then!" St. George pleadingly broke out. "Let me see before I die the thing I most want, the thing I yearn for: a life in which the passion—ours—is really intense. If you can be rare don't fail of it! Think what it is—how it counts—how it lives!"

They had moved to the door and he had closed both his hands over his companion's. Here they paused again and our hero breathed deep. "I want to live!"

"In what sense?"

"In the greatest."

"Well then stick to it—see it through."

"With your sympathy—your help?"

"Count on that—you'll be a great figure to me. Count on my highest appreciation, my devotion. You'll give me satisfaction—if that has any weight with you." After which, as Paul appeared still to waver, his host added: "Do you remember what you said to me at Summersoft?"

"Something infatuated, no doubt!"

"'I'll do anything in the world you tell me.' You said that."

"And you hold me to it?"

"Ah what am I?" the Master expressively sighed.

"Lord, what things I shall have to do!" Paul almost moaned as be departed.

VI

"It goes on too much abroad—hang abroad!" These or something like them had been the Master's remarkable words in relation to the action of "Ginistrella"; and yet, though they had made a sharp impression on the author of that work, like almost all spoken words from the same source, he a week after the conversation I have noted left England for a long absence and full of brave intentions. It is not a perversion of the truth to pronounce that encounter the direct cause of his departure. If the oral utterance of the eminent writer had the privilege of moving him deeply it was especially on his turning it over at leisure, hours and days later, that it appeared to yield him its full meaning and exhibit its extreme importance. He spent the summer in Switzerland and, having in September begun a new task, determined not to cross the Alps till he should have made a good start. To this end he returned to a quiet corner he knew well, on the edge of the Lake of Geneva and within sight of the towers of Chillon: a region and a view for which he had an affection that sprang from old associations and was capable of mysterious revivals and refreshments. Here he lingered late, till the snow was on the nearer hills, almost down to the limit to which he could climb when his stint, on the shortening afternoons, was performed. The autumn was fine, the lake was blue and his book took form and direction. These felicities, for the time, embroidered his life, which he suffered to cover him with its mantle. At the end of six weeks he felt he had learnt St. George's lesson by heart, had tested and proved its doctrine. Nevertheless he did a very inconsistent thing: before crossing the Alps he wrote to Marian Fancourt. He was aware of the perversity of this act, and it was only as a luxury, an amusement, the reward of a strenuous autumn, that he justified it. She had asked of him no such favour when, shortly before he left London, three days after their dinner in Ennismore Gardens, he went to take leave of her. It was true she had had no ground—he hadn't named his intention of absence. He had kept his counsel for want of due assurance: it was that particular visit that was, the next thing, to settle the matter. He had paid the visit to see how much he really cared for her, and quick departure, without so much as an explicit farewell, was the sequel to this enquiry, the answer to which had created within him a deep yearning. When he wrote her from Clarens he noted that he owed her an explanation (more than three months after!) for not having told her what he was doing.

She replied now briefly but promptly, and gave him a striking piece of news: that of the death, a week before, of Mrs. St. George. This exemplary woman had succumbed, in the country, to a violent attack of inflammation of the lungs—he would remember that for a long time she had been delicate. Miss Fancourt added that she believed her husband overwhelmed by the blow; he would miss her too terribly—she had been everything in life to him. Paul Overt, on this, immediately wrote to St. George. He would from the day of their parting have been glad to remain in communication with him, but had hitherto lacked the right excuse for troubling so busy a man. Their long nocturnal talk came back to him in every detail, but this was no bar to an expression of proper sympathy with the head of the profession, for hadn't that very talk made it clear that the late accomplished lady was the influence that ruled his life? What catastrophe could be more cruel than the extinction of such an influence? This was to be exactly the tone taken by St. George in answering his young friend upwards of a month later. He made no allusion of course to their important discussion. He spoke of his wife as frankly and generously as if he had quite forgotten that occasion, and the feeling of deep bereavement was visible in his words. "She took everything off my hands—off my mind. She carried on our life with the greatest art, the rarest devotion, and I was free, as few men can have been, to drive my pen, to shut myself up with my trade. This was a rare service—the highest she could have rendered me. Would I could have acknowledged it more fitly!"

A certain bewilderment, for our hero, disengaged itself from these remarks: they struck him as a contradiction, a retractation, strange on the part of a man who hadn't the excuse of witlessness. He had certainly not expected his correspondent to rejoice in the death of his wife, and it was perfectly in order that the rupture of a tie of more than twenty years should have left him sore. But if she had been so clear a blessing what in the name of consistency had the dear man meant by turning him upside down that night—by dosing him to that degree, at the most sensitive hour of his life, with the doctrine of renunciation? If Mrs. St. George was an irreparable loss, then her husband's inspired advice had been a bad joke and renunciation was a mistake. Overt was on the point of rushing back to London to show that, for his part, he was perfectly willing to consider it so, and he went so far as to take the manuscript of the first chapters of his new book out of his table-drawer, to insert it into a pocket of his portmanteau. This led to his catching a glimpse of certain pages he hadn't looked at for months, and that accident, in turn, to his being struck with the high promise they revealed—a rare result of such retrospections, which it was his habit to avoid as much as possible: they usually brought home to him that the glow of composition might be a purely subjective and misleading emotion. On this occasion a certain belief in himself disengaged itself whimsically from the serried erasures of his first draft, making him think it best after all to pursue his present trial to the end. If he could write as well under the rigour of privation it might be a mistake to change the conditions before that spell had spent itself. He would go back to London of course, but he would go back only when he should have finished his book. This was the vow he privately made, restoring his manuscript to the table-drawer. It may be added that it took him a long time to finish his book, for the subject was as difficult as it was fine, and he was literally embarrassed by the fulness of his notes. Something within him warned him that he must make it supremely good—otherwise he should lack, as regards his private behaviour, a handsome excuse. He had a horror of this deficiency and found himself as firm as need be on the question of the lamp and the file. He crossed the Alps at last and spent the winter, the spring, the ensuing summer, in Italy, where still, at the end of a twelvemonth, his task was unachieved. "Stick to it—see it through": this general injunction of St. George's was good also for the particular case. He applied it to the utmost, with the result that when in its slow order the summer had come round again he felt he had given all that was in him. This time he put his papers into his portmanteau, with the address of his publisher attached, and took his way northward.

He had been absent from London for two years—two years which, seeming to count as more, had made such a difference in his own life—through the production of a novel far stronger, he believed, than "Ginistrella"—that he turned out into Piccadilly, the morning after his arrival, with a vague expectation of changes, of finding great things had happened. But there were few transformations in Piccadilly—only three or four big red houses where there had been low black ones—and the brightness of the end of June peeped through the rusty railings of the Green Park and glittered in the varnish of the rolling carriages as he had seen it in other, more cursory Junes. It was a greeting he appreciated; it seemed friendly and pointed, added to the exhilaration of his finished book, of his having his own country and the huge oppressive amusing city that suggested everything, that contained everything, under his hand again. "Stay at home and do things here—do subjects we can measure," St. George had said; and now it struck him he should ask nothing better than to stay at home for ever. Late in the afternoon he took his way to Manchester Square, looking out for a number he hadn't forgotten. Miss Fancourt, however, was not at home, so that he turned rather dejectedly from the door. His movement brought him face to face with a gentleman just approaching it and recognised on another glance as Miss Fancourt's father. Paul saluted this personage, and the General returned the greeting with his customary good manner—a manner so good, however, that you could never tell whether it meant he placed you. The disappointed caller felt the impulse to address him; then, hesitating, became both aware of having no particular remark to make, and convinced that though the old soldier remembered him he remembered him wrong. He therefore went his way without computing the irresistible effect his own evident recognition would have on the General, who never neglected a chance to gossip. Our young man's face was expressive, and observation seldom let it pass. He hadn't taken ten steps before he heard himself called after with a friendly semi-articulate "Er—I beg your pardon!" He turned round and the General, smiling at him from the porch, said: "Won't you come in? I won't leave you the advantage of me!" Paul declined to come in, and then felt regret, for Miss Fancourt, so late in the afternoon, might return at any moment. But her father gave him no second chance; he appeared mainly to wish not to have struck him as ungracious. A further look at the visitor had recalled something, enough at least to enable him to say: "You've come back, you've come back?" Paul was on the point of replying that he had come back the night before, but he suppressed, the next instant, this strong light on the immediacy of his visit and, giving merely a general assent, alluded to the young lady he deplored not having found. He had come late in the hope she would be in. "I'll tell her—I'll tell her," said the old man; and then he added quickly, gallantly: "You'll be giving us something new? It's a long time, isn't it?" Now he remembered him right.

"Rather long. I'm very slow." Paul explained. "I met you at Summersoft a long time ago."

"Oh yes—with Henry St. George. I remember very well. Before his poor wife—" General Fancourt paused a moment, smiling a little less. "I dare say you know."

"About Mrs. St. George's death? Certainly—I heard at the time."

"Oh no, I mean—I mean he's to be married."

"Ah I've not heard that!" But just as Paul was about to add "To whom?" the General crossed his intention.

"When did you come back? I know you've been away—by my daughter. She was very sorry. You ought to give her something new."

"I came back last night," said our young man, to whom something had occurred which made his speech for the moment a little thick.

"Ah most kind of you to come so soon. Couldn't you turn up at dinner?"

"At dinner?" Paul just mechanically repeated, not liking to ask whom St. George was going to marry, but thinking only of that.

"There are several people, I believe. Certainly St. George. Or afterwards if you like better. I believe my daughter expects—" He appeared to notice something in the visitor's raised face (on his steps he stood higher) which led him to interrupt himself, and the interruption gave him a momentary sense of awkwardness, from which he sought a quick issue. "Perhaps then you haven't heard she's to be married."

Paul gaped again. "To be married?"

"To Mr. St. George—it has just been settled. Odd marriage, isn't it?" Our listener uttered no opinion on this point: he only continued to stare. "But I dare say it will do—she's so awfully literary!" said the General.

Paul had turned very red. "Oh it's a surprise—very interesting, very charming! I'm afraid I can't dine—so many thanks!"

"Well, you must come to the wedding!" cried the General. "Oh I remember that day at Summersoft. He's a great man, you know."

"Charming—charming!" Paul stammered for retreat. He shook hands with the General and got off. His face was red and he had the sense of its growing more and more crimson. All the evening at home—he went straight to his rooms and remained there dinnerless—his cheek burned at intervals as if it had been smitten. He didn't understand what had happened to him, what trick had been played him, what treachery practised. "None, none," he said to himself. "I've nothing to do with it. I'm out of it—it's none of my business." But that bewildered murmur was followed again and again by the incongruous ejaculation: "Was it a plan—was it a plan?" Sometimes he cried to himself, breathless, "Have I been duped, sold, swindled?" If at all, he was an absurd, an abject victim. It was as if he hadn't lost her till now. He had renounced her, yes; but that was another affair—that was a closed but not a locked door. Now he seemed to see the door quite slammed in his face. Did he expect her to wait—was she to give him his time like that: two years at a stretch? He didn't know what he had expected—he only knew what he hadn't. It wasn't this—it wasn't this. Mystification bitterness and wrath rose and boiled in him when he thought of the deference, the devotion, the credulity with which he had listened to St. George. The evening wore on and the light was long; but even when it had darkened he remained without a lamp. He had flung himself on the sofa, where he lay through the hours with his eyes either closed or gazing at the gloom, in the attitude of a man teaching himself to bear something, to bear having been made a fool of. He had made it too easy—that idea passed over him like a hot wave. Suddenly, as he heard eleven o'clock strike, he jumped up, remembering what General

Fancourt had said about his coming after dinner. He'd go—he'd see her at least; perhaps he should see what it meant. He felt as if some of the elements of a hard sum had been given him and the others were wanting: he couldn't do his sum till he had got all his figures.

He dressed and drove quickly, so that by half-past eleven he was at Manchester Square. There were a good many carriages at the door—a party was going on; a circumstance which at the last gave him a slight relief, for now he would rather see her in a crowd. People passed him on the staircase; they were going away, going "on" with the hunted herdlike movement of London society at night. But sundry groups remained in the drawing-room, and it was some minutes, as she didn't hear him announced, before he discovered and spoke to her. In this short interval he had seen St. George talking to a lady before the fireplace; but he at once looked away, feeling unready for an encounter, and therefore couldn't be sure the author of "Shadowmere" noticed him. At all events he didn't come over though Miss Fancourt did as soon as she saw him—she almost rushed at him, smiling rustling radiant beautiful. He had forgotten what her head, what her face offered to the sight; she was in white, there were gold figures on her dress and her hair was a casque of gold. He saw in a single moment that she was happy, happy with an aggressive splendour. But she wouldn't speak to him of that, she would speak only of himself.

"I'm so delighted; my father told me. How kind of you to come!" She struck him as so fresh and brave, while his eyes moved over her, that he said to himself irresistibly: "Why to him, why not to youth, to strength, to ambition, to a future? Why, in her rich young force, to failure, to abdication to superannuation?" In his thought at that sharp moment he blasphemed even against all that had been left of his faith in the peccable Master. "I'm so sorry I missed you," she went on. "My father told me. How charming of you to have come so soon!"

"Does that surprise you?" Paul Overt asked.

"The first day? No, from you—nothing that's nice." She was interrupted by a lady who bade her good-night, and he seemed to read that it cost her nothing to speak to him in that tone; it was her old liberal lavish way, with a certain added amplitude that time had brought; and if this manner began to operate on the spot, at such a juncture in her history, perhaps in the other days too it had meant just as little or as much—a mere mechanical charity, with the difference now that she was satisfied, ready to give but in want of nothing. Oh she was satisfied—and why shouldn't she be? Why shouldn't she have been surprised at his coming the first day—for all the good she had ever got from him? As the lady continued to hold her attention Paul turned from her with a strange irritation in his complicated artistic soul and a sort of disinterested disappointment. She was so happy that it was almost stupid—a disproof of the extraordinary intelligence he had formerly found in her. Didn't she know how bad St. George could be, hadn't she recognised the awful thinness—? If she didn't she was nothing, and if she did why such an insolence of serenity? This question expired as our young man's eyes settled at last on the genius who had advised him in a great crisis. St. George was still before the chimney-piece, but now he was alone—fixed, waiting, as if he meant to stop after every one—and he met the clouded gaze of the young friend so troubled as to the degree of his right (the right his resentment would have enjoyed) to regard himself as a victim. Somehow the ravage of the question was checked by the Master's radiance. It was as fine in its way as Marian Fancourt's, it denoted the happy human being; but also it represented to Paul Overt that the author of "Shadowmere" had now definitely ceased to count—ceased to count as a writer. As he smiled a welcome across the place he was almost banal, was almost smug. Paul fancied that for a moment he hesitated to make a movement, as if for all the world he *had* his bad conscience; then they had already met in the middle of the room and had shaken hands—expressively, cordially on St. George's part. With which they had passed back together to where the elder man had been standing, while St. George said: "I hope you're never going away again. I've been dining here; the General told me." He was handsome, he was young, he looked as if he had still a great fund of life. He bent the friendliest, most unconfessing eyes on his disciple of a couple of years before; asked him about everything, his health, his plans, his late occupations, the new book. "When will it be out—soon, soon, I hope? Splendid, eh? That's right; you're a comfort, you're a luxury! I've read you all over again these last six months." Paul waited to see if he would tell him what the General had told him in the afternoon and what Miss Fancourt, verbally at least, of course hadn't. But as it didn't come out he at last put the question.

"Is it true, the great news I hear—that you're to be married?"

"Ah you have heard it then?"

"Didn't the General tell you?" Paul asked.

The Master's face was wonderful. "Tell me what?"

"That he mentioned it to me this afternoon?"

"My dear fellow, I don't remember. We've been in the midst of people. I'm sorry, in that case, that I lose the pleasure, myself, of announcing to you a fact that touches me so nearly. It *is* a fact, strange as it may appear. It has only just become one. Isn't it ridiculous?" St. George made this speech without confusion, but on the other hand, so far as our friend could judge, without latent impudence. It struck his interlocutor that, to talk so comfortably and coolly, he must simply have forgotten what had passed between them. His next words, however, showed he hadn't, and they produced, as an appeal to Paul's own memory, an effect which would have been ludicrous if it hadn't been cruel. "Do you recall the talk we had at my house that night, into which Miss Fancourt's name entered? I've often thought of it since."

"Yes; no wonder you said what you did"—Paul was careful to meet his eyes.

"In the light of the present occasion? Ah but there was no light then. How could I have foreseen this hour?"

"Didn't you think it probable?"

"Upon my honour, no," said Henry St. George. "Certainly I owe you that assurance. Think how my situation has changed."

"I see—I see," our young man murmured.

His companion went on as if, now that the subject had been broached, he was, as a person of imagination and tact, quite ready to give every satisfaction—being both by his genius and his method so able to enter into everything another might feel. "But it's not only that; for honestly, at my age, I never dreamed—a widower with big boys and with so little else! It has turned out differently from anything one could have dreamed, and I'm fortunate beyond all measure. She has been so free, and yet she consents. Better than any one else perhaps—for I remember how you liked her before you went away, and how she liked you—you can intelligently congratulate me."

"She has been so free!" Those words made a great impression on Paul Overt, and he almost writhed under that irony in them as to which it so little mattered whether it was designed or casual. Of course she had been free, and appreciably perhaps by his own act; for wasn't the Master's allusion to her having liked him a part of the irony too? "I thought that by your theory you disapproved of a writer's marrying."

"Surely—surely. But you don't call me a writer?"

"You ought to be ashamed," said Paul.

"Ashamed of marrying again?"

"I won't say that—but ashamed of your reasons."

The elder man beautifully smiled. "You must let me judge of them, my good friend."

"Yes; why not? For you judged wonderfully of mine."

The tone of these words appeared suddenly, for St. George, to suggest the unsuspected. He stared as if divining a bitterness. "Don't you think I've been straight?"

"You might have told me at the time perhaps."

"My dear fellow, when I say I couldn't pierce futurity—!"

"I mean afterwards."

The Master wondered. "After my wife's death?"

"When this idea came to you."

"Ah never, never! I wanted to save you, rare and precious as you are."

Poor Overt looked hard at him. "Are you marrying Miss Fancourt to save me?"

"Not absolutely, but it adds to the pleasure. I shall be the making of you," St. George smiled. "I was greatly struck, after our talk, with the brave devoted way you quitted the country, and still more perhaps with your force of character in remaining abroad. You're very strong—you're wonderfully strong."

Paul tried to sound his shining eyes; the strange thing was that he seemed sincere—not a mocking fiend. He turned away, and as he did so heard the Master say something about his giving them all the proof, being the joy of his old age. He faced him again, taking another look. "Do you mean to say you've stopped writing?"

"My dear fellow, of course I have. It's too late. Didn't I tell you?"

"I can't believe it!"

"Of course you can't—with your own talent! No, no; for the rest of my life I shall only read *you*."

"Does she know that—Miss Fancourt?"

"She will—she will." Did he mean this, our young man wondered, as a covert intimation that the assistance he should derive from that young lady's fortune, moderate as it was, would make the difference of putting it in his power to cease to work ungratefully an exhausted vein? Somehow, standing there in the ripeness of his successful manhood, he didn't suggest that any of his veins were exhausted. "Don't you remember the moral I offered myself to you that night as pointing?" St. George continued. "Consider at any rate the warning I am at present."

This was too much—he *was* the mocking fiend. Paul turned from him with a mere nod for good-night and the sense in a sore heart that he might come back to him and his easy grace, his fine way of arranging things, some time in the far future, but couldn't fraternise with him now. It was necessary to his soreness to believe for the hour in the intensity of his grievance—all the more cruel for its not being a legal one. It was doubtless in the attitude of hugging this wrong that he descended the stairs without taking leave of Miss Fancourt, who hadn't been in view at the moment he quitted the room. He was glad to get out into the honest dusky unsophisticating night, to move fast, to take his way home on foot. He walked a long time, going astray, paying no attention. He was thinking of too many other things. His steps recovered their direction, however, and at the end of an hour he found himself before his door in the small inexpensive empty street. He lingered, questioning himself still before going in, with nothing around and above him but moonless blackness, a bad lamp or two and a few far-away dim stars. To these last faint features he raised his eyes; he had been saying to himself that he should have been "sold" indeed, diabolically sold, if now, on his new foundation, at the end of a year, St. George were to put forth something of his prime quality—something of the type of "Shadowmere" and finer than his finest. Greatly as he admired his talent Paul literally hoped such an incident wouldn't occur; it seemed to him just then that he shouldn't be able to bear it. His late adviser's words were still in his ears—"You're very strong, wonderfully strong." Was he really? Certainly he would have to be, and it might a little serve for revenge. *Is* he? the reader may ask in turn, if his interest has followed the perplexed young man so far. The best answer to that perhaps is that he's doing his best, but that it's too soon to say. When the new book came out in the autumn Mr. and Mrs. St. George found it really magnificent. The former still has published nothing but Paul doesn't even yet feel safe. I may say for him, however, that if this event were to occur he would really be the very first to appreciate it: which is perhaps a proof that the Master was essentially right and that Nature had dedicated him to intellectual, not to personal passion.

About Author

Henry James OM (15 April 1843 – 28 February 1916) was an American-British author regarded as a key transitional figure between literary realism and literary modernism, and is considered by many to be among the greatest novelists in the English language. He was the son of Henry James Sr. and the brother of renowned philosopher and psychologist William James and diarist Alice James.

He is best known for a number of novels dealing with the social and marital interplay between émigré Americans, English people, and continental Europeans. Examples of such novels include The Portrait of a Lady, The Ambassadors, and The Wings of the Dove. His later works were increasingly experimental. In describing the internal states of mind and social dynamics of his characters, James often made use of a style in which ambiguous or contradictory motives and impressions were overlaid or juxtaposed in the discussion of a character's psyche. For their unique ambiguity, as well as for other aspects of their composition, his late works have been compared to impressionist painting.

His novella The Turn of the Screw has garnered a reputation as the most analysed and ambiguous ghost story in the English language and remains his most widely adapted work in other media. He also wrote a number of other highly regarded ghost stories and is considered one of the greatest masters of the field.

James published articles and books of criticism, travel, biography, autobiography, and plays. Born in the United States, James largely relocated to Europe as a young man and eventually settled in England, becoming a British subject in 1915, one year before his death. James was nominated for the Nobel Prize in Literature in 1911, 1912 and 1916.

Life

Early years, 1843–1883

James was born at 2 Washington Place in New York City on 15 April 1843. His parents were Mary Walsh and Henry James Sr. His father was intelligent and steadfastly congenial. He was a lecturer and philosopher who had inherited independent means from his father, an Albany banker and investor. Mary came from a wealthy family long settled in New York City. Her sister Katherine lived with her adult family for an extended period of time. Henry Jr. had three brothers, William, who was one year his senior, and younger brothers Wilkinson (Wilkie) and Robertson. His younger sister was Alice. Both of his parents were of Irish and Scottish descent.

The family first lived in Albany, at 70 N. Pearl St., and then moved to Fourteenth Street in New York City when James was still a young boy. His education was calculated by his father to expose him to many influences, primarily scientific and philosophical; it was described by Percy Lubbock, the editor of his selected letters, as "extraordinarily haphazard and promiscuous." James did not share the usual education in Latin and Greek classics. Between 1855 and 1860, the James' household traveled to London, Paris, Geneva, Boulogne-sur-Mer and Newport, Rhode Island, according to the father's current interests and publishing ventures, retreating to the United States when funds were low. Henry studied primarily with tutors and briefly attended schools while the family traveled in Europe. Their longest stays were in France, where Henry began to feel at home and became fluent in French. He was afflicted with a stutter, which seems to have manifested itself only when he spoke English; in French, he did not stutter.

In 1860 the family returned to Newport. There Henry became a friend of the painter John La Farge, who introduced him to French literature, and in particular, to Balzac. James later called Balzac his "greatest master," and said that he had learned more about the craft of fiction from him than from anyone else.

In the autumn of 1861 Henry received an injury, probably to his back, while fighting a fire. This injury, which resurfaced at times throughout his life, made him unfit for military service in the American Civil War.

In 1864 the James family moved to Boston, Massachusetts to be near William, who had enrolled first in the Lawrence Scientific School at Harvard and then in the medical school. In 1862 Henry attended Harvard Law School, but realised that he was not interested in studying law. He pursued his interest in literature and associated with authors and critics William Dean Howells and Charles Eliot Norton in Boston and Cambridge, formed lifelong friendships with Oliver Wendell Holmes Jr., the future Supreme Court Justice, and with James and Annie Fields, his first professional mentors.

His first published work was a review of a stage performance, "Miss Maggie Mitchell in Fanchon the Cricket," published in 1863. About a year later, A Tragedy of Error, his first short story, was published anonymously. James's first payment was for an appreciation of Sir Walter Scott's novels, written for the North American Review. He wrote fiction and non-fiction pieces for The Nation and Atlantic Monthly, where Fields was editor. In 1871 he published his first novel, Watch and Ward, in serial form in the Atlantic Monthly. The novel was later published in book form in 1878.

During a 14-month trip through Europe in 1869–70 he met Ruskin, Dickens, Matthew Arnold, William Morris, and George Eliot. Rome impressed him profoundly. "Here I am then in the Eternal City," he wrote to his brother William. "At last—for the first time—I live!" He attempted to support himself as a freelance writer in Rome, then secured a position as Paris correspondent for the New York Tribune, through the influence of its editor John Hay. When these efforts failed he returned to New York City. During 1874 and 1875 he published Transatlantic Sketches, A Passionate Pilgrim, and Roderick Hudson. During this early period in his career he was influenced by Nathaniel Hawthorne.

In 1869 he settled in London. There he established relationships with Macmillan and other publishers, who paid for serial installments that they would later publish in book form. The audience for these serialized novels was largely made up of middle-class women, and James struggled to fashion serious literary work within the strictures imposed by editors' and publishers' notions of what was suitable for young women to read. He lived in rented rooms but was able to join gentlemen's clubs that had libraries and where

449

he could entertain male friends. He was introduced to English society by Henry Adams and Charles Milnes Gaskell, the latter introducing him to the Travellers' and the Reform Clubs.

In the fall of 1875 he moved to the Latin Quarter of Paris. Aside from two trips to America, he spent the next three decades—the rest of his life—in Europe. In Paris he met Zola, Alphonse Daudet, Maupassant, Turgenev, and others. He stayed in Paris only a year before moving to London.

In England he met the leading figures of politics and culture. He continued to be a prolific writer, producing The American (1877), The Europeans (1878), a revision of Watch and Ward (1878), French Poets and Novelists (1878), Hawthorne (1879), and several shorter works of fiction. In 1878 Daisy Miller established his fame on both sides of the Atlantic. It drew notice perhaps mostly because it depicted a woman whose behavior is outside the social norms of Europe. He also began his first masterpiece, The Portrait of a Lady, which would appear in 1881.

In 1877 he first visited Wenlock Abbey in Shropshire, home of his friend Charles Milnes Gaskell whom he had met through Henry Adams. He was much inspired by the darkly romantic Abbey and the surrounding countryside, which features in his essay Abbeys and Castles. In particular the gloomy monastic fishponds behind the Abbey are said to have inspired the lake in The Turn of the Screw.

While living in London, James continued to follow the careers of the "French realists", Émile Zola in particular. Their stylistic methods influenced his own work in the years to come. Hawthorne's influence on him faded during this period, replaced by George Eliot and Ivan Turgenev. 1879–1882 saw the publication of The Europeans, Washington Square, Confidence, and The Portrait of a Lady. He visited America in 1882–1883, then returned to London.

The period from 1881 to 1883 was marked by several losses. His mother died in 1881, followed by his father a few months later, and then by his brother Wilkie. Emerson, an old family friend, died in 1882. His friend Turgenev died in 1883.

Middle years, 1884–1897

In 1884 James made another visit to Paris. There he met again with Zola, Daudet, and Goncourt. He had been following the careers of the French "realist" or "naturalist" writers, and was increasingly influenced by them. In 1886, he published The Bostonians and The Princess Casamassima, both influenced by the French writers he'd studied assiduously. Critical reaction and sales were poor. He wrote to Howells that the books had hurt his career rather than helped because they had "reduced the desire, and demand, for my productions to zero". During this time he became friends with Robert Louis Stevenson, John Singer Sargent, Edmund Gosse, George du Maurier, Paul Bourget, and Constance Fenimore Woolson. His third novel from the 1880s was The Tragic Muse. Although he was following the precepts of Zola in his novels of the '80s, their tone and attitude are closer to the fiction of Alphonse Daudet. The lack of critical and financial success for his novels during this period led him to try writing for the theatre. (His dramatic works and his experiences with theatre are discussed below.)

In the last quarter of 1889, he started translating "for pure and copious lucre" Port Tarascon, the third volume of Alphonse Daudet adventures of Tartarin de Tarascon. Serialized in Harper's Monthly Magazine from June 1890, this translation praised as "clever" by The Spectator was published in January 1891 by Sampson Low, Marston, Searle & Rivington.

After the stage failure of Guy Domville in 1895, James was near despair and thoughts of death plagued him. The years spent on dramatic works were not entirely a loss. As he moved into the last phase of his career he found ways to adapt dramatic techniques into the novel form.

In the late 1880s and throughout the 1890s James made several trips through Europe. He spent a long stay in Italy in 1887. In that year the short novel The Aspern Papers and The Reverberator were published.

Late years, 1898–1916

In 1897–1898 he moved to Rye, Sussex, and wrote The Turn of the Screw. 1899–1900 saw the publication of The Awkward Age and The Sacred

Fount. During 1902–1904 he wrote The Ambassadors, The Wings of the Dove, and The Golden Bowl.

In 1904 he revisited America and lectured on Balzac. In 1906–1910 he published The American Scene and edited the "New York Edition", a 24-volume collection of his works. In 1910 his brother William died; Henry had just joined William from an unsuccessful search for relief in Europe on what then turned out to be his (Henry's) last visit to the United States (from summer 1910 to July 1911), and was near him, according to a letter he wrote, when he died.

In 1913 he wrote his autobiographies, A Small Boy and Others, and Notes of a Son and Brother. After the outbreak of the First World War in 1914 he did war work. In 1915 he became a British subject and was awarded the Order of Merit the following year. He died on 28 February 1916, in Chelsea, London. As he requested, his ashes were buried in Cambridge Cemetery in Massachusetts.

Biographers

James regularly rejected suggestions that he should marry, and after settling in London proclaimed himself "a bachelor". F. W. Dupee, in several volumes on the James family, originated the theory that he had been in love with his cousin Mary ("Minnie") Temple, but that a neurotic fear of sex kept him from admitting such affections: "James's invalidism ... was itself the symptom of some fear of or scruple against sexual love on his part." Dupee used an episode from James's memoir A Small Boy and Others, recounting a dream of a Napoleonic image in the Louvre, to exemplify James's romanticism about Europe, a Napoleonic fantasy into which he fled.

Dupee had not had access to the James family papers and worked principally from James's published memoir of his older brother, William, and the limited collection of letters edited by Percy Lubbock, heavily weighted toward James's last years. His account therefore moved directly from James's childhood, when he trailed after his older brother, to elderly invalidism. As more material became available to scholars, including the diaries of contemporaries and hundreds of affectionate and sometimes erotic letters written by James to younger men, the picture of neurotic celibacy gave way to a portrait of a closeted homosexual.

Between 1953 and 1972, Leon Edel authored a major five-volume biography of James, which accessed unpublished letters and documents after Edel gained the permission of James's family. Edel's portrayal of James included the suggestion he was celibate. It was a view first propounded by critic Saul Rosenzweig in 1943. In 1996 Sheldon M. Novick published Henry James: The Young Master, followed by Henry James: The Mature Master (2007). The first book "caused something of an uproar in Jamesian circles" as it challenged the previous received notion of celibacy, a once-familiar paradigm in biographies of homosexuals when direct evidence was non-existent. Novick also criticised Edel for following the discounted Freudian interpretation of homosexuality "as a kind of failure." The difference of opinion erupted in a series of exchanges between Edel and Novick which were published by the online magazine Slate, with the latter arguing that even the suggestion of celibacy went against James's own injunction "live!"—not "fantasize!"

A letter James wrote in old age to Hugh Walpole has been cited as an explicit statement of this. Walpole confessed to him of indulging in "high jinks", and James wrote a reply endorsing it: "We must know, as much as possible, in our beautiful art, yours & mine, what we are talking about — & the only way to know it is to have lived & loved & cursed & floundered & enjoyed & suffered — I don't think I regret a single 'excess' of my responsive youth".

The interpretation of James as living a less austere emotional life has been subsequently explored by other scholars. The often intense politics of Jamesian scholarship has also been the subject of studies. Author Colm Tóibín has said that Eve Kosofsky Sedgwick's Epistemology of the Closet made a landmark difference to Jamesian scholarship by arguing that he be read as a homosexual writer whose desire to keep his sexuality a secret shaped his layered style and dramatic artistry. According to Tóibín such a reading "removed James from the realm of dead white males who wrote about posh people. He became our contemporary."

James's letters to expatriate American sculptor Hendrik Christian Andersen have attracted particular attention. James met the 27-year-old Andersen in Rome in 1899, when James was 56, and wrote letters to Andersen that are intensely emotional: "I hold you, dearest boy, in my innermost love, & count on your feeling me—in every throb of your soul". In a letter of 6 May 1904, to his brother William, James referred to himself as "always your hopelessly celibate even though sexagenarian Henry". How accurate that description might have been is the subject of contention among James's biographers,   but the letters to Andersen were occasionally quasi-erotic: "I put, my dear boy, my arm around you, & feel the pulsation, thereby, as it were, of our excellent future & your admirable endowment." To his homosexual friend Howard Sturgis, James could write: "I repeat, almost to indiscretion, that I could live with you. Meanwhile I can only try to live without you."

His numerous letters to the many young gay men among his close male friends are more forthcoming. In a letter to Howard Sturgis, following a long visit, James refers jocularly to their "happy little congress of two" and in letters to Hugh Walpole he pursues convoluted jokes and puns about their relationship, referring to himself as an elephant who "paws you oh so benevolently" and winds about Walpole his "well meaning old trunk". His letters to Walter Berry printed by the Black Sun Press have long been celebrated for their lightly veiled eroticism.

He corresponded in almost equally extravagant language with his many female friends, writing, for example, to fellow novelist Lucy Clifford: "Dearest Lucy! What shall I say? when I love you so very, very much, and see you nine times for once that I see Others! Therefore I think that—if you want it made clear to the meanest intelligence—I love you more than I love Others." To his New York friend Mary Cadwalader Jones: "Dearest Mary Cadwalader. I yearn over you, but I yearn in vain; & your long silence really breaks my heart, mystifies, depresses, almost alarms me, to the point even of making me wonder if poor unconscious & doting old Célimare [Jones's pet name for James] has 'done' anything, in some dark somnambulism of the spirit, which has ... given you a bad moment, or a wrong impression, or a 'colourable pretext' ... However these things may be, he loves you as tenderly as ever;

nothing, to the end of time, will ever detach him from you, & he remembers those Eleventh St. matutinal intimes hours, those telephonic matinées, as the most romantic of his life ..." His long friendship with American novelist Constance Fenimore Woolson, in whose house he lived for a number of weeks in Italy in 1887, and his shock and grief over her suicide in 1894, are discussed in detail in Edel's biography and play a central role in a study by Lyndall Gordon. (Edel conjectured that Woolson was in love with James and killed herself in part because of his coldness, but Woolson's biographers have objected to Edel's account.)

Works

Style and themes

James is one of the major figures of trans-Atlantic literature. His works frequently juxtapose characters from the Old World (Europe), embodying a feudal civilisation that is beautiful, often corrupt, and alluring, and from the New World (United States), where people are often brash, open, and assertive and embody the virtues—freedom and a more highly evolved moral character—of the new American society. James explores this clash of personalities and cultures, in stories of personal relationships in which power is exercised well or badly. His protagonists were often young American women facing oppression or abuse, and as his secretary Theodora Bosanquet remarked in her monograph Henry James at Work:

> When he walked out of the refuge of his study and into the world and looked around him, he saw a place of torment, where creatures of prey perpetually thrust their claws into the quivering flesh of doomed, defenseless children of light ... His novels are a repeated exposure of this wickedness, a reiterated and passionate plea for the fullest freedom of development, unimperiled by reckless and barbarous stupidity.

Critics have jokingly described three phases in the development of James's prose: "James I, James II, and The Old Pretender." He wrote short stories and plays. Finally, in his third and last period he returned to the long, serialised novel. Beginning in the second period, but most noticeably in the third, he increasingly abandoned direct statement in favour of frequent

455

double negatives, and complex descriptive imagery. Single paragraphs began to run for page after page, in which an initial noun would be succeeded by pronouns surrounded by clouds of adjectives and prepositional clauses, far from their original referents, and verbs would be deferred and then preceded by a series of adverbs. The overall effect could be a vivid evocation of a scene as perceived by a sensitive observer. It has been debated whether this change of style was engendered by James's shifting from writing to dictating to a typist, a change made during the composition of What Maisie Knew.

In its intense focus on the consciousness of his major characters, James's later work foreshadows extensive developments in 20th century fiction. Indeed, he might have influenced stream-of-consciousness writers such as Virginia Woolf, who not only read some of his novels but also wrote essays about them. Both contemporary and modern readers have found the late style difficult and unnecessary; his friend Edith Wharton, who admired him greatly, said that there were passages in his work that were all but incomprehensible. James was harshly portrayed by H. G. Wells as a hippopotamus laboriously attempting to pick up a pea that had got into a corner of its cage. The "late James" style was ably parodied by Max Beerbohm in "The Mote in the Middle Distance".

More important for his work overall may have been his position as an expatriate, and in other ways an outsider, living in Europe. While he came from middle-class and provincial beginnings (seen from the perspective of European polite society) he worked very hard to gain access to all levels of society, and the settings of his fiction range from working class to aristocratic, and often describe the efforts of middle-class Americans to make their way in European capitals. He confessed he got some of his best story ideas from gossip at the dinner table or at country house weekends. He worked for a living, however, and lacked the experiences of select schools, university, and army service, the common bonds of masculine society. He was furthermore a man whose tastes and interests were, according to the prevailing standards of Victorian era Anglo-American culture, rather feminine, and who was shadowed by the cloud of prejudice that then and later accompanied suspicions of his homosexuality. Edmund Wilson famously compared James's objectivity to Shakespeare's:

One would be in a position to appreciate James better if one compared him with the dramatists of the seventeenth century—Racine and Molière, whom he resembles in form as well as in point of view, and even Shakespeare, when allowances are made for the most extreme differences in subject and form. These poets are not, like Dickens and Hardy, writers of melodrama—either humorous or pessimistic, nor secretaries of society like Balzac, nor prophets like Tolstoy: they are occupied simply with the presentation of conflicts of moral character, which they do not concern themselves about softening or averting. They do not indict society for these situations: they regard them as universal and inevitable. They do not even blame God for allowing them: they accept them as the conditions of life.

It is also possible to see many of James's stories as psychological thought-experiments. In his preface to the New York edition of The American he describes the development of the story in his mind as exactly such: the "situation" of an American, "some robust but insidiously beguiled and betrayed, some cruelly wronged, compatriot..." with the focus of the story being on the response of this wronged man. The Portrait of a Lady may be an experiment to see what happens when an idealistic young woman suddenly becomes very rich. In many of his tales, characters seem to exemplify alternative futures and possibilities, as most markedly in "The Jolly Corner", in which the protagonist and a ghost-doppelganger live alternative American and European lives; and in others, like The Ambassadors, an older James seems fondly to regard his own younger self facing a crucial moment.

Major novels

The first period of James's fiction, usually considered to have culminated in The Portrait of a Lady, concentrated on the contrast between Europe and America. The style of these novels is generally straightforward and, though personally characteristic, well within the norms of 19th-century fiction. Roderick Hudson (1875) is a Künstlerroman that traces the development of the title character, an extremely talented sculptor. Although the book shows some signs of immaturity—this was James's first serious attempt at a full-length novel—it has attracted favourable comment due to the vivid realisation of the three major characters: Roderick Hudson, superbly gifted but unstable and unreliable; Rowland Mallet, Roderick's limited but much more mature friend and patron; and Christina Light, one of James's most enchanting and maddening femmes fatales. The pair of Hudson and Mallet has been seen as representing the two sides of James's own nature: the wildly imaginative artist and the brooding conscientious mentor.

In The Portrait of a Lady (1881) James concluded the first phase of his career with a novel that remains his most popular piece of long fiction. The story is of a spirited young American woman, Isabel Archer, who "affronts her destiny" and finds it overwhelming. She inherits a large amount of money and subsequently becomes the victim of Machiavellian scheming by two American expatriates. The narrative is set mainly in Europe, especially in England and Italy. Generally regarded as the masterpiece of his early phase, The Portrait of a Lady is described as a psychological novel, exploring the minds of his characters, and almost a work of social science, exploring the differences between Europeans and Americans, the old and the new worlds.

The second period of James's career, which extends from the publication of The Portrait of a Lady through the end of the nineteenth century, features less popular novels including The Princess Casamassima, published serially in The Atlantic Monthly in 1885–1886, and The Bostonians, published serially in The Century Magazine during the same period. This period also featured James's celebrated Gothic novella, The Turn of the Screw.

The third period of James's career reached its most significant achievement in three novels published just around the start of the 20th century: The Wings of the Dove (1902), The Ambassadors (1903), and The Golden Bowl (1904). Critic F. O. Matthiessen called this "trilogy" James's major phase, and these novels have certainly received intense critical study. It was the second-written of the books, The Wings of the Dove (1902) that was the first published because it attracted no serialization. This novel tells the story of Milly Theale, an American heiress stricken with a serious disease, and her impact on the people around her. Some of these people befriend Milly with honourable motives, while others are more self-interested. James stated in his autobiographical books that Milly was based on Minny Temple, his beloved cousin who died at an early age of tuberculosis. He said that he attempted in the novel to wrap her memory in the "beauty and dignity of art".

Shorter narratives

James was particularly interested in what he called the "beautiful and blest nouvelle", or the longer form of short narrative. Still, he produced a number of very short stories in which he achieved notable compression of sometimes complex subjects. The following narratives are representative of James's achievement in the shorter forms of fiction.

- "A Tragedy of Error" (1864), short story
- "The Story of a Year" (1865), short story
- A Passionate Pilgrim (1871), novella
- Madame de Mauves (1874), novella
- Daisy Miller (1878), novella
- The Aspern Papers (1888), novella
- The Lesson of the Master (1888), novella
- The Pupil (1891), short story
- "The Figure in the Carpet" (1896), short story
- The Beast in the Jungle (1903), novella
- An International Episode (1878)
- Picture and Text
- Four Meetings (1885)
- A London Life, and Other Tales (1889)
- The Spoils of Poynton (1896)

- Embarrassments (1896)

- The Two Magics: The Turn of the Screw, Covering End (1898)

- A Little Tour of France (1900)

- The Sacred Fount (1901)

- Views and Reviews (1908)

- The Wings of the Dove, Volume I (1902)

- The Wings of the Dove, Volume II (1909)

- The Finer Grain (1910)

- The Outcry (1911)

- Lady Barbarina: The Siege of London, An International Episode and Other Tales (1922)

- The Birthplace (1922)

Plays

At several points in his career James wrote plays, beginning with one-act plays written for periodicals in 1869 and 1871 and a dramatisation of his popular novella Daisy Miller in 1882. From 1890 to 1892, having received a bequest that freed him from magazine publication, he made a strenuous effort to succeed on the London stage, writing a half-dozen plays of which only one, a dramatisation of his novel The American, was produced. This play was performed for several years by a touring repertory company and had a respectable run in London, but did not earn very much money for James. His other plays written at this time were not produced.

In 1893, however, he responded to a request from actor-manager George Alexander for a serious play for the opening of his renovated St. James's Theatre, and wrote a long drama, Guy Domville, which Alexander produced. There was a noisy uproar on the opening night, 5 January 1895, with hissing from the gallery when James took his bow after the final curtain, and the author was upset. The play received moderately good reviews and had a modest run of four weeks before being taken off to make way for Oscar Wilde's The Importance of Being Earnest, which Alexander thought would have better prospects for the coming season.

After the stresses and disappointment of these efforts James insisted that he would write no more for the theatre, but within weeks had agreed to write a curtain-raiser for Ellen Terry. This became the one-act "Summersoft", which he later rewrote into a short story, "Covering End", and then expanded into a full-length play, The High Bid, which had a brief run in London in 1907, when James made another concerted effort to write for the stage. He wrote three new plays, two of which were in production when the death of Edward VII on 6 May 1910 plunged London into mourning and theatres closed. Discouraged by failing health and the stresses of theatrical work, James did not renew his efforts in the theatre, but recycled his plays as successful novels. The Outcry was a best-seller in the United States when it was published in 1911. During the years 1890–1893 when he was most engaged with the theatre, James wrote a good deal of theatrical criticism and assisted Elizabeth Robins and others in translating and producing Henrik Ibsen for the first time in London.

Leon Edel argued in his psychoanalytic biography that James was traumatised by the opening night uproar that greeted Guy Domville, and that it plunged him into a prolonged depression. The successful later novels, in Edel's view, were the result of a kind of self-analysis, expressed in fiction, which partly freed him from his fears. Other biographers and scholars have not accepted this account, however; the more common view being that of F.O. Matthiessen, who wrote: "Instead of being crushed by the collapse of his hopes [for the theatre]... he felt a resurgence of new energy."

Non-fiction

Beyond his fiction, James was one of the more important literary critics in the history of the novel. In his classic essay The Art of Fiction (1884), he argued against rigid prescriptions on the novelist's choice of subject and method of treatment. He maintained that the widest possible freedom in content and approach would help ensure narrative fiction's continued vitality.

James wrote many valuable critical articles on other novelists; typical is his book-length study of Nathaniel Hawthorne, which has been the subject of critical debate. Richard Brodhead has suggested that the study was emblematic of James's struggle with Hawthorne's influence, and constituted an effort to place the elder writer "at a disadvantage." Gordon Fraser, meanwhile, has suggested that the study was part of a more commercial effort by James to introduce himself to British readers as Hawthorne's natural successor.

When James assembled the New York Edition of his fiction in his final years, he wrote a series of prefaces that subjected his own work to searching, occasionally harsh criticism.

At 22 James wrote The Noble School of Fiction for The Nation's first issue in 1865. He would write, in all, over 200 essays and book, art, and theatre reviews for the magazine.

For most of his life James harboured ambitions for success as a playwright. He converted his novel The American into a play that enjoyed modest returns in the early 1890s. In all he wrote about a dozen plays, most of which went unproduced. His costume drama Guy Domville failed disastrously on its opening night in 1895. James then largely abandoned his efforts to conquer the stage and returned to his fiction. In his Notebooks he maintained that his theatrical experiment benefited his novels and tales by helping him dramatise his characters' thoughts and emotions. James produced a small but valuable amount of theatrical criticism, including perceptive appreciations of Henrik Ibsen.

With his wide-ranging artistic interests, James occasionally wrote on the visual arts. Perhaps his most valuable contribution was his favourable assessment of fellow expatriate John Singer Sargent, a painter whose critical status has improved markedly in recent decades. James also wrote sometimes charming, sometimes brooding articles about various places he visited and lived in. His most famous books of travel writing include Italian Hours (an example of the charming approach) and The American Scene (most definitely on the brooding side).

James was one of the great letter-writers of any era. More than ten thousand of his personal letters are extant, and over three thousand have been published in a large number of collections. A complete edition of James's letters began publication in 2006, edited by Pierre Walker and Greg Zacharias. As of 2014, eight volumes have been published, covering the period from 1855 to 1880. James's correspondents included celebrated contemporaries like Robert Louis Stevenson, Edith Wharton and Joseph Conrad, along with many others in his wide circle of friends and acquaintances. The letters range from the "mere twaddle of graciousness" to serious discussions of artistic, social and personal issues.

Very late in life James began a series of autobiographical works: A Small Boy and Others, Notes of a Son and Brother, and the unfinished The Middle Years. These books portray the development of a classic observer who was passionately interested in artistic creation but was somewhat reticent about participating fully in the life around him.

Reception

Criticism, biographies and fictional treatments

James's work has remained steadily popular with the limited audience of educated readers to whom he spoke during his lifetime, and has remained firmly in the canon, but, after his death, some American critics, such as Van Wyck Brooks, expressed hostility towards James for his long expatriation and eventual naturalisation as a British subject. Other critics such as E. M. Forster complained about what they saw as James's squeamishness in the treatment of sex and other possibly controversial material, or dismissed his late style as difficult and obscure, relying heavily on extremely long sentences and excessively latinate language. Similarly Oscar Wilde criticised him for writing "fiction as if it were a painful duty". Vernon Parrington, composing a canon of American literature, condemned James for having cut himself off from America. Jorge Luis Borges wrote about him, "Despite the scruples and delicate complexities of James, his work suffers from a major defect: the absence of life." And Virginia Woolf, writing to Lytton Strachey, asked, "Please tell me what you find in Henry James. ... we have his works here, and

I read, and I can't find anything but faintly tinged rose water, urbane and sleek, but vulgar and pale as Walter Lamb. Is there really any sense in it?" The novelist W. Somerset Maugham wrote, "He did not know the English as an Englishman instinctively knows them and so his English characters never to my mind quite ring true," and argued "The great novelists, even in seclusion, have lived life passionately. Henry James was content to observe it from a window." Maugham nevertheless wrote, "The fact remains that those last novels of his, notwithstanding their unreality, make all other novels, except the very best, unreadable." Colm Tóibín observed that James "never really wrote about the English very well. His English characters don't work for me."

Despite these criticisms, James is now valued for his psychological and moral realism, his masterful creation of character, his low-key but playful humour, and his assured command of the language. In his 1983 book, The Novels of Henry James, Edward Wagenknecht offers an assessment that echoes Theodora Bosanquet's:

> "To be completely great," Henry James wrote in an early review, "a work of art must lift up the heart," and his own novels do this to an outstanding degree ... More than sixty years after his death, the great novelist who sometimes professed to have no opinions stands foursquare in the great Christian humanistic and democratic tradition. The men and women who, at the height of World War II, raided the secondhand shops for his out-of-print books knew what they were about. For no writer ever raised a braver banner to which all who love freedom might adhere.

William Dean Howells saw James as a representative of a new realist school of literary art which broke with the English romantic tradition epitomised by the works of Charles Dickens and William Makepeace Thackeray. Howells wrote that realism found "its chief exemplar in Mr. James... A novelist he is not, after the old fashion, or after any fashion but his own." F.R. Leavis championed Henry James as a novelist of "established pre-eminence" in The Great Tradition (1948), asserting that The Portrait of a Lady and The Bostonians were "the two most brilliant novels in the language." James is now prized as a master of point of view who moved literary fiction forward by insisting in showing, not telling, his stories to the reader. (Source: Wikipedia)

NOTABLE WORKS

NOVELS

Watch and Ward (1871)

Roderick Hudson (1875)

The American (1877)

The Europeans (1878)

Confidence (1879)

Washington Square (1880)

The Portrait of a Lady (1881)

The Bostonians (1886)

The Princess Casamassima (1886)

The Reverberator (1888)

The Tragic Muse (1890)

The Other House (1896)

The Spoils of Poynton (1897)

What Maisie Knew (1897)

The Awkward Age (1899)

The Sacred Fount (1901)

The Wings of the Dove (1902)

The Ambassadors (1903)

The Golden Bowl (1904)

The Whole Family (collaborative novel with eleven other authors, 1908)

The Outcry (1911)

The Ivory Tower (unfinished, published posthumously 1917)

The Sense of the Past (unfinished, published posthumously 1917)

SHORT STORIES AND NOVELLAS

A Tragedy of Error (1864)

The Story of a Year (1865)

A Landscape Painter (1866)

A Day of Days (1866)

My Friend Bingham (1867)

Poor Richard (1867)

The Story of a Masterpiece (1868)

A Most Extraordinary Case (1868)

A Problem (1868)

De Grey: A Romance (1868)

Osborne's Revenge (1868)

The Romance of Certain Old Clothes (1868)

A Light Man (1869)

Gabrielle de Bergerac (1869)

Travelling Companions (1870)

A Passionate Pilgrim (1871)

At Isella (1871)

Master Eustace (1871)

Guest's Confession (1872)

The Madonna of the Future (1873)

The Sweetheart of M. Briseux (1873)

The Last of the Valerii (1874)

Madame de Mauves (1874)

Adina (1874)

Professor Fargo (1874)

Eugene Pickering (1874)

Benvolio (1875)

Crawford's Consistency (1876)

The Ghostly Rental (1876)

Four Meetings (1877)

Rose-Agathe (1878, as Théodolinde)

Daisy Miller (1878)

Longstaff's Marriage (1878)

An International Episode (1878)

The Pension Beaurepas (1879)

A Diary of a Man of Fifty (1879)

A Bundle of Letters (1879)

The Point of View (1882)

The Siege of London (1883)

Impressions of a Cousin (1883)

Lady Barberina (1884)

Pandora (1884)

The Author of Beltraffio (1884)

Georgina's Reasons (1884)

A New England Winter (1884)

The Path of Duty (1884)

Mrs. Temperly (1887)

Louisa Pallant (1888)

The Aspern Papers (1888)

The Liar (1888)

The Modern Warning (1888, originally published as The Two Countries)

A London Life (1888)

The Patagonia (1888)

The Lesson of the Master (1888)

The Solution (1888)

The Pupil (1891)

Brooksmith (1891)

The Marriages (1891)

The Chaperon (1891)

Sir Edmund Orme (1891)

Nona Vincent (1892)

The Real Thing (1892)

The Private Life (1892)

Lord Beaupré (1892)

The Visits (1892)

Sir Dominick Ferrand (1892)

Greville Fane (1892)

Collaboration (1892)

Owen Wingrave (1892)

The Wheel of Time (1892)

The Middle Years (1893)

The Death of the Lion (1894)

The Coxon Fund (1894)

The Next Time (1895)

Glasses (1896)

The Altar of the Dead (1895)

The Figure in the Carpet (1896)

The Way It Came (1896, also published as The Friends of the Friends)

The Turn of the Screw (1898)

Covering End (1898)

In the Cage (1898)

John Delavoy (1898)

The Given Case (1898)

Europe (1899)

The Great Condition (1899)

The Real Right Thing (1899)

Paste (1899)

The Great Good Place (1900)

Maud-Evelyn (1900)

Miss Gunton of Poughkeepsie (1900)

The Tree of Knowledge (1900)

The Abasement of the Northmores (1900)

The Third Person (1900)

The Special Type (1900)

The Tone of Time (1900)

Broken Wings (1900)

The Two Faces (1900)

Mrs. Medwin (1901)

The Beldonald Holbein (1901)

The Story in It (1902)

Flickerbridge (1902)

The Birthplace (1903)

The Beast in the Jungle (1903)

The Papers (1903)

Fordham Castle (1904)

Julia Bride (1908)

The Jolly Corner (1908)

The Velvet Glove (1909)

Mora Montravers (1909)

Crapy Cornelia (1909)

The Bench of Desolation (1909)

A Round of Visits (1910)

OTHER

Transatlantic Sketches (1875)

French Poets and Novelists (1878)

Hawthorne (1879)

Portraits of Places (1883)

A Little Tour in France (1884)

Partial Portraits (1888)

Essays in London and Elsewhere (1893)

Picture and Text (1893)

Terminations (1893)

Theatricals (1894)

Theatricals: Second Series (1895)

Guy Domville (1895)

The Soft Side (1900)

William Wetmore Story and His Friends (1903)

The Better Sort (1903)

English Hours (1905)

The Question of our Speech; The Lesson of Balzac. Two Lectures (1905)

The American Scene (1907)

Views and Reviews (1908)

Italian Hours (1909)

A Small Boy and Others (1913)

Notes on Novelists (1914)

Notes of a Son and Brother (1914)

Within the Rim (1918)

Travelling Companions (1919)

Notebooks (various, published posthumously)

The Middle Years (unfinished, published posthumously 1917)

A Most Unholy Trade (1925, published posthumously)

The Art of the Novel : Critical Prefaces (1934)

CPSIA information can be obtained
at www.ICGtesting.com
Printed in the USA
LVHW050045271020
669864LV00014B/169

9 781662 715969